BY LAWRENCE SCHOONOVER

To Love a Queen

Walter Raleigh and Elizabeth R

Lawrence Schoonover

Little, Brown and Company · Boston · Toronto

FIRST EDITION

T02/73

Library of Congress Cataloging in Publication Data

Schoonover, Lawrence L
    To love a queen.

    1. Raleigh, Sir Walter, 1552?-1618--Fiction.
    2. Elizabeth, Queen of England, 1533-1603--Fiction.
I. Title.
PZ3.S3728To [PS3569.C527]   813'.5'4
ISBN 0-316-77461-8   72-8887

Published simultaneously in Canada
by Little, Brown & Company (Canada) Limited

PRINTED IN THE UNITED STATES OF AMERICA

TO MY CHILDREN

Judith, Elizabeth, Caroline, Virginia:

*with love abiding
I dedicate this book.*

NOTE

The contemporary most frequently quoted is John Chamberlain, a highly respected diplomat of independent means, resident at the English Court. His letters comprise two large volumes and were written to a favorite nephew, who was in the Foreign Service and usually absent from England. Chamberlain sought successfully to advance his nephew's career.

A. L. Rowse says of *The Chamberlain Letters*, "These two large volumes are used by all who undertake scholarly study of the period between 1597 and 1626."

John Chamberlain had ready access to all the latest news. Being a superb reporter he was able to pass it on to his nephew as no other man could have done, or so fast.

Mixed with Chamberlain's hard and accurate news there are also court gossip and incredible trivia, amusing and charming to read. We do not know how much of the gossip, the trivial, he actually believed, for he does not say. We do not know, for example, whether he actually believed that an Irish rebel, having died, "on being opened, there was found in him a serpent with two heads of eight foot long"; or whether he believed that "an ingenious fellow in Berkshire sailed over a high steeple in a boat all of his own making and, without other help than himself, conveyed her above twenty miles by land over hills and dales to the river, and so down to London."

CHAPTER I

IT WAS a wonderful age, a breathless age, an age of ferment, when everything was new; a youthful age, sure of itself and its future.

It was an age when a terrible new disease ravaged Europe, where men possessed no immunity to its spirochete. It was called the Great Pox, and the iniquity of the fathers was visited upon the children unto the third and fourth generation, if so many survived, which was seldom. Before it killed, the Great Pox caused excruciating agony and often ended in madness. King Henry VIII, Elizabeth's father, suffered from this disease, which is now known as syphilis.

Men lived hard, fast and loose. Men loved their wives devotedly but whored widely; and men could die under the executioner's axe with a cheery pun upon their lips, lips that would shortly speak no more from severed heads stuck on the steely points of ceremonial halberds. Said Sir Walter Raleigh, when reproached for his levity in "taking tobacco" at his beheading: "It is my last mirth in the world. When I come to the sad parting you will find me grave enough."

It was an age when it was equally good to live or die. Manly, fast, flamboyantly they lived, and fearlessly they died.

It was the age of Elizabeth.

Elizabeth's sea-captains blasted the Spanish Armada.

Her seamen were superb navigators and deadly gunners; Sir Walter was one of them. Imperial Spain, haughty, cruel, bigoted, declined and faded from that moment of history into the impotence that has been her fate to this day. Spain did not know that her glory was departed, that her future was naught but a fond and futile memory, sterile and dead as the ethos of her people, dead as some fossil dinosaur print in a Cambrian seam of coal.

It was the youth of the English language. Young William Shakespeare was writing his plays and his sonnets, stringing out multiple negatives, no-not-neither-nors; using language as wild and exuberant as that of Elizabeth's own mariners. They were the first to fix that vigor and manliness that has lasted for four hundred years. Little did they suspect how soundly they wrought; but their lives live today in the genius of the English language and the seamanship of every ship that sails the seas.

It was also the beginning of youth's end. With the death of the Virgin Queen came a decline of England's preeminence, the twilight of a dazzling age, the *Götterdämmerung* of Elizabethan glory.

Raleigh was the last Elizabethan.

CHAPTER II

HE WAS born a selfish child, with a sense that the world was against him. All his long flamboyant life he remained convinced that his merit went unrecognized, that enemies were thwarting his plans, that people were stealing from him.

He would be extremely talkative one day, initiating startling and grandiose schemes, always with himself as the author; then silent and withdrawn the next, his face a mask, his eyes half-closed, brooding heavy-lidded over his wrongs—nor were all his wrongs imagined. Such a man, with so many wide-ranging capacities, possessed also the capacity for making deadly enemies, for attracting few friends and those only in fair weather, ready to leave him when the wind changed. A modern psychiatrist, with modern understanding of the thin line that separates genius from madness, would use the word "paranoid" to describe him. It was incipient, it was not incapacitating; but it was there and it colored his judgment.

He nearly wasn't born at all. Bloody Mary, deeply Catholic, was Queen. His native Devonshire, bony and barren like her, was in armed rebellion against her; she was busily burning Anglican Protestant bishops, and Devonshire was deeply Protestant. Worse, she was violently in love with Philip II of Spain, and shortly she married him though she was eleven years older than he;

she was hot-blooded and romantic; he was cold as a fish.

Devonshire and Cornwall, the maritime shires, were convinced, not without reason, that the Spanish marriage would reduce England to a mere province of Spain. They rose in revolt. They were mercilessly put down.

At the height of the revolt, to street cries of "No Popery! Down with Spain!" Walter Raleigh was born, with a hatred of Spain in his blood like all Westcountry men—Drake, Gilbert, Grenville, to most of whom he was related.

Even to men of his own age Westcountry men were a breed apart. Raised on the barren moors, where will-o'-the-wisps made weird fires at night among the menhirs, cairns, cromlechs and other stone monuments of the prehistoric Celts, they were superstitious and violent, often cruel. The land offered them nothing. Only the sea provided a livelihood, great hauls of fish for the sober sort; a highway to adventure, wealth, fame, often by way of piracy, for the young and daring. And to some depraved men the seashore of Devon and Cornwall was a source of murderous loot. These men were the notorious "wreckers." They would extinguish navigational shore lights and, with lanterns and flares, lure unsuspecting ships to rocky coves. There, when the ship foundered, they would murder the crew, steal the cargo and burn the hulk. The Westcountry was decidedly no place to be found helpless in. True, Westcountry men often rose to fame and fortune, but they were too wild, too eccentric to be trusted with positions of great responsibility in the kingdom.

Such men are useful, however, and always used when a state is in dire peril. It was so with Raleigh.

When he was rich and famous, at the height of his power, he was sorely irked that he was a commoner. By then, however, he could buy men, favors, monopolies, almost anything. He sought out an antiquarian, an expert in pedigrees, and in no time he had heraldic papers to prove that he was of royal blood, a Plantagenet, descended from Henry the Lion—a bit on the female side it is true. Even Raleigh's vaulting ambition was tempered by the fact that it would be dangerous to claim direct royal descent, lest his enemies murder him as a pretender to the throne. He had troubles enough. He would not put *that* weapon in their hands.

Meanwhile, if he was to rise he must rise on his own, beat the world at its own selfish game, out-subtle the subtlest, outbrave the bravest, seek "for fame, for gold, for glory," as he candidly avowed later on.

He did all these things, with a flair, an élan, that was unmatched even in his own age, an age of megalomaniacs whose astounding contributions to literature, poetry, history, philosophy, the art of war, even the design of a new kind of ship—the kind that whipped the Spanish Armada—seem incredible. In all these varied endeavors Walter Raleigh played a conspicuous part, vocal, strident, superbly articulate.

Westcountry men sometimes looked in wonder at the cromlechs and menhirs the ancient Druids had left, high rocks weighing many tons, and mused: There were giants in those days.

They themselves were the giants, unknown to themselves, and their influence is with us today after four hundred years.

Bloody Queen Mary died at the early age of forty-two, on a dreary winter's day. Her last days were pitiful. Philip had deserted her. A peculiar delusion of her terminal illness caused her to believe that she was pregnant. Prayers of thanksgiving were offered in all the churches where Popish priests, many of them Spanish, burned incense on Popish altars and praised God and the saints that King Philip would now have his long-desired son, for then, with England added to his other globe-circling domains, Spain would rule the world. Months passed. The poor queen's belly continued to swell, but there was still no baby. Protestant skeptics mouthed cruel obscenities: "The Spanish bitch is taking twelve months to drop her whelp—ain't any, sez I, just water and wind."

Her delusion persisted almost to the end. Still hoping for an heir and fearing the dangers of childbirth, she drew up a will designating Philip as Regent of England during the minority of their son.

Then hope was gone, Philip was gone, and a few weeks before her death she added a codicil to her will entreating "the next heir to the Crown according to the laws," whom she could not bring herself to name, to follow all her policies, restore the Old Religion and accept Philip of Spain as King of England. The next heir was Elizabeth and Elizabeth had no intention of following Mary's policies, far less of accepting the King of Spain in any capacity—though it turned out that Philip would have been more than willing to accept her. Mary was ugly, sick and old before her time; Elizabeth was beautiful, young, fresh as a daisy; she had lips like a rose, with honey-colored hair and most beautiful hands, hands like the lily-white hands of Spanish ladies, who never exposed them to the sun. It was enough to set a small fire in Philip's fish-cold blood. She would be pliant, this beautiful youngster; he could bend her to his will. He instructed his ambassador to make cautious advances even before Mary's death.

Well might Elizabeth be proud of her beautiful hands. Her unfortunate mother had always worn a glove of peculiar shape to hide an extra finger; Elizabeth had the proper five, exquisitely formed; and she displayed them on every occasion.

Of these biological and imperial doings Walter Raleigh had no knowledge: he was six years old, listening to sea tales told by rascally old salts returned from some prosperous venture, some of them wreckers, listening to ghost stories and believing them all, for the "weird" was on the moors, as it always had been since time out of mind. And he was growing like a weed.

"He'll be a handsome nimble lad," said his mother, who had been married before and had had other children and knew whereof she spoke.

"Aye, that he will," said his father, who had been married twice before.

That he was.

CHAPTER III

BIOGRAPHERS are constantly confronted with weasel words like the following:

"We find him next in England again after a lapse of fifteen years during which time his whereabouts remain a mystery. . . ."

We "find him" indeed!

Where was he all this time, all these youthful critical plastic formative years? What was he doing? What mentors shaped his character?

How was it he went away a boy and came back a fighting man?

If we know the age in which he lived it is not so hard to fill in the gaps.

When Pompeii was buried under burning ashes and boiling mud by an eruption of Mount Vesuvius, a time so long ago that men who were then still living could remember what the face of Jesus Christ looked like, at that time when that awful convulsion of nature occurred, the bodies of men were carbonized, as happens now when the dead are cremated. Nothing remained, not even bones. Over the empty spaces where the bodies of men, women, children, pet dogs had been totally consumed, over this emptiness the boiling mud flowed, blazed, cooled and solidified, sealing them in. They were gone, but they left hollow places in the tufa where their bodies had evaporated into gas.

But we know exactly what they looked like. We have statues of them, depicting precisely the posture in which they died: the dog, tortured, gasping for breath in the suffocating sulphurous atmosphere; the child, open-mouthed, screaming for a mother to help; the money-lender, his bag of minted gold under his body in the garden where, too late, he tried to escape and fell poisoned by the breath of Vesuvius.

Into the hollows in the tufa left by the victims, modern engineers have pumped liquefied plaster of paris; in a little while it sets into a hard mold; carefully the tufa is broken away and the mold removed and we see them as they died. It is a painstaking archaeological procedure but it is absolutely accurate. The unthinkable lapse of time flashes away. We see them as they were. We see them as of today. In such a reconstruction it makes no difference whether the time-lapse is two thousand years, as in the case of Pompeii, or a mere four hundred years as in the case of Raleigh. If we know the age, as we do, if we know the devious statecraft, the disguising of motive as Elizabeth constantly disguised it, we know where young Raleigh was, what he was doing, whom he admired, what he hated and how it was that he went away a boy and came back a man.

CHAPTER IV

WALTER RALEIGH went to France an obscure young soldier in a fighting unit of volunteers captained by one of his many Westcountry relatives.

The mission of these "volunteers" was to help out the French Huguenots, a Protestant minority group, intensely hated by the militant majority of French Catholics. When the French caught them, they hanged them with placards nailed onto their chests, saying, "Not as heretics but as rebels against the good friend of France, Elizabeth, Queen of England."

Elizabeth backed the volunteers, but unofficially. She supplied funds, but she withheld approval: Philip of Spain was suing for her hand in marriage. She could not afford to sanction his enemies. So she helped them on the sly. No record of her support of Admiral Coligny, leader of the Protestant Huguenots, ever appeared in her official papers. Philip could never say, "You are subsidizing my enemies, the enemies of God." Blandly she could have replied, "No, Philip, I am not."

But she was. At any moment she could repudiate the volunteers and say, "This happened without my knowledge. They did it on their own. I am in no wise responsible."

This elaborate double-dealing was repeated again and again throughout her long and glorious reign, till she outwearied the Spaniards while deceiving them and made for England a place in the sun never equaled in statesmanship since the Empire of the Romans, and all with so smiling, so innocent and demure a countenance that her worst enemies never reproached her with duplicity. How little they understood her intuitive grasp of kingcraft in a world in flux, how little Spain and the world grasped the tremendous fact that a beautiful little woman was out-manning them all.

The Huguenots of France were a sober industrious sect, possessed of curious and unusual skills in a world that lacked and needed such skills: they were expert weavers of carpets, of woollen cloths, of beautiful tapestries to hang on the cold dank walls of gorgeous but drafty castles; they were superb metallurgists, fashioners of beautifully designed and thoroughly practical maces, bills, pikes, swords and crossbows in a world that had need of these weapons; they were above all devoted to the Protestant religion, sworn enemies of the Spanish Inquisition – it was then in its last days but still a terrible menace. They looked to Elizabeth for help, knowing well that she could not help them officially.

Leader among the Huguenots, whom Raleigh admired almost to the point of worship, was old Admiral Coligny.

Coligny, Count Gaspard de Chatillon, Admiral of France, had fought all his life and sustained serious wounds in the cause to which he was devoted. He had achieved the distinction of once being held to ransom for fifty thousand crowns when he lost a battle in the Huguenot war; he was ransomed and got a letter of congratulation from sour old Calvin in Switzerland, saying that his captivity was all for the best and God had favored him for his bravery. Brave he was, but not especially favored, for in the end the white-haired old warrior was defenestrated: they threw him out of the window, having first stabbed him in the throat. The unfortunate man, broken of bone and suffering what would now be called internal injuries, died on the cobblestones of his own residence, his ribs shattered, his skull fractured, his blood slowly forming a crimson puddle around him, incapable of uttering a word, though imaginative chroniclers have attributed to him one last dying battle cry: "Fight on! For God! No Popery!"

These are convenient words to put into the mouth of a victim incapable of uttering a syllable. Convenient words are almost never true. But in the case of Coligny they voice an ideal that he had espoused by the actions of an entire life. So perhaps they are true after all. Pontius Pilate had trouble with Truth too. Queen Elizabeth believed that Coligny spoke these last words; so did Walter Raleigh, whose idol Coligny was.

Raleigh had served under him in a number of vicious battles characterized by abominable cruelty on both sides. He had seen Coligny with his jaw half shot away by a musket ball—it was months in the healing.

Iron-willed, the Admiral fought on, directing his troops as if he felt no pain. Perhaps he didn't; fanatics often do not.

Raleigh had seen Coligny's prisoners slaughtered by the Papists. These were grim lessons for a very young soldier. In Raleigh's later years, on his spacious estates in Ireland, his similar treatment of the Irish rebels, cruel in the extreme, recalls the military severity he witnessed in the French Wars of Religion. One is reminded of the Roman legionaries who, if they shirked, were "decimated," that is, one out of every ten was killed as an example to others regardless of whether that one was a shirker or not, and one is reminded also of Winston Churchill's suggestion that capital punishment be meted out to soldiers who didn't quite measure up to his impossible directives.

In those battles, the iron entered into Raleigh's soul to remain with him all his life. It was here that he learned his warrior-craft.

When Raleigh himself came to die under the executioner's axe he possessed considerable legal knowledge. At his trial the prosecuting attorney marveled at his expert defense of his case. Yet Raleigh spent only one year at Oxford and left without a degree. It was not in his nature to submit to university discipline.

A story comes out of his college days demonstrating his touchy temper. He was in a tavern one day, wearing some borrowed finery, and a candle-maker laughed at it. Raleigh scooped up the candle-maker's wax, rubbed it in the man's hair, pulled at his beard and stuffed the stuff into the candle-maker's mouth. "Sealing it," the spectators said, "he retired laughing."

There is another story, demonstrating his tact and inordinate pride.

A Westcountry youth about his own age approached him one day and said, "I have been challenged to a duel, and I'm not much of a swordsman. What shall I do?"

Raleigh bethought himself of the laws against dueling. He said, "When honor is involved, one fights."

"But I'll be killed, and nobody will care."

"Are you not of royal blood?"

"Oh, I don't know . . ."

"Are you not a Westcountry man?"

"You know I am."

"Then you are of royal blood. We all are. All Westcountry men. And to fight a lesser breed is beneath our dignity. Challenge the rogue to a shooting match."

The youth did: he shot his arrow square into the middle of the target; his honor was redeemed. Even the University Chancellor permitted himself a wry smile that no blood was shed, for ofttimes it was, and Elizabeth, whose edicts against dueling were severe, was always "discontented," since it was daring hot-angry blood that was shed in these youthful brawls and she had need of such men.

What Raleigh learned he learned largely on his own: French, the classics, mathematics, navigation, gunpowder, ballistics. His proficiency in Latin helped him immeasurably, as it did Queen Elizabeth, who spoke it fluently and, once, vehemently harangued a Hungarian diplomat for forty minutes in Latin. Latin was not only the language of the hated Mass; it was the *lingua franca* of all learned men. The Hungarian was astounded that a mere woman, sovereign though she was, could hurl it back at him, and reported to his Hungarian king that the Majesty of England was a formidable female whom one would be wise to be cautious with.

And now, in France, at daybreak on Sunday, August 24, 1572, there came the hideous massacre of Saint Bartholomew's Eve. Bartholomew was one of the twelve apostles. He had watched Jesus walk upon the water without getting His feet wet, though Saint Peter sank. He had beheld the shining face of the risen Christ, eaten meals with Him; he was noted for his learning, humility and humble faith, but it did him no good: he was flayed alive and crucified, like his Master. Michelangelo, in an unpleasant painting, painted Bartholomew with folds of his own skin draped over his hands.

Slaughter of the Protestants continued for three weeks, Cologny being the first to die. There were fifty thousand others. King Philip, on hearing the news, ordered Te Deums of thanksgiving in the churches and joyous bonfires in all his Spanish possessions from Madrid to Mexico to commemorate the elimination of so many heretics.

Raleigh took refuge in the residence of the British ambassador. That in itself would not have saved him: all British were heretic Protestant dogs, and diplomatic immunity was yet to be heard of. But there is an enduring and likely story that a very highly placed French Protestant also took refuge in the British residence: he was Henry of Navarre, heir to the French throne, later King Henry IV, at that time a Protestant. Even for Philip it was not politically expedient to have *him* murdered, and he exerted his enormous influence to save the British compound.

Thus it was that Elizabeth's volunteers saved their lives until, shortly, they were deported home to England.

CHAPTER V

HISTORIANS have speculated endlessly without much success concerning Raleigh's ambition to plant an English colony in America, wasting much ink and taxing brain cells that could have been put to better use.

Granting that Raleigh's imagination was more daring than most men's, more poetic, less fearful of failure, the historians still wonder, "Where did this island Elizabethan with so many other ambitions, get the idea of settling Englishmen in the New World?"

Once again, the idea came from Coligny, who shaped his young mind.

Coligny had sent to Brazil a colony of Huguenots, years before the Puritans set foot on Plymouth Rock, in a feat of forethought that verges on genius. The Huguenots were expelled because they were Protestant and kind to the Indians, but they told stories of a place full of boundless resources. This was the seed. In Raleigh's mind it sprouted and took root; in imagination he elaborated and glorified it.

The beckoning vista of far-stretching American horizons haunted him throughout his life. He determined to get all this for Englishmen.

There, in fabulous America, was the gold of Montezuma, a mountain of pure silver that the Spaniards were stealing, endless savannahs, docile natives, a new and nutritious grain called maize that would feed whole populations with very little effort, a tuber called the potato, that proved very good for the Irish when Raleigh came to rule them, a weed that grew wild in the fields called "tobacco" that seemed to have soothing properties second only to those of wine and not nearly so addictive as whisky, which was ruining the Scotch, and gin, which was ruining the Dutch. Thus Coligny broadened a mind that was born to be broad. He did not teach Raleigh brutality; brutality was everywhere in that violent age; he taught him to accept it as a fact of life, and abhor it with a shrug and a smile, and fight back.

There were many Spaniards left to fight.

In that age of spectacular butchers Philip had a butcher that out-butchered them all, namely, the bloodthirsty Duke of Alva.

Whenever there was a job too abhorrent for anyone else to undertake Philip entrusted it to Fernando Alvarez of Toledo, Duke of Alva.

In France Alva had fought the French Huguenots. This was predictable, old religion against new religion.

In Italy, however, Alva had also fought the Italian Catholics. This was not predictable. They were of the same religion. It was occasioned by Philip's far-ranging policy of treating as enemies all who stood between him and the extension of his empire: sometimes his allies were the unspeakable Turks; sometimes his enemies were Catholic Italians; but sometimes he did veer toward alliance with the uncommitted English, pretty little Elizabeth being an added attraction.

Alva pitched his tents at the gates of Rome. The Pope, the greatest landholder in Italy, feared another invasion, such was the reputation of the terrible Duke of Alva. Quaking in Castel Sant'Angelo, the Holy Father prayed for a miracle.

It would not have been the first time Rome had been at the mercy of vandals. There was that other barbarian chieftain who, when the Romans pleaded, "Our tribute is all we have," threw his sword into the scales and retorted, "Vae Victis!" "Woe to the vanquished," and demanded and got more.

To the astonishment of the Pope, who was a practical man, the miracle occurred.

Alva, with Rome at his feet, was suddenly commanded by his King to do penance, to go barefoot into the presence of the Pontiff, to beg absolution on bended knee for the sin of unsheathing the sword against the Vicar of Christ.

Philip's was the first empire on which the sun never set. When it was growing dark in the eastern reaches of his Spanish possessions the sun was just rising on Mexico, Florida, California, the New World. Philip's was the first world outlook to be global in scope. Only one thing held him back from the excesses of a Hitler, and that one thing was religion. When Alva reduced the Pope to a cipher, when the Pope was a humbled beaten Sovereign-of-Nothing, Philip sustained a queer turnabout of conscience. He could not stomach Alva's brutality, though he had used him. All the world wondered when Alva made his submission.

But this, at the time when Raleigh fought him, was some years in the future.

When Raleigh took arms against the Spaniards in the Netherlands, Alva was at the height of his power, Captain-General and Regent of Holland, boasting that he had slain eighteen thousand Protestant heretics and burned, for the salvation of their souls, some thousands more of witches who, as all good Spaniards knew, were prevalent in the north of Europe.

Raleigh had a remarkable half brother, Sir Humphrey Gilbert, some years older than he and highly respected. Gilbert wore no pearls in his ears, he was a Member of Parliament, he was sober in dress and deportment and he, like Raleigh, had a vision of the boundless opportunities for England in the New World. He sought and received permission to plant colonies in America. Queen Elizabeth, officially for once but supplying the scantest of funds, authorized him, "his heirs and assigns, to discover, occupy and possess such remote heathen lands [as are] not actually possessed of any Christian prince or people," in America. This was a munificent grant with far-reaching results for Raleigh when Gilbert came to die.

Gilbert's death has a singular attraction for naval persons. Churchill quotes his last words. So does Sir Charles Wilson, Churchill's doctor, author of the penetrating *Anatomy of Courage*.

Gilbert was returning in a ship called the *Golden Hind* from his "western planting" of a colony of Englishmen in America, a venture he financed by selling some of the property of his extremely rich wife.

For the sake of rounding out the remarkable character of Raleigh's brother we stray a bit from strict chronology.

A violent tempest arose on the way home from the western planting. Gilbert could have saved his life if he had consented to transfer from the *Golden Hind* to a larger ship, part of his convoy and near at hand, but he refused.

"Suddenly," the captain of the larger ship observed, "her lights were out, and in that moment of the tempest the *Golden Hind* was devoured and swallowed by the sea," but Sir Humphrey, the convoy report continues, "with a book in his hand called out above the storm, 'We are as near to Heaven by sea as by land.' " Another Elizabethan, blood brother to Walter Raleigh!

In a letter to Gilbert on the occasion of his voyage to America, Raleigh writes:

Brother:
I have sent you a token from Her Majesty. [It was a picture of the Queen.] She wishes you good-hap and safety to your ship as if herself were there in person.

For the rest, I commit you to the will and protection of God, Who sends us such life or death as He shall or hath appointed.

Your true Brother,
W. Raleigh

In the afterlight, when all was known, Raleigh's letter had an eerie foreboding ring.

CHAPTER VI

THE MOST difficult lesson Raleigh ever had to learn in his whole life was to hold his tongue.

He was by nature nimble of speech, querulous, quick to take offense, quick to retort and more than a little seduced by the sound of his own words. All who heard him, whether friend or foe, conceded his words to be deep, vigorous, reasoned and above all poetic. To this day, after four hundred years, Raleigh's poetry finds a place in the anthologies of Elizabethan literature, no small accolade when one considers that Shakespeare was a contemporary.

While he was fighting the Spaniards in Holland Raleigh learned, but only half-learned, to hold his tongue: the example of William, Prince of Orange, Stadholder of the Netherlands, for whom he fought, taught him the lesson.

Mortal enemy of the Spaniards, William was known as "The Silent," because he never committed himself when emissaries came to him from other countries to offer, in private, what would now be called "deals": secret treaties, lordships of provinces, Mexican silver, Spanish gold, Catholic troops, Protestant troops, mercenary troops to fight on his side in return for William's support for their own interests.

William would smile, hold his tongue and say he would consider the matter.

Meanwhile he outwitted the Spaniards by opening his dikes and letting sea water inundate half of Holland.

This posed a food problem elsewhere in the Netherlands, and the Dutch were already known for their love of good lengthy meals washed down with the best beer in the world. Lest there be a famine, William decreed: "Let no one slaughter any animals, neither oxen nor calves nor sheep nor geese nor chickens," and his loyal Dutch subjects obeyed him, though as a result of his opening the dikes, many in the inundated provinces were drowned in the waters of the cold North Sea that rose four feet above the tiles of their homes, leaving only the windmills above water, their sodden sails motionless and forlorn.

Defeat and exile had overwhelmed the Huguenots of France. The English "volunteers" had fled, hardened warriors now, inured to the brutality they witnessed every day and burning with hatred for everything that smacked of Popery, everything Spanish.

From France Raleigh went to Holland, there again to fight against the ever-mounting power of Spain, in the suite of a French Royal Duke, whose bravery and fatuity have seldom been equaled in the annals of history. The Duke was defeated, and Holland underwent such a horror of sickening cruelties as never again were to be seen by a shuddering world till Hitler, with his all-but-successful maniacal dream of world conquest, arose to plague the planet.

In Holland, as in France, Queen Elizabeth encouraged all Spain-haters who would fight, but always unofficially and at little cost to herself—in truth her own treasury had little to spare. Unofficial wars were costing her dear. And there was always in her mind her supreme concern: that if she could keep Philip dangling for her hand the fortunes of England would prosper. Nothing must come before that, not even her interest in men or her love of dancing.

Raleigh returned to England, and from England he departed for Ireland, there again to fight against Papists and rebels.

And this time he made his fortune.

CHAPTER VII

"THE IRISH," said Lord Macaulay, in whose veins ran Celtic blood, "are distinguished by qualities which tend to make men interesting rather than prosperous. They are an ardent and impetuous race, easily moved to laughter or to tears, to fury or to love. Alone among the nations of northern Europe they have the susceptibility, the vivacity, the natural turn for acting and rhetoric which are indigenous to the shores of the Mediterranean Sea," and he adds, "The Irish alone of the people of northern Europe remained true to the Old Religion."

It was this unswerving fidelity to the Church of Rome that endeared the Irish to Philip of Spain and threatened to topple the throne of Elizabeth of England. "Jesus!" she was heard to remark. "The Spanish spider thinks he can bed me or burn me. He shall do neither, by God!"

But she muttered these imprecations under her breath. Only old Burleigh heard her, her trusted Prime Minister; and he merely smiled and never breathed a word, neither of her lusty curses, to which he was accustomed, nor of her crafty foreign policy, which he knew, had helped shape and approved: "*Video et taceo*"—I see all, I say naught—and waited upon events.

In Ireland there ruled a turbulent lord, owner of a huge ancestral estate comprising six hundred thousand acres of lush green farmland, tall forests of valuable timber, prosperous hamlets, ancient castles with towering keeps swathed in emerald-green ivy but still capable of vigorous and prolonged defense. Mineral wealth lay under the deep rich soil. Edible fish swarmed in the Blackwater, a placid river that added its shimmering beauty to the countryside, though there was little need of fish food except during the season of Lent among the well-fed inhabitants. Little need until a storm of disaster burst upon them with horrors like the apocalypse.

The name of the lord of all this wealth and promise was Gerald Fitz Gerald, fifteenth Earl of Desmond. For a thousand years the Desmonds had been a power in Ireland, violent, cruel, possessed of a singular aptitude for creating havoc and anarchy. Englishmen firmly believed that this trait in the Earl's character was a blood-legacy from the founder of the Desmond Clan, one Thomas, "the Ape," ten centuries before.

Seeing a chance to rid Ireland forever of the curse of the English, Desmond opened his seaports to any nation willing to fight against them. English "colonists" in Ireland held many prosperous towns and estates confiscated from the aboriginal inhabitants by Henry VIII and confirmed in their holdings by Elizabeth. They lived as English colonists have always lived and as they would continue to live throughout conquered lands down to our own times, surrounded by aliens whose culture they did not understand, whose language they did not comprehend or try to comprehend, and whom they lumped into one all-inclusive category: savages.

France cautiously declined Desmond's invitation to send fighting men to Ireland. France had too recently witnessed the merciless power of Elizabeth's "volunteers."

But Spain responded with Philip's blessing, and Italy, with the blessing of the Pope, who quoted the Papal Bull which solemnly declared Queen Elizabeth excommunicate and a bastard, disqualified from ruling, and freed all Englishmen from their oath of allegiance to her.

Elizabeth at first refused to credit the rumor that

Desmond was in revolt. She herself had received his homage as an Earl. But shortly the news arrived that her town of Youghal, a small but beautiful place on the Blackwater Estuary, smack in the Desmond domains, had been viciously plundered by Desmond, who there earned the nickname "the Rebel Earl." He devastated the surrounding countryside; he slaughtered the cattle; he sank the little pleasure boats of the English colonists. As for the colonists themselves in the town, he slew all within reach of his soldiers' swords—men, women, children— and the few who escaped to England brought home such tales of rape and rapine that all England shuddered.

To add to the horror came fear, fear of an actual invasion of England. It was rumored that a force of five thousand Spaniards and Italians had landed in Smerwick in Ireland. What was to prevent this formidable army of Papists from taking over all of Ireland? Such a takeover could hardly be called a conquest. The indigenous Irish were already inclined to welcome their coreligionists and might flock to their banners, might visit the horrors of the Spanish Inquisition on all loyal Englishmen in Ireland, and cross the narrow Irish Sea, a half-day sail if the Devil sent a Papist wind, in a fleet of Spanish vessels, and land on English shores, restore the Old Religion, depose and kill the Bastard Queen and put King Philip on the English throne.

The Italians and Spaniards had indeed actually landed at Smerwick. But their number did not exceed eight hundred. Still, they constituted a dangerous army, especially in a country disposed to be friendly. Worse still, the foreigners brought with them a large supply of arms —maces, pikes, muskets, swords, suits of Spanish armor, even cannon and gunpowder and shot, enough to equip an Irish army ten times the size of the invaders' own.

Small wonder there was fear in England. Small wonder the ancient hatred of the Irish was exacerbated to a frenzy of fanaticism.

Elizabeth did not dare risk a war with Spain. Not yet.

[27]

But she had at her command a terrible weapon of reprisal, her reckless war-hardened corps of "volunteers," fanatically devoted to her person, deeply Protestant and blazing with hatred and scorn of everything Spanish.

This was the weapon she hurled against Ireland.

Among her volunteers was Walter Raleigh, now a captain.

CHAPTER VIII

ELIZABETH'S terrible army of veterans struck against the Rebel Irish Earl first at Youghal. They landed unopposed.

Heartsick, Captain Raleigh looked upon the devastation of the countryside. The forests were chopped down. Around the trunks of such trees as the rebels had not had time to chop down they had cunningly cut circles in the bark, so that the trees would die of themselves. Slaughtered cattle lay bloated in the fields. Many had been cut up for food despite their putrefaction. All the colonists had fled to England or lay slaughtered in the fields, bloated like the cattle. Fish still swarmed in the Blackwater and might have fed the few remaining farmers of the vicinity. But Desmond had searched for their fishnets, found them, and burned them. It was in Desmond's nature to create anarchy. Out of anarchy for a thousand years his clan had prospered; and, reasoned the Earl, how did it happen that senseless anarchy had always brought power to his clan? It must not be senseless. So he scorched the earth.

Captain Raleigh reasoned otherwise. If you feed the starving you win people over to your side. And there was another reason.

Flint-hard as he was where his own interests were concerned, he could not stomach the pitiful hands of children (he had a weakness for children and pretty women) outstretched for a morsel of food and these children were orphans, victims of Desmond's scorched earth.

To feed the orphans, to win the survivors to his side, to thwart the Rebel Earl and to pacify the countryside in accordance with his orders, Raleigh devised a plan.

He appealed to Sir Humphrey Gilbert, his half brother. "Dear Brother," he wrote, "the tuberous vegetable called 'potato' would do well in this rich Irish soil, and of this comestible you possess an abundance in your Virginia plantations in America. Dispatch, dear brother, some hundredweight of these tubers to me here at Youghal, that I may have them planted here to their speedy increase, that they raise up a rich harvest to feed many who are starving, who otherwise would rebel out of hopelessness, to our own great dishonor and the detriment of our Cause." Raleigh added, "The cost would be small and will be doubtless paid out of general military funds allotted to the expedition." He did not of course offer to pay the cost himself or intimate that the Queen should do so. There was always plenty of leakage into the pockets of highly placed military leaders during a war, and the leakage might as well be used for potatoes as for a commander's sudden wealth. And he hoped that Sir Humphrey, through his wife, would defray the cost: she was always willing to spend her wealth to advance the career of her impecunious husband.

Raleigh sent the letter to Elizabeth's Court, not knowing where Sir Humphrey was at the moment.

Sir Humphrey was not at Court. He was at sea. It was a long time before there were any potatoes in Youghal.

Humphrey Gilbert's fame, passed down to us over the centuries, rests solely on the final beautiful words he spoke when his ship went down, words much quoted and patently true. No man has ever denied them, the last brave words of a brave man, facing death like a true Elizabethan. Least of all would his younger brother, Walter, have found fault with them, Walter who looked up to him.

But, "This would be scanned"—words which another Elizabethan put into Hamlet's mouth.

To scan the life of Humphrey Gilbert is to descend into the abyss.

He was a deplorable navigator. He seldom knew where his ship was. His captains pulled him through. He was inordinately covetous. He was cunning, like Raleigh. His goal was glory, gold and advancement, no matter how acquired. But in Gilbert's blood, half-shared with Raleigh, was a quirk Raleigh never had: an unthinkable cruelty.

A few years before, Elizabeth had sent Gilbert to Ireland to put down one of the perennial Irish uprisings. Gilbert put it down in a way that in our day would be called pathologically sadistic.

On either side of the path that led to his tent he placed a row of rotting human heads. Some were very little; they were the children. Some had once been beautiful women. Some still glared their fury from ant-covered eyes, and these were the severed heads of the Irishmen he had slain. Gilbert's purpose was to teach a salutary lesson to anyone else who might be tempted to rebel.

There were fewer rebels after that, for a while; but only for a while.

For his stern measures in Ireland Elizabeth knighted him. Thenceforth he was Sir Humphrey Gilbert. She showered honors upon him. But she deemed it wise to recall him from Ireland lest he become too powerful, saying, "It is never politic to give a horse his head, or he may throw you." Among his honors was the authorization to plant colonies of Englishmen in America where she did not care how powerful he became, for if he did, she did; and it would keep him out of England for a long time.

Thus, Sir Humphrey Gilbert, whose blood was the same, but only half-same, as the blood of Walter Raleigh; and this is the reason potatoes were so long in coming to Youghal, where Walter and his men landed unopposed.

Youghal was pacified. To replace her veterans, who were needed elsewhere, Elizabeth sent a force of men to occupy the town.

The replacements were a shoddy lot, offscourings of the streets and some prisoners released from London jails, guilty of only minor offenses and now offered freedom for service in Ireland, with further promises of benefits to come if they kept the town peaceful and prevented reoccupation by the rebels. They leaped at the chance.

They came from the poorest class. Many had known hunger in London; they could not stand to see hunger among the orphans, even though the orphans were Irish.

They fashioned fishlines from ivy strands that hung from the dying forest trees. They made fishlines by unraveling hangman's ropes, that Desmond had prepared in great quantity, a quantity greater than he had had a chance to use. They made fishhooks of stray bits of wire and baited the hooks with rotting pieces of flesh from any source available. There was a lot of that, and they were not overfastidious what sort of flesh. Only a fish could have eaten some of it with appetite. They fashioned crude fishnets of "withies," the long flexible strands of willow that poor Irishmen used in place of rope.

Soon the shores of the Blackwater took on the aspect of a holiday outing, with good fat fish broiling over scores of campfires day and night, happy children laughing and singing and gorging themselves with the first good meal they had had in weeks and thanking God and these Protestant Englishmen who were suddenly so friendly. It did not much bother the English that the Irish orphans crossed themselves. What could you expect from kids that had been brought up wrong? It was good to see them fed, even Papist kids.

The delectable fragrance of broiling fish wafted over the countryside; now out of the dying forests crept hundreds of famished Irishmen, formerly, but no longer, the friends of the Rebel Earl. There were pitiful scenes of parents who recognized their lost children and rushed to clasp them to their bosoms, sobbing. There were heart-sickening scenes of parents who never found their own.

In the main it was a successful operation. Desmond had never fed them; these English did; and, as Raleigh had predicted, they came over to his side, bringing with them hidden stores of survival food, ample skills and a newborn tolerance of the Bastard Queen. Youghal was secure. But Raleigh was gone.

He had gone overland with his troop of horse toward Smerwick where the Spaniards and Italians had landed.

He sent a letter to the Queen, praising her in high-flown poetic terms, extolling her beauty, wisdom and foresight, but especially her statesmanship in achieving the unopposed reoccupation of Youghal, amply implying that he, as captain, deserved no small share of credit for the operation.

Elizabeth liked the tone of his letter. She said to her Prime Minister, "If this stripling captain continue as he start, I will advance him. What does he look like?"

Burleigh answered, "He is said to be tall and handsome, Your Majesty; but reckless, reckless, ambitious, ambitious."

"There are worse qualifications," Elizabeth said.

"Perhaps there are. They are, at any rate, universal in our time, Your Majesty."

Elizabeth patted his ancient shoulder. "My old, my dear, my wise, my very good friend. You never say anything to discontent me, even when you smell a rat."

"I smell no rat, Your Majesty."

"Is he dangerous?" She glanced sidewise, as if apprehending an assassin behind the arras.

Burleigh said, "Dangerous? Not to you, Your Majesty. The tone of his letter bespeaks naught but devotion to your person and Cause. And a rat? Not this man. Not a rat that deserts a sinking ship. This young captain comes from one of your loyal maritime counties, seamen all, half brother to Sir Humphrey Gilbert."

"Ah yes, Sir Humphrey," mused the Queen. "A cruel man."

"But very efficient, Your Majesty."

"I had to recall him. Is young Raleigh like Sir Humphrey?"

"Much like, unless the future prove him less like."

"How looks his face, this Raleigh?"

Here old Burleigh smiled broadly and said, "I would that my own son looked like Walter Raleigh."

Burleigh's son was sickly.

"A clear olive complexion that flushes scarlet when he is angry, which is often; piercing black eyes that bewitch the ladies, of whom he is very fond . . ."

Elizabeth scowled.

". . . a short pointed black beard . . ."

Elizabeth nodded approval. Only Puritans shaved their chins.

". . . which I think he waxes . . ."

Elizabeth chuckled. She was already coloring her hair. Men were as vain as women.

". . . and in his ear, like many English mariners, a pendant earring with a shining sea pearl, snatched, it is said, from a Spanish sea captain whose ship he just happened upon, which he scuttled and looted, a ship now in Your Majesty's Royal Navy. He received, unofficially of course, a small bounty for the capture. Your Majesty received the ship's treasure."

"What did he do with the Spanish crew? I expect they went down with the Spanish ship, unofficially of course. Did they?"

[34]

Burleigh said, "On the contrary, he put them all in a longboat, gave them food and a compass and bade them sail off to the nearest port of the Spanish devil, King Philip."

Elizabeth mused, "He is not at all like Sir Humphrey."

"Equally valuable, equally unpredictable, Your Majesty," the Prime Minister said.

"Can he dance?"

Burleigh said, "I should think he'd be the sort of man who would, expertly, even on a tightrope."

Elizabeth said, "He has made no mistake so far, and he did write a most beautiful letter."

From Youghal to Smerwick the overland route lay through thickly wooded country, beautiful and green in the sunlight, interspersed with numerous patches of marshland. Here the Irish farmers delved with spades into the peat bogs, furrowing long ditches and piling up brick-shaped cuttings of peat, to drain dry and subsequently use as fuel. Excellent fuel it was, cheaper and cleaner than British sea coal and so fragrant that it imparted an unforgettable flavor to Irish whisky when distilled over peat fires. The whisky of Scotland, said the Irish, could not compare with it.

But no Irishmen worked the peat bogs now. They had heard that the British were coming and they had slunk off into their forests, to watch and wait and wonder whether Desmond or the British would prove the more deadly enemy. In the end there was little to choose. Terror of both was justified.

Captain Raleigh, leading his troop of cavalry, had with him a fellow Westcountry man named Henry Moyle, a close friend whom he greatly admired.

One day as they approached a shallow ford in a river, Raleigh said idly, "It is curiously quiet, Henry. I could almost think it were too quiet. Are there none to oppose our passage?"

Henry Moyle answered with a good round oath, "The

stupid Irish kerns have all run away, disappeared, back to their pigs and their priests. Did we not land unopposed? Unopposed we shall proceed."

"Aye, Moyle; I hope so. But keep a sharp eye."

The horses waded knee-deep into the ford. The silence was broken only by the plashing of the beasts in the crystal clear water or the good-natured halloos of the riders when some horse paused to snuffle and drink.

Then, without warning, silently, the bushes stirred, parted. Shots rang out and Moyle's horse went down.

Raleigh opened his mouth and gave vent to an oath of such fury that the Queen, when it was reported what he had said, chuckled with admiration.

Yelling a volley of curses and threats at the Irish, he called them such names as would have made their pigs, if pigs could blush, blush to hear and tremble some porcine tremblings, sensing in Raleigh's threat some new and novel termination of their valuable existence.

The smoke of the Irish guns betrayed the Irish positions. Raleigh whipped out his musket and fired. His aim was accurate. Dying groans and yells of pain greeted his fusillade. He hurled from him his musket, both barrels now empty; water was up to his stirrups, and there was no time to reload. But he had a handgun, and he fired that also, spotting his targets by gunsmoke in the bushes. that also, spotting his targets by gunsmoke in the bushes.

His handgun empty, he threw that away also. Now he was armed only with a dagger, a sword and a stout stick, which Shakespeare—if the stripling young genius had been there to witness the encounter—would have called a "quarterstaff." Raleigh had it handy: a five-foot length of hickory, not only a convenient means of measuring the depth of bog-water and the soundness of the soil beneath, but also the traditional English weapon of self-defense that had been carried by Englishmen since Chaucer's time. Armed with this he felt, with racial memory, a full sense of security.

He turned to Moyle, whose horse was dead, scooped him up in his arms and sat him pillion on his own mount and said, "Are you wounded?"

"Only my poor horse."

Then another shot rang out and Raleigh's horse too fell down dead, and he found himself floundering in the water with his friend.

"That was meant for you," Moyle said, coughing up water out of his stomach.

"Or you, or us both," Raleigh said, bearing him up. "They missed the mark, but mark you this: I will slaughter these Irish beasts like the beasts they are and like the beasts they slaughter."

Now it was quiet again. The invisible attackers had faded again into the forest. The bushes were motionless, and the smoke from the encounter drifted lazily up into the treetops and became one with the crystal air, as if it never had been, as if nothing had happened, though much had happened in Captain Raleigh's mind and in his acutely sensitive soul: the revenge he had sworn against the Irish hardened and blazed.

He re-formed his troops and led them forward toward Smerwick.

Very shortly thereafter Henry Moyle, Raleigh's friend from the Westcountry, collapsed and died. But whether the bog-water in his lungs or some obscure disease brought about his demise Raleigh never knew. There was much disease, virtually a plague, epidemic throughout Europe, deadly and never before seen. Nobody knew who might be afflicted next, one's closest friend perhaps. It was widely rumored that Columbus, suffering from it himself, had contracted it in America. Most of his crew were likewise afflicted, especially the lusty and young.

Raleigh buried his friend under a yew tree that grew in a bog by the side of the slow-winding overland route toward Smerwick. "Kinsman, farewell," murmured Raleigh. "I will avenge thee." And all the while Raleigh in another part of his mind was calculating what Moyle might have possessed that he could legally claim.

But poor Moyle possessed nothing, nothing but an honorable death in the English cause.

"I will avenge thee," said Raleigh, and his hatred of the perfidious Irish grew ever more virulent.

By a courier he sent back to Queen Elizabeth a description of the Irish:

"Madame: The Irish kerns come upon us when we are least aware. They lie in ambush, then spring like hyenas with unearthly cries like demoniac laughter, then having fired and wrought death and dole upon Your Majesty's subjects, they disappear.

"Madame: I proceed overland to Smerwick, to defend Your Majesty against the heretic invaders of your Isle, Italians and Spaniards who even now are in Smerwick fortress defying Your Majesty. Our English force is small, and the castle of Smerwick is strong, circled by frowning thick walls and possessing many guns and largely provisioned withal. God bless Your Majesty."

Elizabeth said to Burleigh, her Prime Minister, "There is a touch of self-martyr in this missive, an *ave atque vale* in his tone. Good my lord Burleigh, let me not permit handsome young Raleigh, so pirate a poet with pearls in his ears, to bring about his own death in our service, which would accomplish nothing but his own glory; but let us rather save him for the future in our service. Suggest something, lest he foolishly destroy himself like a self-doomed hero in a theatrical play: there is much of the hero about him. And inasmuch as he is tall and comely and self-seeking, preserve him. Wise Burleigh, my trusty good friend, suggest a means, lest I lose him prematurely, for in the end I fear I shall lose him like all the others." And she sighed, and for a moment her hard eyes were misted over with a softness.

"Give him his head," Burleigh replied. "He still hath much within him to serve you withal. But strengthen him, for he is much overpowered in Ireland."

Thereupon Elizabeth sent out her Admiral, Sir William Winter, to be Raleigh's commander, with reinforcements of men and heavy siege guns to act against the rebel fortress of Smerwick, which now was full of alien Spaniards and Italians.

Raleigh, on his own, with his paltry hundred horse, pressed forward, seething with fury and mourning his kinsman, unaware that the Queen had sent reinforcements.

With his keen ability to copy others' tactics, he muttered to himself, "If the Irish can ambush, the English can ambush also," and he lay in wait, silently, one afternoon when some Irish kerns appeared, not many but bellicose, thinking themselves unopposed and keen to plunder. They came swaggering out of the forest. The English were hidden, covert, watching. There were about a score of the Irish.

The Irishman who strode toward the English looked to them like a demon out of hell: his gait was lithe, his blue eyes flashed, there was a curse on his lips and there was that in his manner that bespoke a bellyful of good Irish whisky. "On we go," he shouted, "to overthrow the heretic Queen, bitch, bastard, whore! We will smash her to smithereens."

To the English mind the Irish kerns were a queerish folk. They wore their hair in a sheep-dog droop down over their brows. It was believed by the English that this was to differentiate them from their pigs, whose foreheads were smooth and white. The kerns dressed in rags and smelly untanned leather; they could neither read nor write; with cows, pigs, rats and garbage they shared their hovels of wattle and daub, honoring with racial memory not only the Stone Age Druids but the cross of Christ, King Philip of Spain, Bloody English Queen Mary and his dead wife, and all the Mediterranean invaders who now occupied the fortress of Smerwick. Thus the Irish kerns.

The kern who swaggered down the route that led to

Smerwick had around his neck for easier carriage a string of withies.

"Now!" Raleigh shouted. To the astonishment of the Irish they found themselves confronted by the guns and swords of a determined band of Englishmen.

Raleigh stepped forward and cried, "How comes it to be that my way is blocked by a kern with some withies?"

The kern shouted back, eyes blazing with scorn, body quaking with terror at the death that he knew was upon him, "To hang Englishmen withal!"

"Seize him up," said Raleigh; and, punning upon a word as one day he would do at his own death: "With these withies so wither and dangle and die all Papist rogues and enemies of the Queen!"

Shortly there dangled and died, hanged by the neck with the strands he had wound 'round his shoulders, the unfortunate kern, from a tall tree that grew by the bog-side. His feet twitched for some minutes, as hanged men's always do.

The Irish, momentarily stunned by the sudden execution of their leader, turned to fly, and some escaped, but not before a volley of shots from the English had cut down many of them.

"Shall we kill them all, here and now?" Raleigh's lieutenant asked.

"There'll be time for that later," Raleigh said. "Tie them neck to neck in a string, shoot any man who attempts to break out and march them with us to Smerwick. Prisoners of war are negotiable currency."

The English jubilantly obeyed, the Irish submitted. Only a couple tried to break out and were instantly shot. The Irish were even more submissive after that.

Raleigh turned his head away from the queer-angled head of the dead man, whose eyes were glazing over but whose mouth still seemed to move.

"Curse me not," Raleigh muttered. "Peace, thou clay. You swore to hang me, so I hanged you. Had you lived to manhood you might have learned to be less rash." The victim looked about sixteen years of age.

Sobered, leaving the lad to hang as a warning to other traitors, Raleigh pressed on, followed by his string of captives.

He had an eye out for more prisoners, but word quickly spread abroad throughout the boglands that an English captain of singular cunning and devious tactics was beating them at their own game. They feared him greatly, sensing in him an implacable hatred, and they did not attempt to ambush him again lest they be ambushed themselves. Thus his way was unobstructed until he arrived at Smerwick.

There stood the castle, provisioned, defiant, confidently waiting for reinforcements they could not know would never arrive, from Italy, from the Pope, and above all from Philip of Spain.

Screaming insults from the battlements, laughing, scornful, they boasted, "Neither you nor anybody else can get in! Soon the great King of Spain will send us his fleet from overseas. Then look to yourselves in England."

Raleigh shouted back, "Nobody can get in, do you say? I have with me a string of captured kerns. I am loath to hang them. Will you let them in, or shall I hang them here in your sight?"

The kerns came forward, begging to be let in, telling the castle that the terrible English captain who addressed them had already hanged dozens of them, swearing that they had witnessed the executions with their own eyes.

There was a hurried consultation behind the walls. The kerns would strengthen the castle garrison and there was plenty of food for them.

"We shall let them in," came the reply.

"Then open your gates and let them in."

There was no hesitation. Raleigh's troop was observed to be small. The English could not possibly rush the castle while the gates were open. The prisoners filed into the fortress and were received with shouts of acclamation and many a good bottle of welcoming cheer.

Raleigh grinned. "Now we need neither feed nor hang them," and he laid out a plan for a system of siege trenches to be dug 'round the castle. His cavalrymen were not at all willing to dig trenches, but he silenced them with a threat. "Would you gentlemen care to go in also? I conceive they would gladly welcome you within the castle."

It was a vain threat and Raleigh knew it. It would have been high treason to turn Englishmen over to the enemy. But the cavalrymen did not know it. They had seen their captain knee-deep in the ford, his horse shot dead under him, bullets whizzing around him, bearing up a friend, utterly careless of self, rash and importunate. They had seen him hang the kern, immobilizing by his swift action the forces around him. He had led them seventy-five miles through enemy country, and after the incident of the hanging not another shot had been fired against him. He was rash and hard but he protected his men. His rashness and hardness, they feared, might actually cause him to turn them over to the Irish if they disobeyed.

Knowing their fate if Raleigh carried out his threat they fell to work with unaccustomed picks and shovels. Laughter greeted them from Smerwick's walls, but they were not fired upon. It was more amusing to watch English cavalrymen laboring like Guinea slaves. Besides, they would all be killed soon enough by the reinforcements from overseas.

Queen Elizabeth quickly kept her promise. A great shout arose from Smerwick Castle as watchers descried from the walls the many white sails of an approaching fleet glistening on the waters of the bay. In Spanish and in Italian they shouted welcome to their countrymen, mocking the ridiculously small force of their English besiegers, hard at that menial work on those ridiculous siege trenches.

Then suddenly there was a silence from the walls, then shouts of confusion, then a mighty wail. For, as the fleet drew closer they saw flying from the masts of the ships not the red and yellow flag of King Philip of Spain, not the Triple Crown of the Pope and the Golden Keys of Heaven, but Queen Elizabeth's royal English standard, the dreaded Red Cross of Saint George. Here were formidable reinforcements indeed, but not for the Irish. Throughout the afternoon and long into the evening twilight, ominously red in a gathering mist after a spectacular sunset, the watchers saw men, guns and work beasts being ferried ashore from the ships. They fired a few nervous shots from the battlement cannon, but quickly ceased when Admiral Winter, expecting resistance, treated them to such a vicious broadside of grapeshot that they withdrew to cover. The work went on.

If his men thought Walter Raleigh hard and rash they were soon to learn what true hardness and rashness was: the merciless cruelty of Admiral Winter.

Raleigh paid his respects to his new commander, who congratulated him on his safe march overland, especially on the hanging of the kern, and approved his sketched plan for the siege trenches, ordering them even closer to the castle.

Raleigh was surprised at the somewhat meager supplies which the Queen had sent to her Admiral. "Does Your Lordship deem your force sufficient for a quick victory?"

Winter eyed him stonily. "I deem it sufficient if wisely employed."

But before Winter had left England the same doubt had occurred to him. He had even ventured to ask the Queen for more.

Elizabeth, with an oath, snapped, "No! More, more, you ask me for more. Why do you need this 'more'?

There is no treasure in Smerwick Castle. If no treasure, what is to be gained? You have guns, powder, shot. Use them. Fire them out, starve them out till the confounded foreigners capitulate or are dead!"

Herein she spoke angrily like that other petulant English sovereign Henry II, her remote ancestor, who heedless of the consequences, said of Thomas Becket, "Are there none to rid me of this troublesome prelate?"—a thoughtless remark pregnant with terrible results, which has echoed down the centuries.

"King Philip may send reinforcements," the Admiral demurred.

"You may leave King Philip to me," said Elizabeth, with a ghost of a smirk on her painted lips, coyly lowering her eyes.

Her Prime Minister reassured the Admiral. "King Philip hopes to be King of England again, this time in truth and power, by espousing another English Queen. Her Majesty deems it prudent, in the interest of the State, not to discourage his hopes completely lest he send an armada against England, an armada which we know he is already building. Do not trouble yourself with high diplomatic matters outside your sphere, my Lord Admiral. You are a soldier, tried and true and trusted, amply fit to deal severely with enemies of the Queen, as she knows you will do. Do you see now, Admiral Winter, how it is that King Philip will send no reinforcements to Smerwick?"

"I do indeed," the Admiral replied.

He had caught a glimpse of Elizabeth's wily foreign policy, far-flung and invariably successful: she would use every stratagem her fertile mind could devise; hazard every penny in her treasury, if it were not wasted; commit every fighting man in her armed forces, if they were loyal; and into the arsenal of her weapons she threw her undoubted charm and the enormous prestige of her own person in marriage—if she didn't have to marry. For the lucky prince who married Elizabeth would rule England, and with England the world.

"I do see indeed," the Admiral said, face grave and respectful but inwardly smiling with admiration.

Like the knights who set out to murder Becket, he knew now exactly what he would do, though he had received no positive orders. A resolution hardened in his mind, a resolution congenial to his severe temperament. There would soon be no defenders in Castle Smerwick.

He said to Raleigh, "Today I shall bombard the castle. I shall fire from the sea. I put you in charge of the land forces, and you will fire from the land." The siege guns were already in place.

"I will not fail you, my Lord Admiral," Raleigh said, preening himself at his commander's recognition of his ability. "Was it my scheme for the trenches?"

Remembering his interview with the Queen, the Admiral, quick to discern whom the Queen might favor, replied, "Your trenches, yes indeed, Captain Raleigh. You laid them out like an engineer. I doubt not you could design a battleship. But I put you in charge because I conceive that Her Majesty trusts you always to do your duty."

For three whole days and nights the castle of Smerwick was caught in a cross-fire bombardment. It defoliated the ivy-covered walls. It sent up blood-colored smoke from the crumbling ancient stones.

Inside the foreigners cowered. "How can we get out of this alive, we and our women and our children?" For they did not wish to die, abandoned in a foreign land where nobody came to save them despite all the promises; and the ships that should have been Philip's and the Pope's turned out to be Elizabeth's.

"How?" counseled the leaders of the Italians. "Here is how. Negotiate. Promise anything. String out the parleys. The Holy Father absolves us from whatever, in our peril, we promise this heretic Queen."

But it irked them sore that the ships below in Dingle Bay were Elizabeth's, not Philip's, and they wept at the Spanish King's failure to act.

The bitter bombardment continued. Those who ventured out on the walls died in a deadly hail of grapeshot. Some who sought to escape by the sewers were caught in the fire of Raleigh's guns.

Raleigh had always been fascinated by chemistry. He had studied the ancient and mysterious substance known as "Greek Fire." He experimented; he hit upon the secret. "By God! It is not so mysterious after all. It is naught but gunpowder mixed with quicklime."

Quicklime was nothing but burnt limestone, a crumbly substance easily produced. One had only to burn a few statues of Papist saints and shovel up the dust that remained. Of statues of saints, in every chapel in Ireland, there was aplenty.

The superstitious Spaniards and Italians, to say nothing of the Irish within the walls, were awestruck to behold the effect of Raleigh's fire: everywhere that there was a sewer, a moat, water of any kind, even the slightest moisture on a human body, the hellish dew that spewed out from Raleigh's guns took fire. No water could quench it. The more water the hotter it burned.

Observing the burning bodies, the Admiral asked, a little in awe, "With what witchcraft have you loaded my guns, Captain Raleigh?"

"Your guns forsooth!" thought Raleigh. "They are mine!"

Those of Raleigh's troop who had marched with him from Youghal to Smerwick already were certain that Raleigh was a witch. No mortal man could have done what he had done, nay, now was doing.

Raleigh said amiably, "You put me in charge, my Lord Admiral. I but loaded them with loyalty, and loyalty is no witchcraft."

To join the Admiral now came an exalted personage,

Lord Grey de Wilton, the Queen's viceroy for all of Ireland, eager to participate in the reduction of Smerwick Castle. Grey was one of the despised sect of Puritans, but his military record was so brilliant that Elizabeth deemed him just the proper person to put down the Irish Papists. No one, not even Raleigh, hated Spaniards, Italians and Catholics so virulently as Lord Grey de Wilton. His hair was lank, he spoke with a nasal twang, he kept his hat on in the presence of superiors, he never swore but would only "affirm," and his common speech was full of Old Testament metaphors: Smerwick was "Babylon." He had named one of his daughters "Shun-Fornication-Patience-de-Wilton," which caused the Queen, when she heard of it, to give vent to a hearty "Faugh! What a filthy mind has this Puritan!" Raleigh suspected he never read the New Testament: "For such a man it reads too soft." But Lord Grey was useful to Elizabeth, and she used him.

He instantly took over command of all operations against Smerwick, superseding the Admiral and of course Captain Raleigh, who was almost beneath his exalted notice.

There exists to this day in Ireland a spitting curse, when anyone fails to keep his word: "The faith of Grey."

Raleigh was now far down in the chain of command and vastly irked. Everyone else was here to get in on the kill, "and I shall get no credit." Anger rose within him against Lord Grey.

Grey ordered him to confine himself to quarters and to write out a detailed report to explain the unusual burning effect of the guns.

Raleigh did no such thing.

Calling upon his knowledge of the Old Testament, Raleigh reported, "I conceive 'twas the presence of Your Lordship that brought down the fire and brimstone upon Smerwick, as sometime the Lord did rain fire and brimstone on Sodom and Gomorrah."

Lord Grey thought that must be exactly right and, by a courier, recommended Captain Raleigh to the Queen's preferment. "This Captain hath much in him of invention, for his guns bring down unquenchable fire upon the Papists of Smerwick."

When Elizabeth read the report she said to her Prime Minister, "From Lord Grey this is praise indeed."

Burleigh agreed, but shook his wise old head. "There will never be peace in Ireland."

"I will get Captain Raleigh out of the bogs, if he die not, the obstreperous young fool, when Smerwick falls," Elizabeth said.

"Die he just might," the Prime Minister said. "In him is just that sort of rashness."

"He is mad," said Elizabeth, and lapsed into Latin, polyglot as she was: "Whom the gods would destroy, first they make mad."

"Shall I recall him?"

"First let's see if he can survive, then recall him."

"Young as he is, he is of all Your Majesty's subjects the most devoted."

"Burleigh, am I so terribly old?"

"Dear my most gracious Majesty! Thou'lt never be old!"

"Thou 'thouest' me, Burleigh? No one else dares." She plucked at the ribbons that attached her green sleeves to her bodice. She had four thousand pair of them in her wardrobe. "I would thou wert younger."

"Madame, were I younger I would not understand you."

"And now that you're older, nay, ancient, you do?"

"I think I do."

"Dear Burleigh, my very dear Burleigh!" She kissed his withered cheek. "Think again."

That night she danced, and her dancing was sedulously reported by her Spanish ambassador, who was a spy, to King Philip of Spain, who sent a copy of the report to his

[48]

father, the Holy Roman Emperor Charles the Fifth, him of the out-jutting Hapsburg jaw. Nothing Elizabeth did but was reported, written down and analyzed throughout all the chancelleries of Europe, and many a grasping prince, graybeard or stripling, panted, "Does this mean I have a chance?"

"Very high danced Her Majesty," the Spanish spy reported, "and her partner who clasped his hands around her slender waist as he lifted her in the 'jump,' as the English phrase it, was an olive-complexioned youth, broad in the shoulders with a most pleasing leg, rounded and muscular, and very white teeth. Her Majesty's teeth are somewhat dark, as is usual amongst the English, who in this are like their horses. One will look into the provenance of Her Majesty's partner and report further."

But it turned out that Elizabeth's partner was only a Spanish musician who played the guitar. He got with child one of her ladies-in-waiting, eloped with the girl and disappeared into Hungary. "The dirty swine!" swore Elizabeth. "Why do they all desert me? Men, oh phaugh! Pigs, pigs, pigs!" and she straightway confiscated the estate of the bed-happy lady-in-waiting; and since it was considerable consoled herself, for who could get it back from Hungary, that far-away diocese of the Empire? In Latin, composed by herself, she sent a letter of outrage to the Emperor deploring the decline in the morals of the age, suggesting that she would overlook the incident if His Imperial Majesty would make restitution for the money she had laid out to give music lessons to the guitarist and room and board to the lady-in-waiting.

Also in Latin, which was the diplomatic language of princes in their correspondence, His Imperial Majesty, who was about to become a monk, replied that he too deplored the decline in the morals of the age; he sent her some thousands of pounds to compensate her for her expenses and stated, in passing, that his son, King Philip of Spain, held her in highest esteem.

[49]

"Goddamn to hell King Philip of Spain," said Elizabeth, answering, however, the Emperor with a "God will prosper Your Holy Roman Imperial Majesty" (such was the Emperor's title), "with infinite prosperity, long life and ineffable benediction for all the good you have wrought."

The Emperor believed her; he wrote to his son that Elizabeth of England was at heart a true daughter of the Faith, needing only a Catholic husband to bring her back into the fold, appending as was his careful wont detailed notification of all the benefits that would ensue therefrom, namely, the consolidation of all the Old World and the New into one grand united and universal Empire throughout the confines of the whole round globe of earth. Thus she delayed the Spanish Armada for a somewhat longer time.

Now, in Smerwick, there came about a killing that Tamerlane in his Persian grave would have envied. "Never did I heap up so many skulls," he, who had heaped up so many, might have said. "And the perpetrators of this slaughter are naught but Europeans, far away in the mysterious West, where they know not Allah. How very, very instructive."

During the night while Raleigh sat studying in his quarters with no responsibility for the war and brain-deep in a tariff problem—how the new weed called "tobacco" might redound to England's benefit if a proper tax could be placed upon it—Lord Grey sent an ultimatum to the defenders of Smerwick Castle.

"Come out with all honor," offered Lord Grey. "I will send you home to your own countries. Come out, but leave your weapons behind."

"With all honor?" questioned the garrison.

"All," promised Lord Grey.

There was a consultation. Many had been killed by the fire from sea and from land. More had suffered painful burns from Greek Fire that water could not extinguish, even holy water, for they had tried that too, with the result that it simply burned the hotter.

"Why must we leave our swords behind?"

"You surrender them only temporarily, signifying your capitulation as honorable enemies. They will be returned to you; but pile them up in my sight, lest you slit my throat withal, then take your swords and yourselves and begone, into the ships that will carry you back to your homeland."

It seemed, especially to the Italians, that this was a reasonable request. They had a tradition of centuries of throat slitting to their credit in Italy. "We will pile them up," they whispered among themselves, "and if he doesn't put us aboard the ships they'll be easy to get at, and then we will slit his throat indeed."

"Will you honor a flag of truce?" they asked from the walls.

"My gallant friends, enemies though you be, was ever an Englishman who did not?"

No, they agreed; and no Englishman ever had refused to honor such a flag.

Never till now, never till Lord Grey, as the next hours would prove.

They opened the gates of the castle and piled up their swords, very neatly it seemed to Raleigh, who watched: hilts all to one side as if to grasp at a moment's notice.

"There be helms and armor too," shouted Lord Grey. "Pile them up also."

"We need them, my Lord."

"To what purpose? Pile them up. My ships are few. Armor is heavy. Armor will overload them. Do you wish to sink in the sea?"

They did not so wish, and so piled up their armor and helms with the swords. The gate of the castle was still open.

"Now file out, my good friends, and go aboard the

ships that I provide to take you home, for in truth you are going home."

Virtually naked, bereft of weapons, the hopeful defenders of Smerwick filled out of the castle; with them their women and children, the Irish captives and the slatternly females who attached themselves to an army, loudly bewailing their fate, screaming that their protectors had abandoned them, tearing at their bodices and exposing their breasts in a Biblical rending of garments, hoping that the charms thus laid bare might gain them new protectors among the English, who were obviously the victors of the day; nor were they all unsuccessful in their naked stratagem, especially the more comely.

Once the garrison had passed its weapons, at a prearranged signal, it was set upon.

Cannon blazed, hidden soldiers with swords slashed, pikes rained from nowhere and the eerie whfft-whfft-whfft of arrows pierced them dead. Some few, in a welter of corpses, found themselves miraculously alive when day dawned.

"There be some that still wiggle," Lord Grey mentioned to Raleigh. "See that they stop their wiggling."

Raleigh asked, "My Lord, is it again my tour of duty?"

"Yes, it is," said the commander. "Since daybreak. Where have you been? Drawing a plan for new trenches? There is no need; they have sufficed. Sniffing at your alembics? You need sniff no more. Your Greek Fire has burned more Papists than ever King Henry VIII burned at the stake." With his keen sense of the probable, Grey guessed that young Raleigh was likely to rise in the Queen's favor. "You are now to do your duty," Grey said. "I will send you subordinates to assist you in your duty."

"What is my duty?"

"Your duty is to exterminate all those who opposee the Queen."

"All?"

"All. It is an order."

"It is a hard order."

"It is a command. Why do you hesitate, Captain Raleigh? Are you laggard in the Queen's service?"

"Not I."

"Then strike, strike down the Queen's enemies."

On the embankment, where they had waited in vain to be put aboard the ships, lay heaps of the slain garrison.

"There seem none here, my Lord, that need to be struck down further."

"In the castle, Captain Raleigh."

Into the castle Captain Raleigh entered, followed by the assassins under his command, who had higher orders from Lord Grey; but the command was his, and the shame. And there, with them, he did his duty.

In all his voluminous writings he never once referred to the slaughter.

Pikemen thrust so that at times two bodies were impaled on the pike. Cavalry sabres hacked off heads, arms, legs and let them lie where they fell, so that the ancient stones reeked with the queer sweet-sour odor of fresh-let blood. Neither women nor children, nor doddering graybeards nor nubile virgins—none, none were spared.

Whether Raleigh himself took part in the slaughter history does not specifically state, but history leans toward the thesis that he did. Perhaps he thought it more merciful to put them quickly out of their misery, forestalling the inevitable death that he knew awaited them. Perhaps he conceived himself only an agent, obeying military orders. So Herod may have conceived himself at the Massacre of the Innocents.

But it is more probable that Raleigh's hatred of the Irish, inborn and thoroughly English, caused him to use his sword in the dismal slaughter at Castle Smerwick, and that his afterthoughts were mere excuses to exculpate his behavior: the Queen's instructions to Lord Grey, Grey's zeal to exterminate, the ghoulish glee of the subordinates as they went about the task. Raleigh's kindliest biographers find nothing to praise in his action at Smerwick, nothing but his silence and shame.

To Lord Grey Raleigh now could report, "There are none that wiggle, my Lord, not one."

"All are dead?"

"All but a few . . ."

"I commanded you to slay them all."

Raleigh said, "Some few Spanish grandees, my Lord, strutting themselves erect and proud as is their wont, spat in my beard like the highborn Spanish gentlemen they are and I conceived them rich, so them I held to ransom."

"Why?"

"Because it is profitable to the Queen."

When the report reached England Lord Burleigh said, "Raleigh finds treasure everywhere, even in the most unlikely places. There was, after all, treasure in Smerwick."

"I should never have thought it possible in Smerwick," Elizabeth said, rapidly calculating in her mind what the ransom would amount to.

But only reluctantly did she agree to let them be ransomed.

This ransom King Philip promptly paid, still scheming to marry her and glad to get back some of his most capable soldiers, whom he would send against her if marry her he did not. Philip's prompt payment of the ransom greatly eased her perpetually embarrassed exchequer.

Frightened Elizabeth never was. But her ambassadors continued to report that King Philip continued to build the ships of a mighty armada even while he was proffering his hand in marriage.

"Raleigh should not have spared the grandees," Elizabeth said. "I ordered Grey to kill them all."

"The increment to the Treasury is most welcome," Burleigh said, "One could hardly do without it."

"Oh, aye, aye, aye. Goddamn the damned increment. We need it, yes, but Grey should have slaughtered them all as I told him to; and who is this soft Raleigh to spare them!"

"Majesty," sighed Burleigh, "there hath been very very great slaughter."

"I am truly sorry for that. The dead are so helpless." Then she drew herself up and her eyes blazed. "But England is first in my heart."

"So it is first in the hearts of all Your Majesty's loving servants—"

"Loving, my Burleigh?"

"Aye, loving, Your Majesty. They do deeply love you."

"Do you love me too, my Burleigh?"

"My gracious Queen, most gracious Majesty, the theologians, whom Your Majesty readeth more sapiently than I, state and declare that 'love' is a slippery term belonging first to God, as *latria, dulia, hyperdulia* and some other *dulias* that escape me for the moment, all appertaining to the devotion to God and His Saints and to those rulers whom He hath set over us like Your Majesty."

Her father, King Henry VIII, more Catholic than she, had brought her up wise in the complex Latinity of the Church and she was not at all confused by the Prime Minister's *dulias*.

"My father would have agreed with you, Burleigh, even when he summoned the chopper to chop off the head of my poor six-fingered mother, as was said, though in truth it was only a hangnail. Thou knowest naught of love, my Burleigh. In future confine thyself to the little thou knowest."

He bent his grizzled head and did not reply.

Impulsively she tripped 'round him, light as a feather on her quick tiny feet, and tweaked his beard and planted a smacking kiss on his cheek.

"Blood of God, you slog-witted old well of such infinite wisdom, I would there were more like you, more I could trust."

"Most gracious Madame!"

"Look to it. Since this rash Captain Raleigh presumes to take unto himself to hold to ransom certain Spanish grandees, though I sanction him not, do thou, Burleigh, receive into my treasury their Spanish gold, biting it first to be sure it's gold—"

"Madame, my teeth! But others have bit it, and chemists have assayed it and I can assure you it is gold."

"—and divulge naught, especially to King Philip, ten thousand devils [the next word would have made a sailor blush] and blister his Spanish ass!" Burleigh chuckled.

"Madame, do I ever divulge that which I am privileged to hear in Your Majesty's presence?"

The horror of the massacre at Smerwick trumpeted 'round the world. The Mediterranean nations were outraged, since it was their citizens who had been killed. The Pope dusted off the Bull excommunicating Elizabeth but did not publish it, still hoping for better times and a compromise with the eccentric Majesty of England.

The northern nations, sniffing a Protestant wind out of England, sent fulsome congratulations through their ambassadors, hoping for an English alliance.

Elizabeth smiled and held her tongue and encouraged them all.

"Bring him home, Burleigh. 'Twere a pity for so resourceful a man to get himself killed."

Thus Raleigh was recalled, and so was Lord Grey, and Elizabeth placed Ireland under the heel of ever more stern commanders.

CHAPTER IX

ALL DURING the night it rained. Sometimes the downpour was heavy, other times intermittent, but the total precipitation was great, more than enough to turn the streets into torrents of mud and rotting vegetables, liberally laced with the contents of chamber pots which canny housewives waited for just such a cleansing rainstorm to sluice away.

Now, on this glorious spring morning a golden sun shone down, burnt off the haze in the upper air; the wet streets rapidly began to dry. The atmosphere was pellucid, crystal clear, invigorating, full of the fragrance of flowers just bursting into bloom.

Some puddles remained however, and the Queen hesitated. Under her breath she swore, "God's Blood! I will walk straight through. I was never afraid of water. Water is my friend, my island-girding moat that confounds the bloody Spaniards."

But still she hesitated, gazing down fondly at her jeweled slippers, slippers whose cost would have ransomed a prince of the blood, slippers blazing with rubies and pearls. She was loath to befoul them. She would dance in those slippers tonight.

As she hesitated, wrinkling her sensitive high bridged nose at the sight of an especially noisome puddle directly in her path, there advanced from the crowd behind her a tall man whom she had never seen. He was strikingly handsome. He towered above the others; he was over six feet high, an astounding stature at a time when a man was accounted tall if he was bigger than five and a half feet. Her own father, Henry VIII, the most imposing figure of his time, had not been so tall as this.

The man was gorgeously garbed in a spectacular cloak that scintillated with a rainbow spectrum of jewels, all red and green and gold. The Queen, an expert in jewels, knew them all; but "Pish!" she thought, "cat's-eye-green emeralds, golden amethysts, bloody-red rubies, they can all be counterfeited in glass and cheap paste to make a display."

But yet . . . there were the pearls.

Pearls were her favorite jewel; pearls were alive; pearls could not be counterfeited. "He interests me. So many men are puny, little, feeble and don't know a pearl from a pig's snout."

He had a short pointed beard, intensely black and waxed to a point.

It was just such a beard—so went the popular belief, and the Queen shared it—just such a beard as the Devil adopted when he chose to make himself agreeable to unsuspecting females whose husbands were away and whose place he would take in their beds and upon whose bodies he would beget a race of changelings; an uncanny beard but devilishly seductive.

There were other handsome men in her suite; Elizabeth's fondness for them was notorious and chuckled at: what could be more fitting than that a woman who doted on beauty in clothes should dote upon manly beauty also? One such handsome was the stripling Earl of Essex, with big brown dreamy eyes and a beard still soft with the texture of youth. She knew, of course, it would stiffen in time. Meanwhile it was remarkably like her own hair, more red than blond.

Essex bore himself with the pride of his distinguished ancestry, as the proud, the privileged young aristocrat.

It took no sovereign's instinct, however experienced, to see that he was already uncommonly attractive to women, for she felt it in herself. Tonight, she decided, she would permit him to dance with her, and watch with contempt the jealousy of her waiting-women. She was more than twice his age. But she was the Queen.

But suddenly those soft young dreamy eyes blazed with fury. The tall man did an astonishing thing.

Removing his hat with a flourish, Raleigh cast off his cloak and spread it, pearls down, over the surface of the puddle. Its velvet fabric trembled on the surface of the stinking mud as if it were outraged by the insult. Its costly fur collar began to wilt and absorb the stain of the filth.

Elizabeth hesitated to put her foot down on it. It was a garment she herself would have been proud to number among the two thousand gowns, the four thousand pair of sleeves that comprised her wardrobe, along with countless pairs of footgear; and none of this did she ever wear twice, but she knew them all and knew to a penny what they were worth.

Raleigh murmured a Biblical reference, "Majesty, I have parted the Red Sea, that you be not wetted," and he offered his arm, which she took.

"Thou'rt a saucy rascal," she said, "thou"-ing him to signify displeasure, smiling archly to signify she was actually not at all displeased; and she stepped lightly dry-shod to the other side of the puddle while her suite looked on enjoying the spectacle and Essex choked down his fury, red in the face and envy a-borning in his heart, envy that would endure as long as he lived. The Queen said, "How are you called?"

"Raleigh," he answered, "Walter Raleigh, to serve Your Majesty."

Punning upon his name the Queen replied, gazing at the puddle, "I shall call you 'Water.' I have heard good report of you, Captain Raleigh."

They were at the gateway of the splendid mansion she had built for Lord Burleigh.

She glanced back at the cloak, now lying sodden and soiled in the puddle, and sighed. She was never one to waste a penny, far less a costly garment sown with living pearls. Raleigh divined her thought. "It is nothing," he said, smiling, shrugging. "It has done its duty."

"Nothing, do you say? It is nothing? Look back, my Water."

Raleigh looked back. A raggedy beggar was fumbling with the cloak.

"Great Jesus, it is nothing that rogues put stolen pearls into their thieving pockets? Ho there! My guard!"

The Captain of her Guard approached.

"Most gracious Majesty?"

"See to it that no gallows bird steals the pearls from the cloak lying yonder. And if he do, cudgel him roundly and take the pearls away from him."

"Majesty, if a rogue snatch a single pearl that Your Majesty has made doubly precious by the touch of your foot, that rogue shall not see another day."

"Nay," said the Queen, "he would not steal were he not desperate. Feed the scoundrel and let him go. He looks like an Englishman."

"You are lucky," the Captain of the Guard said to the beggar. "I am hungry," said the thief, quaking with terror. The penalty for stealing was hanging.

"Feed the poor man and let him go with my benison. Alas, that Englishmen should hunger! It is the whoreson Spaniards that bring me this grief."

"All right, I'll feed you now," said the Captain of the Guard.

The beggar rose and waved his tattered hat. "God bless Your Majesty, God bless you, Ma'am!" and in a quavering voice, "She is an angel!"

"Art truly an Englishman, rogue?" said the Captain of the Guard.

"Aye, none other."

"Then eat, rogue, and thank God that Her Majesty is compassionate."

Wolfing down the mutton and beer that was proffered him, the thief kept murmuring, "She is an angel."

"What is your name, rogue?" asked the Captain of the Guard, for it was part of his duty to report all contact with malefactors.

"Derrick. My name is Derrick."

"Derrick," said the Captain of the Guard, "see to it that you do no further wrong," and he made a note in a tablet, for he could write.

A good-looking young lackey fetched Raleigh's cloak, the pearls all accounted for, and Elizabeth thanked him coyly and tousled his curly head and watched with pleasure the blush that suffused his beardless cheeks. "Sweet of you, child," she said. She caused the cloak to be hung by a fire to dry, then had it put away in a clothes press. "I shall keep it by me always," she said to Raleigh, "as a remembrance of my madcap Captain's gallantry." He winced a bit, hiding it with a smile. He had lost a costly cloak, but he had gained something far more valuable: the Queen's favorable notice.

She mused as she rested her hand lightly on his arm, "What a formidable face my Lord of Essex put on! Such an undisciplined youngster." And to herself, "And how handsome!" One day, when he grew older she would make a man of him, this highborn youth with his still-too-soft beard, so promising of passion she itched to stroke it, so deliciously like her own hair.

As yet Elizabeth had no need of false hair, though hers was thinning, thinning, the cruel legacy of her father, whose head, in his latter days, the spirochete had balded like a razor, clean down to the skull. Patchy-bald too had been the scalp of his daughter Bloody Mary, Elizabeth's half sister, who had reigned in England before her, ingloriously, pathetically, and had died barren.

[61]

Nor could Elizabeth, she feared, hope for progeny, despite her fervent prayers. The curse of the Tudors.

Just as Elizabeth kept peace in the vast world of Europe among proud and self-seeking princes, so she kept peace in the little world of her own court among equally proud and self-seeking aspirants for her favor.

She danced that night indeed, but not with Raleigh, not yet.

Referring again to the "formidable face" of Essex, she said to Raleigh, "He truly admires you, Water, and he envies your soldierly conduct in Ireland, for as yet he has soldiered nowhere. Such an emotional lad, so ambitious to rise! But youth and fate have so far denied him the opportunity. Smooth the ruffled feathers of this somewhat unstable boy. Smile upon him, my Water, praise his grace in the dance when he dances with me and you will make him your friend for life, mark my word for I know him well."

No one, of course, could go up to the Queen and say, "Ma'am, may I have the next dance?" Elizabeth would inform an equerry who her next partner would be and the favored partner would present himself with a low bow, take her pretty hand and try not to let his face betray how superior he felt to the courtiers whom she had not as yet honored or, worse, did not honor at all; while her waiting-women whispered and gossiped among themselves that So-and-So must be about to be granted a troop of horse, a knighthood, a ship or a monopoly, or that So-and-So was being publicly snubbed, and didn't it make you wonder what dreadful thing he had done to incur her displeasure—tradesmen would cut off his credit, foreign ambassadors would report to their sovereigns that the unfortunate gentleman no longer had the Queen's ear. These little favors cost her nothing and she bestowed them with consummate art, minutely calculating their value to the great goal of her statecraft:

peace at home and abroad while she built up the strength of her island kingdom. So charmingly did she accomplish her ends that she kept the whole world guessing throughout her long and glorious reign. Few men and fewer women have given their name to an entire age.

Raleigh's calculating mind was so like her own that he instantly divined and applauded her little strategy for the evening, and decided to make himself agreeable to Essex: He was already at odds with Lord Grey; he could not afford to make another enemy. "I shall," he determined, "make myself as invisible as a shadow at dawn, and when I greet my Lord of Essex, 'twill be with honey words." Forthwith he chose a more lustrous pearl for his earring, put on a more gorgeous suit of court dress and chose a ruff of Flemish lace for his wrists—he had picked it up for a song in Holland from a pretty little wench who was bewitched by his favors, and returned them.

After the Queen had danced with Essex, Raleigh joined with the others who clustered 'round him to praise and fawn upon his high step in the "jump"; who observed how a strong a man must be to jump so high, what a good, what a handsome leg he had—but Raleigh made all these flattering remarks in such humble and delicate language that Essex found them not in the least offensive. He thought to himself, "This commoner puts a proper value on my worth; he speaks better than the country-born rustic that he is; no doubt he has good qualities and I will not deny him my friendship, particularly since the Queen shows him none. She hasn't so much as glanced at him all evening, big as he is." So Essex smiled his handsome smile at Raleigh and shook his hand and said he hoped they would meet again, and Raleigh bowed respectfully and melted into the background where he made himself inconspicuous among the unknown courtiers and hangers-on whom nobody ever noticed.

But it is difficult to be inconspicuous when one dresses

like a prince and towers head and shoulders above everybody else in the room. Shortly Raleigh slipped out of
the court and went to his rooms, where he stayed up
late, writing by candlelight a sheaf of notes to prepare
his mind for a confrontation with Lord Grey. Elizabeth
had summoned both Raleigh and Grey to attend her in
Privy Council next morning to apprise her of the
present state of Ireland and recommend the best measures to take against the rebels.

"I hope that fool Grey doesn't try to keep his hat on
in Her Majesty's presence," Raleigh thought with a grin,
half hoping the bigoted Puritan actually would. "She'd
be vastly discountenanced." Raleigh's gallantry was so
deep and instinctive that he would doff his hat to a
flower-girl in the street—if she were pretty or pert or
looked tired or helpless.

Lord Grey would come to the Council with his secretary at his elbow to jog his memory and supply him
with names, places, dates and military precedents for all
the stern measures he had taken in Ireland. Raleigh had
only his excellent memory and fertile mind.

Elizabeth rose early and went early to bed, a custom
prevalent also among the New England colonists and fos-
silized in Puritan tradition long after the mother country
had adopted laxer manners: it was supposed to make one
healthy, wealthy and wise.

Punctual at the sunrise Lord Grey arrived at the
door of the Privy Council with his tall black Puritan hat
jammed down tight on his forehead, and was met by the
Captain of the Queen's Guard, who told him to take it
off.

Grey jammed his hat down tighter and said it was the
will of God that he keep it on.

The Captain of the Guard said he did not know the
will of God, being neither a theologian nor a Puritan.
He eyed Lord Grey stonily and pronounced that he *did*

know the will of the Queen however, and that it was precisely her will that men remove their hats in her presence.

Scowling, sensing the prejudice against his sect, knowing how much he had to lose if he incurred the Queen's displeasure, Lord Grey took off his hat. Raleigh watched the comedy with a wry grin.

Raleigh himself had dressed with meticulous care, but how different he looked from the flamboyant creature of the night before: he had on his simple captain's uniform, clean but much worn from the Irish campaign, with a patch neatly sewn on the sleeve of his sword arm, covering, as everyone supposed, a rent from a bullet or sword—except that there was no rent underneath. "But there easily might have been," Raleigh thought, justifying the theatrical patch. "God knows I've seen action enough." It was just his bad luck that he had neither wounds nor a torn garment to prove it.

Following Lord Grey came his secretary, Edmund Spenser, another Puritan, a nervous little man who habitually lived with his mother. He had a fumbling manner and a very bad cough that he tried to suppress in a small red handkerchief. Raleigh wondered why it was red and thought he knew: to hide the red spots that sometimes resulted from the cough. Raleigh's compassion, like his fury, was easily aroused. "Poor man," he thought, "there is death in that cough." His cheeks were too thin, and too pale except for hectic red spots on the prominent cheekbones. But Raleigh felt drawn to him nevertheless, for Spenser was wretchedly poor, poorer than Raleigh ever had been. Besides, it took courage to be a Puritan in Elizabeth's age, and Raleigh admired courage. Moreover, Spenser was known to be a poet, with a sharp wit and a superb command of the English language, "a bit over-educated, to my way of thinking," Raleigh had decided, "a bit over-fraught with allegory, leading you oftentimes through so labyrinthine a maze that his meaning is hard to discover—but superb withal."

Lord Burleigh looked up from the long table at which the Privy Council were sitting awaiting the Queen. He saw Spenser, and his face took on a look of dislike which he seldom displayed in public. Edmund Spenser had had the temerity to pen some satirical verses with Lord Burleigh the butt of his satire. Though he circulated them only in manuscript among a few friends, they instantly came to Burleigh's attention; Burleigh never forgave him; and from Burleigh they came under the eye of the Queen. Elizabeth's devotion to her great Prime Minister verged on the pathological; she equated an attack on him with an attack on herself; before she entered the Council Chamber Edmund Spenser had already lost his secretaryship.

Elizabeth sat herself down in the throne-like chair at the head of the table and welcomed her Privy Council. Pearls shone in her carefully coiffed hair. Her dainty white hands sparkled with jeweled rings. She greeted many of her Council by name. Her welcome to Lord Grey was especially warm and apt: "My Lord," she said, "you have subdued Egypt and destroyed it; you have scattered your enemies abroad with your mighty arm," and the dour Puritan, recognizing the words of the 89th Psalm, could not restrain a startled, "God bless Your Majesty."

It was now apparent to everyone that, though she was asking advice, she had already made up her mind what to do about Ireland.

She did not once look at Spenser and glanced impatiently in another direction whenever he whispered some pertinent data into Lord Grey's ear as he made a long speech in defense of his Irish policy.

Somewhat dispiritedly Raleigh had to concede that Grey's defense was remarkably good, and found himself wishing that Edmund Spenser were on his side. First there was flattery, which was always sweet music to Elizabeth's ear and could only have come from Spenser. Then there was iron, which could only have come from Grey.

Under their wise and gracious Queen, Grey said, England possessed the most just laws and the purest religion known to the civilized world, where even dissenters were free to follow their consciences. Irish laws and Irish religion should be made to conform to England's. But first the Irish rebels must be thoroughly subjugated. An army of ten thousand foot and a thousand horse should be immediately dispatched to Ireland. The rebels should be given no more than twenty days to surrender. Those who refused or were slow to submit should be made to suffer the just desert of Her Majesty's displeasure, hunted down like animals, extirpated root and branch, branded as the traitors they were till their spirit was broken. Then and only then, if they repented and threw themselves on her mercy, might a more liberal viceroy be appointed and pardons granted. But until that time, if it ever came, the Irish must be treated as they always had been, as beasts, corrupt, traitorous, idolatrous.

Grey sat down. Elizabeth smiled winningly toward nim. Heads nodded around the table, all but Raleigh's. He slowly shook his head, sorely bemused. He found himself in agreement with everything Lord Grey had said, except, perhaps, that he disliked slaughtering children. By God! How he would have liked to head such an army as Grey had projected! It was easy to see that Grey hoped to command it and win reinstatement as viceroy. Raleigh did not begrudge him that. In his place he'd have done the same.

It was the sheer logistical impossibility of Grey's grandiose operation that appalled him. Grey was a soldier. He should have known that 10,000 soldiers would require 10,000 muskets plus spares; 100,000 pounds of gunpowder at the start plus an assured source of renewal when they became engaged, as they were certain to be; 10,000 swords, daggers at the very least; 10,000 good woollen blankets, unless the men were to catch a consumption from sleeping in the noisome Irish bogs; 10,000 pair of sturdy marching shoes; 10,000 uniforms, since the common soldier habitually dressed in rags till the army clothed him; 5,000 canvas tents, for assuredly there was no shelter that Ireland could afford them; plus rations, since food was getting scarcer every day in Ireland. Rations meant bread, and bread meant bakers, and bakers meant ovens—all this would have to be supplied at enormous cost.

As for the 1,000 horse—1,000 saddles, 1,000 bridles, 1,000 suits of harness with harness-men to repair them; 4,000 horseshoes, with blacksmiths to re-shoe them and adequate supplies of iron for new ones; and blacksmiths meant forges and bellows. Tons of fodder to feed the animals—the requirements were endless. It would take weeks of careful planning just to set up the operation, as Grey, the soldier, should have known; but Grey was proposing that everything be dispatched to Ireland immediately.

Raleigh doubted whether there were enough skilled craftsmen in all of England to meet such fantastic requirements, and if there were, whether they would be willing to leave their hearth and homes and go. There was no law to compel them. Conscription into an army had not yet appeared in the civilized world to solve this awkward problem. Courts martial did not exist. If a common soldier struck his commanding officer he was tried by a jury of his peers, and his peers were usually poor farmers like himself and they usually let him off. If, perchance, they found him guilty, they levied a fine against him for such damage as his blow had inflicted, which usually wasn't much. And if the man didn't like the verdict he was perfectly free to go home after his forty-day tour of duty was done.

Competent as he was, brilliant as was his record, Lord

Grey was only a soldier. Raleigh was both a soldier and a sailor. He knew, as Lord Grey could not know, the enormous tonnage required to keep up a constant flow of replacements of all the supplies that Grey's expedition would eat up and wear out, and this too at a time when the Queen was trying desperately to build up a navy of fighting ships.

At the head of the table the Queen was looking at him, displeased. She had not especially minded his thoughtful mien and the slow negative shake of his head. What really irked her was a sense that Raleigh and that scurrilous Edmund Spenser seemed to have something in common. How was it possible, the one so seductive and the other so repulsive!

"Captain Raleigh, you hold a different view from the view of Lord Grey?"

"With humble duty, Ma'am, I do," Raleigh said, and attempted to explain the deplorable logistics of maintaining a constant flow of supplies to Ireland.

"Pish, pish," said Elizabeth; but she did not swear in front of the Puritans as she might have done if they had been absent.

"And the cost, Your Majesty, would probably exhaust Your Majesty's treasury."

This hit her hard. "Would it?" she whispered to Lord Burleigh.

"To the very last penny," he replied in a whisper, his face never changing.

Elizabeth made a quick and characteristic decision. She would let the matter rest for the moment, do nothing, and wait upon events.

Graciously she dismissed her Council, thanking them for their advice, smiling at everyone, Raleigh included—everyone but Spenser. Ireland, she said, was in competent hands at the moment. She had had word that the rebels were being progressively routed; no doubt the Irish would soon come to their senses.

Later she said to Lord Burleigh, "Get that scribbling poet out of my sight!"

"Which one?" Burleigh said blandly.

"That ugly sickly wheezing Puritan runt, Edmund Spenser."

"Aye, that one," said Burleigh. "Nothing would pleasure me more. Would it please Your Majesty to send him back to Ireland? There is famine there, and it is increasing."

"Good!" said the Queen. "Lord Grey did his work well. Famine is cheaper than his scheme for an invasion. Send Spenser there by all means and let him enjoy it, though the wretched man looks half starved already."

So Edmund Spenser was packed off to Ireland to starve, lodged in a tumble-down house that had been confiscated from the rebels. He got it rent free on condition that he harbor no traitorous Irishmen and that he keep them out in the bogs, a condition easily met, since the Irish were already in the bogs, digging for edible roots and counting it a feast day if they happened upon the corpse of an animal not too far gone in putrefaction. That he did not actually starve was due entirely to Walter Raleigh, who sold a jewel and gave him a small sum of money.

"Farewell," he said, "though I fear your fare will prove a fast. I would this were more, but I know not my own future."

"I do," Spenser said. "I read it in the Queen's eyes."

There in Ireland, in his lonesome house, Spenser wrote dismal poetry by the smoky light of a guttering rush candle. He was too poor to afford real candles. Wax candles were all in Popish churches; tallow candles, made of good mutton fat, had all been eaten. But rushes grew in the bogs, and when dipped in grease too sickening for even a starving man to eat, could be made into "rush-lights."

Rush-lights do not keep you warm. Sometimes he imagined he would die of the cold and the dampness that winter soon would bring. There was firewood aplenty close by, but he did not have the strength to cut it; peat too, but to dig it was even a harder task. Listless and sick, he did not much care whether he lived or died.

He ate almost nothing at all. Illness had totally suppressed all natural hunger, and thus he did not die of starvation while all around him, first by the score, then by hundreds, Irishmen starved to death—men, women and, pitifully, children. In the extremity of their hunger, as the famine deepened, people turned into beasts. Mothers who at first had deprived themselves to feed their children, now snatched the food, ignoring the piteous cries and imploring hands of their little ones, ate it themselves and, having swallowed it, wept at the thing they had done. There were even uglier rumors, that cannibalism existed, that people were eating each other; but Spenser did not believe the rumors and did not include them in his history of the famine, on which the above account is based.

Then, oddly, as his body wasted, a strange change came over him. Like the Buddha, when he saw a corpse for the first time and was first aware of human misery; like Mohammed fasting lonely in his cave; like Saint Simeon, fasting lonely on his pillar; like Saul, who beheld a great light and became Saint Paul—so it was that the change came over Edmund Spenser with the strength of a revelation.

His depression ebbed away. The venom drained out of his pen. He no longer resented his personal disgrace. He no longer thought of Lord Burleigh as a spiteful old man. And as for the Queen, who had so petulantly exiled him, he viewed her as one more struggling human being, cast in a role she had not chosen, set upon by ravening enemies, valiantly trying her poor human best to bring order and peace to a wolfish world.

Compassion had entered into the soul of another great poet, as it did to John Milton when he went blind.

CHAPTER X

SURELY a wolfish world it was. Famine was decimating the population of Ireland, where Spenser languished, the fire of his consumption burning out all that was dross in his soul and his poetry.

Elizabeth did nothing, sat by and let the famine run its course. She did not reinstate Lord Grey, but neither did she dismiss him. He remained in high repute and a Privy Counsellor. In Ireland her roaming bands of murdering soldiers ambushed and killed the rebel Earl of Desmond. They cut off his head and sent it to her pickled in a butt of brine, like a cabbage. She thanked them in gracious language and caused the head to be impaled on a pike and exposed for all to see on London Bridge, where it remained till the eyes melted out and the jaw sagged open in what looked like a scream or a curse. Ravens came and carried away the hair and flew off with it in their beaks for some raven-purpose of their own, perhaps to line their nests, then pecked at the whitening skull till it no longer interested them.

Famine and Desmond's head served as an object lesson: Ireland was so thoroughly broken in spirit that the Irish did not rise again in revolt even when, some time later, the Spanish Armada arrived.

Spain was climbing toward the pinnacle of her power. From America silver and gold in enormous quantities poured into her treasury, despite heavy losses from privateers. Pearls, gems, spices and precious silks came in her high-decked galleons from her possessions in the Orient. In manpower, wealth and territory she dwarfed all other nations. Nor was Spain rent by religious dissension. The Inquisition saw to that. Throughout the Iberian peninsula Catholicism was monolithic under the never-sleeping eye of the Holy Office. This was the heartland of the Spanish Empire. Seven hundred years of fighting the Moors and finally expelling them had forged the Spanish character. God had prospered their swords; to lay them down was unthinkable; to spare the infidel, the heretic, the Protestant, was to betray God. Chaos might reign among nations on her borders, but in the heartland of Spain all was granite law and religious order.

But there lurked a creeping menace, unknown and unsuspected. The population of Spain, once so fertile, insidiously ceased to grow. Too many Spaniards had made too many voyages to America, where there was pox, and to the East Indies, where there were yaws, gleet, tapeworm, ague, inguinal granuloma, disabling diseases, several of them venereal. Many healthy young Spaniards, deprived of their Spanish women for two or three years on a voyage, raped or bought the native women, and returned home with the sickness in their bodies; and this while in northern countries the populations were booming.

There was no such religious order in the Protestant Netherlands. Since Spain claimed the Netherlands she sent an army to fight the Protestants. In their never-ending struggle to free themselves from the Spanish menace the Dutch suffered many reverses but never gave up. One encounter involved Walter Raleigh.

He contrived to twist it to his personal advantage.

There was a flighty worthless French Duke named Francis of Anjou with nothing to redeem him in

English eyes except that he was Protestant. But with all his faults he was brave. Duke Francis was rich, blood relative to half of Europe's rulers, bored with life, and perpetually scheming to do something spectacular. He never could stick to anything.

It suddenly occurred to him that it might be amusing to go fight the Spaniards in Holland, and he began collecting an expeditionary force of volunteers.

Raleigh was at Elizabeth's court. More and more she was coming to relish his companionship. When she was weary after an exhausting day she would lie back on her bed and relax and listen to him read his poems. They were all addressed to her.

He called her his goddess, heaven's queen of beauty, radiant Diana, the moon, blessing the earth beneath with celestial rays:

> *Praised be Diana's fair and harmless light,*
> *Praised be the dews wherewith she moists the ground;*
> *Praised be her beams, the glory of the night,*
> *Praised be her power, by which all powers abound.*
>
> *Praised be her nymphs with whom she decks the woods,*
> *Praised be her knights, in whom true honour lives,*
> *Praised be the force by which she moves the floods,*
> *Let that Diana shine, which all these gives.*
>
> *She beauty is. By her the fair endure.*

She beauty is. By her the fair endure. But Diana was far, far away, untouchable as a star. Her lover could only sigh.

It was courtly poetry. Many gentlemen attempted it. It had its provenance long ago in Dante's love of Beatrice, whom, though he married someone else and had children, he adored all his life long. Other poets, good and paltry, took up the theme. The wandering minstrels, singing for their supper in the lord's castle, addressed similar love poems to the lady of the manor. Some were quite explicit:

> *I naked, thou naked, in bed would we lie*
> *All night long;*
> *Touch thee would I not, but praise thee in song.*

The lord of the manor never took offense, since such poetry had a long and respectable tradition behind it.

Few gentlemen of her court possessed Raleigh's skill as a poet. Not one had his good looks. Elizabeth began to demand more and more of his time and gave him nothing in return but her smiles, which made him enemies and put not a penny in his purse. Vexed by her possessiveness he begged her permission to join the Duke of Anjou and go, at his own expense, to fight the Spaniards in Holland. He was a proven captain. She was always glad to fight the Spaniards. It would cost her nothing. Reluctantly she let him go.

"Do not get yourself killed, my Water," she said, and there was unwonted affection in her eyes. "It is my wish to keep you by me."

The Duke's expeditionary force was ill-equipped, ill-provisioned and payment was slow when it came at all. They were no match for the disciplined Spaniards and died in droves. Many others deserted.

The Duke quickly tired of the land war and decided he could accomplish more by a sea war. Knowing that Raleigh was a sailor, he gave him letters of marque to prey upon Spanish shipping. The actual document was engrossed on vellum and sealed with the Duke's gorgeous Angevin crest. It gave Raleigh, his heirs and assigns, unlimited authority to sink, capture and loot Spanish ships and kill or hold to ransom their crews. The document was legal, couched in the usual terms and everywhere acceptable in Europe. Raleigh had no ships, but he knew the value of letters of marque.

The Duke also fancied himself an ambassador of good-will. It would help no end, he thought, if he should pay a courtesy call on the Prince of Orange, struggling so valiantly to unite the Netherlands against the Spanish menace.

"Cousin William will never forgive me if I fail to come and see him and cheer him up," he said to Raleigh. "You speak French, do you not?" Since he and Raleigh had never spoken anything else and were speaking it at that very moment, Raleigh simply smiled and said, Yes, he did.

"Good," said the Duke. "Cousin William speaks no English, in fact he hardly ever speaks at all, which must be why they call him William the Silent, yes, I am sure it is. How droll. But he hobbles along with a sort of Dutch-French that assails the ear like a pump—how do you say it, my sailorman friend?—like a bilge pump choked with beer. There. I have something."

"Monseigneur," Raleigh said, "You certainly do. There is nothing that assails the ear so formidably as a bilge pump choked with beer."

"So you must come with me, *mon ami*, and explain the importance of sea war to my good Cousin William. It is arranged. I have arranged it, have I not?"

"Masterfully," said Raleigh. "Like Don John of Austria, the victorious admiral at Lepanto."

"Ah yes," said the Duke, vastly pleased to be classed with the hero. "Dear Uncle John. A *very* great man. I've never been ashamed that he was a bastard, though of course some of our family. . . ."

"I understand," Raleigh said.

William the Silent, Count of Nassau and Prince of Orange, Stadholder of the Netherlands, greeted his cousin with a geniality that belied his name. Raleigh sensed that the Prince was silent only on political matters, like Elizabeth herself, *Video et taceo*. William was

[76]

a strong-faced man with a sturdy build and a short Dutch beard prematurely gray. He quite understood the importance of sea warfare. What Dutchman did not? But he let Raleigh explain it as if it were new to him.

"Above all," Raleigh said, "let the ships be fast, heavily gunned and full of seamen, not soldiers. Soldiers only add weight. Let the weight be gunpowder and cannon."

Raleigh warmed to his subject.

"And oars? No oars! Lepanto was a glorious victory, but we'd have had it at half the price except for those confounded oars on the Venetian galleys. They got in the way of Don John's ships and he had to sheer them off before he could maneuver."

The Prince of Orange nodded his head. Raleigh had described exactly the sort of ships he was building. "Captain Raleigh is right," he agreed. "Oars are no good in the Atlantic. The sea is too rough. But I expect they'll be used in the Mediterranean for a long time to come."

"Of a certainty, Cousin," said the Duke, whose French ships also had oars. "Where in the world would one put one's galley slaves but on oars?"

Raleigh said shortly, "I will have no galley slaves on *my* ships."

"You have ships, Captain Raleigh?" asked the Prince of Orange.

Raleigh's imagination soared. In his mind he already had. "Sir," he said, "I propose to man and outfit a considerable fleet."

"To what purpose, Captain Raleigh?"

"To search out new lands, to plant colonies like my brother Sir Humphrey Gilbert; but especially and most immediately to fight the Spaniards on the sea."

"I myself have granted to Captain Raleigh my letters of marque for his laudable venture," said the Duke. "Would it not be in your interest, Cousin William, to grant him yours also? One cannot have too many friends; King Philip cannot have too many enemies."

It would cost the Prince of Orange nothing to authorize one more privateer to prey upon the Spaniards. He readily granted his letters of marque.

Yet in the end it would cost him his life. King Philip was increasingly irked at the steady persistent tenacity of the Dutch. Everywhere they were stirring up enemies against him. Openly or covertly the pressure against him mounted, and he laid the blame squarely where it belonged: on the doughty stubborn Prince of Orange. Philip turned to a device he had successfully used before: political assassination. He offered a rich reward to anyone who would murder William. He found a likely agent, paid him half the reward, sent him secretly to Holland and there, in the Prinsenhof at Delft, William's own residence, the assassin shot him dead. On the murderer's return, King Philip gave him the other half of the blood-money muttering, "William now is silent indeed," and ordered Te Deums of praise sung secretly in his private chapel. King Philip never advertised the means by which he gained his ends.

Raleigh returned to England within the month with two valuable letters of marque snugly tucked away in his purse. The reason for his sudden return was the unexpected death of the Duke. Duke Francis of Anjou slipped out alone one beautiful moonlit night to take a farewell look at the picturesque countryside which he had decided to leave. It was peaceful in the moonlight, with silvery canals and lazily turning windmills. "But what a soggy country; not at all like home." He was bored to death. He conceived that he had done his duty. He would disband his little group of volunteers, those who had not already deserted. He would go home and turn his talents to something more glamorous, something less tedious and sweaty.

In that night there suddenly appeared before him a squad of Spanish scouts reconnoitering the countryside, silvery moonlight glistening on their silver helmets, touching with silver the tips of their pikes, a cold fore-boding light such as appears in lunar rainbows, such as appears on tombstones of the dead, ashen.

He drew his sword and dashed at them shouting for help, "*à moi*," and they ran him through.

"Who is this?" said the squad leader.

Looking at the corpse another replied, "Blessed Mother of God! 'Tis the Duke himself."

The Duke looked handsome in the moonlight, be-jeweled and beribboned like the royal prince that he was, and on his face an expression of profound peace.

"Touch him not," ordered the squad leader, his eye on the Duke's rich attire.

"Not I, sir."

"We shall send him back to King Philip as he is."

Then the squad leader stripped the corpse of all that was valuable and sent the body back to King Philip, who praised God that one more enemy was dead and made no mention of the incident, no more than he did of the handsome reward that he gave the squad leader.

On Raleigh's return from his short-lived campaign in the Netherlands, Elizabeth commanded him to appear at a dance, for which the Earl of Leicester, a faithful but fading old admirer long reputed to have been her lover, cheerfully paid. She danced with Leicester, she danced with Essex, but more than with anyone else she danced with Raleigh.

Lord Burleigh smiled, sitting by the fireside in the shadows, and mused, "One would think she was honor-ing a general just back from winning a war instead of the ill-fated expedition it was." But everyone could see that Raleigh had caught the Queen's eye, and the waiting-women chirruped behind their fans and wished they could catch his. "His star is in the ascendant," Burleigh mused. "Oh well, better him than a rogue."

As Raleigh lifted Elizabeth high in the "jump"—

[79]

higher than Essex, the darling but so soft!—she felt herself light as a feather, as indeed she was in his powerful arms, with his strong sword-hardened hand tight against her jeweled stomacher, pressing against the secret parts of a body that was the mystery and hope of so many European princes and her own great personal grief. As he danced with her she threw her head back and blushed and laughed and sang an accompaniment to the tune of the fiddles; and the fiddlers, taking their cue from the obvious enjoyment of the Queen, played faster and louder, tapping their feet till at last, dizzy and panting with pleasure, she whispered, "Walter, put me down. I am thirsty. Stay me with flagons, comfort me with apples—" Just in time she caught a warning glance from Burleigh's wise old eye and did not complete the exquisite verse—"for I am sick with love." He put her down and she fanned the perspiration from her brow.

Raleigh too was acquainted with the sensuous love poetry of the Song of Songs, but he dared not presume to answer her in kind, answering only, "Behold, thou art fair, my love; behold thou art all fair, there is no spot in thee. Thy lips are like a thread of scarlet; with comely speech, with myrrh and aloes, great Diana hath ravished my heart."

He crooked a jeweled forefinger. The cellarer approached, white-haired and dignified, with a ceremonial key to the wine cellar hanging from a golden chain around his neck. Raleigh uttered a curt order. Shortly the cellarer returned with a crystal goblet on a silver salver which he presented to Raleigh, who presented it to the Queen, who tossed it off at a gulp, like a parched guardsman who had marched too long in the sun, and she looked as pleased for more. But she bethought herself, for there were some Puritans in the room. She favored them with a glare, for they would not have been at a dance if they did not want something, like Lord Grey, hoping for reinstatement. Puritans did not disapprove of wine, for the Bible said it was good "for the stomach's sake," and in fact they were heavy drinkers. They merely disapproved of dancing. Dancing gave so much pleasure to so many people, and pleasure was sinful, giving rise to carnal desires. In justice to the Puritans it must be stated that this has never been disproved. It was certainly true of Elizabeth.

Elizabeth had noted the rich ring on Raleigh's forefinger when he summoned the cellarer but she deemed it too spectacular to be real. It was a large cabochon ruby set 'round with a sparkling halo of chip diamonds. He could not have bought it on his "pay" in the Netherlands, for he had served without pay, and it wasn't likely that anybody had given it to him, nor did she think him the sort to steal such a thing, which would surely have involved murder. Ergo, it must be a fake. It was easy to fake rubies and little chip diamonds. Insofar as she was able to feel compunction she did. It was sad that her "Water" with his love of true finery should be reduced to wearing counterfeit jewels. Somehow she would make it up to him.

But it was not counterfeit. It was real and extremely valuable. Raleigh had quietly got himself a good round sum of money by selling both his letters of marque, though he felt it wise not to tell the Queen or anyone else.

The transaction was simplicity itself. One had only to ride down to London Bridge, where anything could be bought, anything sold.

London Bridge was an ancient structure dating from the Dark Ages, weighted down by dwellings and shops, and smack in the middle, a chapel, which the pious builder, inspired by a vision, had built to the glory of God.

Raleigh rode his horse to the center of the bridge and there, in the shadow of the chapel, he found the dwelling he sought: a cleaner-than-most little shack of half-timberwork. Over the door hung the three gold balls, signifying to those who could not read that this was the shop of a moneylender.

There was a hitching post by the door, but the reputation of the bridge was such that Raleigh was afraid his horse would be stolen. He called to a raggedy little beggar, assuming from his small stature that this must be one of those homeless unwanted waifs that cluttered the London streets till they lapsed into thievery and ended their miserable lives on the gibbet. But the man turned out to be a dwarf with one monstrous leg where two were fused to form a single grotesque limb. He propelled himself with difficulty on a little wheeled platform to where Raleigh stood.

"Alms!" he begged. "Alms, for the love of God. I have not eaten all day."

Physical ugliness repelled Raleigh; he avoided it when he could; it was the converse of his great attraction to physical beauty.

The beggar stank of stale beer, and a half-gnawed hambone stuck out of his pocket.

Raleigh pointed to it. "Haven't eaten, eh, you lying jackanapes!"

Hurriedly the beggar sought to hide the hambone in his pocket.

"It is my last bit of food in this world. On it I must subsist for a week, and then I starve. It is God's truth I am telling Your Lordship."

It was probably not God's truth, but it just might be, and the word "starve" had a horrid meaning for Raleigh since Ireland.

Somewhat relenting, he said, "If I let you hold my horse will you be here when I return, not sell him, not run off with him?"

A lifetime of pain looked out of the beggar's eyes and he replied with some dignity, "Sir, I have never run in my life. I pray God that I shall in the next."

"Here then," Raleigh said, reaching down the reins to the dwarf. "Guard him well, and when I come out I will make it worth your while. Meanwhile, better hide your hambone from Father Abraham in there."

"He gave it to me," the beggar said, smiling for the first time. "You do not know Isaac Ehud."

Raleigh knocked at the door. "I know of him," he said. He was the richest Jew in London.

On the door, on a well-shined name-plate, was boldly engraved in *niello* work the name *Isaac Ehud*.

No Jew could live legally in England. England had expelled them four hundred years before and repeatedly since that time, whenever their talents and skills were not needed. Then when they were needed again they were tacitly permitted to return. Outwardly obsequious, inwardly proud and contemptuous, they bought and sold and prospered greatly and bilked the Christians who mocked them in the streets and called them dogs —and used and needed them. Strangers in many strange lands, as they had been strangers in Egypt five thousand years before, they had developed a capacity to survive that bemused Christian theologians, who tried to forget that Christ was a Jew. But wherever they were permitted to live they were aliens, without citizenship, without civil rights, viciously taxed, aliens who never knew when a new turn of fate might expel them again, or when a mob might appear in the night, batter down the door, steal, burn, murder. Thus it was that they invented ingenious devices to transfer worldly goods quickly without actually moving them, like the letter of credit: by means of a few words written on a scrap of paper a London Jew could convey thousands of pounds to a brother overseas and not one ounce of gold would have moved. At the moment, in Elizabeth's England, the Jews were needed and safe.

Isaac Ehud opened the door himself and let Raleigh in. In the clear light of many wax candles Raleigh saw lying on the table from which the Jew had just risen an abacus and a sheet of paper covered with Hebrew characters. From the neatly arranged columns he guessed it was an accounting of some sort. The Jew was an elderly man with gray streaks in his beard, gnarled hands and a back much bent with habitual bowing. Through a pair of strong spectacles he shot Raleigh an appraising glance, learned much and guessed more.

"In what can I serve your gracious Lordship? Come you to buy? I have many excellent things for sale. Do I say *sale?* Rather I should say I will practically give them away for the honor of your Lordship's favor."

"I am not a lordship, Isaac Ehud." He managed to convey the contempt that all right-thinking Christians felt for Jews simply by pronouncing the name. Isaac would have been suspicious if he had not.

"Sir, it was a natural mistake—your soldierly bearing, your commanding presence, your magnificent suppression of the Irish rebels—"

"You know me?"

"Who does not know the renowned Captain Raleigh? Noble Captain, permit me to show you my priceless for-saleables. For you I will price them so cheap that I beggar myself. Will it be a handsome sword? I have one here that I guarantee lethal, the tiniest nick of the edge and your enemy falls dead at your feet—there is a certain substance on the blade."

Raleigh's face showed that his interest in chemistry was aroused.

"Ah, Captain, I see you take my meaning. You will not betray me? Perhaps it is slightly illegal. No, I read in your handsome face that you will not betray me. Why then, I shall sell you the poison itself if you wish. No? No poison today? Perhaps some other time. Other curious medicaments do I have: elixirs that make old men lusty in venery—but you do not need that, rather the other kind, which I have also. Ha! Once there came to me a desperate young man whose rival stole his lady-love; the desperate young man still loved her and wanted her back, so I sold him the impotent-making elixir, which he put into his rival's wine. All thankful and happy he came to me afterwards and he told me the change was remarkable."

Raleigh laughed. "Did he buy some of the venery elixir for the lady?"

"It wasn't necessary. It was she who was desperate after that. Now they are blissfully together again. Always I try to do good. But if you desire no medicines, perhaps fabrics? I have cottons sheer as silk and silk so sheer it cannot be seen at all, very suitable for nightgowns. No? No fabrics either? Jewelry? Behold this case of beautiful rings, pendants, bracelets, every one a bargain. No? Gloves perhaps, perfumed with musk of the Orient guaranteed to stay fragrant forever? Sleeves, all colors, stockings? No? No garments either?"

Raleigh said, "I come to sell, not to buy."

In Isaac Ehud's veins ran all the guile of the Levant from whence he sprang. He was of mixed Armenian, Greek, Lebanese, Turkish and Cretan blood, and far far back, he claimed descent from the Phoenicians, the canniest traders of whom history preserves any record. He was always willing to buy anything, but first he must know where he could dispose of it at a profit.

Cautiously he asked, "What do you have for sale, Captain Raleigh?"

"These."

He smoothed out his letters of marque on the table. In the golden glow of the candles they looked like Imperial patents of nobility or priceless illuminated manuscripts rifled from the library of some cathedral.

Isaac was bending over them. "Beautiful, beautiful," he murmured.

"Not the mere documents," Raleigh said, mistaking his remark. "I came to sell what they contain, what they authorize me to do, namely, to prey upon Spanish shipping, hold crews to ransom—oh, read them yourself if you can."

The polyglot Jew had already done so. He was casting about in his mind where to sell them, and he hesitated only a moment. He knew exactly where. They were the handsomest windfall that had come his way in a very long time. His whole manner changed.

"They are unquestionably of great value, Captain Raleigh. What are you asking for them?"

Raleigh named a preposterously high figure, expecting the Jew to haggle and cut it in half. Out of habit the Jew did haggle, but surprisingly little, and Raleigh came off the richer by five thousand pounds. He never found out that Isaac Ehud, through various intermediaries, promptly sold both letters of marque to King Philip of Spain, who paid twenty-five thousand for them and thus quashed at one blow and quite cheaply for him a huge increase in the Dutch and French privateering that was costing him more every year.

But the letters bore the name Walter Raleigh, and *Walter Raleigh* was etched forever in acid in King Philip's mind. He marked him for extinction, now or sometime, anywhere, by any means he could contrive.

And he hardened in his resolve to build an armada of ships that would be invincible, to humble once and for all the Queen he had hoped to marry and the England he had hoped to rule. King Philip, the most patient of monarchs, found his patience wearing very thin.

Isaac Ehud looked with compassion upon Walter Raleigh. Never before, thought Isaac to himself, did I murder a man! For he knew in his heart that once he sold the letters to Philip poor Captain Raleigh was as good as dead—but stay: Philip might die first, or Raleigh might meet a natural death. Or he might fall in a battle or a brawl in which Philip had no hand. Anything might happen to this reckless Englishman. But still his conscience smote him.

[86]

Raleigh was speaking. "What are you saying, Captain Raleigh?" asked the Jew.

"Are you deaf? I was saying, my good man, that I'd like to take another look at that tray of jewels. There was a ring there. . . ." He could afford it now.

"At once, at once, sir, here is the tray. All are superb, all genuine, shining like stars, and for you . . ."

Raleigh laughed. "I know. For me you will ask only twice what they are worth. How much for this?" He picked up the cabochon ruby with the halo of diamonds.

"For you, Captain Raleigh, it is a gift from old Isaac Ehud." He seemed to speak very seriously. "Live long, and wear it in good health."

Raleigh took it and pressed it down on his forefinger. Maybe I sold too cheap, he thought; the Jew is un-Jewishly generous.

But on the whole he was satisfied. He had no ships, and had he had, there were the tedious logistics of manning them, gunning them, provisioning them, finding captains who would not steal from him, and waiting endlessly for prize money to come in. And there was always the risk of the Queen's displeasure if she found out that he had not confided in her. Better as it was, with no responsibility and ready funds.

"Thank you," he said. "And now, Master Isaac, my five thousand pounds. I shall want it in gold."

The Jew looked troubled. "Tonight? Here? Now? Is that wise? You would be set upon before you got off the bridge and your saddlebags rifled. No, no, Captain. I beg you, let me send it to your lodgings."

Raleigh thought quickly, balancing the hazards: the now-dark streets, the thieves who frequented them and the heavy gold in his saddlebags—a certain invitation to violence. On the other hand the Jew might simply default and leave him with only a ring to show for the sale of his letters.

"I'll have it here and now," he decided.

The Jew shrugged, nodded. "It will take some few moments," and he rang a little bell and scribbled something on a sheet of paper. A young clerk appeared, looking the very image of a younger Isaac Ehud. "Take this," said the Jew, "and see that this amount is put in Captain Raleigh's saddlebags. And see that he comes safely to his lodgings with it."

The young man said, "Yes, Father," and disappeared.

Shortly he returned. About him was the vague smell of incense, as from a church.

Isaac chuckled. "I keep certain funds on deposit in the chapel," he said. "Far safer there than in a Jew's house, and of course tax exempt."

"The gold is in the Captain's saddlebags, Father."

"And the escort?"

"It is formed and mounted."

The patient beggar held the reins of Raleigh's horse up to him, smiling. "Now you know Isaac Ehud," he said. Raleigh pressed a gold piece into his hand and replied, "A man of unwonted resource and profoundest invention." He was just the sort of man Raleigh admired.

Raleigh took his leave. Riding beside him was the Jew's son, and around him rode the escort armed with pikes and guns with flaming torches aloft; and the street rabble slunk back into the shadows as they did when the nightwatch appeared.

"My father will like your appreciation, Captain Raleigh," he said, smiling; then the smile disappeared. He knew where his father would sell the letters. "He conceived that you might want protection, and that is why we are here."

"I laud it and thank him."

At the door of his lodgings the young man said, "Perhaps you will meet him again."

"Perhaps I shall."

Thus it was that the Queen need have wasted no sympathy because poor Walter Raleigh was reduced to wearing counterfeit jewelry. She would have been furious if she had known he had come by "found" money from abroad which he had cunningly deprived her of. The Crown possessed ancient rights to a share of such money, and Elizabeth sorely needed it for England. It was the first time he had ever deceived Diana, but it was not the last or the worst.

He had always chafed at inaction. Now he must spend much time at court, often closeted privately with her, soothing her petulant moods, reading her love poems when her mood was romantic, which was often, praising her singing when she was gay—and Elizabeth sang beautifully albeit with a somewhat husky voice—and always there was the dancing, to which she was addicted as to a drug. Sometimes she would jump up from her chair, pirouette 'round the room dancing alone, tap Raleigh on the cheek with her fan, pucker her lips in a teasing kiss and display such wantonness that Raleigh's natural instincts were aroused. Then a mixed look of withdrawal and triumph would come over her face and she would gently chide him for his "venery."

"If my role is to be the role of a lover," he mused, "I had rather play it to the hilt!" Boundless possibilities opened to his vivid imagination and for one wild moment he shared with many princes the hope of espousing this passionate elusive woman. But only for a moment.

The role he must play he saw only too clearly: that of the minstrel-lover, to sigh, seek, pant, praise, aspire, but never to touch.

He played it to perfection. But the air of the court was stifling and close, full of the perfume and chatter of women, full of spying envious eyes of noble courtiers who watched with mounting anger his mounting intimacy with the Queen.

"I would to God I could breathe fresh air," he grumbled to himself.

Sometimes he could. The Queen loved archery and could outshoot many a man. Laughing gaily when she sank her shaft she would cry, "Behold, my Water! Square in the center of the white!" If she missed the mark she would be equally loud in her curses. Her own father, loving the sport himself, had got her a famous marksman, Roger Ascham, to perfect her skill, and he was so pleased with her that he wrote a book about it, *Toxophilus*, the first book on archery ever written in the English language.

She also loved horse riding and rode like the wind, sometimes with a hawk on her wrist, loosing the bird at small quarry in the fields, clapping her hands in delight at the kill. Raleigh, always happy in the saddle, liked the strong sharp smell of the horse, which filled him, like the smell of gunpowder, with fond and familiar memories of successful action on the field of battle, and he welcomed the hunts with the Queen. Her energy was astounding. The age to which Elizabeth gave her name was decidedly vigorous. And at night she was never too tired to dance.

So Raleigh occasionally did breathe fresh air, but still he felt thwarted. Whatever he had he always wanted more, and always was sure that somebody else was getting that more, and at his own expense.

"If only my good brother Humphrey had taken me with him to America. Ha! *There* is a glorious adventure! But I am caught in a silken cocoon spun by my Queen, motionless as a grub, useless as her lapdog."

Elizabeth said, "Your brother was always unlucky at sea. I was wise to refuse your request—nay, how you begged me!—to go with him to America. For now the poor man is dead and you are still alive, and I can still keep you by me." She smiled fondly at Raleigh.

The remnant of Sir Humphrey's little fleet had straggled home.

In that quick and endearing change of heart which is so characteristic of the English, Humphrey Gilbert now rose to the stature of a national hero. All of his savageries, all of his covetousness, all his ineptitude—all, all instantly flashed away. Only his death was remembered, and the sublime words on his lips as he, another great Elizabethan, faced final moments of life. Other great Elizabethans had done, and were still to do the same, before the Age of Elizabeth closed.

"Yet in life he served England well," said the Queen.

"England, aye; and England's Queen," Raleigh said, "for Elizabeth is England, England is Elizabeth."

"Grieve not too sorely, my Water," she said, comforting him. Raleigh was weeping. He had loved his brother. His cheeks were wet with tears.

"Serve England, as did Sir Humphrey."

"Madame, I will so serve." He kissed the palm of her hand, a Spanish gesture he had picked up in the Netherlands; it sent shivers down her spine. "And England's Queen," he said, thinking fast. Behind his heartfelt human tears rose a vision of unmeasurable personal benefits to be gained by the death of his nearest kinsman.

Humphrey Gilbert had indeed done much to enhance the prestige of England.

Landing in the wasteland of what is now Newfoundland, which obviously was "possessed of no Christian prince," he had, in accordance with the terms of his charter, taken legal possession of the place and of "all lands six hundred miles in any direction whatsoever, to colonize, possess, govern and occupy in my own name and the names of mine heirs and assigns forever," subject only to the overlordship of the Queen and to the renunciation of a one-fifth share of any gold that might be discovered therein. In honor of the Virgin Queen he called the place "Virginia."

There was no gold in this vast northern "Virginia."

Only the beginnings of Empire.

He took aboard some sassafras bark, which grew wild in the place, and tobacco, which the fishermen bought from the Indians. Both herbs were in great demand. Sassafras was a pleasant flavoring for tea, much favored by little old ladies for its powerful diaphoretic properties; and tobacco was soothing to the nerves. Over and above these minor benefits was a fact well known to all doctors, namely, that sassafras and tobacco were positive cures for the Great Pox.

This huge expanse of land, Raleigh calculated rapidly, amounted to more than eight times the area of England, Scotland, Ireland and Wales. All was Sir Humphrey's to colonize, govern, possess—and now that Sir Humphrey was dead, did it not devolve upon his nearest kinsman, Walter Raleigh himself?

He put forward his claim. The Queen was willing. It would cost her nothing. Gilbert had served her well. Raleigh would do the same. And he was much more interesting.

But despite his poetic "England is Elizabeth, Elizabeth is England," flattering as it was, it was not strictly so. In France it was so, and in Spain it was so—there the monarch *was* the state: but not in England, not since Magna Carta. In England there was always the power of Parliament to constrain and delimit the will of the Crown, a confounded nuisance to Elizabeth's way of thinking but so firmly entrenched in the English Constitution that no sovereign, not even her father, had ever been able to eradicate it.

But it could be bypassed, especially by a clever woman.

"The charter is mine to bestow," she said, "but Parliament must confirm. I will do what I can."

Forthwith she appointed a committee to consider Raleigh's claim and make its recommendation to the House of Commons.

On the committee were Sir Francis Drake, Sir Richard Grenville, other Westcountry men, mariners all, who knew Raleigh's worth as a seaman, all friends, many

[92]

relatives—and Walter Raleigh was promptly confirmed.

Now he had power. Now he had ships. Now the vast reaches of the New World were open to him, and he lusted to go adventuring there if for no other reason than to escape the lapdog bondage in the perfumed atmosphere of the court; and for a season the Queen let him think that his escape was at hand.

"What are you thinking of, Walter?" she asked him one day. He was drawing something on a sheet of paper.

When she called him "Walter," keeping the "l," he knew she was formal, all Queen; when she dropped the "l," as if it were "water," like the puddle, like the ocean, she was kittenish, cuddly, all woman, no Queen in her manner. "Walter" she called him this time, and he answered, "Your Majesty, I am designing a ship."

"You already have ships—Sir Humphrey's."

"Yes, Madame, but none like this." He showed her.

She knew a great deal about ships, as had her father, whose cannon of bronze, stamped with his name and the royal Tudor crest, were still the deadliest in the world.

She looked at the sketch. "Yes, Walter, this is truly a formidable ship. Have you not, however, decked her a bit too high above waterline?"

"Not at all," said Raleigh. Had he dared he would have embraced her. What woman but Elizabeth knew what a waterline was or could have understood his scribbled drawing?

"High she is, Madame, but not too high. With this height, when the cannon fire, we have a choice. We can blast into the sails, with chain-shot and grape, dismantling the drive, cutting the canvas to ribbons, chopping the spars to splinters; or, contrariwise, we can fire into the hulls, puncturing the timbers, letting in the sea, and down, down, down they go! Ha! Had I but a hundred such ships, what could I not do for you!"

"And what would you christen such a ship, if you

had one?" asked the Queen. Surely he would answer the *Queen Elizabeth.*

"The *Ark*, Madame; for in my *Ark* lies the future of all English sailormen!"

"Vaunt on," she thought. "Vaunt yourself up big as a bloater, big as a king." But she liked big words.

"The *Ark*, Walter? No further?"

"The *Ark Raleigh*, Ma'am; since she is mine own conceit."

"Not mine too, Walter Raleigh? Were I to give you such a ship, have I no part in her?"

"Most gracious Majesty! You will? You will?"

"I will, but one only."

"Then, Madame, to your honor and glory she shall be Royal, like you: the *Ark Royal!*"

And so she was built, and so christened; and she became the flagship of the British Royal Navy; and her name was terror on all the seas of the world for four hundred victorious years, till a German submarine torpedoed her namesake, an aircraft carrier, in the Mediterranean on November 14, 1941. Four hundred years is a very long time for a pearl-earringed Elizabethan mariner to have perpetuated his seafaring genius.

Every day Raleigh rode down to the dockyards to supervise and inspect the building of the *Ark Royal.* Her timbers were seasoned English oak, hard as iron. He had determined her to be, and so she became, the fastest ship in the world. He fell in love with her. She was part of himself, arrogant, flamboyant, devious, deadly. Lovers of ships and lovers of women—Raleigh loved both—have always found that women and ships have much in common. That is why ships are always female. To this day a sailor would be laughed at if he referred to his ship as "he" instead of "she."

She was slender in the waist, to give her more speed, like a young girl and also like a wasp, "for she can sting!" exulted her builder. Three decks of murderous bronze cannon lurked behind her ports (which were counterweighted to open instantly at a touch, an invention of Raleigh's), cannon numbering eighteen to a broadside, an incredible firepower for a ship of her time. Some of the gunports were camouflaged, to look as if she had fewer; some were false, merely painted on, to look as if she had more. "Devious, deceitful, ready to surprise, ready to kill, thoroughly female;" thought Raleigh. "How I love her!"

She had no oars, no banks of benches where galley slaves sweated out their lives as in French and Mediterranean ships. Long since Raleigh had looked upon galley slaves as an encumbrance, and not entirely for humanitarian reasons: "Replace them with sails, for motor power; replace them with cannon, which never turn upon you and revolt as do slaves." Thus the *Ark Royal* was all speed, all firepower, prototype of the English warships that not too long hence were to whip the Spanish Armada.

She carried an unheard-of press of sail. Some who saw her a-building, noting her slender waist and towering masts, said "She will broach to with a gale abeam," but she never did. Raleigh had rigged her half like a square-rigger, half like those Dutch schooners he had seen in the Netherlands, which could sail closer to the wind than any other ships. Square-rigger or schooner, the *Ark Royal* could change into either at a command.

Nor did he forget how Spanish ships carried hundreds, sometimes a thousand or more "marines." Marines were land soldiers, not sailors. It was their job to board an enemy ship and fight hand to hand as if on land, as if their ship were nothing but a platform on which to maneuver. Their ignorance of seafaring was notorious and ludicrous. English sailors scoffed, "When nobody else will believe you, tell it to the marines!"

To kill marines, especially their captains and leaders, Raleigh built "roundtops" high up on his masts. These were basket-like contrivances. Sharpshooters by the dozen could hide in them, then suddenly rain down a deadly hail of musket balls upon the unsuspecting marines that swarmed the enemy decks.

But suppose all this were not enough. Suppose wind and sea and luck went against him. Suppose some towering Spanish galleon actually grappled the *Ark Royal* and a thousand Spanish marines—everyone conceded their bravery—sought to swarm aboard. Raleigh had thought of that too.

Air-tight buckets of sulphur, naphtha and quicklime he caused to be slung to the tips of his spars. Sure-footed English sailors, who daily with naked feet stood upon the slender lines of the topmost sails with never a fear of falling to make or shorten sail as in all English vessels, could release these buckets at the slice of a dirk, which all English sailors carried stuck in their belts. The dirk was a long sharp dagger. A sailor was lost without it. With it he cut his salt pork at mealtime, cut leather for his hat and soles for his shoes, patches for sails and patches for his clothing and fuses for bombs and grenades. He carried it with him ashore, where it was useful in tavern brawls. So much a part of the sailor was his dirk that there was a bawdy sea-chanty about it which sailors sang at their work. It went like this: "Like a Jew without 'is money, Like a whore without a cunny, Like a cas-ter-HATED Turk, is Jack Tar without 'is dirk." This was how the common sailor of Elizabeth's time thought that certain things were absolutely certain, unalterable.

At the slice of a dirk the buckets would fall, spewing out their horrible contents.

Raleigh again with his lifelong interest in chemistry. Raleigh again with his astounding rediscovery of the Ancients' Greek Fire.

And when the buckets would fall and burst, there would spread out on the deck an agonizing unquenchable terror, rising up, covering the shoes, ankles, knees, groin, the privy parts of the Spanish marines.

For on contact with the slightest moisture, be it blood or water—there was certain to be one or the other—a terrible flame that could not be put out would envelop, consume the Spaniards, reducing them to ashes.

Thus it was that the *Ark Royal*, built under Raleigh's loving and critical eye, product of his fertile imagination, sound as her oaken timbers, fleet as a greyhound, deadly as a scorpion, became the model and mold for all British warships of his generation, embodying the qualities that all future generations of British warships strove, and successfully strove, to emulate.

But no description of the *Ark Royal* would be complete if it dealt with her warlike aspects only. There was another side to *Ark Royal*. There was another side to Walter Raleigh: the gorgeous side. He had built for himself in her aftercastle a sumptuous Captain's Cabin. Tall windows of imported Venetian glass looked out upon the sea. A costly Turkey carpet, part of the spoils of Lepanto, covered the flooring from bulkhead to bulkhead, which in turn were hung with Flemish tapestries depicting—a pretty compliment to the Queen—the legend of the Virgin and the Unicorn. There was a rack to hold wine bottles and comfits and bottles of scurvy-grass. There was a polished brass brazier to take off the chill in cold weather. There was a teak-wood bathtub and, beside it, artfully concealed, a flush toilet activated by a silver-handled pump. And—"Thou Sybarite!" said the Queen when she saw it (there was to one side under the windows a four-poster bed)—"Do you expect company in your voyaging?" She smirked and tapped his cheek with her fan. "Dared I but dare!" he replied, and she frowned. "Dare not too far." But she was only displeased on the surface.

Abaft all this luxury he caused there to be constructed an "Admiral's Walk," the first in the British Royal Navy, an innovation in naval architecture. only recently abandoned. It was actually a balcony sticking out from the body of the ship over the waves just above the rudder. There he conceived he might take the air and commune with the stars and smoke his pipe and perhaps write a little poetry if no enemy action impended and if he felt so inclined. Generations of seafaring epigoni enjoyed such Walks and some noble admirals had four-poster beds, but their poetry is not recorded and none dared kiss a Queen.

Raleigh returned to his lapdog bondage. Never had the Queen so smiled upon him. But he was sick to death of wasting his days and nights paying court to her. America called him, and she let him feel that soon she would let him go adventuring thither, though she had no intention of doing so. To everyone he boasted that Her Majesty had entrusted him with Gilbert's charter to explore the New World and plant a colony there; and he exhibited the *Ark Royal* to the Admiralty with justifiable pride: here was a ship, he said, that would speedily enhance the prestige of the English Royal Navy and counter the Spanish aggression in America.

The Admiralty readily agreed, for *Ark Royal*, though only half built, was launched and running her sea trials. The Admiralty were astounded at her power and speed.

Courtiers, who believed him soon to sail, jealous of the favor he enjoyed with the Queen, were delighted that he soon would be out of the country and hoped that *Ark Royal* would sink to the bottom and Raleigh with her, never to be heard of again.

He had spent much of his secret hoard to provide the luxuries in the Captain's Cabin. The Queen would not pay for the tapestries and demanded that he recompense the Royal Treasury for them, since they were spoils of war—"if you can," she said doubtfully, still thinking he was poor. "Madame," he said, "I placed in pawn some jewels"; and to prove his point he wore fewer every day, till she saw him reduced to half his usual finery. "Poor Water," she thought, "you are beggaring yourself on vanities," but she took the money. And she thoroughly disliked the four-poster bed. Who would be in it with him? Nobody! In fact he would not be in it himself if she had her way, as she always did when she suspected some female was charming away some favourite.

She was seconded by her Admiralty in her determination not to let him go: *Ark Royal* was far too valuable, as the most powerful fighting ship in the Royal Navy, to waste on a trumpery voyage to America where there was no one to fight but Indians and fish and seals and where it was not yet politically expedient to fight Spaniards.

With her Admiral of the Fleet at her side to argue the Navy's need for the ship, which was patently valid, she communicated her decision to Raleigh that he must stay. With a tug at her heartstrings she beheld the distress on his face, for she had arrived at another decision that would distress him even more.

"Then I must go in brother Humphrey's ships," Raleigh said stoutly. There were only two small ones left. The Admiral, a distant relative, admired his singleness of purpose but was deeply conscious of his value to the Navy and shook his head when Elizabeth glanced at him as if she were asking advice in a purely naval matter, as if she had no personal interest in whether Walter Raleigh went or stayed.

The Admiral said, "Captain Raleigh, I conceive it far wiser for you to remain in England, to prepare the fleet against the ever-rising Spanish menace. England, not America, is threatened. Serve England, Captain Raleigh," he said, unconsciously repeating the words that Elizabeth had said.

"Aye, and England's Queen," Raleigh replied; but disappointment still showed on his face.

The Queen said, "But your voyage of discovery need

not be canceled. Depute two trusted captains to sail Sir Humphrey's ships to the New World. The crossing will be short, the project is worthy. We know little and must know more of America and seek out likely sites for your plantation." She glanced imperiously at her Admiral of the Fleet. "The Admiralty can readily spare two small ships for a short while, can it not my Lord Admiral? And the cost to you will be small in view of the discoveries: the coastal surveys, the weather, the rivers, harbors, soundings that will be made, the temper of the natives, samples of timber suitable for ships—who knows what benefits to England?" Here was Elizabeth talking sea language, in which she was as adept as in Latin; and everything she said was true. But the Admiral was ruefully aware that she had skilfully contrived to shift the entire cost of the expedition from herself to him. He nodded his head in agreement, marveling at her fiscal acumen no less than her grasp of naval affairs. Here was a sovereign, and only a woman, with a larger view than most kings. Small wonder she had won the hearts of her subjects. Everyone knew the story of the drunken helmsman who had grounded a ship on a reef. Justice was swift; the hangman lopped off his erring right hand. Yet with the hand that still remained he lifted his hat in a cheer and shouted, "God bless the Queen!"

Raleigh deputed two sea captains to command Sir Humphrey's ships and wrote them a list of detailed instructions:

Item: To explore the coast of North America as far south as time and provisions might permit, making accurate charts.

Item: To plant English seeds and see if they would grow [it was summer, the season was propitious] with a view to make self sustaining the colonies he projected.

Item: To make friends with the natives, to trade with them fairly; to bring home samples of what they had to sell that might be valuable to England, and find out what England might supply that they valued in return.

Item: To bring home some Indians, to be taught the English language that they might be employed as interpreters on future voyages and instructed in the true Protestant religion, with special emphasis on its superiority to the Catholicism of the Spaniards, who made slaves of them.

And in a verbal and confidential instruction to his captains Raleigh commanded them to turn over all information so gathered to himself before anyone else saw it, in order that he might personally edit it, paying them well for their secrecy and promising them more when they delivered the material.

The ships sailed, and Raleigh was left behind, disconsolate. Now he must play the role of the courtier again. His spirits sank and his manner became petulant even to the Queen, even when she graciously accompanied him to inspect the building of the *Ark Royal*.

She was patient with his moods, knowing whence they sprang. She was distressed at his display of poverty. And she could not abide a doleful countenance in a favourite, especially in as handsome a countenance as Raleigh's. Unless her own spirits were to flag she would have to do something to cheer him up.

This she did, at no cost to herself, but it made Walter Raleigh rich as a lord in his own right, with the first steady income he had ever enjoyed in his life.

Among the many monopolies at the disposal of the Crown was the exclusive right to sell wine and to fix its price. Every ounce of wine consumed in England meant income to the holder of the monopoly, and since the amount consumed was enormous, so was the income. Queen Elizabeth gave the wine monopoly to Walter Raleigh; Parliament instantly confirmed it, as was traditional. The price of wine would not go up. The working man would still tipple at his favorite tavern, the great lord in his castle would still set out hundreds of bottles at his feasts—nothing would change. But overnight Walter Raleigh found himself with an income of two thousand pounds, more than many a landed gentleman who lived high, kept his own stable and rode to hounds.

Thus Elizabeth kept him by her, and his spirits certainly improved, though he *did* think she might have shown her appreciation sooner. Till his ships returned from America (when he would ask for more) it was easier now to stay at court, where not an eyebrow was raised, not an envious frown appeared. Only Lord Essex, precociously mature and already the object of many a lady-in-waiting's amorous glance, was seen to look hurt at times, not because of the monopoly but because he was jealous of Raleigh's favor with the Queen.

Elizabeth was delighted with Raleigh's change of mood. Already his jewels were reappearing from the strongboxes where he had hidden them: "I redeemed them from pawn, Your Majesty, thanks to your gracious favor." They laughed gaily together in the evening: he praised her when she sang, she applauded when he read her his love poems; he sat in her pavilion when she went to watch bearbaiting and cockfights, sports which everyone greatly enjoyed and where she bet heavily on winners. When she won she clapped her hands and counted the purse. When she lost, nobody dared ask her to pay. Raleigh would have liked to bet too, big amounts. She forbade it. "Such grandiose notions! I make you rich and you lust to be richer. Have a care, Walter Raleigh, lest you displease me. No, you shall not bet." For she knew that if he lost, he, unlike herself, would have to pay.

When he took her aboard the *Ark Royal* his eye would grow sharp and his bearing decisive and soldierly. She was interested in everything. She asked him, "What is scurvy-grass? Does it cure scurvy or cause it?"

"Both properties would be valuable, Ma'am, if skilfully employed, the one to kill enemies, the other to help friends. It is this," he said, showing her the bottle in which the herb was preserved.

"Is it truly effective?" She was suspicious of the complicated medicaments of the time and never took any herself except the purges that everyone took and which her tense nervous body occasionally required.

"It is naught but a cress, Your Majesty, such as one eats in a salad, here preserved in brandy. I deem it utterly useless. And yet—" he stroked his beard thoughtfully—"sailors beg for it when their gums begin to rot, and all sea captains carry it. It soothes the pain, and remissions have been known to occur upon taking it. But I suspect it's the brandy that soothes the pain and the cress that causes the remission. Sailors who eat onions and garlic, when available, seldom succumb to scurvy. But scurvy-grass never cured scurvy or saved a single sailor's life." He was much more interested in the subject than the Queen, who shrugged and said, "If it eases the poor men's passing out of this life, captains are well advised to carry it."

Sometimes he amused her with trivia. One misty day she rode hunting too long in the damp and developed a nasty head cold and aches in her joints. She was furious. Joints got older every year and she dreaded the time to come when she could no longer dance.

He could see she was out of sorts when she croaked, "Walter, is it true as they say that tobacco smoke clears a stuffy nose?"

"Madame, it has always cleared mine, and soothed my nerves also, but I do not know how it might affect others."

"Call for your pipe," she commanded. "I detest the stink, but I couldn't be more miserable than I am now."

Raleigh summoned a servant, who shortly returned with his pipe and a pouch of tobacco.

"Now smoke the stuff," said the Queen, "and see if it helps."

Raleigh took a coal from the fire, lighted his pipe and puffed out a great cloud of blue smoke.

"Blow it over here, you coward. It is I who have the stuffy nose."

Raleigh directed a cautious puff in her general direction.

"Not there, rogue! Here in my face!"

Oh very well, you petulant Majesty, thought Raleigh. It shall be as you ask.

He bent his face down very close to hers and blew a long jet of smoke directly upon her high-bridged patrician nose. It washed over her face and she had to shut her eyes lest they water more than they already did from her cold. But she did not draw back and, by sheer power of will, she conquered the impulse to choke as the irritant fumes struck the tender membranes of her nose and throat.

When she could speak she gasped, "Brandy!"

Raleigh poured her a generous measure. He was aghast at her appearance. Beads of sweat stood out upon her brow and her cheeks were white as a sheet, save only where the rouge burned red like fever spots. "What have I done!" he moaned, and to himself, though she heard, he murmured in genuine concern, "I have hurt the fairest lady that ever lived, I have hurt my precious Diana!" Tenderly he patted the glow from her brow, the tears from her eyes, with his own silk handkerchief.

Elizabeth sat up, took the handkerchief, noted that no rouge had come off on it and, confidence restored, she said fondly, "I thank you. Your medicine does indeed seem to possess a certain virtue."

The brandy had narcotized the pain in her throat; the smoke had struck such a violent blow to the membranes of her nose that feeling had disappeared. The smoke also made her feel dizzy, but not unpleasantly so. If she had not been giddy she would have jumped up and danced.

"So diaphanous a fume, so weightless like a cloud, weightless it makes me feel; aye, it has virtue!"

"Nay, Madame, it has weight also."

"Smoke? Weight?"

"Weight, Madame, and I'll wager a penny I can demonstrate it to you."

"Only a penny? Pish, pish! You have little faith in your demonstration."

"A hundred angels then, to convince an angel!" Raleigh said, naming a very valuable gold coin.

"Done!" said the Queen.

He called for a scale and measured out an ounce or so of tobacco. He burned it, and the smoke drifted up to the ceiling, till nothing was left on the scale but a little pile of white ashes.

"Your weighty smoke has escaped you, vanished, and some went up the chimney. How will you conjure it back to weigh it?" asked the Queen, who had carefully watched the experiment and was vastly amused.

"I shall simply weigh the ashes," he said and he did so. "For it is plain to see that the ashes weigh less than the tobacco, which contained both ashes and smoke. Ergo, it is evident that the difference in weight between the ashes and the tobacco is the weight of the smoke, quod erat demonstrandum." He swept her a lordly bow.

She laughed with delight and had to agree. It was logical, scholastically logical. She called for her purse bearer, who counted out a hundred gold angels in front of Captain Raleigh.

"Thou'dst make a most persuasive schoolman," she said, "thou-ing" him fondly. She was glad he had won, glad to confer one more mark of favor upon him. "And how many angels do you suppose can dance on the head of a pin, my sailorman-scholar? The old question is still debated by learned scholastics in the universities. Nay, but I'll give you no pin, lest your angels dance away like your smoke and you have them no more."

"Madame," said Raleigh, "I know but one angel who can dance, and divinely, the angel whose hand her devoted servant and subject makes bold to kiss."

She shivered again at the salutation.

Spenser had read Raleigh's future aright in Elizabeth's eyes.

CHAPTER XI

RALEIGH's two captains sailed in their little ships with a strong following wind. Their mission was purely to gather information; it was an exploratory operation. They made a speedy crossing, sedulously following Raleigh's instructions: to avoid all foreign ships, scamper away from any sail they sighted, disappear as quickly as possible in the vast and trackless expanse of the Atlantic.

Coasting up the North American shoreline they came upon Roanoke Island, a place they deemed suitable for a permanent colony since it was easy to fortify and proved to have other advantages.

There they found a population of Indians, who took them for gods because of their white skins and at first seemed quite docile, thoroughly scared. They fled into the forests; then, when they discovered that the white gods did not instantly annihilate them, they filtered back to the shore to worship them, and found them friendly, laden with gifts: tin plates, copper bangles, shiny little metal disks you could see a face in (a handsome Indian who did everything you did); and even more precious things: kettles, hammers, hatchets, axes, knives. And all they would take in return for their gifts were some deerskins and skins of ermine and mink and other common wild animals, and a handful of sea pearls. The Indians wore a few gold ornaments which they got in trade from Spanish Indians from the south, but the English,

acting on Raleigh's orders, affected to disdain gold, not
accepting any but carefully noting its existence.

The surrounding countryside abounded in game, some
of which they shot, prizing especially the venison. They
feasted gloriously on wild boar, hare and the succulent
flesh of a large strange-looking bird that made a ludicrous noise like "gobble-gobble-gobble" and which they
called a "gobbler."

Seeing the English shoot game and bring down birds
at a distance far beyond bow-shot, the Indians fell to
the ground and cried out for mercy, sure in their savage
hearts that the white gods were displeased and would
shortly kill them too. But seeing the English start to
plant seeds, like squaws, they had second thoughts. Perhaps the white gods were humans after all.

Presently a sailor took sick. He sweated and shivered
alternately and grew even whiter. Concern showed on
the faces of his comrades, who did not know the disease.
The Indians did and prepared an infusion of bitter bark
and gave it to him to drink. Shortly the symptoms
ameliorated, though his skin now took on a yellowish
tinge like an Indian's. Now the Indians were sure that
the English were human, and, though they still feared
them, their bargaining became cannier after that, exhibit-
ing a preference for weapons, though the English would
give them no guns.

Since gunpowder was the source of the white men's
power—muskets seemed to be only hollow tubes that
any Indian could make—they asked for a quantity, signifying by sign language that they proposed to plant it
and raise up a crop as with any other seed. The English
laughed and gave them a cupful, which they planted in
a hole, carefully wetting it down to make sure it grew.

The English had better luck with their own seeds,
which sprouted in the fertile soil and grew rapidly, as
if pulled up by the tips by the sun and salubrious air.
Food would assuredly be no problem in America. In

the forests were bowers of grapevines, purple with lush wild grapes. There were acorns for pigs, nuts and uncountable varieties of fruits for men, acres of hay-grass for fodder. There was little need to exaggerate the self-sustaining potential of such a delightful spot for a colony.

Two brighter-than-average Indians were readily persuaded that it would be in their interest to go back to England with the ships: they would return to their homes rich and famous with the next expedition that was soon to set out. They dressed themselves in their finest feathers and supplest leather; their moccasins glittered with colorful beads; bracelets and armbands of massy gold shone against the red-brown skin of their muscular arms; sea pearls and seashells were sewn in fantastic patterns to their soft deerskin jerkins. Like Raleigh himself the American savages loved finery.

Raleigh's captains faithfully lived up to their instructions. Raleigh boarded the ships as soon as they reached England and scrutinized their manifests with an eagle eye, expecting to be bilked as was customary. Surprisingly, the manifests matched the cargoes down to the exact count of the sea pearls, three hundred and sixty-five. Nothing had been stolen except a small crock of cucumber pickles and a demijohn of beef-brandy-and-wine, a popular summer tonic. The captains cheerfully acknowledged the shortage but professed to have given it to the Indians; one had required the tonic to cure a bad case of seasickness; the other had never tasted pickles before and incontinently wolfed down the whole crockful. "On which, I suppose," said Raleigh, "he also became seasick and needed the tonic to cure him?" "Exactly what happened!" said the captain, glad of so plausible an excuse to account for the demijohn, which had a capacity of two and a half gallons. Raleigh chuckled and let it go at that.

He listened to their enthusiastic description of Roanoke Island, its impregnable site as a fortress, its wholesome climate and fruitful soil, its abundant food supplies, the precious furs, the gold that the natives valued no higher than copper, the surrounding sea alive with edible fish and sea pearls to be found in every one of the millions of oysters in beds only ten feet down.

It was easy to write an account of these wonders for the Queen. Indeed, Raleigh exaggerated very little, save perhaps in regard to the pearls. But she loved them, even as he did himself; he let his captains' story of their abundance stand as they had related it; Diana must not be disappointed or suffer doubts about the fabulous wealth of America.

No sea captain since Columbus had had such tales to tell a Queen as Captain Raleigh, and none had been listened to with more favor; but he thought her somewhat grasping when she graciously accepted every one of the three hundred and sixty-five pearls for herself— surely she could have spared him a score or two. He grumbled to himself, "Was ever there lady so niggardly of favors!"

Grumbling, self-commiserating, never satisfied, while favors were actually showering upon him like a golden rain! And yet he'd have died for her.

Not only Elizabeth but the Admiralty read his account of the Roanoke voyage. They were convinced, and advised her to send out a second and larger expedition. Uppermost in their minds was the fear of the Spaniards, with their mighty armadas and world-clutching claims. Anywhere that the Spanish could be thwarted on land or on sea, there, with dogged English resolve, the Admiralty vowed that thwarted they should be. On King Philip's empire the sun never set; but neither did it set on the English Royal Navy.

No one was surprised, though some were jealous, when the Queen dubbed Raleigh a knight. Thenceforth he was Sir Walter Raleigh.

He and his dead brother Sir Humphrey had climbed high for two Westcountry men of obscure family. Sir Walter chose for his crest the arms of his ancient Plantagenet ancestor, adding some fanciful flourishes of his own, which went unchallenged. Heraldry had declined since the invention of gunpowder; blazoned shields no longer served to identify warriors on the field of battle so hidden in armor as to be unrecognizable. Coats of arms were now put to more decorative uses and appeared in gorgeous embroidery on bedcovers, pillow slips, window curtains, the livery of servants and the harness of horses.

The Queen did more. She conferred upon him, pursuant to Sir Humphrey's charter, the exclusive right to possess, occupy, rule and colonize all the territory his exploratory expedition had laid open to the English, and gave him the magniloquent title, "Lord of Virginia." (Some prurient courtiers snickered, "In sooth he is! Sir Walter doth swive * the Queen." Of course he didn't; perhaps no man could, though the gossip went that many had tried and that now, at the age of fifty, she was peevish and frustrated because of her impenetrable virginity.)

Sir Walter Raleigh now owned the entire continent of North America from Spanish Florida to the North Pole. And, as was like him, he cast a covetous eye on South America too, lusting after the whole hemisphere, as will appear in its proper place. No one of Walter Raleigh's age appreciated the enormous extent of his holdings and influence, and few realize even now that but for this one complex Elizabethan poet-and-mariner we would all be speaking Spanish today instead of an English that is far more like his than the "British" of present-day England.

---

* *Footnote:* An earthy Elizabethan term, now disused in favor of a nastier one, meaning: "to copulate with."

CHAPTER XII

THE BUILDUP of the English Royal Navy continued at an ever-accelerating pace. King Philip's resolve to invade the heretic British Isles became each month more apparent. Everywhere along his continental coasts English spies reported huge Spanish galleons a-building, secure, as Philip thought, from attack, to be hurled against England when their numbers and heavier armament should render his armada invincible. Hence it was that in England every warship, every ship that could be built or converted into a warship was at a premium.

Pitted against King Philip's resolve was the resolve of Sir Walter Raleigh, whose prophetic vision of an English colony in America took on the character of an obsession.

Raleigh's tiny exploratory expedition had brought home great promise, of gold, glory, trade and unmeasurable territorial expansion for England, a veritable empire. And, in his vision, the American creeks and estuaries would surely prove to be a passage to the Pacific, probably only a few miles away. The Isthmus of Panama was well known to be only a few miles wide—unfortunately there was no water passage through it. Sir Walter reasoned that there must surely be an Isthmus of Virginia, *with* a water passage. And once you burst into the Pacific the way lay open to India, China, and the Spice Islands where pepper—that in England was measured against its weight in gold dust—was cheap. Sir Francis Drake,

another of his Westcountry kinsmen, the first Englishman ever to circumnavigate the globe, had gone the long
way 'round through the Straits of Magellan, taking more
than two years for the voyage, a deplorable waste of
time in Raleigh's opinion. How much more efficient to
sail straight through! –if once the passage were found.

He presented his case to the Admiralty, arguing its
validity with eloquence and conviction, the more persuasive because his case was tightly reasoned and his
own belief shone through; while Elizabeth stood by,
inwardly pouting, "I dub him knight; he dubs me his
precious Diana; but he cannot hide his haste to leave
me!"

But she held her peace and merely nodded assent when
her Admiral said No.

"No, Sir Walter. England cannot spare the ships."

"Then give me a dozen, nay, half that, little ships,
pinnaces of no fighting value, anything that will swim,
to the end that England secure a foothold in the New
World and discover the short passage to India!"

"We have such ships, if they don't sink," said the Admiral, half convinced. "I myself would be wary to hazard my skin in those ancient hulks–shallow draft, leaky,
unlikely to survive in the stormy Atlantic."

"Shallow draft is precisely what is required," Raleigh
said. "The passage is sure to be shallow in spots."

"If Sir Walter is in them they won't sink, I'll warrant
you that," said the Queen, smiling prettily at him.

So seven small ships of questionable quality were
assembled. Raleigh spent liberally of his personal funds
to replace the rotting timbers and mildewed sails, and
he somewhat improved their seaworthiness.

The Queen discovered he was laying out money
of his own from his wine monopoly, and sighed heavily.
Soon her "Water" would be short of funds again.

Still, it was for an English venture, and England was
closer to her heart than any favourite, any lover. And

she didn't have to pay for it. That always pleased her.

For a while she let him believe he would personally lead the expedition, in which she found another pleasing aspect—there would be no women, only men: traders, cartographers, engineers to construct and arm a fortress on Roanoke Island. Nor would large supplies of food, always a costly item in outfitting ships, be necessary since Virginia was reputed to be abundantly supplied.

Then once again at the last minute she said to him sweetly, "I have other plans for you, Sir Walter."

There was finality in her tone. "Other plans, Your Majesty?"

"For the moment I cannot let you go. I need you here and the Admiralty agree." She did not add, but she sorely feared, "Your little fleet is unsafe, and a nightmare rides me daft at the spectre of your corpse at the bottom of the sea, gnawed at by fishes, phaugh! Such an end for such a man!"

He bowed his head in submission, striving to keep his face straight, hoping she had not seen him bite his lip in disappointment, but she had. "Forever and always I am Your Majesty's servant," he said.

"For Christ's sake, Walter, don't fall into one of your surly moods! I cannot abide you when you are peevish."

She would make it worth his while. She would bribe him to keep him by her. It was shortly announced that Sir Walter Raleigh, knight, had had bestowed upon him by the Crown the monopoly of wool: that is to say, the tax on every yard of woollen goods exported from England went into his pocket, a formidable sum.

"Your expedition is not canceled," she said more gently. "It is simply that another must command it. Choose whom you will."

He chose a Westcountry cousin, Sir Richard Grenville.

Grenville was a veteran of the Irish rebellion, like Raleigh's brother, Humphrey Gilbert. He had all of Sir Humphrey's distaste for the Irish without Sir Humphrey's pathological pleasure in cruelty which was twisted and queer.

He was fanatically brave, so brave in fact that in many a battle his disregard of personal safety bordered on hysteria.

Unlike Sir Humphrey he was a superb navigator.

There was popularly supposed to be a "weird" in the fate of these Devonshire mariners. The sea was their life, the sea was in their blood; and the sea was believed to finally claim them. Grenville's father, captain of a ship called the *Mary Rose*, had drowned in the wreck of his vessel.

The Queen shrugged off all this as superstitious nonsense, but the pattern was there. Too many of her Devonshire sea-captains, able devoted men, had been drowned in the sea for her to disregard the matter completely.

Disconsolate, disgruntled, feeling as useless as a man forced to retire from action, Raleigh now found himself victim of a black overwhelming depression. He was actually lonesome, though suppliants daily surrounded him suing for his favor, though the Queen smiled upon him as never before. Often at midnight in his dreams he returned to his childhood, at play with his brothers when everything was new and bright and full of promise. He wanted to go home.

But he had no home.

The house where he was born had long since passed out of his family. All his mature life he had lived in rented abodes, sometimes in penury, sometimes, like now, rich and courted; but still the places were rented, not his.

He watched his little flotilla sail away without him; and as the ships faded from sight in the misty distance his depression deepened. He wrote to an acquaintance in his native county of Devonshire:

My Friend:
  I write to you to ask you to act for me touching the purchase of some farmland and a house that was once in the possession of my father. I will most willingly give whatsoever you in your conscience shall deem it worth. And in return, should you have occasion to ask a favor of me, you shall find me a thankful friend to you and yours. I am moved to purchase the place by a natural desire, for I was born in that house. I had rather possess it as a country seat than any other elsewhere.
  And so I take my leave, ready to countervail all your courtesies to the uttermost of my power.
                    I subscribe myself,
                    from the Court, this
                    26th day of July, 1584,
                              Your most willing, and
                              friend, in all that I
                              shall be able,
                                        W. RALEIGH.

Little escaped the Queen's vigilant eye. Since the day of her birth she had been surrounded by enemies who plotted against her throne and her life. For years she had kept in commodious prisons the royal person of Mary, Queen of Scots, that much-married and appealing lady whose past was dark with murdered lovers and who remained a menace as long as she lived, to the life, the Crown and religion of England, to all that Elizabeth held dear.

For years, for her own protection, Elizabeth had maintained a network of spies who intercepted, read, copied, sealed again and delivered to the addressee all letters sent to prominent persons of her court.

Raleigh received the answer to his letter, the seal intact and apparently unopened. It stated that the purchase of his old home could be easily arranged. But the Queen had already read it.

Her Tudor temper flared. Her Tudor prudence restrained her. "Alas, my Water is in a pet and, if I let him, the saucy rascal will leave me. But he shall not!" And she bribed him with a bribe that set courtiers' tongues to wagging and made him more enemies, one a most formidable one, the Right Reverend Lord Bishop of Durham. "If my Water wants a home he shall have one. But near me!"

Durham was a county that lay far to the north of London on the Scottish border. The people worked hard in coal mines and iron mines, sweaty work that bred a race of tough and hardy men. They had little time for learning, their speech was rough and their tempers easily aroused. During the long northern winter nights they kept themselves warm with the excellent Scotch whisky available tax-free from just over the border if one had the wit to smuggle it in, as virtually everybody did. They might go hungry but never cold. A Durham clergyman with a bent for comedy celebrated their expertise:

> *I cannot eat but little meat,*
> *My stomach is not good;*
> *But sure I think that I can drink*
> *With him that wears a hood.*

The county was ruled by a bishop, who, in ancient times had possessed all-but-sovereign power; but now that England was Protestant only the title and a few innocuous privileges were left of his feudal rights.

Among those rights was the right to maintain a luxurious manor house in London, whose upkeep was paid for by the Church. The Bishop made it his principal residence and never appeared in his distant episcopal see except to discharge a few ceremonial duties. Durham

House had a famous rose garden with fountains and fish ponds and pleasant walks through its close-cropped turf among flowering hedges cared for by a corps of gardeners. Its ample stables had stalls for forty horses. A staff of cooks and servants took care of the Bishop at his table and a truly superb wine cellar contributed to the cheer of his guests. In short, the Lord Bishop of Durham lived like the lord that he was, at no expense to himself or the Queen or anyone else except the coal miners and iron miners who supported the Cathedral at Durham two hundred and fifty miles away.

Queen Elizabeth was Head of the Church of England with ample power to make or break bishops as she pleased. It pleased her to suggest to the Bishop of Durham that he return to his faraway bishopric, and no pleading on his part that the inclement weather was hazardous to his health could move her.

He departed in a rage, and the Queen graciously installed Walter Raleigh in Durham House.

"I want you to have a real home," she said.

Thus she kept him by her.

CHAPTER XIII

RALEIGH's second expedition to Roanoke went wrong
from the start.

Sir Richard Grenville's success in dealing with the
Irish gave him the notion that those other savages, the
American Indians, could be successfully dealt with in
the same way. And Grenville banked heavily on some
verbal instructions from Raleigh given him just before
he sailed, instructions virtually certain to assure a profitable voyage no matter what happened at Roanoke.
"As you know, my dear cousin," Raleigh said, never
batting an eye, never mentioning he had sold them, "I
hold valuable letters of marque signed by the Prince of
Orange and a royal French Duke, giving me free rein
to privateer against Spanish shipping and hold to ransom any prominent Spaniards I can catch. Naturally you
have the same privilege, since you command in my
place." Grenville had nodded, pleased. Raleigh added,
"Your ships are slow perhaps, but you have seven of
them, and guns enough for a big fort."

Raleigh had added one further bit of news, a secret
known only to the Queen and high personages in her
Admiralty. "Things are not what they were. Her Majesty no longer frowns upon Englishmen who fight the
Spaniards even in their own domain. I can tell you in
strictest confidence that our kinsman, Sir Francis Drake,
is even now at sea with a powerful fleet on a secret mission, with the Queen's tacit consent and approval—and

'tis said that his course is southward toward the Spanish Main."

So Grenville too bent his course southward with a weather eye peeled for likely prizes. Several huge galleons, all sailing east to add their might to the gathering Spanish Armada, he let go by; they were too dangerous. But then, off Spanish Florida, he came upon two lumbering unescorted freighters. His little flotilla got the wind of them. And suddenly the astounded Spaniards were greeted by a murderous hail of fire from the hundred cannon destined for the Roanoke fort.

The freighters instantly surrendered, their masts splintered, their sails shredded, hulls riddled like a sieve. One of the Spanish captains, sorely smitten in his vanity, surveyed the ruin of his vessels and said sourly, "We did not expect fire like that from those—those—those contemptible scows!" He pointed a shamed and tremulous finger at Grenville's tiny flotilla.

Sir Richard merely smiled. "It is never wise to underrate the English Royal Navy, Señor Captain."

Thereupon, for time was short, he forced all the Spanish crewmen still able to stand to transfer the cargoes of the two ships to his own: sugar, molasses, bales of exquisite mink pelts, a hogshead of ambergris, a casket of pearls and gold ornaments obviously stolen from the Indians, a chest of exotic New World drugs that he knew would delight Raleigh, who was fascinated by the muscle-crippling substance that the Indians used to poison their arrows and which in their language was called *ourari* (corrupted by the English into "curare"); and there were some sizable bars of silver, stamped with King Philip's crest, which Raleigh, when he got them, promptly stamped with his own. Not a tremendous haul; but enough, with the ransom of the Spanish captains, to augur Sir Richard a prosperous voyage, a voyage which was only beginning.

"Put your wounded into boats, Señor Captain," he

said. "Your ships won't float much longer. If the fire from my contemptible scows has damaged your compasses I will provide you with navigational instruments of my own. Your crews will all get safely ashore, which is just over the horizon. Quickly now!"

Courtesy and cruelty were curiously commingled in the Spanish character. The captain swept him a courtly bow and said without a trace of sarcasm, "You have treated us like caballeros. One is astonished at the heretic English pirate! I shall request in my report to my King that Don Ricardo Gren-veeya, because of his consideration, be strangled before they hang him. And now, adios." He bowed again and made a step as if to board the last of the lifeboats.

"Your report will have to wait a while," Grenville said. "I am taking you and the other captain with me back to England as my guests, where, no doubt, ample arrangements will be made with your King to repatriate caballeros of your worth."

Grenville continued to treat them as guests. They dined with him in his cabin, and were not even forced to accommodate their delicate palates to English brew since Sir Richard graciously allowed them some of their own excellent sherry looted from their ships.

Grenville proceeded at a leisurely pace northward along the coast. Occasionally he would remember that his primary mission was to construct a fort on Roanoke Island, but his good luck with the two ships made privateering more attractive. The attitude was even more pronounced in the minds of his crews: it is highly exciting to fight, to sink, to loot, activities which are all over in an hour or two with the prospect of rich rewards in your share of the prize. But to build a fortress, chop down trees, raise walls, cut, hammer, saw, mount heavy cannon—that was a different matter entirely, sweaty tedious work, far fitter for peasants and slaves than brave English freebooters flushed with victory and greedy for more.

But no likely prizes appeared. Grenville reluctantly left Spanish Florida behind and sailed north to Roanoke Island, determined to do his best to carry out Raleigh's orders.

He was met by a group of wary but not yet hostile Indians, who greeted him with smiles and held out gifts that they knew the white man liked, signifying a desire to trade. Grenville accepted a few pearls and some gold ornaments but shook his head when they pointed to muskets, swords, armor, halberds and daggers that they wanted in exchange. He gave them a large iron kettle. He had no intention of wasting the valuable time of his men, not with so many savages to do the menial work, which might as well start with cooking for the whole flotilla as with anything else.

The Spanish captains proved invaluable at this juncture. They barked imperiously at the Indians in the Carib tongue as if they were used to ordering Indians around and being obeyed. Not unreasonably the Spaniards calculated that their own chances for a quick ransom and return to their homeland depended on collaborating with the heretic English to enslave the pagan Indians.

Hopelessly outnumbered and out-weaponed, the Indians went wooden in the face, expressionless; what they were thinking nobody knew, and the English assumed from their passive obedience that they were not thinking at all.

"What docile servants they would make!" Grenville remarked.

"Sí, Don Ricardo," one captain agreed.

The other said, "Sí?" and smiled. "But I always wear armor when I go among them, Señor Capitan, and I'd advise you and your men to do the same."

"It is very hot," Grenville said.

"It stops poison darts," said the Spaniard.

"Good Lord!" Grenville said, remembering. There-after, despite the heat, which got worse, all the English wore armor.

Even with cowed and helpless slaves it took a long time for the pharaohs to build the pyramids, as Raleigh would write when he came to write his *History of the World;* and it took a long time to build the fort at Roanoke, though the Indians were unmercifully lashed if they faltered. Before the last tier of timbers was laid atop the walls of the fort, beautiful orchids were flowering on the first.

Most of the Indian squaws had quietly disappeared in canoes over to the mainland, but a few seemed to have chosen to stay with their men. Noting that they were the youngest and comeliest of the lot, Grenville thought, "They are probably recent brides, poor things," and honestly wished Raleigh had provided the expedition with a proper Anglican priest to instruct them in the Protestant faith and marry them to their braves, as an example of English superiority over the Spaniards who, as he knew, never bothered to civilize the Indians. "But Cousin Walter is lax in religious matters," he remembered, smiling indulgently. (Walter Raleigh indeed was so lax in religion that all his life enemies called him an "infidel.")

Grenville was an efficient organizer. He put the young Indian squaws to cultivating the field of English seeds planted by the first expedition, noting with pleasure how they had grown, planting additional seeds of different kinds in accordance with his instructions. And he let it be known that if, by chance, the field should be sabotaged, the girls responsible would be "sternly dealt with" and their men would be shot before their eyes. Needless to say the field throve after that. The Spaniards nodded, "We know, we know; the Moors were good gardeners too."

Grenville was equally stern with his own men. When he saw some of his all-male company looking hungrily at the Indian girls—it was early one Sunday morning while he was reading the Morning Prayer—he cheerfully announced that anyone caught molesting them would be given a fair hearing, instantly adjudged guilty and promptly hanged. His men knew the reputation he had acquired in Ireland. They knew he would do exactly that.

Then, confident that all was going well, he divided his company, taking the ships with the shallowest draft to explore the mainland, leaving behind his well-disciplined and well-organized work parties.

There were some storms, which seemed to rise without warning out of the Caribbean, but they didn't seem serious. He asked about the weather, but the mainland Indians were uncooperative and fled at his approach. His reputation had preceded him. Fugitive Indian women had told how he flogged and enslaved the Indians on the island. In their simple savage minds they could detect no difference between Spaniards and Englishmen.

The Spanish captains told him, "The weather will hold for some time yet, Don Ricardo."

In sweltering heat, armed cap-à-pie, he drove his reluctant adventurers up every creek, every estuary that seemed to hold promise of passage to the Pacific a few miles away, taking soundings, meticulously charting the coast, noting in his log how the Indians constructed fish weirs, planted maize, built their dwellings. Grenville was a thorough man. But no passage led to the Pacific and the dwellings were deserted; but deserted only recently and it seemed only upon his approach, for campfires still smoked. He was confused, frustrated, furious.

The Spaniards advised him, "They are lurking nearby,

Señor Captain. In such cases it is customary to burn a few habitations. We always do. Squaws and *pique-niños* are usually left behind till we pass."

Grenville swore, "By God, it is Ireland all over again!"

His men applied the torch to some squalid Indian hovels. Instantly there was a shout of rage from the forests, shrill female screams of panic as women clutched babes to their breast and fled to the safety of the woods. Then out of the woods a host of painted savages charged recklessly upon the English, who promptly mowed them down with muskets prudently charged with heavy game-slugs that would stop a bull.

Grenville surveyed the damage he had wrought.

"Shoot the wounded," he said compassionately. "They have suffered enough." The others fled into the forest, where now there was naught but a great silence and glaring-red eyes.

He wrote in his log for Raleigh to see, "Cousin: I have charted the coast insofar as the time I allotted therefor would permit, but as yet have discovered no passage through to the Pacific, the natives requiring pacification. I doubt not I have taught them good manners by now, smoothing your path against the time when you yourself shall adventure hither. Now I repair to Roanoke to oversee the construction of the fortress you bade me build, the weather having changed for the worse."

And later: "The fortress on Roanoke Island is complete and very neatly made, with spacious outbuildings for the housing of the native workers. You would be pleased, I think, could you but see the impregnable citadel we have caused to be built in Virginia. We have wrought all this with but one casualty, a most curious incident."

It was curious. It was ominous. Its implications were not at first fully grasped.

One of the young English engineers, more used to the bear-gardens and tavern maids of London than sweaty and celibate work in Virginia, had raped one of the female Indian gardeners. She submitted without a whimper. His own eyes were closed in long-pent-up physical delight; but if he had opened them to look into hers he'd have seen death in them, *his* death. He actually thought she enjoyed it.

Next day he was found, looking up at the sky, and on his face an expression of peace and relaxation as if he had died while enjoying a pleasant dream. But one of the Spaniards pulled out of his neck a little dart and said, *"Ourari";* and crossed himself to the disgust of all right-thinking Protestants who looked on.

Then in the log there appears a record of a qualm: "Good Cousin: Here in Virginia there is a weird upon the land, which was sometime so plenteous and fruitful. In the rivers, no fish. In the forests, no game. Our supply of food is scant. Two human heads rolled into the fort today bouncing like bowling balls—our men, alas, two feckless youths who went scavenging into caches where the Indians bury their winter food supply in wicker hampers, and who were caught and beheaded.

"Naturally, I have taken appropriate countermeasures, to wit: the Indians having failed to deliver the perpetrators of these most foul and treasonable murders although repeatedly ordered to do so, I have caused twenty of their number chosen at random from among the fort workers to be hanged (shooting them first out of pity) and their bodies flung into the wilderness, thereby teaching a salutary lesson to the savages, besides reducing the number of useless mouths, our food supply causing ever greater concern, as it dwindles daily."

The odds against the expedition were desperate from the start and got worse as the season advanced. Grenville's Irish-type treatment of the natives now turned against him. Far from making friends of them as Raleigh had instructed, he had turned them into deadly and cunning enemies. Far from demonstrating the superiority of Englishmen over Spaniards he had inextricably confounded the two in their minds.

His men tried to live off the game in the forests. Seldom now was an animal found alive, only rooting carcasses stuck full of darts and so laden with poison that scavenger buzzards that ate the remains dropped dead on the wing. His men rooted in the Indian buried food supplies only to find them befouled with dung. They raided the fish weirs and found them broken up—there was no food in them either. In their desperation they ate their horses and dogs and pounded unskilfully at the sea rocks for oysters and clams, and cursed when big fat crabs scuttled out of reach.

Grenville tried to cheer them and encourage them to harder work. "In a land so plenteous and fruitful as Virginia," he said, "you need never lack for sustenance"; and indeed there was actually a plenty to be had; the Indians couldn't spoil it all. But the English were averse to work even if they had had the skill. Survival in a wilderness is not for the city bred, who long only to return to the city.

Worse now fell upon them. The hurricane season. A storm such as never was known in England came howling out of the Caribbean uprooting trees and washing away the field of crops planted by the English. Nothing was left but a dismal swamp, looking for all the world like an Irish bog; and after it dried the soil was caked hard. All plant life was dead, not a grain of wheat could be salvaged, it was too late to plant another crop.

Grenville, with wonderful navigational foresight, had anchored his flotilla under the lee of the island and thus saved it from complete annihilation. But he was disheartened. He conceived he had done his duty. And in truth he had honestly tried, insofar as light was given him to see his duty, conscientiously, bravely in the face of unknown and unexpected hazards. Now it was time to go home and report to Cousin Raleigh, with his Spanish loot and his Spanish captains.

He left a hundred men to man the Roanoke fortress, bidding them be of good cheer: the fort was impregnable, there were plenty of guns and ammunition, virtually all the Indians had run away or been killed and such few as remained could be easily forced to gather food. And he promised to return in the spring with supplies and reinforcements of men. In this Grenville asked them to hazard no more than he himself would have done if he had been in their place.

With anything but good cheer in their hearts his disconsolate men watched his sails dip over the eastern horizon toward a rising sun on a perfect autumn day.

Grenville's career as a privateer prospered greatly on the voyage home. He captured a richly laden Spanish ship, the *Santa Maria*, with a cargo of gold, silver, pearls, and dyestuffs, and proudly sailed her into Plymouth with her cargo intact and more Spanish prisoners to be ransomed. Then he rode posthaste up to London to report to his cousin Sir Walter, now living in style in Durham House.

Raleigh flew into a rage when he heard of the doings in Virginia, but he quickly sobered when he beheld the honest sun-seamed countenance of his hardworking cousin. Grenville had left undone, as the Anglican Prayerbook so lucidly set forth, those things which he ought to have done and done those things which he ought not to have done, but there had been terrible provocation. "Aye," Raleigh had to agree, " 'twas Ireland all over again." He embraced his cousin, especially when he saw the ships' manifests of all the rich booty that Grenville had brought home, and sat him down to a lordly feast in the great hall at Durham House. The Deputy Mayor of Plymouth was there (Sir Francis Drake being the Lord Mayor but largely away on ventures at sea), and some other influential notables, all suing for Raleigh's favor now that he stood in such favor with the Queen. They dined and drank far into the night from silver stamped with the Raleigh crest served by servants wearing the Raleigh livery, drinking excellent wines of dusty vintage from the Lord Bishop's ample cellars.

But next day, when the guests were gone, he took his cousin aside and said gravely, "Richard, I must send you back at once with a relief ship. I'll get you a fast one— I can, I have influence with the Admiralty; I *must;* for I fear me sore there be mischief afoot in Virginia. Nay, do not make your face stern, good cousin. The men you left behind have not your invention, stamina, your high sense of duty, your skill in dealing with revolt, and above all your bravery. Go back I say, with a relief ship, now, tomorrow, then come home to me and the rich reward you so dearly deserve for your exploit, in the Queen's greater advancement and favor."

Grenville departed within the week in a fast fighting ship with a crew of fighting Royal Navy men, and safe in the hold a heavy cargo of foodstuffs, expertly chosen as only the Royal Navy knew how, to be life-sustaining and nonperishable for a considerable length of time.

On Roanoke Island the colonists who were left behind considered themselves abandoned, marooned, with a starving winter ahead, surrounded by hostile savages. By night they could smell the smoke and catch flickering glimpses of Indian campfires through the trees of the forests; by day they could hear Indian dogs barking and Indian yells of derision, mocking them. It was a time of hunger and fear. Nerves wore thin. Imagination magnified dangers already too great to exaggerate.

Then, when panic seemed likely to render them irrational, they descried a close-packed fleet of twenty sail bearing menacingly upon them from the south. After the first spasm of terror that it might be Spanish, they saw, through perspective glasses, Queen Elizabeth's battle flags streaming from the masts, and sent up a shout of joy, relief at salvation-unlooked-for. It was the absentee Mayor of Plymouth, Sir Francis Drake.

They welcomed him with such fare as they had, but when Sir Francis saw how scanty it was and its deplorable quality, he ordered a feast sent ashore from his ships: pineapples, bananas and other exotic tropical fruits; freshly butchered mutton and veal; rum, sugar loafs and vintage Spanish wines; for he had been plundering Spanish islands and the Spanish Main, burning whole cities, looting and sinking ships, taking Spanish prisoners for ransom and freighting his fleet with Spanish pearls, bars of silver, nuggets of gold and precious East Indian spices looted from Spanish warehouses before he burned them down. Now he was sailing victoriously home to lay his plundered treasures at Queen Elizabeth's feet, with only this casual pause at Roanoke to see how Sir Walter's venture fared. He was distressed at the sight of it faring so ill.

He loaded a barge with a two-year supply of food and gave it to the colonists. A storm arose and sank it. He offered them another, but a deputation approached him and begged him to take them back to England, away from the accursed island. There would be no relief till spring, they told him; only in spring had Grenville promised to send them relief and reinforcements. Meanwhile, though they might not starve, they would surely be massacred by the Indians.

He looked into their faces and saw the signs of desperate strain. These were not disciplined Royal Navy men, sturdy and dependable to the last drop of blood. These were overspecialized engineers, tried to the breaking point by hardship and privation. He agreed to take them home to save their lives, excepting such as might volunteer to remain. Not a man volunteered.

Shortly Sir Richard came charging across the Atlantic in Raleigh's relief ship with large supplies of food and reinforcements of men.

The gates of the fort were open. Inside there was not a soul. Nor were there signs of violence. Nothing but eerie silence and the squeak of hinges as the gates swung idly in the wind. Fearless, even rash in battle when he could see what he was fighting, his stout heart quailed at terror of the unknown. Surely a weird *was* upon this deserted place.

He put a good face on the matter. The absent garrison was probably on the mainland punishing the Indians after chasing all the savages away from the island. Shortly they would return, he said. Meanwhile his fast ship was needed in England, where great events impended. "Now I must return to Sir Walter and give him this good report," he said. He said there was no need to leave extra men and extra mouths to feed since the mainland party would soon make their reappearance.

He delegated a party of a mere twenty men to hold the fort and keep it tidy, leaving food aplenty for them and the "mainland force." Then he departed, sealing their doom.

For in the night on which he sailed, the Indians crept out of the forest and slaughtered two sleepy sentries. The other eighteen men fled to the beach and crowded into a little boat and set off in a heavy surf into darkness and oblivion. They were never seen or heard of again. Their tragedy did not become known for two years.

This was the first "Lost Colony" of Roanoke.

There was to be another.

CHAPTER XIV

MODERN psychiatrists, who can boast the distinction of having achieved the highest suicide rate of all medical practitioners, gravely assure us that women, upon entering into their fifties, exhibit one of several variants of female sexuality, namely: they grow gentle, resigned, Whistler's-Motherish, happily spoiling their grandchildren; or, they become troublesome nags, the butt of the comedian's mother-in-law jokes; or else, if they are exceptionally strong, like Queen Elizabeth, they refuse to abdicate their lost youth and fall into a sexual trap: they fall passionately in love with very handsome young men, fondleably son-like, unstable, weak and pitifully anxious to please. Such was Lord Essex, such the Queen.

There were no psychiatrists in Elizabeth's day, nor would she have laid herself on their couch had there been, and so she was spared all vexatious feelings of guilt.

But fall into the sexual trap she did, and the man who trapped her was Robert Devereux, young Lord Essex, the highborn aristocrat, soft-eyed, full-rosy-lipped, whose curly head she had tousled when he was little, running her fingers through his little-boy beard, now prickly and stiff, Essex, now grown up, broad in the shoulders, built like an inverted triangle, all rippling muscles on top, sensually seductive, down to a narrow brace of hips that left Elizabeth's waiting-women breathless with their promise—handsome, handsome young Essex, as manly as ever he would be, who one day would go mad and to the block. That was why, for the moment, Diana was not quite her usual sober self.

With Walter Raleigh the case was quite otherwise. He was entering upon the happiest years of his life, happiest because they were the busiest. Ceaseless activity left him little leisure to indulge his mental bent toward a brooding self-pity. It is hard to be paranoid when everybody wants you.

Increasingly the Admiralty turned to him to help out in a difficult problem: how to get full value when captured prisoners were ransomed. Raleigh had acquired a reputation for scrupulous honesty in such matters. He had captured prisoners himself, and so had the commanders of his expeditions, who served under him. He had always turned over to the Queen's treasury every penny of the ransom. But many other prisoners were being captured by many other English privateers, and profit from their ransom had a habit of leaking away into the pockets of corrupt local officials. There was always some obscure jailor or ship chandler or alderman who declared he had claims against the ransom money. The Admiralty turned to Raleigh to resolve these complex financial matters and force the corrupt officials to disgorge their ill-gotten gains, a task requiring long hours of research into the facts of each case.

On one occasion, typical of many, he wrote to the Admiralty reviewing the case of an English captive ransomed out of the hands of the Barbary pirates of North Africa:

May It Please Your Good Lordships:

> Twice have we heard the plea of this complainant, a rich linen merchant, who states upon his oath that his ransom money hath not been paid; nay, further, that certain charges have been levied by local authorities

against his own pocket, purporting to be for room and
board whilst he was detained in the African prison,
whereby, as we take it, this complainant is much
wronged. And we find the hardness of the case to con-
sist in this: That the ransom paid by the Pirates for the
redemption of this English Captive hath been withheld,
against all equity, from Her Majesty's Treasury, and
that the Complainant himself hath been penalized in his
pocket for his own misfortune.

> Your Lordships' Humble Commandment,
> (signed) W. RALEIGH.

Actions like this naturally made Walter Raleigh many
enemies among the officials involved, all of whom he
named in an enclosure with the letter and all of whom
were forced to pay. And all of whom considered Raleigh's strict construction of fiscal honesty highly unrealistic. In justice to the corrupt officials of the far-off
age in which Raleigh lived, it must be admitted that
they were *expected* to eke out their slender salaries with
a little well-placed graft, and that Raleigh was much
stricter in applying fiscal honesty to them than to himself.

Lord Essex, constantly in attendance upon the Queen's
person, took every occasion to undercut his rival. He
would muse aloud for her ear, "One misses that over-
dressed upstart with his witty sallies and the pearls in
his ears, one really does"; and Elizabeth, who truly did
miss him a little, would glower inwardly, "Wasting his
time upon trivia—linen merchants, Barbary pirates, pish!"
and would dance with young Essex far into enchanted
evenings, while courtiers too quickly concluded, "Sir
Walter's goose is cooked."

For a little while Raleigh wrote her every day, hastily
scrawled letters full of contractions and Westcountry-
isms—"the missive I wrat [wrote] to Your Majesty
ystdy, is hit yet com . . . ?" but she answered curtly
—never in her own hand—or not at all.

Always sensitive to displeasure, especially the Queen's, Sir Walter fell into the sulks and exiled himself to his 50,000-acre estate in Ireland. If Diana didn't want him by her, by her he would not be, drat her!

There, throughout a weary summer, vainly awaiting the London mails, he brooded, bored, inactive, feeling put-upon, experimenting with medicinal formulas, planting New World potatoes and New World tobacco. Both flourished, and he saw with satisfaction that the Irish developed a taste for both: potatoes to feed them cheaply, tobacco to soothe their savage Irish breasts. Thus it was that the "Irish" potato first made its appearance in Ireland.

Edmund Spenser was also living in Ireland, also upon an estate confiscated from the rebel Irish Earl; but Raleigh carefully avoided him. He could not use him; Spenser was in even greater disfavor with the Queen than Raleigh himself.

For Elizabeth's eye he wrote a sonorous doleful poem, one of his loveliest, instinct with the loyalty and courtly love he bore her all his life long; and it detracts not a whit from its beauty that he hoped it would serve a useful purpose: to help restore him to favor.

What else is hell, but loss of blissful heaven?
What darkness else, but lack of lightsome day?
What else is death, but things of life bereaven?
What winter else, but pleasant spring's decay?

Unrest what else, but fancy's hot desire,
Fed with delay and followed with despair?
What else mishap, but longing to aspire,
To strive against earth, water, fire and air?

Heaven were my state, and happy sunshine day,
And life most blest, to joy one hour's desire;

Hap, bliss, and rest, and sweet springtime of May,
Were to behold my fair consuming fire.

But lo! I feel, by absence from your sight,
Mishap, unrest, death, winter, hell, dark night.

Mollified but unreconciled, the Queen accepted this tribute with a smile, as her due. It was pleasant that Sir Walter grieved at her loss—but couldn't the stiff-necked rascal have presented it in person, contrite, on bended knee with a tear or two? Darling Essex could weep so charmingly! Ah well, let him suffer a little longer, and then one day, probably sooner than he deserved. . . .

But it was the Royal Navy that cut short Raleigh's Irish exile.

Raleigh's native Westcountry lay squarely athwart the invasion route of the Spanish Armada, now massing across the Channel. Hundreds of miles of unprotected shoreline of Devon and Cornwall, with deep estuaries where heavy-draft galleons could safely anchor, offered a perfect landing site for the galleons to disgorge a formidable army once they had crossed the Narrow Sea. Never since William the Conqueror had England faced such peril. For behind those unprotected southern shores there was nothing to oppose an invader. No army, no militia, a sparse population of farmers and mine workers, hardy but undisciplined and long unused to war.

It was to the Westcountry seamen, fishermen with salt water in their blood, privateer captains like Drake and Walter Raleigh, that the Admiralty now turned.

Prompted by her Admiralty, seconded by her Privy Council, her Prime Minister and all her closest advisers except Lord Essex, Queen Elizabeth was now advised to bestow upon Walter Raleigh an office of trust and responsibility no commoner had ever held before. With a prissy pout and a self-satisfied smile she agreed. (The pout was because he was stiff-necked. The smile was because others recognized the worth of her "Water"— she had been right all the time.)

And Sir Walter Raleigh now became Vice Admiral for Devon and Cornwall. His star was rising fast. His titles and honors were growing apace. "Admiral Sir Walter Raleigh, Lord Warden of Devon and Cornwall," had his own battle flag to fly from his ships.

Fast also rose his duties, more onerous than one man, no matter how energetic, could easily discharge. It was Raleigh's responsibility to arm the Westcountry against invasion. He had ample authority by reason of his new appointment. He used his authority without stint.

Militia: Westcountry farmers and miners learned the use of guns. Crops might go unreaped, the production of tin from the mines might go down, but every man had a musket and learned how to load it with Spaniard-killing slugs. "They will come upon us in formation, most arrogant and visible," he said. "Do not attempt to shoot at their backs, though the armor be thin there, a tempting target. They never turn their backs. Hide yourselves behind rocks and shoot at their bellies. Then, as I think, they shall have no stomach left to fight." "Aye, Water," they said, grinning. "We know. And thank'ee."

Taxes: They thanked him for their soldiers' pay. The Lord Warden of Devon and Cornwall was responsible for collecting the Queen's taxes. Most Lord Wardens had hitherto pocketed the monies. Raleigh poured it all back into the militiamen's pay. He collected it unmerci-fully. His methods were unorthodox. A good many Westcountry landowners complained that their manor houses had been broken into, their silver plate stolen and melted down into shillings. Walter Raleigh could now add them to his lengthening roster of powerful enemies. But the militiamen loved him. He was one of their own. He spoke their provincial language. They blessed him and blessed the Queen. When Elizabeth heard of his depredations she snapped, "He is perfectly legal. Who are the rogues that withheld my taxes beforetime? Punish them!" and then bethought herself, "Nay, punish them not. They are Englishmen. England hath need of every man in the clear and present danger. Nor shall you punish Sir Walter either. Give him his head, so long as my taxes are got and the south prepared." So the taxes continued to be got and the militiamen continued to be paid; and they improved their marksmanship, which was already good from long years of illegal poaching.

Fiery beacons: Raleigh told his men, "You will spot the galleons by their high hulls and lumbering gait and the Popish crosses on their sails. They must not get ashore, lest it go hard with us. Signal when you see them. Sir Francis Drake, Sir Richard Grenville, kinsmen to us all—they are lying in wait in hidden coves to pounce upon them ere they land when we sight them," and he caused to be erected a line of fiery signal beacons, high poles with tar buckets on top all along the southern coast, some on church steeples, where keen-eyed watchmen stood watch with fire-matches burning day and night, sending up a sulphurous incense to heaven that brought hearty chuckles from the good Anglican priests whose houses of worship were turned into watchtowers: "A pillar of cloud," they said, "to guide the Popish dogs to destruction. Now if only we mined some salt in these parts to turn them into Lot's wife!"

Raleigh was everywhere at once in the Westcountry, gathering taxes, impressing seamen into the Navy, drilling militiamen, warning, exhorting, running himself ragged and everyone under him. No, not ragged. Not Raleigh. He went about decked in finery as flamboyant as ever. Subordinates needed an example in neatness. How could one expect men to follow a leader who dressed as dirty as they did?

The worst dressed, the dirtiest and the most unruly of all the Westcountry men were the miners who worked underground in the "stanneries," the tin mines of Devon and Cornwall. Twelve hours a day they toiled in the subterranean gloom. The skinny mules that pulled the ore carts were blind from the dark, eyes white with cataracts, hide bleached gray, hoofs swollen and soft with damp and disease; the stench was appalling. When the miners climbed out of the pits at sundown they shielded their eyes against the gentle twilight as if from a glare. The pure clean air struck their unaccustomed nostrils as a most unpleasant smell. They welcomed the soothing new palliative tobacco, and laid out hard-earned wages for it when they could get it.

This confirmed Walter Raleigh, who himself was fond of the weed, in his belief that tobacco was a medicament of wonder-working potential; and he cast about in his mind how to make it cheaper and more available: perhaps he would bring back a whole shipload when he sent his next expedition to Virginia.

He had read the classic French treatise on tobacco, published some years before. In France tobacco was called *Nicotiane* in honor of the French diplomat, Jean Nicot, who introduced it into that country. Having described the delights and therapeutic benefits of smoking and "drinking" tobacco, Seigneur Nicot went on to describe its other virtues:

This strange plant [he wrote] was brought from Florida. I planted it in my garden, where it grew and multiplied marvelously. One of my servants told me that a kinsman of his had a deep ulcer in the gristles of his nose, very sore and painful. My servant took a leaf of the plant and pounded it into a poultice, the fibres of the leaf and the juice, and applied the resultant ointment to the ulcer of his kinsman, who found himself marvelously eased thereby. I caused the sick young man to be brought before me and the said herb to be applied for eight or ten days, whereupon the said young man's sore was utterly healed and extinguished, nor hath he felt it since.

And further:

> One of my cooks, having almost cut off his thumb with a great chopping knife, my steward ran for the Nicotiane and dressed him therewith five or six times, and so in the end he was healed.

And another case:

> The father of one of my servants, who was troubled with an ulcer in his leg, having had the same for two years, came to me for my herb, and used it in the same manner as the others, and at the end of ten or twelve days he was healed.

And another:

> A woman with her face covered with ringworm as if she were wearing a visor on her face came to me and begged, "Monseigneur, pray let me have some of your herb," which I gave to her and instructed her how to use it; and at the end of eight or ten days she was healed and came to me to show me her healing.

And another:

> A captain whose son suffered from the King's Evil, his face a mass of sores, came to me; and having applied my herb to his son's face, his son in a few days was cured of the King's Evil.

Jean Nicot gave an elaborate formula for compounding the ointment. Raleigh brewed up a kettleful and held his nose in disgust. "The Frenchman is surely exaggerating the efficacy of this sorry mess." And yet Raleigh himself had long had it in mind to concoct a healing elixir no less elaborate; when he had more time he proposed to perfect it. He had to concede, "There just *may* be some virtue in the Frenchman's ointment; but I suspect he praises it simply because it perpetuates his name."

In the true scientific spirit he tried the Nicotiane poultice on a miner's mule that the harness had galled. The sore did not heal and the mule died.

The miner, a surly fellow, shrugged, "Hit'ud be daid by now anyhow. Don' nothin' live long in a stannery."

Raleigh gazed at his rags, his grimy face, his gaunt and bony body. "Why not?"

The miner gazed at Raleigh, his gorgeous dress, his immaculately clean face. "Ever see a stannery, *Sir* Water?"

"No. But I propose to. This instant. And you shall be my cicerone."

"Yer wot?"

"My *guide*, skeleton!"

Something in Raleigh's manner did not offend the miner despite his rough words. He was, after all, the first Lord Warden who ever had noticed that stannery mules were sick and stannery miners thin.

Clothed as he was, Raleigh clambered down the ladder into the pit and saw at first hand the conditions under which man and beast were forced to work. Using his formidable powers he set about putting things right. Humanitarianism had nothing to do with it. It was all just too damnably inefficient.

He shortened the miners' hours. He raised their pay. He recruited extra work shifts. The mules he could do nothing about, nor did he try. He simply ordered more into the mines.

Rumors of Raleigh's exorbitant expenditures reached the court. Essex said, "Our over-dressed jack-a-dandy is a long time away, he really is. But I suppose it will take a while to deck all those miners in velvet and pearls." "Oh, shut up," said the Queen, who was all business these days. Sometimes at night she was even too tired to dance.

She too had heard complaints from the Westcountry. She too had fretted about the new Lord Warden's high-handed methods and wild outlay of monies. She consulted her trusted Prime Minister, wise, thorough old Lord Burleigh. "Dear Burleigh, has my Water gone mad?"

"Madame, as to that I cannot say," But he could reassure her. He held a sheaf of papers in his hand. "The Treasury reports that he is collecting Your Majesty's taxes at an unprecedented rate. True, he has expended large sums on equipment and healthier clothing for the miners, but he delivers to your Treasury as much as ever it got under former Lord Wardens. Moreover, he seems to have made the stanneries actually popular places for the Westcountry men to work in, and the output of the tin mines is up."

He had all the facts, all the figures. He glanced at another paper.

"And the Admiralty reports him successful in massing a force of well-armed and well-trained militiamen, in impressing hundreds of able seamen, in inventing a new and ingenious system of beacons to alert the countryside when the Armada is sighted."

The Queen looked grave. "He cannot work miracles. Pray God the Armada never lands."

Burleigh nodded, equally grave. "All England is praying, Your Majesty."

Elizabeth struck the table with her clenched fist and cursed all Spaniards. "God rot 'em, rot 'em, *rot 'em!* And to think that whoreson Philip once wanted to wed me!"

To lighten her mood Burleigh said, smiling, "And here is a curious report. The miners have got up a petition, all duly and neatly signed with hundreds of names, more than are necessary, and not only miners but farmers, fishermen, militiamen: they want to be represented in Parliament by Walter Raleigh, and he accepted! Of course I shall declare the petition illegal at once—unauthorized signatures, something to void it."

A cunning look came into the Queen's eye. "Why?"

"Why? Why, Madame, he—he—he is much too valuable where he is, his duties! How can he bury himself here in London in Parliament . . . he is sure to win, you know."

The Queen said sternly, "My people have the right to elect whom they please to represent them. There are greater lords and greater admirals in Parliament than Sir Walter Raleigh. If the Westcountry wants him to serve in Parliament, serve he must."

Burleigh repressed a smile. He understood now. Elizabeth wanted her poet-sailorman back. Ah well, he was better than Essex. Or would she have them both? Probably both. "Sir Walter will serve I am sure, Your Majesty."

No one campaigned against him. No one challenged his seat. And so it came about that Sir Walter Raleigh, Vice Admiral of Devon and Cornwall, Lord Warden of the Stanneries, could add one more title of honor to his name: Member of Parliament. And thus Diana had him again by her side.

The first thing he asked of her when she received him was a fleet of ships to plant another colony in Virginia.

CHAPTER XV

THOSE who knew Queen Elizabeth best were always struck by the fact that the more she had to do the more she was capable of doing. Her body, growing older every year, to her intense irritation, might tire, but never her mind. In the afternoon, after her main meal of the day, taken at eleven o'clock in the morning like everyone else's, she might seem to retire to relax among her waiting-women, listening to their prattle and the music of a lute strummed softly in an anteroom, usually some love *ballade* written by her father, who had possessed among his other accomplishments, that of being an excellent composer.

But let there come a courier with news from any part of her threatened realm, news good or bad—a rich prize taken from the Spaniards, a rising of the Irish, or some recent plot against her by Queen Mary of Scotland—and Elizabeth was all action. The waiting-women withdrew. The lute ceased to strum and the lutist tiptoed away. Her mind expanded, her vision broadened, all thought of relaxation vanished. She was taut as a bow-string and her mind could hold a dozen conflicting schemes simultaneously. At such times the Queen felt capable of anything.

This remarkable capacity was the result of a lifetime of danger. As a little girl she had never known whether that which stirred the curtains around her bed, the arras on the walls, was a gentle breeze that breathed over the moors or a hired assassin after her blood to eliminate her right to the throne. It was also the result of the genes in her blood, where Tudor courage and Tudor caution were so curiously commingled. That is why her chosen motto, *Video et taceo,* was so apt. Had Elizabeth been simpler she might have been less tragic, but England less great.

It was with this feeling of taut alertness that she granted Walter Raleigh his audience. All had withdrawn except Essex, who had the run of the palace even to her bedchamber.

She sensed at once exactly how to handle the situation. She could not dismiss Essex without offending him, which she could not bring herself to do. She could not refuse to see Raleigh without offending *him*, which she did not wish to do. Therefore she would simply let Essex stay when she received Raleigh. If any unpleasantness resulted she would know how to handle it, twist it to her benefit and if, in the process, there might occur some spinoff of comedy, enjoy it, learn from it.

The two proud men confronted each other, her lovers both but in such different ways! How beautiful Lord Essex looked, bursting with youth, how easily he wore his costly clothes; he was born to elegance, he had never known anything else. And how handsome was her "Water," older, maturer, more proven, his pale poetic face intense, his elegant costume cunningly contrived, calculated, that of the man who had risen, would rise, rise or die. And she was the source, the fountainhead of all honors, titles, patents of nobility, the favors they sued for, her ancient feudal right, the right of all English sovereigns: she was England's Queen! It was a delicious thought.

She knew how deeply Essex hated Raleigh. How would he react?

With an impulsive gesture Essex held out his hand and greeted Raleigh with a smile.

"Breeding will out," thought the Queen, pleased. There would be no unpleasantness.

Raleigh accepted the proffered hand, shook it, bowed stiffly, dropped it and turned away to face the Queen and unburden himself of what was on his mind.

"Ships, ships, ships!" interrupted Essex, who knew nothing of them. "How can you ask for ships with Spain at our throats?" Shortly he wearied of Raleigh's impetuous monologue and begged leave to retire. Elizabeth kissed him lightly on the cheek—kissing was a common form of greeting and leave-taking in England, abhorrent in Spain where any bodily contact was considered a work of the devil—and said, "Sweet, noble heart, Sir Walter lusteth after ships as most men lust after women," and smiled him out of the door. He departed, wondering how much she knew, whether she guessed he was vioently attracted to one of her prettiest waiting women, and he decided she didn't.

She didn't.

Not yet.

Raleigh continued his request for ships. There were men in Virginia, he said, brave Englishmen, holding the fort on Roanoke Island. All the others had panicked, come home; he would explain how it happened. But these were stalwarts, valiantly maintaining a foothold in Her Majesty's New World, which was rich in gold, pearls, silver, seed of an empire, a British Empire that would grow and grow and grow. "In the teeth of the furious storms, surrounded by savages that Spain hath subverted but yet may be tamed into friendship and allies, cut off from home, alone, without wives, children, all the roots that anchor a man to a spot of earth, these men, Your Majesty's subjects, keep watch and ward day and night in Your Majesty's fortress, ever lifting their eyes to the eastward over the ocean seeking the sails of Your Majesty's ships to bring them your favor and relief in their present peril." And he added in a more practical vein, "Holding a foothold in Virginia will assure Your Majesty a fortified flank against the monstrous presumptions of Spain."

She said, "My ships are needed here, Sir Walter, against the Armada. The Spanish Armada does not sail against Roanoke Island."

He said, "Madame, the fault was mine. I sent out my expedition without thought that men alone are footloose; my expedition was composed entirely of men. That was wrong. For men with wives establish true homes, beget families, root themselves like oaks to the soil and fight to the death to preserve all."

He touched her there. "Aye," said the barren Queen, thinking of Mary of Scotland, so fertile, so dangerous to her throne, "There is value in what you say."

He would form a group of colonists composed of men *and* women, he said, transport them with food, guns, ammunition, agricultural tools, seeds, trinkets to barter with the natives. "It will be," he said, "as fruitful and stable a colony as ever Your Majesty could wish," and he added with a touch of pride, "Not even Your Majesty's Westcountry could be more loyal!"

"Yes, you have done well there, Sir Walter," she said, smiling.

But it could not be, she said. "There are no ships, no captains. And you yourself cannot go; my Admiralty specifically forbid it. It is a goodly dream, but it must wait."

Raleigh had known the Admiralty would forbid him to lead the expedition—he had already consulted them —nor was he particularly disappointed. The Queen had spoken patent truth when she said that the Spanish Armada was not sailing against Roanoke. It would sail against England. Here in England would be the battle, here the chance for glory; he would fight the Armada here. But the colony need not necessarily wait. He was prepared with answers to her objections.

There were ships in Her Majesty's Navy, he assured her, good for nothing but barging coals from Newcastle to London, staunch shallow-draft vessels, no good for fighting but seaworthy and, with a few guns for protection, amply fit to transport the entire colony to Virginia. Might he have them?

"What good are ships without captains, my Water?" She knew he would have an answer. She was prepared to listen.

He said, "Captains are scarce, Ma'am, as is right and commendable in times like these. But I have the very man, an alien I frankly concede, but a man who hates Spain with a hate that out-hates old Cato's hatred of Carthage—one Simon Fernandes."

"Faugh! I will have no truck with Spanish traitors!"

"Simon Fernandes is not Spanish, Your Majesty. He is a Portuguese."

Elizabeth raised her penciled eyebrows, smiled broadly, "Good!" and thanked God for Portugal.

Recently Philip of Spain had coolly taken over the proud and helpless Kingdom of Portugal. The Portuguese, smarting under their Spanish masters, looked to England, with whom they had ancient ties, to free them from his iron hand. Among the bravest of the Portuguese fighters for freedom were their sea captains, nurtured in the traditions of Henry the Navigator, violent, unruly, very much like Elizabeth's own Westcountry sea captains.

Simon Fernandes, he told her, would pilot the expedition to Virginia. But he would not entrust the governorship of such a venture to any foreigner, no matter how skilful, but only to an Englishman.

She encouraged him, "Say on, Sir Water, say whom you wish."

He said, though he knew she would refuse, "My cousin, Sir Richard Grenville."

She shook her head, No; he had known she would; she waited.

He repressed a sigh and said, "There is another man, an excellent man, an imaginative man, inventive, a staunch and loyal Englishman, an artist in fact. . . ."

"With words? Like you? Like a poet? Oh come, not a poet! Are you wheedling yourself back into a captain's cabin, my Water?"

"Not with words, this artist, but with a paintbrush, with a pencil, Ma'am. He will limn you the land of Virginia in living portraits, as though you yourself were there to behold it with your own eyes. He is named John White, of no small renown among artists; and so enamored is he of the adventure that he takes with him his own dear daughter and the good young man who is married to her, to settle permanently in America. Such is the measure of his faith in Your Majesty's New World of Virginia!" And he played upon the name of the son-in-law, which was "Dare." "All that is dear to him, all does he dare in Virginia."

It was good to have him back, kneeling at her feet, kissing her hand, so persuasive, so effusive with gratitude. She pursed her lips. "If indeed there are ships to be spared, if my Admiralty consent. . . ."

The Admiralty consented.

But the Admiralty exacted conditions: there were not to be fighting ships.

And the Queen exacted conditions also: there were not to be harlots among the women, nor the contrary either, no women of high degree; but honest working women of the poorer sort, lest the first families of Virginia be sluttish wantons or lily-fingered aristocrats like her waiting-women.

Raleigh realized that such women, neither highborn nor giddy, were precisely the sober dependable unimaginative sort who would prefer to stay snugly at home. He'd have liked a smidgin of yeastier leavening, somewhat as he concocted his chemical formulas: a bit of the base, a bit of acid, mixed with the bland neutral ingredients.

But one did not say things like that to Queen Elizabeth. He said the safest thing: "Your Majesty is exactly right."

"And maybe she is," he mused. "The women must not be wild, like Captain Simon Fernandes, nor yet artistic and impractical, like Governor John White."

At length two little ships were found and an assembly of ninety men and twenty women, who were required to produce marriage certificates, and some ten or so children legitimately born, with others demonstrably on the way. And there was a friendly Indian of the Croatan tribe who had attached himself to the colonists that Drake had brought back to England, a clever inscrutable savage, who now wanted to go home and who everyone agreed would be valuable as an interpreter. Sir Francis Drake, the Mayor of Plymouth, now in residence, and Admiral Sir Walter Raleigh, M.P., waved them farewell.

Snug in the strongbox of Governor White was a charter for a new city, the city of Raleigh. It had cost Queen Elizabeth nothing to bestow; she knew it would tickle Sir Walter's fancy to have a city in the New World named after him.

In the strongbox were also the Governor's instructions: he must trade honestly with the Indians, and on no account antagonize them; he was to seek out a broader tract of land than Roanoke Island for the first permanent colony, so that it might have room to expand.

There was such a place a few miles to the north on a salt water bay, called Chesapeake by the Indians, fertile as Roanoke but possessing an additional advantage in that it was sheltered from the hurricanes that yearly ravaged the island. There, in the city of Raleigh, would be planted the first English colony in America, the seed of the British Empire that Raleigh had promised his Queen.

With high hopes the colonists watched, as the sails of the two crowded little ships bellied out in the cool strong breath of a fair and following breeze, their prows bisecting the golden ovoid orb of a sun sinking in the west whither lay their hopes, as the ships' bells chimed for evensong and prayers wafted up like an incense beyond the sun to the throne of the Providence that held them in the palm of His Hand, a Providence inscrutable, beyond the ken of mere mortal, holding for them a fate that no man could foresee.

Raleigh had done his best with the meager means at his disposal. He himself, once again, was forbidden to lead the expedition that he genuinely believed was composed of colonists who, this time, would take permanent root in the New World and prosper. And so they might have, but for Governor White and Captain Fernandes.

Meager had been his choice of captains, meager the number of good men to act as governors. The ablest Englishmen, like Raleigh himself, were all ordered to stand fast in England, to ready the Island against the impending strike of the Armada.

White and Fernandes were the best he could get.

No two men ever born ever understood each other less. In their characters there was no meeting ground, no overlapping area of mutual understanding. Both men were brave, both good, both dedicated to the cause; these were no inconsiderable virtues. But they were born so different in makeup that they were completely unable to communicate. It was these men, not the colonists, that lost the cause and the colony.

The following wind held fair and strong; the ships made a speedy passage.

One day they sighted a Spanish cargo vessel, her masts ripped out by some recent storm, wallowing slowly toward Spain under a jury-rigged jib, helpless, unescorted, an easy and profitable prize.

Fernandes exulted, Ha! Here was loot! Here was a cargo ripe for the taking, a cargo that would make him rich for life, for he knew something of the cargoes that sailed home to Spain and filled King Philip's coffers with treasure. But stronger even than his greed for gain was his hatred of Spain and his desire to use this unexpected opportunity to vent it upon this helpless Spanish ship.

"No," said Governor White quietly. He was carefully applying the undercoat to a canvas for a picture he had a mind to paint. It would depict the natives at their interesting activities, with their canoes, fish weirs, costumes. So far only descriptions were available in England; he would paint them to the life, as Raleigh had asked him to. "No," he said, "you must understand, Señor Fernandes. . . ."

Fernandes bristled. "Señor" was Spanish. Could these heretic English never learn to say "Senhor"?

". . . that my orders permit of no privateering. Sir Walter's orders bind us all." He made the mistake of trying to reason with the fiery Portuguese. "We are to proceed with all dispatch to Virginia, plant these good colonists there in a fair and fertile spot sheltered from storms, nor stop for a moment for any other purpose. Look you, good señor, how fast we sail, how providential the wind! Were we to tarry to take this Spanish vessel who knows, mayhap the wind would fail whilst we tarried, so press we on, señor, press we on!"

Fernandes glared, bit his nether lip. Francis Drake would have tarried, Richard Grenville would have tarried, Walter Raleigh would have tarried he knew, and taken the ship; and if the wind failed would have explained it away with golden explanations! But Governor White seemed not at all like them, and he talked too much. Would he never stop talking in that bland voice of his, oh damn him and his damned paintbrushes!

"Furthermore," said the Governor, "we should not burden ourselves with Spanish prisoners, our ships are already crowded, they would trouble our women, husbands would get jealous, fights would break out, no, no, no, Señor Fernandes, we shall pass the troublemakers by."

Fernandes said, "Then at least while the ship is close, let me fire my cannon into her and sink her!"

"To what end, my good captain? I dislike killing helpless human beings, and what is the gain? No, no, we press on."

Fernandes stalked aft and spat in the wake of his own ship; and in the wake was the face of Governor White, the water imparting a motion to the brain-projected visage as if the lips were still speaking sweet reason. "That to you, you damned artist!" Governor White was not aware of this aqueous insult to his image and calmly continued preparing his canvas.

Fernandes watched the prize slip away astern. Over the widening gap of water came hearty male voices, singing.

"What is that singing?" the Governor asked. "It is very beautiful; it sounds like a hymn of some sort."

"Sir," said Fernandes, "It is a Spanish Te Deum of praise. The Spanish dogs are praising God that a stupid English Puritan did not have the wit to take them when he could."

White said stiffly, "I am not a Puritan; I am a good Anglican."

"To them you are a Puritan. To them only a Puritan would pass up such a chance," and he thought, "I cannot make out this man."

"It was a beautiful hymn," White mused aloud. "Press on, Fernandes, press on."

"Why am I fated to obey this lunatic artist!" Fernandes asked himself gritting his teeth and vowed that, come the time, he would not. "Weak as a fish! For a man like me!"

The following wind held fair, and shortly they beheld before their bows the Island of Roanoke, fog-shrouded in one of those peculiar atmospheric phenomena that beset the waters of "Virginia," not yet called "Carolina." The place still looked pleasant and green though the season was well advanced, and up from the island could be seen smoke from fires, easily distinguishable by their different coloring from the fog, which soon burnt away under the rays of the morning sun. If smoke, then people; and if people, probably the doughty twenty men Grenville had left, still manfully holding the fort, probably signaling after sighting their sails.

But they were not smoke signals from the fort. White, when he landed to look around, saw that the smoke arose from soggy brushfires smouldering in the wet underbrush. The storm that had dismasted the Spanish vessel must have had lightning in its clouds. Some scrubby-looking Indians were rooting in the ruined English garden.

White sent Fernandes to see what had become of the Englishmen in the fort. The Indians shouted insults at him in a language he did not understand. One made a threatening gesture. Fernandes promptly shot him dead.

"He tried to kill me!" Fernandes said to White.

White believed him. His English blood was up. He was suddenly terribly angry, as only a sensitive artist can be, with an anger as irrational as his creative moods. Unarmed he walked alone into the interior of the fort. It was weird, it was illogical, it was frightening.

It was totally deserted. Yet totally lacking in signs of violence: there had been no struggle, no massacre; the cannon were in working condition, loaded and primed, yet not one had been fired.

Still in his angry mood he summoned his interpreter, the friendly Croatan. Sternly to him, "Identify this savage!" pointing to the dead Indian's corpse. "Hostile Indians have wrought with guile upon the English in the fort, tricked them away, made off with them. Who knows what dastardly deed they have done! The wretch lying here was one of them; he threatened my captain. Well, man, speak, identify his tribe, which I swear by God I will slay to the last man. Speak, man!"

For a moment the interpreter's soft brown eyes

seemed to blaze red with a fiery glare as he gazed at the corpse at his feet. White's artist eye caught the color change, but attributed it to a reflection from a little flame that a gentle breeze had momentarily kindled in a brush fire, which instantly went out as did the light in the Indian's eyes.

With face impassive the Indian said, "He is a Croatan, Master White."

"Confound it, man, there are no Croatans on Roanoke Island! You are a Croatan. Look again. You are mistaken. The Croatans are friends. What is the tribe of this savage?"

With exquisite irony, lost on the furious Governor, the Indian said, "This *savage* was a Croatan."

White's anger melted away as quickly as it had flared up. Contrition took its place, heartfelt sorrow. "Oh my friend, my friend!" Impulsively he flung his arm around the interpreter's shoulder. Indians do not like to be touched, but he did not draw back. No one but another Indian could have guessed what he was thinking. "My dear good friend, what a ghastly mistake! I will make amends. He shall be given a fitting funeral. With full military honors. His family shall be cared for. I will erect a statue to his memory. I will reprimand my captain." He wrung his hands, tears ran down his cheeks.

The interpreter said, "Thank you."

Fernandes looked on, suppressing a cynical sneer.

The dead Croatan was placed in a coffin of good English oak taken from one of the ships, which were plentifully supplied with this necessary item, and gently lowered into a grave. A salute was fired and the stately prayers of the Anglican burial service were duly read. White supposed that since the dead Indian must have been a pagan, not properly baptized, the burial was probably invalid, perhaps even forbidden. But he wished to demonstrate the respect with which the English were ready to honor their friends and allies.

The Indians had quite different ceremonies when they

disposed of their dead; but they held their peace, said nothing and thought their own thoughts.

White was to see the grave once again, much later, when much had happened to England, to Spain, to both the Old and the New World. It would seem to him at that time that the grave had been disturbed. He would have it dug up. No coffin would be found. Coffin and Indian, like much else, had disappeared into legend. But that was to come, not now.

Now White simply, honorably buried Fernandes's fatal mistake, his own colossal error of judgment.

Shortly White made more.

He sailed to the mainland in one of the ships with a small party of armed men, leaving Fernandes with all the colonists huddled into the other.

On the mainland there was a little Indian village. "They are Croatans," the interpreter said, "friendly."

But they fled at his approach. "They are afraid we will steal their winter supply of food," the interpreter explained after some moments of colloquy with one of their number, who came slinking back, making frightened gestures of supplication.

It seemed to White, who could make nothing of their gibberish, that the conversation took longer than was necessary to elicit this meager information.

There had been famine among them, the interpreter said. A series of drenching rains had ruined their garden plots, as had happened on Roanoke Island; it had rotted the fruits in the forests; the grapes were musty and foul; even the acorns had not developed; wild pigs had died from eating them; all the game had disappeared, no one knew whither, guided by some obscure animal memory that told them that this was a time to seek healthier feeding grounds. Only the sea still seemed to be fruitful.

"Tell them," said White, "we do not come to steal, but as friends; we will gather our own food," and to prove his good faith he set some men to gathering oysters and clams among the rocks along the shore. It was heavy work without proper tools; the men had only their swords to pry loose the shellfish, only musket butts to smash the agile crabs. They cursed and complained and sweated.

Seeing the English engaged in so peaceful a pursuit, and so clumsy at it, the Indians came as near to laughing as ever they did and turned more friendly.

Then it was that White learned the fate of the men Grenville had left behind. His suspicions were aroused. That twenty strong men, unless panicky with terror, should trust themselves in a tiny boat to the open sea with nowhere to go, seemed incredible.

In broad daylight he found himself glancing over his shoulder, fearful of what might be lurking there, his palms went wet with sweat—then suddenly he straightened, drew himself up, ashamed of himself. "There is nothing to be afraid of," he said. But his heart still pounded. "At least nothing that I can see, so nothing is there."

Then, out of nowhere, there was the hiss of a poisoned dart in the air like the hiss of an angry snake, and one of the crab fishermen grabbed at the back of his neck and collapsed, gave a series of labored breaths, then ceased to breathe and fell face down in the water among the crabs, which scurried away, uninterested.

Even the wooden face of the interpreter registered a human flicker of surprise as he shot a glance, scowling, in the direction of the Indians, who took to their heels, shouting something. "Ah," he said slowly nodding his head, "that was unfortunate, Master White. But it is over now. The Croatans are friendly, like me. I am friendly. I know my people. I can speak for them. It is a death for a death, that is all. It is over now."

He explained that an old man, untaught in the White Man's civilized ways and higher sense of values, still clinging to the ancient traditions of the tribe, had simply exacted a death for a death, the death of the Indian Fernandes had shot. "He was his father," the interpreter said. "Naturally he knew no better. He is very old."

White was no longer afraid. Here was murder, here was something he could see, could fight. He was furious. Combined with his fury, making it twice as fierce, was his sense of guilt and shame. A moment before he had reacted like a coward. His whole body craved action, revenge.

He shouted orders at his men. With a ringing cheer they clapped on their helms, blew on their match-fuses till they flamed and made toward the Indian village, shouting, firing their muskets. It was a welcome relief from crab fishing.

They burned the village down. It didn't take long. There were only a dozen or so miserable little thatched hovels. They were disappointed to find them deserted. All the Indians had fled. No one was killed.

When White regained his composure he was glad, on sober reflection, that he had done nothing to start a war. "I meant only to teach your people a lesson," he carefully explained to the interpreter. "Accidents like this sometimes happen among friends. I will bury my dead Englishman next to your dead Croatan, both innocent victims of a misunderstanding." He held out his hand. "We are still friends?"

The Indian took it. "We are still friends."

They sailed back to Roanoke Island.

Here all was surprise and confusion. Fernandes had peremptorily ordered all the colonists ashore, them and their household goods and chattels, everything they owned, down to the last baby crib, the last pet puppy, the last rag doll.

With the mood of action still strong upon him, Governor White soundly berated his Captain. "You are a rogue and a scoundrel, Señor Captain! You take too much upon yourself! Our orders are explicit. You understand them as well as I. We are to sail north to Chesapeake Bay. The colonists were not even supposed to land here on the island, only a few men are to reconnoitre the place. Damme, man, you are in mutiny! I could have you hanged. Francis Drake hanged a mutineer for less than this mutiny of yours! Well? Well? Well?"

For answer Fernandes calmly pointed to the lowering sky. Rain was beginning to fall, big slow drops. The surf was beginning to rise, long lazy swells such as sailors know outrace the storm that begets them. On the distant horizon there was lightning, and a black waterspout snaked down from the clouds, lazily coiling, to disappear in a white welter of mist on the surface of the leaden sea.

"If the Governor were a navigator," Fernandes said, exquisitely polite, "he would realize that a tropical storm is approaching. Perhaps when it arrives the Governor will paint it. Already it presents a certain dramatic aspect. I deemed it wise to disembark the colonists. The ship would have foundered with all aboard, heavily laden as she was. Now, with the Governor's permission, I will sail the ships 'round under the lee of the island and anchor them with four anchors apiece and pray God they ride out the storm." He added, "If you'd been ten minutes later I'd have done it anyhow, no matter what happened to you," and he cursed something in Portuguese that reflected unkindly on White's maternal forebears to the third generation.

White sighed, appeased. He knew he was no navigator, and the approaching storm certainly did look ominous, albeit with a queer foreboding beauty of its own. "Too late, too late," he mused. "We arrived too late."

The storm raged for three days. The ships rode it safely out, though some anchors were lost.

Safe in the solid fort the colonists were not uncomfortable and grew to like the place; it afforded them refuge from the elements; Chesapeake Bay was unexplored, an unknown distance away, there was no fort there. Surely no shelter. Probably no food. Probably surrounded by hostile savages.

"Here at least we can subsist," they told Governor White. There was seafood. There were supplies from the ships. The Indians were friendly. "Go back to England," they begged, "and send up a shipload of victuals; and *then* we shall be prepared to search for a suitable location at Chesapeake Bay. But not now."

There was logic in what they said. White himself scarcely dared face the hazards of seeking a better location so late in the season. Reluctantly he agreed to go back with one of the ships and return in two months, God willing, with supplies to see them through the winter. But he did not go yet.

His daughter was nearly at term, and he could not bring himself to leave her till his grandchild was born; so he tarried some weeks till it was.

It was a blond blue-eyed little girl, whom he christened Virginia Dare, the first English child ever born in the New World. Kissing her rose-petal cheek he whispered, "Virginia, thou'rt named for a Queen! I will paint your pretty face and show it to Her Majesty. She will be proud, and I have no doubt she will send a present for you and your children and their children to cherish forever."

Then he sailed, leaving baby Virginia Dare, his daughter, his son-in-law and all the other colonists safe and sheltered on Roanoke Island, as worthy and hopeful a lot as ever left England to seek new homes in America.

But he did not come back with the shipload of "victuals," nor did he set eyes on Roanoke Island for a very long time. God and Spain intervened. All normal traffic with America stopped. All England now rallied to face one tremendous event.

No white man ever saw Virginia Dare again.

The Spanish Armada struck.

CHAPTER XVI

KING PHILIP's overall strategy to conquer the Kingdom of England was simple, as all great conquests are simple, appealing to the military mind. Clausewitz would have approved it; and Bismarck; and Tamerlane; and William the Bastard of Normandy, the only man who ever actually accomplished it. And Sir Winston Churchill, who wrote, "At the top there are great simplifications."

The trick was to secure the sea lanes, lest the island be nourished by reinforcements of food and men; then to put ashore an overwhelming army of infantry. In this way the difficult deed could be done and the troublesome islanders would trouble the continent no more.

Ancillary precautions were also to be taken as a matter of course: make sure that there be traitors among the English, bribe their hereditary foes, the Irish, the Scots. Convince those close to the seat of power, the English throne, that they will benefit by the overthrow of that power. All these precautions were duly taken. Success seemed certain, the mighty Armada invincible. The Pope in Rome, along with his blessing, actually so christened it, *Invincible*. This gave King Philip much comfort. He commanded prayers to be said in all the churches of his global domains from Madrid to Mexico, prayers of thanksgiving, and confidently waited for the will of God to be made manifest to the world in a Spanish victory.

Patient as a spider he wove his web, took all the usual

political precautions, made all the correct military dispositions. He had an army waiting in the Spanish Netherlands ready for transport to England as soon as the Armada secured the sea lanes.

He sent spies with Spanish gold to bribe English Admirals and Members of Parliament, Sir Walter Raleigh among them. "Good!" said the Queen when they instantly reported the incident. "Take his gold and learn his plans!" And every English spy became a counterspy, with some Spanish gold for his pains, though naturally Queen Elizabeth required that all such bribes be turned over to her.

He sent emissaries with large promises to Scotland where young King James, a weak and effeminate man, tried vainly to rule a race of fierce and turbulent clans. Vainly men tried to puzzle out his character. How was it possible for so unpleasant a creature as King James to be the son of the beautiful fastidious Mary, Queen of Scots! Lord Macaulay says of him, "His fondness for worthless minions, his cowardice, his childishness, his pedantry, his ungainly person and manners, made him an object of derision. It was no light thing that royalty should be exhibited to the world stammering, slobbering, shedding unmanly tears, trembling at a drawn sword and talking in a style alternately of a buffoon and of a pedagogue" — for James had had a good education and spent much time at acrostics, a sort of crossword puzzle popular among the old-maidish sort of country vicar.

To King James King Philip promised nothing less than the throne of England, after, of course, he dethroned Queen Elizabeth and after his mother, Queen Mary, died.

This was a tempting offer to James. His right to succeed to the throne of England was absolutely valid and absolutely legitimate; he set great store by it. Scotland was poor, England was rich. Scotland was unruly, England was stable. Best of all, in England he would be physically safe.

But Queen Elizabeth also sent emissaries to King James, promising the same thing, only sooner, "for it is well known," the emissaries were authorized to state verbally, "that the health of Your Majesty's royal mother is much decayed." When, regrettably, Queen Mary should pass from this earthly scene, he, her son, King James, would be King of England, after Elizabeth too should die; and the emissaries, shrugging eloquently, had only to mention the advancing years of the aging Queen to remind the prospective heir that even royalty is mortal. Yes, James's expectations were great; he couldn't lose, whether the Armada conquered England or England conquered the Armada.

That night he walked hand in hand in the moonlight with a dimpled young courtier of his suite and spoke of the warmer climes to the south and how pleasant it would be to be king there. At one point, drawing back from his companion, he sniffed and said, "Mon, mon! Ye didna take tobacco the noo, did ye? The stink of it gars me sair!" The young man, who had, said he hadn't; and resolved never to do so again, at least not when he was likely to walk with King James.

King James was not greatly perturbed that the health of his mother was "much decayed." In a queer stuffy way he did not approve of her. Too many gallant men had died too gladly for love of her. In the epicene chill of his dark and twisted soul there was no light, no warmth, no love, far less the consuming fire that drove his mother into all her indiscretions. His memory of her was dim; he had not set eyes on her during all the years of her captivity in England; she was a stumbling block, not a stepping-stone on his road to the throne of England.

In this way Elizabeth secured her northern border against a Scottish invasion, effectively canceling King Philip's schemes with her own far subtler statecraft. She took other precautions. There was another coast to secure, another nest of hereditary foes to smash: Ireland. What was there to prevent the Armada from anchoring in one of the beautiful spacious Irish harbors and launching the invasion of England from there, there where their Catholic brethren would welcome them with open arms and the blessing of the Pope of Rome? There was nothing, nothing at all.

She must either bribe or subject the Irish. The Irish were too proud to bribe. So they had to be subjected, the traditional English method of dealing with those strange unrealistic people, who were highly emotional and superstitious, who believed in fairies and leprechauns, who drank too much and lived in a happy middle zone where the real and the unreal merged and commingled in a manner totally incomprehensible to the English.

The Queen sent Raleigh with a large force of men, horses and guns to Ireland. It was familiar territory. He knew the castles and coasts, the weak spots and the strong spots, the hidden coves and the likeliest landing beaches. He set up his headquarters on his own Irish estates on the Blackwater and there, in sumptuous leisure, he directed the disposition of his English troops so effectively that Ireland was soon as prepared and secure as his own native Devonshire.

It irked this man of action that he was doomed to play a subordinate role behind the scenes, away from the glory of battle, while all his kinsmen and sea-faring friends were being given command of fighting ships; and his mood was surly and withdrawn in the presence of the Queen. Again he felt put upon, deprived of the chance to be spectacular.

But the Queen had said soberly, "Once you called me 'England,' Sir Walter."

He was puzzled, taken aback. "Aye, Ma'am, and so you are."

She smiled winningly, fondly. "And should not England be protected, Sir Walter . . ." here she consciously copied his sailor speech, ". . . protected fore and aft?"

"Assuredly, Ma'am; that is an elementary naval tactic."

"Protect me then, dear friend, for I conceive myself threatened more by a stab in the back than by a frontal assault."

Before he could phrase an answer Elizabeth said, "I propose to make you Captain of my Guard, as soon as I beat the Spanish dog to his knees!" Her eyes blazed with fury. Never had Raleigh seen her look so regal. In that moment Elizabeth *was* England. He could only kneel and kiss her hand, awed as most Englishmen were awed when Queen Elizabeth was in her imperial mood. Majesty clothed her like a garment. "Majesty" was her title. She had earned it. Her father, King Henry, had been addressed only as "Your Grace." Men died for Queen Mary of Scots for the love of the woman. Men died for Queen Elizabeth for the love of England.

Slowly the import of what she had said sank into his dazzled mind. "What stab in the back, Your Majesty?"

"Traitors! Rogues! Under my very nose. Belike in my very house. Some I already know. They shall be dealt with. Others I know not for sure, but know for sure exist. It would suit their purpose well if Elizabeth were suddenly to be no more." She sighed. "Alas, the murdered kings of England, so many, so woeful many! A crown is a heavy burden, Sir Walter. Who wears it sleeps ill o' nights." She quickly recovered from her momentary fear of the unknown but terrible menace she sensed. She smiled. "That is why you, my Water, shall be Captain of my Guard."

It was an unheard-of honor for a Westcountry squire of low degree. Usually the post was filled by a nobleman of ancient lineage. The Queen's Captain of the Guard was charged with the duty of protecting the Queen's person. He had access to her presence at all hours of the day or night. It was his duty to interpose his own body between her and an attacker, to take into his own breast, if need be, an assassin's dagger before it could reach the Queen. Such a man had to have a keen eye and a wily

suspicious nature in order to sense an assassin lurking behind some innocent-appearing face. Elizabeth knew her
Raleigh. He was the very man. That is why she chose
him.

The Captain of the Guard had other duties of course,
some purely ceremonial such as marching in parades;
others sanctioned by long legal custom, such as standing
on the platform when malefactors were beheaded, or
close to the gallows when they were hanged, and certify-
ing for the court records that Yes, the malefactors were
truly dead.

With so great an honor in store for him Raleigh departed for Ireland with his men, in reasonably high spirits. True, he must act behind the scenes, his name would
never appear among those of the sea captains with fighting commands nor would he shine as a victor in the battle
to come, but when the Armada was beaten—no Englishman doubted it would be—he would return to become
the greatest gentleman of Queen Elizabeth's household.
The future glittered like a star.

The Armada claimed its first victim before it ever fired
a shot, the unfortunate Mary, Queen of Scots. She was
caught red-handed with a casket full of incriminating
letters, written in a childishly transparent code, plotting
the murder of Elizabeth and the restoration of the Old
Religion, and indicating her complicity with King Philip
of Spain in sending over his troops and taking over the
kingdom once Queen Elizabeth was safely out of the
way. A former page of hers, also a Papist, now a handsome young man, acted as go-between.

Queen Mary had plotted before, always ineptly, and
had always been found out. "As long as she lives," said
Elizabeth's advisers, "this realm will have no peace." As
often as Mary's plots were discovered, just so often was
Elizabeth importuned to execute her like any other con-
spirator. And just so often Elizabeth gave her one more
chance. "She is a daft silly girl, I cannot do it," Elizabeth
said.

But now with Spain at her throat, she did.

Public executions, especially of women, were usually an occasion for drunken ribaldry, throwing stones and spitting curses at the victim, and much obscene jesting, but it was not so when Mary died. She died calm, serene, with regal dignity. She died still beautiful, still able to capture the hearts of men. It was remembered how often, how carelessly she had loved. She loved men and children and flowers and little pet dogs, endearing qualities in a woman. She was as different from Elizabeth as a human being could possibly be.

An Anglican priest accompanied her to the block, praying fervently for her soul; no man could doubt that his prayers came from the heart.

Queen Mary raised her sweet clear voice and silenced his English prayers with prayers of her own in Latin.

She knelt, and the executioner, whose black hood was wet with tears, struck off her head, the lovely head that had turned the heads of so many gallant men, spelling their doom. The execution of her coconspirator was more painful.

In Scotland King James caused a formal state paper to be issued which stated that Scotland's Queen Mary was dead, but said not a word of her execution, not a word of blame for Elizabeth; and he raised not a finger to avenge her. He calmly returned to his acrostics and his pleasures.

In Ireland Sir Walter Raleigh, who had never seen Queen Mary, deemed her death a statesmanlike stroke, and longed for the time when he could return and protect his august Queen from other potential stabs in the back.

Now the Armada struck, in nine bloody battles in nine bitter days. And everything went wrong for Spain —winds from the wrong direction, howling storms; but especially disastrous was the deadly gunnery of the English ships. Admiral Sir Walter Raleigh took no little pride in the fact that so many of the ships were his own design, and that some were built at his own expense, including the speedy *Revenge* in which his Westcountry kinsman, Sir Francis Drake, battled the Armada.

Raleigh did not see, took no part in these epic battles. But when a tempest washed some of the Spanish galleons ashore in Ireland and the Spaniards swam from the wrecks to the beach, expecting a welcome from helpful Irishmen, it was Raleigh who was there to welcome them. He slaughtered every one.

The rest of the ships wallowed north on the long way 'round toward home, fighting atrocious weather, some sinking at sea, some breaking up and leaving their smashed and shattered timber-tossed hulks on the rocky coasts of Scotland; and of the mighty Armada that had sailed so proudly from Spain less than a third ever reached home.

Patiently King Philip submitted to the will of God, made manifest in the failure of the Spanish Armada. But his conscience was clear; his faith was strong. He felt very close to God; he thought he knew Him very well; God was undoubtedly Spanish—or at least He was on the Spanish side. There was simply no other explanation for the fact that He had made the arms of Spain prosper for so long. The failure of the Armada must therefore be considered only a temporary halt in God's plans for Spain, and his own, for the Bible said: Whom the Lord loveth He chasteneth. Viewed in this light the failure of the Armada was actually a victory, not a failure at all, a victory of faith. Forthwith King Philip ordered his church bells rung all 'round the world in all his possessions and commanded prayers of thanks to God for the great Spanish victory.

And so slow was the travel of news in those days that millions of people believed him. Even Queen Elizabeth was alarmed. "I haven't beaten the Spanish dog yet!" Probably he had more ships. Probably this first assault was only the vanguard of a larger fleet. She ordered Raleigh to remain in Ireland, to keep a weather eye peeled for the sails of another Spanish armada.

Raleigh was well informed. He replied, "Aye, Your Majesty, he is building more galleons, and some are already at sea. But I deem another descent upon England unlikely so soon. But whatever befall, be assured, Ma'am, that Walter Raleigh holds closer than life itself to his heart the protection of his beloved *England*." She smiled fondly as she always did at his courtly letters, but she did not rescind her order, and kept him in Ireland for a while.

The failure of the Armada put a heavy strain on the Spanish treasury. King Philip's coffers were not inexhaustible. It was prudent to refill them before a second assault upon England, since even Spanish soldiers fought ill when they were not paid, when they got bad news from home, when wives and children were hungry, when rapacious tax collectors dispossessed them from their homes. The King knew that this was very bad for a fighting man's morale. And very bad for the financial structure of a state. King Philip had an eagle eye for a ducat. It was the measure of his genius that he knew exactly how much a man, a nation, could endure before breaking under intolerable strain, be it taxes for the good of the realm or torture for the good of the soul and the glory of God. His Inquisition was busy these days gobbling up the estates of rich Jews. His Turkish and Barbary pirate captives were being ransomed at inflation prices. But this, though it was helpful in the crisis, was only a trickle.

King Philip had at his disposal a mighty flood of revenue—the riches of the New World. If only he could get it home to Spain, it would be more than enough to fill his gaping coffers with silver and gold till it overflowed on his treasury floor.

He set about getting it. He diverted his galleons so they could convoy to Spain his treasure fleets from America, to protect them from waspish attacks by Elizabeth's pestiferous Englishmen, unholy, heretical, excommunicate! Surely God would approve.

It was the custom of the Spanish treasure fleets to pause at the Azores Islands after the long Atlantic crossing, to take on food and water, to bury those who had died of scurvy, to pump the filthy bilges into which, as the most convenient sewer, all the latrines of the ship cheerfully drained. This was the practice in English ships too. Raleigh, whose nose was sensitive to odors, had never succeeded in changing the practice except in those very few cases where he had personally supervised the installation of better sewage arrangements in the captain's cabins of his own ships.

There was sweet pure water in the Azores, fresh meat and game, olive-tree wood for the galley fires that delighted the ships' cooks with the fragrant smoke of hearth fires at home. There were onions and garlic and lemons and citrons and limes, which the sailors wolfed down raw; and those who suffered from scurvy, if they were still alive, promptly got well, much to the gratification of the ships' priests, who saw that their prayers had got through; and much to the mystification of the ships' doctors, who wisely agreed with the priests.

The Azores had been Portuguese for a hundred years, but King Philip had forcibly taken them over along with all other Portuguese possessions; and, noting their value to his ships, had methodically garrisoned the islands with Spanish soldiers, lest the islanders give way to their natural instincts and help the foes of Spain.

The islanders were a mixed breed. Many were full-blooded Portuguese, of course, who fiercely resented the loss of Portugal's ancient sovereignty, the loss to Spain of her once proud and wealthy empire. They hated Spain and hoped for an English victory. There was also a blond northern strain among the islanders. These were descendants of the Flemings who had settled there in earlier happier days. They too hated Spain, remembering how Flanders now groaned under the yoke of a Spanish occupation. But of all the Spain-haters none hated so vehemently as the Moors. Hate was in their blood. They were the descendants of the proud and literate Moors of Granada whom Ferdinand and Isabella had driven into exile. Their fathers had fled from the fury of the Reconquest into tolerant Portugal; thence, when threatened even there, into the island outpost of the Portuguese Azores. Long since they had lost their ancient culture, polish, literacy. Long since they had accepted Christian baptism to save their skins. But they never forgot that Spain was the destroyer of a paradisiacal kingdom, grown lovelier in racial memory, to which they were the only legitimate heirs, and that King Philip was the great-grandson of the destroyers: King Ferdinand, Queen Isabella.

To capture the Spanish fleets before they could reach Spain now became the prime objective of the English Admiralty. There was only one spot in the whole Atlantic where they stopped, only one spot to intercept them. If the islanders had had their way the English ships would have had a hearty welcome, the men feted ashore and their ships supplied with stores. But so strong and alert were King Philip's garrison that the islanders could help very little, only at night, on the sly, and then at great personal risk; and the English ships that had put to sea to intercept the treasure fleets were forced to hide, dodge in and out among the many islands, keep clear of Spanish guns. They waited weeks for a chance at the prey. Inevitably sickness occurred among them, but they dared not leave the scene lest the fleets slip through their grasp.

From Ireland Walter Raleigh begged leave of the Queen to command the ships that would intercept the Spanish treasure fleet. Such a command would well suit his character. There would be action, there would be glory, his name would be in every patriotic Englishman's mouth; he would be a Caesar, a Gideon! Poets would crown his victorious brow with laurel leaves of verse. He might help a little with the verses, a mere bit of editing of course, if the poets proved inept. There would be gold, of which he might justly claim a share, and silver, and pearls. Perhaps he would quietly put aside a handful or two of the best for himself, as a present to the Queen if he got caught.

For reasons entirely her own, with motives as mixed as Raleigh's always were, Queen Elizabeth instantly granted him the command.

For Raleigh had visited Edmund Spenser in Ireland, and brought about as graceful a tribute to an English sovereign as ever was penned by an English poet, praise which she longed for these days more than ever before.

Spenser had done well in Ireland. He had left his shabby cottage. Through influential friends he had been granted the perpetual lease of Kilcolman House at a very low rent, which he never quite found the means to pay. Kilcolman was one of the scores of estates confiscated from the Irish rebels. With it went 3,028 acres of productive farmland. Spenser was one of the scores of Irish-hating Englishmen to be set over them, instructed to keep them in their place.

There, in Kilcolman House, Spenser was living with another relative, not his mother this time but his sister, Sarah, as his housekeeper; and there he was writing *The Fairy Queen*, as lovely an English epic as ever was penned by a great English poet. Queen Elizabeth was the "fairy queen." He dedicated the poem to her. He wrote it from the conviction of his heart. He had no notion of gain by so doing. It was in his nature to write poetry, a compulsive urge. And Queen Elizabeth had become for him, as for most Englishmen, an ideal, the embodiment of England, and in Spenser's poetic mind, a goddess, a Fairy Queen.

When Raleigh discovered that Spenser had friends in Ireland and now possessed an estate of his own, he deemed him safe to visit. Poor Spenser was still sick and very thin, still coughed his handkerchiefs pink; but his mood was cheerful, his mind intent on his poetry. He could hardly wait to read it to Raleigh. "My dear good friend!" he greeted him, unaware or forgetful that Raleigh had avoided him for a very long time. "How wonderful to welcome you to Kilcolman! Now and here we make better cheer than . . . whenever, wherever it was. Harken to this, Sir Walter!"

"No wonder this man lacks the wit to pay rent," Raleigh thought. "He lives in a world of fantasy," and, with a twinge of jealousy, "He will always be a greater poet than I, for he is all spirit, naught else," and he settled back to listen.

He was quick to discern in *The Fairy Queen* not only its superb intrinsic worth as poetry but also something sure to be of personal value to himself.

He sent a copy to the Queen, knowing that she would be pleased, as she was, and begged her to receive the poet who had so honored her majesty and the majesty of English letters. This request too the Queen instantly granted.

"My dear Edmund," he said to Spenser, "Her Majesty will not be niggardly in her reward."

Forthwith Sir Walter, with Spenser in tow, returned to court, where they were graciously received, leaving Sarah in Ireland to look after Kilcolman House and the 3,028 acres of land.

To his delight and astonishment Edmund Spenser found himself something of a lion at court. Courtiers courted him. The Queen smiled upon him. Niggardly she was not, for she recompensed his poetic tribute with a good grant of money, more than he had ever had in his life, promising it would continue on a yearly basis. "I owe all this my good fortune to Walter," he mused. "I had no idea!" He grew a beard like Raleigh's thinking to flatter him, and, for a season, basked in the sunlight of the Queen's favor. Always and gently he gave excellent advice to a host of court sycophants who surrounded him, pretending an interest in poetry and begging him to criticize their verses.

There was a lull in the arrival of the Spanish treasure fleet. Elizabeth said to Raleigh, "Captain . . ." for he was now Captain of the Guard, ". . . my Admiralty tell me that two fleets of the Spaniards have joined together, making for the Azores. Fifty, a hundred perhaps, of galleons convoy and protect them. My ships could never sink so many. I am troubled in spirit, my Water. Did you not, my dear friend, swear to defend your England?"

"To the death, Ma'am, and beyond the grave!"

"Then I will not let you go, nor give you the command, but keep you by me to protect me; for in truth I am sick at heart."

"The command will not be mine? Oh Madame!"

"The Admiralty will intercept the fleets."

There was finality in her voice. She was pale beneath her rouge. There was a mist of tears in her eyes. Sovereign authority had spoken; it was not to be gainsaid; it must be obeyed. Raleigh bowed his head. He thought with a pang, "My Queen is sick, or sick at heart, or heart-sick, belike, and of what I know not. But never before have I seen my beloved Queen go womanly weak." He kissed her white hand, so wont to be warm, but cold, cold today and listless. There was no strength in it.

"Choose whom you will to take your command," she said absently, as if something else mattered much more.

He said, "My cousin, Sir Richard Grenville, if Your Majesty please."

She said, "It is done. Stay by me, my Water. Comfort me."

During the lull Raleigh sent John White back to Virginia to succor the colonists marooned on Roanoke Island since the Armada. Not a soul remained. Presumably the colonists had abandoned Roanoke for greater safety, for protection among the friendly Croatan Indians of Croatan Island. Presumably they were still there. But whether the Croatans were actually friendly, or whether they slaughtered them all, or whether they intermarried —blond blue-eyed Indians were said to be seen by later explorers, Indians who spoke no English and remembered no English forebears—the answers to these mysteries never were known. Nor, as the centuries rolled by, was ever the Island of Croatan ever positively identified. This was Walter Raleigh's second Lost Colony.

At Elizabeth's court Raleigh noted a new and unusual cordiality toward himself on the part of Lord Essex. His suspicions were aroused. "The Earl is jealous of me, as well he ought to be," he thought, for Queen Elizabeth frowned at the Earl and looked away when he came near her, and smiled at Raleigh, and glowered at one of her handsomest ladies-in-waiting. In Raleigh's cunning mind a pattern began to form. He scribbled off a poem, chuckling to himself, but very prudently let no one see it.

> *The Earl is a churl*
> *   With a questing cod;*
> *Methinks there's a girl*
> *   He hath swiven, by God!*
> *Keep that in your britches that itches, my lord,*
> *Or jealous Diana will swing her sword.*

Raleigh's biographers have never ceased to wonder why he, so quick to sense danger to others, so soon fell into the same trap.

But Raleigh could not help liking him. Everybody did.

His personal charm, his truly handsome person, his gracious manners, his noble birth, his youthful impulsiveness which young men shared and old men remembered with sighs made Robert Devereux, Earl of Essex, the most popular young nobleman in England.

Raleigh's prescience was soon vindicated. The trouble soon came out for all the world to see. Essex had secretly married the lady-in-waiting. "No wonder," thought Raleigh, "the Queen was sick at heart! Oh, that foolish, foolish man. He knew not where his fortune lay. I fear he will father his own destruction." He was genuinely sorry: clever men did not do that.

CHAPTER XVII

THE QUEEN's depression was pitiful. Her sleep was troubled. Her attendants withdrew to a safe distance, never showed their faces unless specifically summoned—a summons which, for a while, never came—for they did not know what turn her mood would take: another fit of sobbing? another tantrum? The great Queen, usually so self-controlled, was completely unhinged for the first time that men could remember. Her rages were dreadful, were heard outside her chamber: the ripping of a tapestry, a hurled chair crackling and snapping into kindling wood; once the smashing of a great glass mirror, and volleys of shouted curses: "God rot him! Rot off his filthy cod! God damn him to hell, God damn, damn, damn him! Oh darling, my darling, dear heart I love you so, my beloved. I am betrayed," and when the mirror was heard to shatter, "I cannot look, I am ugly, I am old! Ugly, ugly, ugly, faugh!"

Only old Lord Burleigh dared approach her. When he heard the mirror shatter he limped into her bedchamber, leaning heavily on his staff to favor his gouty foot, tears streaming down his cheeks. He took her hand, "Dear Madame, he isn't worth it. Recollect yourself, I implore you."

She collapsed against her breast. He patted her shoulder as if she were a little child. "There, there, there," he murmured, soothing, comforting. "There, there, Elizabeth, take heart my dear, my dear dear Queen, there, there! No man is worth a single tear of England's Elizabeth, far less this torrent of tears for a very silly man."

Elizabeth whispered, "I raised him from a pup! I fondled his pretty cheek ere ever it grew a beard. How I loved him, still do, oh why? And now my puppy is grown a beast and gone a-bitching after my own lady-in-waiting, here, under my own roof. Abomination of fornication! But what—what is this? Dear my Burleigh, have I wet your beard with my tears? Nay, they are your own! Oh my faithful, my dear good friend, would God I had more like you, even one!"

"Madame, you have many."

She was calmer now.

"More than you know, seasoned, mature, stable, devoted, who love you no less than England itself and would die for you as gladly."

He was recalling her, coaxing her back to the heavy responsibilities that only she could bear as England's Queen. She responded, as she always did, to the call of duty, smiled wryly, and said, "My Captain of the Guard once called me 'England,' and truly he is seasoned, mature, devoted, and in his poems he says he loves me—but stable? I do not know. I do not know *what* I know any more." Drawing herself up: "But this I know, I am the Queen."

The crisis passed. But Lady Essex, despite her high birth and a host of powerful kinsmen among the nobility of the realm, was permanently banned from the Court. The Queen never suffered her to come near her. She never set eyes on her again.

Four months after her secret marriage Lady Essex gave birth, and all England was delighted. Lord Essex, always popular, now became more popular than ever. In taverns, earthy common men chuckled over their beer; in manorial halls, peers of the realm winked at each other over their port, and drank sly toasts to Lord Essex: one of their own had given the Queen the slip! Her over-possessiveness toward her minions they had never quite liked; her undignified infatuation for Essex they had heartily deplored. It was all very well, even commendable, for *her* to be a virgin, if that was what she wanted or couldn't help, nobody quite knew which, certainly couldn't help now at her age—but damme, sirs, did Her Majesty seek to inflict a similar virginity on lusty Lord Essex? Ha!

Naturally all these good wishes were whispered, lest the Tudor temper flare and the good-wisher suddenly find his noble self clapped up in the Tower.

Elizabeth no longer doted on Essex, no longer was madly infatuated. But she loved him still, felt a pull at her heartstrings when, kneeling and fearful, he kissed her hand at their first meeting; blushed when she raised him, when he read in her eyes that he was not to be punished. Thereafter her eyes followed him fondly whenever he walked among her Court, manly, erect, smiling, gracious as always. She was proud of him, proud of her own tethered temper. And to do the Earl justice he behaved very well, never complained that his wife was exiled from Court; and of course no one ever mentioned her within earshot of the Queen, who retained him in all his former posts and honors.

Lord Burleigh nodded his wise old head, approved. He mused, "Here is the measure of the Queen's great statecraft. She senses the mood of her people. They want their Essex, she leaves them their Essex. She will not destroy their idol, not while he remains their idol." Nor was he the least surprised that all prurient gossip ceased. Never had Queen Elizabeth so captured the hearts of her people, risen so high in their awe and esteem; for they saw in her now no shred of womanly weakness, only a sovereign majesty, endowed with wisdom that verged on the divine. Only Lord Burleigh knew what it cost her.

When Essex was restored to favor his cordiality toward Raleigh diminished somewhat. Raleigh felt slighted; once he strode up to him and demanded, "Have I done aught to offend you, my lord?" His voice was hoarse with fury.

The Earl was taken aback. "Nothing, Captain Raleigh, nothing at all, unless . . . ," he tried to pass it off, make a joke of it, ". . . unless you eat too many potatoes."

Everyone knew that Raleigh had discovered the prolific American tuber. He had imported and planted it on his Irish estates, where it flourished. He gave them away free to his Irish tenants, "to nourish their shrunken bellies," he said. For he had observed and grown heart-sick at the illness in Ireland, where the Irish seemed sick, like sailors with scurvy. Ireland was an island that nature had blessed, like Virginia, with green abundance. But Ireland now was so wasted by war and the British occupation that no fresh crops had been gathered for years.

Raleigh's own Irish tenants were happy and fat, full of potatoes, from which, with Celtic ingenuity, they had contrived, besides feeding themselves, to distill a foul-tasting but soul-satisfying liquor unequaled in Christendom, save perhaps in far-away Russia, where the Russians had also discovered the virtue of the potato, very good on those long Russian nights when the darkness was terribly cold and one must keep warm, *spasibo*, no matter how or with whom.

Raleigh was much blamed for his potatoes. He was blamed for the population explosion in Ireland. Why, asked the English, were the Irish so fecund, those bog-trotting muddy baboons that ought to die out, not multiply! Why? It was Raleigh's potatoes. Everyone knew that potatoes were a powerful aphrodisiac. Young William Shakespeare, who was starting to write his plays, put into the mouth of an especially lecherous comedian, "Let the sky *rain* potatoes!"

Raleigh's face was white with anger. He started to

speak again, but Essex stopped him, not unkindly. He said in a low voice, "You are watched, Captain Raleigh, not only by me but by others. Have a care, Captain Raleigh, what you do. Not everyone can do what an Essex can do—and get off so lightly."

For the first time in his talkative life Walter Raleigh was speechless. The white drained out of his face. Red replaced it. One waiting-woman, observing the incident, whispered to another, "Upon my word! The Captain of the Guard is actually blushing. I should have thought it impossible."

The other, whose name was Bess Throgmorton, replied, "I think I shall retire now. I do not feel at all well," and retired to her chamber and vomited, as she had every morning for some time. There could be no mistake about it now: two months had passed.

Despite his high position in the Admiralty, Raleigh was repeatedly frustrated in repeated further attempts to send out even a single ship to search for his Lost Colony in Virginia. Not a single ship could be spared. All were required for the English flotilla that lurked in wait among the Azores to intercept the Spanish treasure fleets. That a mighty sea battle impended no one could doubt. With this overriding naval strategy Raleigh as an Admiral could not but agree. Virginia must take second place. He did what he could, which was little enough, to send medicines out to the ships to ameliorate the sickness that was rife among the sailors. Some of the medicines were of his own concoction, and some might have cured the scurvy; but no one had yet discovered what typhus was, so nothing he did could help those who suffered from that.

Edmund Spenser's popularity at Court lasted only a short while. Lord Burleigh frowned him back to Ireland. He had never forgiven Spenser's satirical verses about the

Queen's flirtation with the French Duke, an episode now long forgotten by everybody except the ancient Prime Minister. Little by little Burleigh quashed the Queen's munificent grant for *The Fairy Queen*. It was not to be renewed annually. The paltry pension of fifty pounds a year he did indeed allow to remain—the sickly poet must have something to sustain him, lest the highly emotional Raleigh come to his aid with his formidable pen and his unpredictable tendency to espouse lost causes, orphaned children, and other helpless creatures of no conceivable value to the State.

So Spenser returned, bewildered, to Kilcolman House, and in Ireland he fell in love. This time he was not refused.

Lord Burleigh—the family name was Cecil—had a sickly son, Robert Cecil, whom the ancient Prime Minister was grooming to take his place when he should die. Burleigh knew there would be a race to fill his shoes when, in God's good time—one never knew when, it could come anytime now—he would pass from the earthly scene and go to whatever reward or punishment awaited him in the world to come. He had carefully pondered the question of whether there really was a world to come, and come to the conclusion that there was. He counted on Queen Elizabeth's good sense to make Robert Cecil Prime Minister in his stead when his time came to die, to prefer and support him against all other hopefuls for the enormously powerful place among the advisers who counseled the Queen and shaped the policy of England at home and abroad: to favor Robert Cecil over the Essexes, the Raleighs, all those ambitious and charming aspirants, in all of whom lurked some character flaw that was sure to warp judgment.

To this end he had trained his son from his youth in the delicate, devious, dangerous art of statecraft, which he himself knew so well, taught him the lessons that he had learned so thoroughly through his many years of primacy.

Robert Cecil seemed to have absorbed his father's wisdom in his genes; he knew as if by instinct whether a man could be trusted, knew that none could be trusted completely, sensed when they would betray their trust, abjure their solemnly plighted word. And he knew by instinct how to use them, like his father before him, in the best interests of England.

To all this inherited sensitivity was added his father's wise and practical training. Robert Cecil was first educated at home under his father's roof by private tutors, then sent to Cambridge, then sent abroad on delicate diplomatic missions. "Seek always to set one nation against another," his father taught, "so that England may hold the balance of power in Europe. Only thus shall our little island have peace, prosperity, take our place in the sun; and belike carve out an Empire whilst the continental nations, especially Spain, devour one another and weaken themselves, leaving the field clear for us." Like all patriotic Englishmen old Burleigh firmly believed that a British Empire, when it should come about, would exist for the good of mankind in general. The financial benefits that would inevitably accrue to Britain were only the spin-off of power, power to enforce an orderly pattern of behavior on a world that didn't yet know what was good for it, was not yet mature enough to govern itself: power, in short, to bring, like God, order out of chaos.

In Scotland the scholarly pedantic King James, to whom all this was reported by double agents, was vastly pleased. He composed an acrostic that spelled out the word *theandric*. How proper and pleasant it was that God and Man should work together (through kings, of course), which is what the word meant, to effect what was best for all. And in James's mind began to take shape the doctrine of the Divine Right of Kings. No

Tudor sovereign had ever dreamt of such a preposterous notion, but Stuart King James did. It would dog the Stuart dynasty to extinction.

Robert Cecil had seen war abroad: he observed and took lessons from battle tactics. As a minister and civilian he took no part in the fighting, but he learned how generals thought and saw how soldiers died. He learned how brave the common soldier was, though unimaginative. He learned how rigid the military mind of the generals could be, dedicated indeed, always willing to die; but incapable of bending or compromising. Cecil's appraisal: both are fundamentally stupid. A successful army therefore required precise orders from an imaginative Commander-in-Chief, a Prime Minister, with broad vision over the entire scene and a weather eye out to spot a shift in the perpetually changing political wind, since today's friends were so often tomorrow's foes. Then if the Prime Minister should give equally precise orders to the generals in a contrary sense—they would obey, fight and die just as proudly.

Cecil never sought to be a soldier. He was all too conscious that his body unfitted him for the field. Thoroughly a realist, he never bewailed his physical shortcomings, never wanted to be a Raleigh or an Essex. "Each man hath his gifts: Samson his strength, poor blinded muscle-bound giant, dead for a blabbermouth; Esau his guile and King David his lust, which brought horrid ill hap to them both. Yet their weaknesses lasted not forever, and their strength was greater than their weakness, so they flourished." Thus Robert Cecil, aware without bitterness of his own physical handicap, soberly hopeful for his own future—which turned out to be brilliant.

He was jealous of Raleigh, so unlike him in body, but he respected and courted him because Raleigh was the Queen's favourite.

Cecil's face was the best part of him, sensitive, handsome in a delicate way, reflecting a subtle intelligence behind a cool and lofty brow. He was Secretary of State, a Member of Parliament, one of the Queen's Privy Council—a power to be conjured with. When receiving suppliants who asked for favors—a regiment, a monopoly, a ship, a pardon—he always faced them, never turning sideways or letting his back be seen, and he sat on a very high chair. The suppliants received their just, their exact due. Cecil was calculatedly, cleverly fair. They went away praising him, but terribly terribly afraid of him. He was *so* different from the Queen's other counsellors.

Raleigh in turn sedulously sought the friendship of Robert Cecil, deeply mistrusting it; Cecil with equal mistrust seemed glad to bestow it, seemed actually to seek Raleigh's. Elizabeth thought, "What a curious couple they are," but weighed their value: *divide et impera*. It had always been her policy, never had failed. "This brace of English worthies will so divide and confuse my covert plotters-for-power, forever seeking each other's downfall, that"—she chuckled up her sleeve, one of her four thousand pair—"that they won't know their front side from their backside. *Divide*, I do, *et impera*, I will. I am the Queen!"

A curious couple they were indeed. Sometimes recently Cecil would pass his arm through Raleigh's, walk unabashedly around the Court, conversing in a friendly fashion. Raleigh tried not to let this happen, he knew how comical they looked; but Cecil was not the least embarrassed and Raleigh could not refuse a little promenade without insulting his little companion.

Walter Raleigh towered six feet three inches high, Robert Cecil scarcely achieved five feet; the top of his head just reached Raleigh's armpits. Raleigh was built like an athlete, a slender more youthful Essex. (Essex had lately gone a bit lardy in the chops.) Raleigh's legs were lanky and long, fit for running, which he was so good at. Cecil's were bandy and pipe-stem, ending in weak ankles and two very large, very flat feet: "splay-foot," they called him behind his back.

His back. That was the worst of his whole misshapen body. There was a hump on his back that no tailor's art could conceal.

For this little man to walk arm in arm, in a friendly way, chatting and smiling up at Raleigh, who smiled down at him, was a spectacle never before seen at Elizabeth's Court. Men tried to puzzle it out, could not, gave up, wondered which to sue for favors, could not decide and fell out among themselves, which was precisely what Elizabeth wanted. Over this somewhat sordid scene she brooded, remembering *Video et taceo;* she was winning, as always. Only Lord Burleigh knew that Elizabeth favored Cecil above all others to succeed him as Prime Minister. Loving his son he envisioned with rheumy eyes a brilliant future for him: "Thanks to Elizabeth my Robert will be a British Empire-builder, a Prime Minister that history will honor," and he blessed Her Majesty's statecraft. *"Nunc dimittis,"* he mused, "and if it turn out to be so, I shall die content." The old man felt himself failing, ready to go; he had no inkling that some years of useful service to his Queen were still vouchsafed to him. He did not resent it that Elizabeth called his son "my pygmy." It was a sprightly pet name from a woman prone to give pet names to those she valued, just as she called Raleigh "my Water."

Raleigh sensed trouble. "She favors him. I must watch my step," and, remembering his history, "Caesar was ill of the falling-sickness, but he rose to rule the world before they killed him. Tamerlane limped, but he conquered many kingdoms. Crafty little humpty-backed Cecil, will he likewise soar to supreme power, tergiversate, turn that camel-humpy back upon me and cast me down without a qualm? My step, I must watch my step! What mystical alchemy lies a-yeasting in cripples, to make them grow so big and bludgeon their betters into all the colors of the rainbow? Walter, Sir Walter, take heed where you tread, lest you sink yourself deeper than an Irish bog and suffocate, faugh! You have made enemies; belike the most dangerous of all is this subtle, sober, half-baked fellow that takes my arm and walks me around the Court, smirking as if he loved me. Be warned, beware. And yet I must put a plausible face on the matter and court him, so powerful he is, this lumpish Secretary of State, son of the great Lord Burleigh."

Raleigh took comfort in his own superb good health, deeming it only his due.

During these days he saw much of Bess Throgmorton, the lady-in-waiting, who, during many evenings, stroked his hot forehead and kissed his dry lips, murmuring, "Water . . ." For she too spoke with a Westcountry accent. ". . . dear Water, 'twill all come out right, and I love you more than God."

"Bess," he said, "you know naught of the perils that comber up around us like a tide"; but she comforted him, soothed him, calmly dismissed the perils he feared, and loved him exceedingly. She came of proud and independent stock: one of her family had had his head chopped off as a traitor; another was currently honored as one of the Crown's most redoubtable generals.

No Throgmorton had ever been afraid of anybody. That the child that Sir Walter had fathered already was stirring within her shamed her not a bit. "I don't give a hoot!" she said. She was only proud, only loved Walter Raleigh the more. "If anybody looks at me crooked when my condition becomes apparent," he heard her mutter, "the lecherous monkey, I'll stare him out of his wits." And so, when it did become apparent, nobody dared "look at her crooked."

She was slender, tall and fair-haired, with remarkably large blue eyes. More than one gallant had set his cap to seduce her, till those eyes snapped blue fire and stared him out of his wits, and her tongue would turn viperish and wilt him back to more pliant prey: "I thought she'd be easy, so pretty she looked, but damme, she looked right through me and sent me packing."

Mistress Throgmorton had in her makeup that courage and daring, that sudden intelligence and quick understanding of men and this wicked world that stemmed from the long line of her militant forebears: rebels, pirates, traitors, generals—but never a dullard among them. No, no easy prey, Bess Throgmorton.

But she was putty in Walter Raleigh's hands. Blue eyes wide open and knowing, unafraid, she welcomed him, body and soul. They were made for each other. After Bess Throgmorton he never slept with another woman but her as long as he lived, he who had slept before with so many. Men wondered then and wonder still at Raleigh's amazing devotion and lifelong fidelity.

Far out in the Atlantic on a course toward the Azores swift little English spy-ships sighted the Spanish treasure fleets, could not make out their number in the mist, or the number of the fighting ships that protected them; but the lumbering high-built treasure-laden galleons were unmistakable. Streaming from their masts could be seen the dreaded flags of King Philip of Spain, the double-headed Eagle of the Holy Roman Empire, the Triple Crown and Keys to Heaven of the Pope of Rome, and crosses, crosses, crosses painted on their sails, boasting to all the world that temporal and celestial power hovered over, blessed and protected these ships, with the spoils of the Indies, East and West, snug in their holds.

Owing to the lack of intelligence regarding the strength of the convoy, Elizabeth deemed it far too big a job for one man, especially a man like Grenville. Forthwith she turned the whole operation over to the

Admiralty, appointed the Lord High Admiral of England as Commander-in-Chief and demoted Sir Richard Grenville to second in command, severely adjuring him to follow the orders of his Commander-in-Chief to the letter.

Crestfallen, but all the more determined to make a name for himself, Sir Richard swore to obey.

He did not.

But in the one-sided epic battle that followed he made for himself a never-to-be-forgotten name.

Grenville captained a ship called the *Revenge*, a strongly built heavily armored craft. The *Revenge*, like so many of the ships that had wrought havoc among the Invincible Armada, was built to Raleigh's specifications—Admiral Sir Walter Raleigh, conceded by all to be the best naval architect in England: the ship had gunpowder and cannon aplenty, towering canvas to give her speed, sharpshooters in her roundtops and sides of iron-hard oak. No one could say that Sir Richard, though second in command, commanded a second-rate ship. Deep in her bowels was a hospital area where, Raleigh genuinely believed, her sick could be salvaged, made well again to fight again, through the efficacy of his medicines, all amply stowed in a large chest for their cure: he never stinted.

As the Atlantic mists cleared, spy-ships sped back to the Lord High Admiral, each with a report more ominous than the last. The treasure fleets were protected by King Philip's most powerful men-of-war, scores of them.

The Admiral cursed the mists that had shrouded the fleets and misled him. But he was a realistic judge of the possible. This was more than he could cope with. There must be no engagement today, lest the entire English flotilla be sunk.

In a prearranged signal he rapidly raised and lowered his mainsail. "Disperse," the signal commanded. "Take cover, watch, scout, dog and be wary."

He knew there would come another day, another chance at the prey; but nothing good for England would come out of this day if the English ships were destroyed.

The captains of the ships under his command instantly obeyed the signal and "fled from the scene like quicksilver" as reported to Raleigh; for they too took stock of the fatal odds against them.

One captain did not obey. Whether he saw the signal or chose to ignore it no one ever knew, for he never lived to tell the tale. Sir Richard Grenville cut out from the scattering English flotilla and drove the *Revenge* square into the thick of the Spanish men-of-war.

The English flotilla thought him mad. One doughty English captain, seeking to save him and his ship from certain destruction, disobeyed orders, scudded out to him, hailed the *Revenge:* "Sir Richard! Sir Richard! The signal is: disengage!" "Then disengage," Sir Richard said. "If that is what some signal says, obey!" "But Sir Richard, the Admiral will be angry." Sir Richard replied, "I am angry myself. This is my own affair. I am not altogether an ass. Go back, my good man, disengage. I will go on, on my own."

In Sir Richard's seething soul at that moment he conceived himself an abler admiral than the Admiral. There was a giddiness in his head, a soaring conviction: he would make a name for himself, for the Admiral, for the Queen, for all England! The doughty captain scudded away. "He is mad as a March hare."

Well-intentioned, impulsive, kindly, erratic Sir Richard Grenville, whose good intentions were always getting him into trouble, as they had in Virginia!

Square into the thick of the Spanish men-of-war he drove the *Revenge*, blasting his cannon to right and left as the Spaniards—amazed and admiring him, much as they admired their saints and martyrs—fought back. Some ships he sank, or so the legend ran in afteryears; but it is not a legend, it is documented that he fought them all off, all fifty-three of them, during the space of an entire afternoon and a night and into the next day.

Slaughter on both sides was ghastly.

The Spanish ships came alongside, grappled the *Revenge;* Spanish soldiers surged aboard, sword-slashing through the English on the deck, slew many and were slain themselves. This occurred often during the long engagement.

Other Spanish ships took their place, swept alongside, blasted holes in the sides of the *Revenge;* and through those holes more Spaniards fought their way in, slashed, slew and were slain.

The Spanish captains, observing the carnage, not having achieved their objective, would sheer off; but more Spanish ships would come up, take their place and continue the fight.

Early in the engagement Grenville sustained a minor flesh wound. His surgeon, treating him on the quarter-deck, was suddenly decapitated by a cannonball. Sir Richard murmured, "Poor soul, you were only doing your duty," and bound up his wound himself. Then, silent in the thunder of the cannonade, a musket ball struck Grenville in the base of the skull, and lodged there, stayed there. Sailors tamponed the hole with oakum to stay the bleeding.

The *Revenge* had taken cannonballs below the water line. Six feet of red water sloshed back and forth in her bilges, where the corpses of Spaniards and Englishmen were curiously commingled, moving with the motion of the water as if they were alive, often, by chance, assuming obscenely erotic postures, face to face, mouth to mouth, breast to breast, a leg slithering up a leg which was often a stump, or a hand grasping a hand as if in farewell, as if whimpering solace one to another in the final injustice of a death that wasn't their fault.

Grenville knew his wound was mortal. He was sinking fast, like his ship. Eternity glittered before him. So did eternal renown, the name he had made for himself. "But why me only?" he thought. "Why not equal renown for all my good Englishmen? Their names must live also, deathless, like mine," and he called his chief gunner, the officer in charge of all the ship's gunpowder, and imparted to him this generous impulse.

"Blow up the ship, Master Gunner," he commanded, "Split her in twain, send us to the bottom. Let the Queen, the whole world, know that Englishmen would rather die than fall into the hands of Spain."

The gunner, a family man, said Yes, he would. He gently cushioned his captain's bleeding head on a coil of rope and considered the matter. He loved Sir Richard, as all men did who knew him well enough; had it lain with him alone he'd have scuttled the *Revenge* then and there. But it didn't look as if he'd have to, so fast was she taking water.

Faithful to his captain's order he called the crew together, those who still could walk, and told them Sir Richard's command. But the men, who so bravely had faced death for thirty-six hours, finding themselves still alive as if by a miracle, now wanted to live. They shook their heads No. "No, we have loved ones, wives, children, sons and daughters. There is still a chance. For them we want to live."

The decision was taken out of his hands. The sturdy *Revenge* seemed likely to sink at any moment. She was a wonderful ship. The Spaniards wanted to save her, copy her novel design. They boarded her, promised the crew their lives, patched up the worst of her leaks and sailed her away for further examination.

They put the English crew, except the wounded whom they left unattended to suffer, aboard their own vessel, treating them with the stately courtesy that Spaniards always accorded the brave. They sought for ransom-likely men among them, but found them to be of the common sort and later exchanged them for equally unnotable Spanish sailors that the English held captive.

When it came to Sir Richard the Spaniards experienced an eerie sense of unease, mixed with a trace of religious awe, as they always did in the presence of those who beheld shining visions that nobody else could see, heard heavenly voices that nobody else could hear, strange men who might be devils or saints or angels in disguise sent to try their faith, or madmen—one never could be sure. Best not to take a chance. Sir Richard was certainly unusual.

They placed him aboard their flagship in the Admiral's own cabin, treated him with obsequious courtesy, till he died of his wound. When he did, and nothing remarkable happened—no comets appeared—they breathed a sigh of relief. Just another English heretic, servant of the Bastard Queen, half out of his wits in his hurry to die for her, not at all like a practical Spaniard. And yet, brave themselves, they respected his foolhardy bravery; and one or two secretly prayed that he wouldn't burn too hot in hell, whither, as all good Spaniards knew, all English heretics went when they died; and were severely scolded by their confessors for weakness and sentimentality.

They buried him at sea.

Thus it came about that the Westcountry "weird" was fulfilled: the sea claimed him in the end, like his father before him.

Later the *Revenge* foundered in a gale, drowning her Spanish prize crew, her English wounded, her bilges awash with corpses now rotten and stinking; and with her went down all of Raleigh's ingenious innovations in naval design that Spain never got a chance to copy. Spain continued to build her ships in the old way, rigidly orthodox, thoroughly Spanish.

Sir Richard's harebrained exploit was the only battle fought that day. Far from being an English victory it was a positive setback for the English navy. The Spanish treasure fleets sailed home intact to Spain.

Queen Elizabeth was distraught, cursed and complained, "The gold, the silver, the treasure that would have solved all my financial problems, Christ! Treasure which so many good English sailors sickened and died to get for me—all, all pours into the coffers of that whoreson Spanish King Philip!" and she added some lusty mutterings of her own as to where she'd like to stuff it.

It remained for Walter Raleigh to turn defeat into victory, a victory that set all stout English hearts swelling with pride. He penned an account of the action, which Elizabeth adopted as a State Paper, entitling it *A Report of the Truth of the Fight at the Isles of Azores Betwixt the Revenge, One of Her Majesty's Ships, and an Armada of the King of Spain.*

The blundering ineptitude of his kinsman was transfigured into glorious self-immolation for England's cause. Grenville was represented as buying time by creating a diversion for the Lord High Admiral to escape, drawing murderous fire upon himself, though he knew it would lead to his own death, so as to afford the whole English fleet an opportunity to retire. And since the whole English fleet did escape, sailed home unscathed, Raleigh was believed. *The Last Fight of the Revenge* was a masterpiece of propaganda. It made the name that Sir Richard Grenville could not have made for himself, perpetuated it for three hundred years. "God of battles, was ever a battle like this in the world before!" exulted Alfred Lord Tennyson in the nineteenth century, thrilling no less than Raleigh's contemporaries to the power of Raleigh's pen. The account of the fight was the first prose piece that Sir Walter signed his name to.

"We, the Queen's true and obedient vassals," he wrote, "guided by the shining light of her virtues, shall always love her, serve her and obey her to the end of our lives. Let the Spaniard and traitor vaunt their false successes."

He continued: "Rumors are diversely spread that the Spaniards, according to their usual manner, fill the world with great appearance of victories, when on the contrary, themselves are most shamefully beaten and dishonored."

And regarding his kinsman: "It is agreeable with all good reason that the beginning, continuance and success of this late honorable encounter of Sir Richard Grenville should be truly set down."

Although Sir Richard had many sick in the *Revenge*, Raleigh wrote, so hard pressed was the Lord High Admiral by the great Spanish warships, that "Sir Richard utterly refused to turn from the enemy, alleging that he would rather choose to die than dishonor himself, his country and Her Majesty's ship, but [would] pass through the enemy squadrons and enforce those of Seville to give way."

He described the ensuing battle, "which continued very terrible that evening," and the Spaniards that vainly attempted to board the *Revenge* and "utterly disliked their entertainment," and were "repulsed again and again and at all times beaten back into their own ships or into the seas."

He paid tribute to Grenville's courage. "Some affirm that Sir Richard was very dangerously hurt almost at the beginning of the fight and lay speechless for a time ere he recovered," but he quoted two of the survivors, "brought home in a ship from the Islands," who "affirm that he never was so wounded as that he forsook the upper deck till an hour after midnight, and then, being shot into the body by a musket was again shot into the head and his surgeon wounded to death withal."

This is precise and factual reporting. Although the Elizabethan phraseology strikes the modern ear as quaint and archaic it has a convincing ring, to the Elizabethans even more convincing. (It is also thoroughly "slanted" as will be seen.)

Raleigh went on: "Sir Richard finding himself in this

[195]

distress, the enemy ships all cast about him in a ring, commanded the Gunner to split and sink the ship, that thereby nothing might remain of glory or victory to the Spaniards; commanded the Gunner to persuade the ship's company to yield themselves unto God and to the mercy of none other, calling them to their duty as he himself was prepared to discharge it, adjuring them that they should not shorten the honor of their nation by prolonging their own lives for a few hours or a few days."

These were the words that so thrilled Tennyson, who practically quotes them:

> Sink me the ship, Master Gunner — sink her,
>   split her in twain!
> Fall into the hands of God, not into the
>   hands of Spain.

But the men, said Sir Walter with deft understatement, "were of a different opinion. They drew back from Sir Richard. It is no hard matter to dissuade men from death to life."

He related how the Spaniards took the men from the *Revenge*, "the ship being marvelous unsavory, filled with blood and the bodies of dead and wounded men like a slaughterhouse," and promised them their lives and put them aboard their own vessels where, he stated, "they used them with all humanity."

His State Paper goes on to give highly exaggerated but heartening news, a device much copied in afteryears by later governments in press releases in wartime. He proceeds to tot up the staggering losses Sir Richard inflicted upon the enemy. In addition to a large but unspecified number of Spanish ships sunk, the body count of the enemy dead came to two thousand, ten times the number of English casualties, "besides several high-ranking commanders."

His State Paper does not end with the last fight of the *Revenge*. Skilfully he wove into the text a ringing call to all Englishmen to unite against their enemies: the Papists, the Jesuits and—always music to English ears —"those blockishly ignorant Catholic rebels and traitors in Ireland, so beggarly unnatural in behavior that they strip their own dead of their ragged garments, yea, even to the very shoes off their feet."

He knew exactly how to summon the compassionate tear, whether relevant to the subject or no. He championed the poor Indians of the New World. "In only one island the Spaniards have wasted thirty hundred-thousand of the natives, besides many millions else in other places of the Indies, a poor and harmless people created by God, who might have been won to His knowledge."

Into the mouth of Sir Richard he put his cousin's last words, words that sound very much like Grenville. (A survivor from the *Revenge* had swum ashore in the confusion and staggered into the warehouse of a resident Dutch merchant; the survivor said he heard Sir Richard speak as he lay a-dying.) The death speech was wordier than a dying man's was likely to have been, but the substance was there, thoroughly in character; and it was common for poetic biographers to give their heroes long-winded last words.

Raleigh quoted: "Here die I, Richard Grenville, with a joyful and quiet mind, for that I have ended my life as a true soldier ought to do, that hath fought for his country, Queen, religion and honor, whereby my soul most joyfully departeth out of this body, and shall always leave behind it an everlasting fame as of a valiant and true soldier that hath done his duty as he was bound to do."

Here Raleigh cut off the quote.

Tennyson had only to echo Raleigh's State Paper three hundred years later in the rousing poem that thrilled a generation of Victorians, when the British Empire that Lord Burleigh had so presciently foretold had become a fact and was at its height:

> *I have fought for Queen and Faith like*
> *a valiant man and true;*
> *I have only done my duty as a man is*
> *bound to do;*
> *With a joyful spirit I, Sir Richard*
> *Grenville, die!*
> *And he fell upon their decks, and*
> *he died.*

But the Dutch merchant averred that Grenville said more. What he said is also in character. Since his men chose not to die with him, he cursed them. "Those others of my company, they have acted like dogs and traitors, for which they shall be reproached all their lives and leave a shameful name forever."

Thus skilfully did Raleigh edit out and suppress a thing that might have reflected on the heroism of his kinsman, muddied his motivation and sullied the sublime and simple image that Raleigh sought to create of Sir Richard: England's paladin. "If he really said that last," thought Raleigh, "it will be easy for me to show that he was out of his wits, poor Richard! Who wouldn't be with a bullet in his brain."

Raleigh's State Paper concludes with a final diatribe against the Spaniards: "Who therefore would repose any trust in this ravenous nation that thirst after English blood because of the many overthrows they have received at our hands, whose weakness we have made manifest to the world, and whose forces at home and abroad, in Europe, in India, by sea and by land (even with handfuls of men and ships) we have overthrown and dishonored. Let the Spaniard beware!"

This eloquent government statement, widely distributed by the Queen, was eagerly read by all Englishmen who could read, and by all the friends and allies of England. It produced the tonic effect of a great English victory. The Queen was immensely pleased. She gratefully bestowed upon Raleigh another monopoly: playing cards. Every deck of cards that was sold added a penny or two to Raleigh's already bulging purse. Englishmen loved to play cards, always asked for a new deck for fear the last one might be "pricked," not wholly reliable. Therefore they bought new ones, Raleigh's, by the thousand.

The Queen did more.

Raleigh felt that his palatial manor, Durham House in London, was sometimes too noisy for his taste when he sat down to think, write his poetry, contrive some new chemical experiment or lay out the design of a swifter, better ship. There were all those neighing horses in the stables, all those chattering servants banging their pots and pans in the kitchens. He wanted a quieter retreat.

He was writing a cookbook. It was eventually printed and distributed among the ships of the Royal Navy. Its purpose was to provide good food for his sailors when the galley fires were out because of bad weather, when no hot food could be prepared. "Ship biscuit hath in it no virtue to sustain strength in the mariner during a tempest, which ofttimes continues for days, not only by reason of the maggots that commonly rot it but also because of the binding effect it hath on the guts." Meticulously listing his menus meal by meal, he prescribed sausages made of salt pork, liberally laced with onions, garlic and raisins; raw potatoes kept white in sugar and vinegar; new-caught fish—sailors were always fishing—with the livers and offal, but purified in a marinade of Jamaica rum to kill the little parasites they often contained—you could see them wiggling about —and beer, "all that a sailor can conveniently put away without addling his brain, to offset the aforesaid binding of the gut. And if the tempest continue," he added,

[199]

"or if there be frost on the deck, raw spirits may be doled out in such measure as shall seem necessary to the commander to heat their blood and bull up their strength." Little wonder that sailors who served under Admiral Raleigh adored him.

No, not Durham House. As for his Irish Estates, how could he live there now that he was Captain of the Guard, every moment on call to protect or amuse Her Majesty?

South of London in his native Westcountry, midway between Plymouth and the capital, was a handsome manor house on a spacious estate called Sherborne, with broad and unobstructed parks and gardens, serenely quiet, with a pleasant view of a cool clear brook where fat trout leaped in the sun out of sheer fishy exuberance and tenant farmers poached to their hearts' content, not a bit afraid of the landlord, for the place was deserted. The owner was the Lord Bishop of Salisbury. But he had displeased the Queen in a financial matter—he thought her demand for a two-third share of his rents unchristian. As Head of the Church of England she simply "translated" him, removed him to another see, so poor that there were no rents to share, where he lived for a good long while in holy poverty, sour as a pickle. Thus, for some years, there had been no bishop to occupy the place. These were full and anxious years for the Queen, busy with greater affairs. She had almost forgotten Sherborne.

But Raleigh had seen it and fallen in love with it. He called it to her attention, pointed out that the gardens were overgrown with weeds, the shrubbery all eaten up by rabbits and deer for lack of a resident bishop to oversee the place, "for as Your Majesty well knows," he said, "that is what the word 'bishop' means, *episcopos*, he who oversees."

She knew as well as he did, but she snapped, "You vaunt your learning. Don't talk like King James, I cannot abide it," and softer, "Ah well, my Water, if you want it you shall have it."

Forthwith she created another bishop, stipulating however that he must be satisfied with his new title, which indeed was extremely valuable, for it made him a Spiritual Peer of the Realm with a seat in the House of Lords besides numerous other perquisites; but on no account was he to reside at Sherborne. He must lease it to her Captain of the Guard for a period of years — Raleigh suggested and got a modest ninety-nine — at an absurdly low rent.

Another estate. Another enemy. They were multiplying fast, like his honors. But his enemies lay low, nursing their grievances. Sir Walter Raleigh was far too influential a figure in the state to topple from his seat of power. All they could do in their jealousy and hatred against him was to whisper behind his back, malicious gossip about his love affair, which everyone already knew, everyone but the Queen; for Bess Throgmorton's condition was obvious by now.

She left the Court and retired to a secluded country estate belonging to one of her noble kinsmen. Out of sight, for Elizabeth, was out of mind; nor did any of her Court dare breathe in her ear that Lady Raleigh was nearly at term.

Yes, Lady Raleigh was her title now. Raleigh had secretly married her four months before, shaking in his pearl-encrusted shoes for fear Diana would find out about it.

Little Robert Cecil, Secretary of State, with his long well-informed ears, caught wind of the gossip. Disclaiming all credence but thoroughly convinced that the gossip was true, he discreetly inquired about it directly of Raleigh himself.

Sir Walter sat down in a panic and penned a reply. He denied everything. "If such a thing were true I would have imparted it unto yourself before any man living. And therefore I pray you, believe it not, but insofar as you are able suppress all such malevolent chatter. For I declare that there lives not one woman on the face of the earth that I would be fastened unto in marriage."

Cecil quietly tucked Raleigh's reply away in a private casket of letters, along with the money he had received from King Philip of Spain in his capacity as a double agent, along with his secret correspondence with King James of Scotland—he was constantly reassuring him that his accession to the throne of England would be smooth and uncontested when the great Queen came to die. Cecil said not a word, waiting to see which way the wind of Elizabeth's favor would veer, remembering that Essex, no less a favourite than Raleigh, had not been punished for a secret marriage.

It was quite within the realm of possibility that Raleigh, like Essex, would simply be smartly slapped on the wrist and retained, like Essex, in all his high offices and powers. "It is not consistent with my duties as Secretary of State," Cecil mused, "to ally myself with them that may lose"; and, warily, in the Court, contrived to continue his show of friendship for Raleigh, waiting upon events.

Prurient lampoons appeared on the streets, were eagerly snatched up still wet from the press, and set all London to laughing.

One of the nastiest, in true gossip-column style read:

WHO ARE THEY?
The lady-in-waiting that cannot wait,
Nor scorns to risk a halter,
But lies abed both early and late
*A-swiving with Sir ******?*

Everyone knew who Sir ****** was. Who else would rhyme with halter? Most people wished him one, and the sooner the better. This little gem of poetastry was widely believed to be from the pen of the Lord Bishop of Durham, still cooling his episcopal heels far away in the foggy north, exiled from his sumptuous London mansion, Durham House, which now was Raleigh's.

And now the story came out. Lady Raleigh gave birth to a son.

To the astonishment of everyone Lord Essex threw his arm around Raleigh's shoulder in full view of the entire Court and publicly congratulated him, later held the child in his arms when the little boy was christened Damerei Raleigh, standing godfather to him. Raleigh named his first son for one of his ancestors who, his genealogist had solemnly assured him, was of royal Plantagenet blood.

Queen Elizabeth retired to the privacy of her chamber and wept. Essex tiptoed up to her door, heard her sobbing, dared not enter. No one had the courage to approach her except her ancient Prime Minister, Lord Burleigh, and Robert Cecil his son, her Secretary of State.

"What burdens Her Majesty most sorely," said Burleigh, sighing heavily, "is that you too, my boy, fell in love and lately your lady hath borne you a son. Impolitic. Badly timed. Alas, my poor Queen!" "But so did you, Father," Cecil replied, "or I wouldn't be here, to love you and serve you and England and her." "Aye, lad, but I timed it better," and then, "'Tis the way of the world and us men, but 'tis not the way of the Queen." "Father, I am never quite sure that I know the way of the Queen." "God knows her way; belike God alone. But 'tis England's."

Then they went in unbidden and whatever they said (no one was there to listen) seemed to restore her to her usual spirits; for after they left she was heard cursing and smashing the furniture. The Queen was herself again.

Almost immediately a detachment of soldiers descended upon Durham House, pounded roughly with musket butts on the door of Raleigh's London residence. They were the Queen's Guard, but without a captain—Raleigh was Captain of the Guard. They were led by a scared young officer who never before had arrested a person of Raleigh's prominence. He said, with a tremble in his voice, "I have orders from Her Majesty to conduct you to the Tower, Sir Walter, to be imprisoned during Her Majesty's displeasure." He spoke the line he had practiced, learned by rote.

Dusk had fallen. The weather was misty, drizzling, the night would be chill. "I am ready," he said. "You needn't have pounded. Don't break down my door. It is Indian rosewood." He thought his days were over. Diana would chop off his head. Essex had been right: a Westcountry squire could not do what a nobleman could do and get off so lightly. A death-feeling of peace and finality came over him. Resignation sustained him. He would die, but he was rich, his family would be amply provided for. Essex had proved a friend; he would see to it they were not deprived. "I shall send for a horse," he said. "It hath brought me ill hap to walk through puddles."

"Not only you, Sir Walter. I am commanded to imprison your wife and your son."

Raleigh's temper flared. "What? What! You cruddy scum! What do you mean, 'my wife'? Lady Raleigh you mean! Instruct your gutter tongue," and with mounting concern, "My Lady too, so lately delivered, my infant son? To the Tower? In this weather?"

The officer stammered, "Such . . . such are my instructions, Sir Walter."

Raleigh caught the hesitation, the fear in the young man's voice.

"Look you," he said, contempt in his voice. "Your doublet is full of holes as a sieve. You come on the

Queen's business in rags. You shame Her Majesty. Go buy yourself better clothes."

"Sir Walter, I am poor."

"Poor, poor, stuff and nonsense! Go buy a new doublet. Look like a Captain of her Guard and perhaps you will be one. Go buy, and make her proud of you."

Dejectedly, "I haven't a ha'penny or I would."

Raleigh detached a pearl from his ear. "Take this, young man. Sell it and buy a new doublet."

The young man's eyes glittered with greed. "But how —where could I sell this costly gem? They would say I stole it and hang me." Ah, he thought, if he only could! It was ten times the worth of his yearly pay. But it would be traced, taken from him; he'd lose it and his place in the Guards to boot, be disgraced to beg on the streets.

"Ride up to London Bridge," Raleigh said, his confidence mounting. "Seek out the rich Jew Isaac Ehud, tell him you come from me. He will buy the pearl, give you full honest value and ask no questions; it will simply disappear, no one will ever know."

The Guardsman slipped the earring into his lean and slender purse and glanced around, but none of the others had heard, they were muffling themselves against the rain. They were neither surprised nor interested that their prominent prisoner protested his arrest, stood there arguing.

"Now bring torches, man!" Sir Walter commanded. They would light the way through the dark streets, add dignity and fend off the miasmic vapors that infected these drenching London fogs and made people sick.

"Are apartments prepared in the Tower?"

"A common one, Sir."

"Uncommon it at once! Is there furniture?"

"The usual sort, I'm afraid."

"Throw it out; and get me bigger quarters."

"If I can. I will speak to the Governor."

"I shall take my own furniture. And here, my good Guardsman who's going to get a better suit, distribute this among your men. They look cold." Gold pieces passed between them. Raleigh wondered how much would filter down to the men, smiled cynically. Just enough, he supposed, to cause them to hold their tongue, greedy for more.

Raleigh gave hasty orders. Preparation for all he required took some little time, but his men were used to obeying him smartly, and did.

Then he called for his coach, a luxurious covered vehicle drawn by four smartly caparisoned horses; it was curtained against the weather; his crest decorated the doors. Damerei Raleigh, swathed in a woollen nightdress, lay cuddled between the fat thighs of his wet nurse. The child had come down with the sniffles, looked wan and frail. Around his little neck was a small cheesecloth bag containing rare and costly spices that all apothecaries swore would protect the wearer against the unhealthy London air—Raleigh had investigated the stuff, doubted its efficacy but found it harmless.

Following the coach came a heavily laden cart with suitable furniture for the prison.

Following the furniture came a van, loaded with kitchen utensils, pots, pans, ladles, soup cauldrons, pigskewers and quantities of food to fill them: live chickens, geese, grouse, quail, pork on the hoof, carp swimming in the soup cauldrons. For Raleigh knew the sad fare doled out in the Tower to prisoners who could not pay, and wanted none of it. Besides, there were his servants to feed.

Following the kitchen van came his servants, in Raleigh's resplendent livery, on horseback: his majordomo, the general factotum of his household, to whom all other servants reported and at whose frown they trembled; his cellarer, who had charge of the buttery with its cheeses, milk, butter and eggs; his butler, a refugee French Huguenot, who knew exactly what vintages to serve in what quantity lest the guests fall under the tables; his stable master, who was said to be a Turk because so many of Raleigh's horses were Arabian; his personal attendants, all sailors, some of whom had been galley slaves of the Barbary pirates, some who had escaped from debtor's prison, fierce, devoted men who loved a master who never scolded them about their past and to whom many owed their lives.

Following the servants came the women of his household: ladies' maids and ladies' maids' maids, for each rated an apprentice; scullery wenches who washed the dishes and polished the marble floors and lay with the stable boys whenever they had a chance, which was often. When occasionally they found themselves with child through inexperience or sheer exuberance, Raleigh encouraged them to marry and gave them money to usher the little ones into the world by the safest of midwives and to give them a good start in life. It would sully his name to have bastards born under his roof. Besides, he loved children. The women servants rode in lumbering country carts, terribly excited and happy, just a bit giddy at the change of residence. "Lor' love 'im, prison'll be just like home."

In the rear of this remarkable procession came packhorses loaded with crates crammed with Raleigh's retorts and alembics, apparatus for his chemical experiments; and bottles and vials of his medicines.

A watchman, walking his rounds, lifted up his lantern, recognized Raleigh, flamboyant even in disgrace, and doffed his sodden hat in a surly salute. He heard the Guardsmen talking. "Bound for the Tower, eh? He is fallen then, and high time too. Bad cess to him!" He continued his round and cried in a cheery voice, "Ten of the clock and all's well!" and hastened to the nearest tavern to spread the news. He raised a mug of beer and proposed a toast: "To the worst hated man in England!"

Everyone knew whom he meant.

CHAPTER XVIII

RALEIGH dispatched a hot-spurring courier ahead of the long train of the Queen's prisoners to apprise the Governor of the Tower that his master, Admiral Sir Walter Raleigh, Member of Parliament, Lord Warden of the Stanneries of Cornwall, Captain of Her Majesty's Guard, having temporarily incurred Her Majesty's displeasure, was about to arrive. Imperiously the messenger demanded that quarters be found for his master's retinue, apartments suitable to his rank be made ready with fires alight in the fireplaces to take off the chill.

This was a naval tactic. In much the same manner Raleigh always instructed his captains to send out fast spy-ships to sniff the wind so as to get the weather gauge of the enemy, report whether the wind was favorable.

It was favorable.

The Governor of the Tower rubbed his hands as if gold was already warming them. "Here comes the most profitable prisoner that ever yet entered my establishment!" Raleigh would enhance his reputation, fatten his purse. Others would follow, no doubt about it; for if the great Raleigh could be imprisoned anybody could, men of equal wealth and power. The Queen must be testy, petulant, suspicious in her old age. Raleigh would set a precedent for vastly higher fees. A lucky day in the life of the Governor. "Aye, aye, he shall have his fireplace fires though I chop up the racks in the dungeons to fuel them!" How glad he was now he had paid so much to purchase his job as the Governor of the Tower!

The Tower of London was one of the most beautiful edifices of Elizabeth's capital city. Ages ago it had served as a fortified camp for Caesar's legions, long before Christ had yet appeared on earth. During the ages that followed, it had grown from a rude military camp to a complex of buildings and walls within walls; and atop the battlements were broad walks where prison guards watched and privileged prisoners could stroll and take their ease.

A wide moat, fed by the Thames, surrounded the whole magnificent complex, full of water lilies and leaping trout, where Londoners were free to fish, on payment of a small fee to the Governor, and little London boys could swim when they wanted, and seldom drowned, for the guards would spot them and have them pulled out.

There were other attractions. Parks and gardens were close at hand, manicured greenswards and ancient trees casting a cool and grateful shade, and nearby a menagerie of caged bears, apes, elephants, monkeys, tropical birds with unbelievable beaks and plumage so fantastically colored that some said, "Somebody painted those feathers." The parks and the zoo were free—on payment of a small fee to the Governor—for any Londoner to enjoy and spend a leisurely afternoon, broadening and educational. Where else but here could the common sort see the exotic tropical flowers and wondrous beasts of the whole world, brought home in the ships of Her Majesty's Navy for their recreation? Who else but the Governor would allow people to come so close to his legendary buildings, over which he was absolute lord? And, if one wished a basket of dinner or supper, one had only to ask it of the Governor's pleasant purveyors of victuals—concessionaires who paid the Governor a fee for the privilege—who circulated among the crowds. Out of the Governor's liberality the hungry or thirsty Londoners could buy anything they wished to eat or drink at a reasonable price, very little more than they'd have paid at home. They were not permitted, of course, to bring their own food, lest they litter the grounds and shame him. Thus the Tower of London and its environs were greatly frequented and thoroughly enjoyed by the common people of London.

The Tower of London was once, and still could be, a royal residence. There had been, still were, palatial suites of rooms. When Elizabeth was a little girl, still in her teens, not knowing if she would ever be Queen, not sure from one day to the next if she would be murdered, she herself had been a prisoner in the Tower in one of those royal apartments.

There was a dark and somber side to the beautiful Tower of London that cast a pall of mystery and fear over all that was sunny and pleasant. Royal blood had been spilt there, a King butchered at the altar in the chapel, screaming for mercy in vain. Little princes of royal blood, inconvenient threats to the throne, had been suffocated to death under secret stairs. Their pitiful little-boy bones have been recently discovered, radio-carbon dated and authenticated. Executions, public and private, had taken place in the Tower and its environs, among them those of Elizabeth's own mother and of some of her father's other queens.

And there were common cells for those who could not pay, damp, unheated, unlit save for the tallow candles grudgingly doled out by the Governor so the prisoners could see when the jailors pushed bowls of gruel under the doors; unfurnished save for a pallet of straw that horses wouldn't eat, where rats, not so fastidious, were wont to nest and produce their litters.

But even these indigent prisoners were sometimes pardoned through the Queen's mercy or the intervention of some powerful politician, so they were kept alive and never died except from disease or some other awkward occurrence such as an unpredictable Act of God; and, on payment for luxuries they had not received, they were released, reputations unblemished. No disgrace darkened the future of prisoners released from the Tower. It was deemed sufficient punishment that they had incurred the Queen's displeasure—and for all anybody knew they might become captains of ships or commanders of regiments the very next day.

Darkest of all the mysteries that cast the pall over the Tower of London were the oubliettes, holes in cellars beneath the cellars. *Oubliettes*—the very name struck terror to the heart. It meant "the abode of the forgotten ones." Here, in slimy cisterns, heavy with chains, were men and women whose existence was deemed incompatible with the welfare of the State. They had never been arrested, never tried before a court of law. They had simply disappeared. If anyone ever asked what had become of them, nobody ever knew. And there, in the oubliettes, they lived out the span of their very very short lives. Occasionally, when he remembered to, a jailor might come and look down, to hurl them a scrap of bread; might hit a skeleton with it, rattling its bony response, "Thank you, good sir; I am no longer hungry." Everyone, even the jailors, professed to believe, vehemently protested, that no such thing as an oubliette existed.

Prisoners like Raleigh entered the Tower through Traitors' Gate, a signal privilege accorded only those of high rank. Raleigh was proud of the distinction, spurned the ordinary and much more convenient entrance; head high he strode into the prison. It irked him not a whit that they called it Traitors' Gate. He knew he was no traitor.

With Lady Raleigh and little Damerei he took possession of a luxurious suite of apartments where, true to the Governor's promise, all the fireplaces were blazing merrily. It was a beastly night. Raleigh was glad of the warmth, though he considered it only his due.

His horses and servants were snugly housed, fed and waited upon by the Governor's staff, the Governor keeping a strict and inflated account of all that Sir Walter must pay for. Luxurious accommodation for the rich was traditional, sanctioned by the system.

The Governor was delighted with his prisoner. Raleigh's retinue were happy, as happy as at home in Durham House.

Damerei Raleigh still had the sniffles, now began to run a fever. Raleigh raged that his medicines were late in coming, complained that the Governor had not provided a chemical laboratory, though he hadn't asked for one, suspected that his medicines were being tampered with, diluted, maybe poisoned.

Lady Raleigh said, "Hush, dear heart. The child hath that in him that only God can cure, and I don't think He's going to."

Wives, children, relatives, guests, mistresses could visit rich prisoners in the Tower, stay as long as they were paid for. Births and deaths occurred; marriages were solemnized.

Damerei Raleigh, that frail little boy, soon wasted away and died. Lady Raleigh wept. Walter Raleigh, heart-stricken but still with an eye on his future, had him quietly buried, and never mentioned in public the death of his first-born son lest it compromise his career. He knew that the Queen would be glad that a child that had shamed her own lady-in-waiting now was no more. She, who could not bear children, could not stomach the thought that others who could, did; but she sorrowed when babies died, even when she heard about Raleigh's, sorrowed and yet was glad. "Would God I had one of my own!"

Raleigh's sorrow at Damerei's death very shortly was

lightened: Lady Raleigh was pregnant again. He smiled, kissed her, "God bless you, dear Bess!"

She loved the bristly feel of his beard against her cheek, but pretended to draw back as if it scratched her. "Must you still wax the points sharp, like one of your marlin spikes?"

He laughed, drew himself up, "That I must, Lady Raleigh. Your Admiral must look his best or they'll think they've out-faced me."

But often at night, glowering by the fire, he wrote savagely bitter poems berating his Queen. Naturally he kept them in manuscript, locked them up with other words he had written, words not for her eyes, words he didn't want her to see.

She never did.

They were some of his finest, some of his best. They were for him the emotional release he could achieve only in his poems. Now, after the passage of centuries, they have come to light, we are privileged to read them. We are bewildered at the vagaries of Sir Walter's mind, more than a little prone to condemn, since it's so different from ours. But vagaries were quite common among the writings of his contemporaries, those amazing Elizabethans.

At the same time he was putting to paper his hatred of the Queen—a hatred so mixed with genuine devotion that it is quite impossible to disentangle the two—he was writing just the opposite to Robert Cecil, Secretary of State.

His letter was phony as a counterfeit coin. Its purpose was transparently clear. He lamented his cruel separation from fair Diana. He lived for the day when once again he could bask in the sunlight of her smile. He wrote:

Never was my heart broken till this day, for my Queen frowns upon me, her whom I have served these many years with love and undying fidelity; and now I am left, forgotten by her, in dark prison all alone. Could I but see her once in two or three days my misery were less, I that beheld her walking like Venus, soft zephyrs wafting her golden hair about her face and fair cheeks, a nymph, a goddess, a very angel! Oh lack, once amiss hath bereft me of all! All wounds leave scars, but none so sore and hurtful as those that come of womankind. Divinity itself is instinct with compassion, seeks not revenge, for revenge is brutal and mortal. All those times past: the loves, the sighs, the sorrows shared, the desires—do they not outweigh one frail misfortune? *Spes et fortuna, valete!* Hope and good fortune, farewell. She is gone whom I loved, and for me hath not one thought of mercy.

He told Cecil:

Do with me therefore whatever you wish. I am weary of life. There are those that desire that I perish. If perish I do, it will be for her, and for her in my death I shall count that day blessed wherein I was born.

He ended:

And so, to my honorable friend, Sir Robert Cecil, Knight of Her Majesty's Most Honorable Privy Council, I subscribe myself
                    Yours, not worthy of
                    any name or title,
                                        W.R.
                    From the Tower

Cecil duly brought this missive to the Queen's attention, as Raleigh knew he would, making no comment. None was necessary. She sniffed in disgust and tossed it into the fire. In other days his courtly rhetoric might have moved her, but not now. Her sense of betrayal was far too great, too bitter. She was weary at playing

[214]

at courtly love with lovers she no longer could hold, who sneaked off behind her back and got married, had children. Empty, empty, empty and hollow now sounded their protestations of love, shaming her in the eyes of all who heard them, making her a laughingstock, butt of cruel jokes, branding her a jealous possessive old woman. She simply said to Cecil, "Keep him where he is." "How long, Your Majesty?" "Till he rots."

Once he had written her love poems that she loved, "Praise to Diana," and all the others, that came from the heart, written when she and the world were younger, when she truly believed that her "Water" would never marry because of his love for her, a love hopeless but ever-aspiring, drowning out all passions less elevated. She would have understood, and so would the poet Sir Walter, the exquisite lines of a poet who lived much later, who gave tender expression to such love: the desire of a moth for a star, of the night for the morrow, the devotion to something afar.

"How I deceived myself, and was myself deceived!"

But it was never her nature to be cruel: Raleigh was in no danger of the oubliettes. He might even be useful someday—she had witnessed many strange turns of Fortune's Wheel in her long insecure life. It was never wise to make an irreversible decision. Rigidity in state-craft was Spanish, not English. For the moment she would let things rest. She smiled sardonically at what it must be costing Sir Walter to keep up his flamboyant state in the Tower. Sooner or later he would have to come to her for money. Not a farthing would he get, the gaudy spendthrift!

But Fortune played one of its wry little tricks, and the matter turned out quite otherwise, as will be seen in its place.

One day the Governor said to Raleigh, "I must ap-point you a keeper, Sir Walter."

Escape from the Tower was by no means impossible,

especially if the prisoner was rich. Therefore a "keeper," a special guard, was set over all prominent prisoners. Night and day the keeper must be alert for any change in the prisoner's behavior—a suspicious furtiveness, a sudden affability, too much talk or too little, any such change might be the give-away sign that the prisoner was plotting escape. Keepers were subject to heavy fines if their prisoners escaped. If the keepers could not pay the fines they themselves were cast into debtor's prison. Hence they were chosen from sober solid men of slender means, intelligent when possible, preferably with large families who would starve if the keeper lost his salary. If a keeper accepted a bribe from his prisoner and helped him escape, the keeper was hanged. Keepers were therefore extremely efficient and, to a man like Raleigh who valued his privacy, they were a confounded nuisance, always underfoot when one wanted, say, to write a poem or the history of the world.

Raleigh said, "Keeper? What have I to do with a keeper? Do you think that I scheme to abscond?" He thought of his numerous retinue. "What would become of my people?"

"I have orders, Sir Walter, orders from the Secretary of State. I am casting about in my mind whom to appoint. I confess that I cannot decide . . ."

Raleigh understood at once. He was being given a chance, in return for a fee, no doubt a large one, to name his own keeper. He said, "There's a Westcountry cousin of mine, a man of unsullied repute, that will suit me. Cousin though he is, he would run me through if I tried to escape, which I won't. It is perfectly conformable with your orders from the Secretary of State, Master Governor, for you to appoint this man as my keeper; for my kinsman is a ship captain that hath won many victories both in Ireland and upon the seas, and is known to Her Majesty's Admiralty as a valiant dependable Englishman."

Raleigh's kinsman was instantly appointed.

It is true that Raleigh's new keeper would have killed him if he had tried to escape. A ship captain had always to consider his own future, never hazard the chance for promotion through some mistaken loyalty to a relative.

So keep him he did, under friendly but strict surveillance. And since his keeper also maintained contact with the Admiralty, Raleigh was shortly the best informed prisoner in the Tower, almost as well informed as if he still were at liberty, still striding the quarterdeck of his men-of-war, receiving reports from his spy-ships of all that was rumored or true in the business of Her Majesty's Navy.

Thus it was that he learned of the *Madre de Dios*, the richest prize the English Navy ever captured.

The reason the Mother of God, the *Madre de Dios*, was so heavily freighted with treasure had directly to do with the state of mind of King Philip of Spain. He was getting old. He was subject to fears that never had troubled him in his youth. He feared the torments of Purgatory. Incredibly, he, the richest man in the world, feared poverty. He had dreadful dreams; in nightmares he starved; there was nothing to eat in all the vast acreage of his magnificent palaces; he gnawed on chapel candles; demonic laughter mocked his sleeping ears at this insult to God.

Always religious, his religion now took a turn toward superstition. Often he read in his Bible: Remember now thy Creator in the days of thy youth—aye, he remembered.

He could easily have read his Bible in English. But he hated the English, his barren English Queen, his lost English throne, English Elizabeth the heretic bastard whom he never quite managed to marry, long safe on the English throne, thwarting him at every turn, stealing his ships—no, he would not read his Bible in English.

He read his Bible in Latin or Hebrew or Greek. The ancient tongues were austere, brutally direct: not a trace did he find in the ancient tongues of the poetic euphemisms which the English embodied in their translation:

"Evil days will come upon you," read the ancient tongues; "You will have no pleasure in living."

"Your eyesight will grow weak, you will no longer see clearly."

He already wore spectacles.

"Strong men will lose their strength, straight backs will grow crooked."

And more: "You will wake up at the first crow of the cock." It was already so, his bladder.

"You will get dizzy, you will be afraid of heights." His gold-headed cane with the gold double-headed Eagle of the Empire atop it—he carried it now not for show but because, if a dizzy spell struck him, he leaned upon it lest he stagger and betray unimperial weakness. He no longer mounted the steps of his many palaces to breathe on their towers the sweet-scented forest-fresh air that wafted over the Escurial. The Bible was true; he was desperately afraid of heights. The somber notes of the organ in the cellar, perpetually dirging a Dies Irae, suited him better.

The English read: "Desire shall fail," but the ancient tongues, "You will become sexually impotent." He already was; how he hated and regretted the rosy lost Elizabeth.

The delicate English read: "And the grinders cease because they are few, and those that look out of the window be darkened." But in the ancient tongues: "Your teeth will get hollow and black and fall out." It already had happened. Philip had always had the outjutting Hapsburg lower jaw. Now that his upper teeth were gone the family disfigurement was painfully more evident. Sycophantic courtiers, even young ones, had their upper teeth yanked out to look like him.

At the end of the passage King Philip's Bibles all read the same: "Then shall the dust return to the earth as it was, and the spirit shall return to God who gave it."

With his upper teeth gone King Philip developed a lisp. It is still heard today after the lapse of centuries among Spaniards who aspire to status, much as the aristocratic "British stammer," legacy of one of the crazy Georges, is heard among butlers and play actors. It is of interest to philologists that the current Queen, another Elizabeth, never stoops to such affectation, her status being secure.

It was King Philip's psychotic dread of poverty that caused him to issue commands that all the gold possible from all his domains, all silver, all precious gems, costly spices, pepper, pearls, musk, ambergris, hartshorn, bezoar stones, shark fins, the lac that grew on the trees of Ceylon, the curious drugs that the Chinese sold (just where and for what he wasn't quite sure), and wines from the isles of Greece that were said to have mystic properties—all, everything that was precious, all this he wanted to be brought close by, stored up for quick sale if the poverty which he so feared should strike him. All this he ordered to be loaded forthwith into the holds of his ships and transported to Spain. So much for the ships.

And as for his soul: to hedge against the fires of Purgatory, he commanded that all the bones that could be found of the more influential saints be scooped up and translated to the Escurial, his palace in Madrid, with their cerecloths and mouldy skulls. He would build shrines, light candles before these precious relics, depute priests to say masses to the end that the relics would intercede for him and cool, if only a little, the purgatorial flames. Philip did not know, no man knows it about himself, but such fears are quite common among eldering men, princes and peasants alike.

That was the reason the Mother of God, *Madre de Dios*, was on her way to Spain with so fabulously rich a cargo.

Raleigh's captains captured her and sailed her intact into Plymouth Harbor.

The moment the *Madre de Dios* tied up at the Plymouth wharf the English prize-crewmen started to steal the cargo. "The fragrance of musk and rare spices hangs sweet over the whole of Her Majesty's city," wrote a contemporary.

They thoroughly rifled the cargo, went rollicking, tipsy, all night long through the streets of Plymouth town, bottles of liquor that only a lord could afford clutched in their tarry hands. Tavern whores suddenly found themselves paid in pearls for a pint. Never had sailors so glorious a homecoming. It was all quite illegal, of course, but all quite of a piece with the boisterous conduct of Queen Elizabeth's sailors. No one was arrested.

Alarmed, the Secretary of State rode down to Plymouth, looked at the mess and promptly rode back to London. It was more than he could cope with. He calculated the worth of the *Madre de Dios* at a million pounds, "but it is frittering away, Your Majesty, like leaves that are torn from trees in a whirlwind." And soon, he doubted, it would all be lost in the pockets of rogues.

The Queen was furious. She could use that million pounds. "Little man, little man," she thought, "thou'rt not thy father," and set about planning to retrieve what she could of the million pounds.

Every moment was vital, every moment more treasure was being squandered.

She asked ancient Lord Burleigh, ailing but still half possessed of his faculties, "Who, dear my counsellor, can I call upon to get me the gold of this Spanish ship?"

"What, little princess? What did you say? There, there, fret not yourself. All will come right in the end."

He was in another world. She gave him a spoonful

of porridge to sustain him. She said, "There's a captured Spanish ship lying in Plymouth Harbor, a cargo worth millions. My silly sailors are stealing it, giving it to whores."

"Aye," said Lord Burleigh, the porridge having strengthened him, "aye," remembering, "that is ever the way of sailors with their whores. Pity, a great pity. Always happens. Too bad, too bad." His head nodded; but whether he dozed or whether he was simply nodding agreement she could not tell.

"Burleigh, Burleigh, come back to me! Counsel me. Whom can I call upon to get me the treasures in the Spanish ship captured by my Navy, now lying in Plymouth Harbor with all my foolish sailormen stealing her treasures? Poor souls, they don't even know the worth of what they steal."

"Majesty," said Lord Burleigh, who was himself again, "call upon that poetic sailor of yours, whom I do not love, no more than I love that other scribbling poet Edmund Spenser. But Walter Raleigh works wonders in naval affairs; the common sailors adore him; and for all that he's quirky and queer, I think you'd best let him out of the Tower, let him go down to Plymouth and stop the thieves that are stealing the guts out of the Spanish galleon called the Mother of God." He shook his hoary head. "Madame, the blasphemy! *Mother of God!* What a foul and counterwrought name King Philip chose for a treasure ship. The veritable Blessed Mother of God was poor as a church mouse."

"She certainly was," said the Queen, who always approved of virgins.

Thus advised, the Queen acted fast. A court courier on a frothing charger galloped up to the Tower gate, demanded and got instant admission to the Governor. He had with him Elizabeth's order for Raleigh's immediate release—it was not a royal pardon, Raleigh

had never been charged with anything, simply imprisoned by her command. Now, just as simply, he was to
be released. The courier had another paper, drawn up
by the Secretary of State, describing the pilfering of the
Madre de Dios and ordering Sir Walter to stop it. Raleigh noticed that Her Majesty's Secretary had addressed him by his title, "Admiral." He understood at
once that he was not to be deprived of his places and
honors. It was scant comfort. He astonished the Governor by struggling in vain to keep tears from his eyes
then flew into a rage.

"Oh, my poor Queen, so gentle, so liberal! So bur-
dened with great affairs of state! Poor careworn Majesty,
they have caught her unaware, unsuspecting, oh vile,
oh foul, the shame of it. And sailors, too!"

The Governor stared at him in disbelief. He didn't
know Raleigh very well. Could this outburst be real?
Yes, he could see it was real: there was no mistaking
Raleigh's sincerity.

Raleigh spat out a rapid-fire succession of orders. To
his relative the ship captain, keeper no longer, he said, "Is
your ship manned, are your crew loyal?" "Aye, Sir Walter, fully manned and as loyal as your own." "Sail her
down to Plymouth, put your men aboard the *Madre de
Dios*, stop the thievery, let no one go ashore."

"I'll clap the whoreson rogues in irons!"

Raleigh shook his head, "No, not that—just take away
their liquor till they sober up. They were long at sea,
they went a little wild when they saw all those Spanish
riches. They are loyal English sailors when they're sober."

To his majordomo: "No doubt the Governor has a
list of expenses I have incurred for the keep of my people. They were well treated, you have heard no complaints? No? Nor have I. Good then, give the Governor
whatever he asks, and add a bit to it."

The Governor was genuinely sorry to see him go. He
had proven a model prisoner, liberal, entertaining and

very good company. Who knew what heights he might rise to now? The Governor was a little afraid of him. He even slightly reduced the amount of the bill he presented to the majordomo, who paid it on the spot, in gold.

The Governor bade him good-bye in a cordial meeting. "Surely it is not necessary for you to depart tonight, Sir Walter. I'd count it a privilege if my honorable guest were to honor my table at a farewell banquet—at my expense, Sir Walter," he hastened to add, "not a farthing of fee." And he intimated, not too subtly, that if the Admiral should happen to get wind of other distinguished candidates for the Tower—one never knew where the axe of Her Majesty's displeasure might chop next, did one—he'd be grateful if the Admiral were to put in a word of praise for the excellent accommodations that he, the Governor, could offer in the Tower and mention the reasonable fees.

Frowning, Sir Walter said, "I know of no such candidates; I must depart this very night. There is business afoot that I must discharge." Then he smiled wryly, "I don't even know if we shall not meet again, Master Governor, here in this very same place."

The Governor contrived to look horrified, an impossibility—and gestured the notion aside, thinking, "Aye, that is possible."

Forthwith Raleigh sent all his retinue back to Durham House, save for a picked party of his best sailor-horsemen, mounted on his fastest horses, all armed; and these he led down to Plymouth to discharge the business that was afoot.

He discharged it with skill and dispatch. Old Burleigh had been right. He was probably the only man in England who could have salvaged so much of the cargo.

Raleigh found the English prize-crew sober, dried out and in terrible fear of hanging. He forced them to

[223]

disgorge all the plunder they had secreted on their person. Some of the more frightened ripped open the seams of their ragged garments, out of which came a hidden pearl or two. "Do not rip open Admiralty uniforms," Raleigh said tartly, looking away, pretending not to see. "Sew that up again at once. For shame! You must still be drunk." They thanked him with their eyes. He made them cleanse the dirty decks with vinegar and salt, pack all the treasures neatly back in the chests; he had the chests securely locked; sentinels picked from his own men sat on top of them night and day. They were in no danger of assault. The crew were thoroughly awed, grateful to their Admiral whom they trusted to conjure them out of the sorry predicament they had got themselves into. This he did when he came to make his report to the Queen: no reprisals were to be taken against them, for the treasure salvaged from the *Madre de Dios* exceeded the wildest estimate. The Queen was appeased. As for the treasure that had disappeared ashore, it seemed nothing could be done about it. There were many of the crew still ashore. They soon heard that their crewmates had been caught, quarantined in the *Madre de Dios*. They feared a thief's death. But then word was leaked to them that no reprisals would be taken if they surrendered themselves and returned the loot, this on the word of their fellow-sailor, Admiral Sir Walter Raleigh himself. Forthwith there was a hasty staggering back to the ship of all but a few; those few were never heard of again, having probably drunk themselves to death or eaten too much opium paste and promptly given up the ghost, not being accustomed to this expensive oriental luxury. And not a few dockside trollops found the beautiful robes of Cathay torn from their backs, much to their annoyance, and found themselves left only with the trinkets—a necklace, an earring, a pearl—that they'd prudently hidden while their companions lay in a drunken stupor beside them. There were hazards in their profession as in any other, and a wise girl put something aside for a rainy day.

Such was the saga of the capture of the fabulous treasure ship, the Spanish *Madre de Dios*.

Raleigh sent a pack train laden with Spanish chests to Robert Cecil with an accurate account of the worth of their contents. It suited Sir Walter's fancy to caparison the horses in gorgeous Spanish harness. The Queen's banner triumphantly waved at the head of the procession. Elizabeth beamed. Raleigh had poured a year's revenue into her treasury. He sent her a letter, thanking her for her gracious permission to be of service. He subscribed it, "With an humble and contrite heart, your poor prisoner of the Tower, Walter Raleigh."

He never saw the inside of the Tower again, never so long as she lived.

At the same time he sent to the Secretary of State a demand for his share of the salvage, to which he was legally entitled by Admiralty law. It was substantial, but not nearly so much as he had expended in the Tower. Cecil promptly paid it.

Spain still had more ships than England. Another Armada invasion attempt still loomed as a threat. The Admiralty could not afford to downgrade an ingenious naval architect who had earned their professional respect and who seemed to command almost mystical loyalty from his seamen.

Queen Elizabeth therefore stripped from him not one of his honors, estates, monopolies or titles. He was still her Captain of the Guard.

Taxes in England were rising; monopolies were an abomination to the common people, on whom they bore most heavily; harvests in Ireland were poor, the Irish peasants were hungry, rebellious; the cost of more and more soldiers to keep them in their place was great. Raleigh's estates in Ireland began to lose money. He could not help his tenants and did not try, his mind far too busy with other matters he deemed more important. He was hated in Ireland, he was hated in England. Never had a man had so many enemies.

While he was a prisoner in the Tower he had heard tales of a region in the mountains of Guiana called Eldorado, unknown to the Spaniards and ruled by an Indian Emperor who every year was ritually smeared with honey and rolled in gold dust. Thither the Indians brought all the treasures they continually stole from the Spaniards. Raleigh believed every word of it. The old urge "to seek new lands, for fame, for gold, for glory," cast its spell upon him. It held him in thrall for years.

Meanwhile he retired to Sherborne, where his good Bess bore him another son, and then another.

CHAPTER XIX

QUEEN ELIZABETH's passion for dancing, verging on a compulsion, never left her. One day Lord Burleigh said to her, "Madame, it is unseemly for you to dance in public." She flared at him, "Burleigh, go hang yourself! Am I so old?"

He said, "Madame, you dance like the pretty princess I loved when you were naught but a rosy little snippet of a girl, high in the jump, seductive like the odalisques that the Grand Turk lusteth after." He bit his lip. "Madame, I beg your pardon."

She kissed his cool old cheek. "Am I, am I still? Thou art my best esteemed friend in this whole naughty world, for you always counsel me true."

Lord Burleigh had begun to present that cherubic aspect of face, a little soft, a little saggy, baby-like, that comes to all men who live to a great old age.

"I love to dance," Elizabeth said softly. "There is music in me. Do not forget, dear my Burleigh, that my father was a notable sweet composer of melodies that pleasured his ladies to dance to. No doubt I have it from him."

But thereafter, since she was realistic, she danced only in the privacy of her chambers where no one could see her; but never was she without a dream-partner; he was always the same, always handsome Lord Essex. She would never forgive him; neither could she forget him.

"If only he'd ask me for something!" Then, drawing herself up, "Maybe I'd grant it, maybe I wouldn't."

Soon he did ask her for something. Grant it she did.

In Ireland another rebellion erupted, as had happened so often in the past. Lord Essex said, laughing, "The cruddy baboons are at it again, Your Majesty, burning your castles, eating up everything in sight as I hear," and indeed there were horrid rumors of cannibalism among the starving Irish. "Let me go over and teach them some decent English manners."

Pleased that he needed her, Queen Elizabeth gave him the title of General, gave him a large company of soldiers —these in addition to those she already maintained in Ireland at so great a cost—and sent him over Saint George's Channel to do what no one had ever been able to do when the Irish turned nasty.

He was worsted at every turn. There was terrible slaughter on both sides. He lost more men than ever were lost before in a punitive English expedition. He returned disgruntled but not in disgrace. When the hated kerns were desperate no Englishman could beat them, far less understand them.

"It could have turned out," mused the Secretary of State, "that Raleigh had handled this matter somewhat more to our advantage," remembering Raleigh's past record in Ireland.

But Raleigh was busy elsewhere on a military mission quite different and far more important.

In Cadiz in the south of Spain King Philip was amassing a great fleet. In his patient methodical mind this was to be another Invincible Armada. This time, God helping, he would win. There were warships, supply ships, ships to transport horses and soldiers. Cadiz was also the safest port for his treasure ships, with the silver and gold that would keep him from starving, and many old bones of the saints that would pray for him. He had collected so many holy relics that he had not yet had time to build suitable shrines for all of them.

Cadiz was an ancient port with buildings whose architecture recalled the Moors who had lived there so long. At low tide there could still be discerned the outlines of Phoenician sea walls and jetties. Cadiz, by reason of its sheltered miles-long estuary had been a commercial seaport since time out of mind. It had a seaport's reputation. In Roman times it was famous: "No town can compare with Cadiz for its cookery and dancing girls," wrote a rapturous Roman who visited it. Now it had a Christian cathedral with a yellow dome; the yellow was gold foil. In it were precious relics of saints long dead, not attractive to look at but patently powerful, since Cadiz was safe from all enemy ships, at least had been so far.

Most of the drinking water was brackish or fouled when the Spanish ships pumped their bilges. But King Philip was sure that God held him in special regard, for under the high altar of the cathedral there gushed a large spring of pure sweet water yielding a volume that was more than enough to supply the whole town. Surely this was a miracle. Of course it had gushed for the Moors too, but the King was assured by his theologians that the earlier gushing had only foreshadowed the coming of his Christian Imperial Majesty.

A tall tower rose in the center of the city. Its purpose was to signal the arrival and departure of ships, with a special cluster of flares if the ships that approached were hostile. But for many years these warning flares had never been lighted. For many years no enemy ships had dared to attack Cadiz. The signalmen had forgotten where the flares were stored or how to light them if they were found, which they never were, having long since been stolen to kindle fires under pots of *olla podrida* or grown so damp with disuse that they had been thrown away.

Raleigh's military mission resulted from a high-level

strategy resolved upon by the English Admiralty, a strategy combining the simplicity of genius with the daring characteristic of the Elizabethan Royal Navy. *Objective:* to forestall another Armada, to fend off the invasion threat that daily grew worse. *The Operation:* to sail boldly into that highly defended hitherto safe harbor of Cadiz, to burn, sink, destroy every vessel in sight and everything that chanced to come under the deadly English guns. The Admiralty commissioned Walter Raleigh Vice Admiral in charge of the expedition.

An expedition required a Commander-in-Chief, a nobleman whether seaman or no; no mere Vice Admiral would do, hadn't the prestige — especially the "worst hated man in England."

Lord Essex was the best loved. Now he asked yet another favor of the Queen. He begged her to give him the command. She did not hesitate, for a political reason: the best loved man in England had suffered some loss of prestige in the public eye because of his many defeats. She could restore him to public esteem by a smashing victory at Cadiz, which her Admiralty assured her was certain. And for a personal reason: she simply wanted to. So Lord Essex led the English fleet to the south of Spain to smash King Philip at Cadiz. Raleigh fretted that he had not been named to command, but he had not opposed the appointment of Essex, who had so recently befriended him. Essex knew so little of sea fighting that he could scarcely be feared to make many mistakes, was so generous of nature that he could easily be talked out of any he might make.

But he did make mistakes. More soldier than sailor, admittedly brave, he ordered hundreds of soldiers into scores of boats as the fleet approached Cadiz and ordered them to row ashore and take the town. It was nothing he would not have done himself. Only his position as Commander kept him aboard ship instead of leading the little flotilla in person. It was an appalling error of judgment.

It was a beautiful June evening, with the soft Spanish air full of the scent of jasmine and the sweet odor of burning cooking fires wafting over the harbor as the Spanish garrison looked forward to supper, and a huge copper-colored sun sank slowly over the Spanish forts. From the walls came the mocking laughter of Spanish sentries. The Englishmen must be mad. Or perhaps the boats were very sensibly deserting to the Spanish cause. Mad, or a trick, or deserters, the maneuver made no sense and posed no danger.

Raleigh thought, "My Lord of Essex greatly underestimates the firepower of the fleet he commands," forgave his inexperience but clearly foresaw disaster. He leaped into a boat and had himself rowed swiftly over to the Commander's flagship. He found Essex looking out of the windows of the captain's cabin, tremendously excited, rubbing his hands, muttering, "Victory! Victory! Victory is at hand for my Queen!"

Raleigh shouted, "For God's sake call them back, you idiot! You're sending them to their death!"

Essex's face flushed red as the setting sun, hot with fury. For a moment his hand grasped the hilt of his sword, then dropped. "You doubt their courage? For shame, Sir Walter." Then, icily, "Be good enough to remember who is in command, Sir Walter."

Hastily Raleigh apologized, mastering his rage and, honey on his tongue, summoned up all his persuasive eloquence. He had simply come over to speak to his Commander, he said, about his Commander's plans.

Later, in a soberly penned account of the action at Cadiz, praising everyone and himself in particular, he mentioned the incident: "I protested against the plan of my Lord of Essex, demonstrating that he risked our general ruin, to the utter overthrow of Her Majesty's expedition. But the Earl would not consent to enter the harbor with the fleet until the town was first taken."

Raleigh then called a conference of all the ships' captains in Essex's cabin. His account read: "All the commanders joined me in my attempt to dissuade the Earl, for they were seamen and foresaw the danger, and said most respectfully to the Earl, 'They will perish in the sea before ever they set foot on the land.'"

Faced with such weight of professional opinion, Essex let himself be persuaded and ordered a signal flag displayed that would call the boats back. Raleigh bowed, said he was sure it would be done at once. He could well be sure! He had already ordered it done. Of all Raleigh's faithful sea-captains not one loved him with such doglike adoration as Lawrence Keymis, a comrade of his youth who had shared most of the years of his master's checkered career, basking in his master's favor when his master was rising to power, serving him without complaint when his master was disgraced. Frequently he protested to his friends, "I would die for him." (One day he would blow out his brains because he would think he had brought his master bad luck.) Raleigh trusted few men. He trusted Lawrence Keymis.

Captain Lawrence Keymis did not attend the conference of captains in Essex's cabin that evening. He was on the quarterdeck of the flagship. "Before that sun sets," whispered Raleigh in his ear, "run up the signal to recall the boats."

If Keymis had had a tail he'd have wagged it. If he'd had the body of a dog instead of a dog's loving nature he'd have licked Raleigh's hand. He simply whispered, "Aye, Sir Walter."

Soon the men were all back safe in their own ships glad to be alive.

The Spanish garrison, having finished their supper, decided with some logic that it had all been a perfidious English trick and went to bed, having primed their guns and prepared for a leisurely victory over the heretic English expedition next morning.

God and the saints were on their side.

[232]

But not the God of Battles.

Next day disaster fell upon Cadiz.

At sunrise the action began. Raleigh and Essex, in their separate ships, vied with each other to be first to enter the harbor. Fire from the Spanish forts was noisy but inaccurate, the Spanish gunners being long unused to their cannon. At every salvo from the walls Raleigh ordered a fanfare of trumpets, ending with an insulting sound like a horse breaking wind—you could almost smell the stink—thus signifying his contempt, disdaining to answer till he was closer in: he had his eye on four huge galleons at the harbor's mouth, coveted them all, the loot in their fat holds, the prize money he could demand for himself.

Fire from the Spanish warships, however, long accustomed to convoy and protect the galleons, was more accurate, and soon there were casualties among the English.

Essex saw with anger that Raleigh's ship, faster than his own, was forging ahead of him; it looked as if Raleigh were going to beat him into the harbor. Essex ordered an English ship which had lost her sails in a hail of chainshot and lay dead in the water to throw a line over Raleigh's stern. It was an unseamanlike command, thought Raleigh, since he would only tow the disabled ship closer to enemy fire—far better to have had some other ship tow her the other way, out of range. He suspected the jealous Earl was trying to slow him down so that he, the Earl, would be first into Cadiz, get all the glory for himself. "A scurvy trick!" Seizing an axe he raced to the offending towline and chopped it off with one stroke. His sailors chuckled, "Derrick himself couldn't have chopped cleaner!" The disabled ship drifted astern, out of danger, while Raleigh's ship shot ahead, firing as she went, her seamen cheering, her guns taking a terrible toll of the Spanish warships.

Soon the Spaniards withdrew their four galleons to

the inner harbor. Not only the English fire but fire from their own warships was damaging them in the crowded sea battle that now raged on all sides.

As the English passed the forts and entered the estuary the Spanish cannon atop the walls became useless: they could not be depressed to aim at the English below them. When the gunners attempted to point them down the cannonballs fell out. Nor could they be turned around. It had never occurred to the Spaniards that they might one day be required to shoot at enemy ships in the estuary.

Within the harbor the sea fight continued for four hours with heavy casualties to ships and men on both sides. The air over Cadiz, yesterday so fragrant, now stank of gunpowder and blood, and the sky grew dark from the smoke of burning ships.

Suddenly Raleigh felt a blow in his leg. He thought he had barked his shin on some piece of equipment dislodged by the gunfire. He looked down, and there, sticking out of a bloody embroidered stocking worth twenty pounds, was a six-inch splinter of wood embedded in his calf. He bent down, yanked it out, still feeling nothing. A sailor wound on a tourniquet. Later the wound was to cause him great pain.

Still in command of himself and his ship he beheld with dismay that two of the galleons had beached themselves and set themselves afire. Essex gave no orders to board and take the other two. But Raleigh did, and was instantly obeyed. "The Earl hath no need of prize money," he grumbled, "but I have." So had all the other English ship captains, which explains why the two galleons were promptly grappled, boarded, overwhelmed and sailed out of the battle on a course to England, with English prize crews and many Spanish prisoners likely to be ransomed aboard.

Now, all over the harbor, Spanish ships began to set themselves afire and scuttle themselves. "The waste is appalling!" thought Raleigh; but, remembering the last fight of the *Revenge*, he could not but admire it. "This is what the crew of the *Revenge* should have done when Sir Richard ordered them to. The brave are always brave, the craven always craven, and betwixt the bravery of English and Spanish seamen I trow there be little to choose."

Ashore, in the town, fires began to break out, some caused by English incendiary bombs, some set by the Spaniards themselves, following the example of their ships. Warehouses, stored with the spoils of the whole world, began to burn.

Now the English crews with their contingent of soldiers stormed ashore. There was terrible slaughter. The English displayed some restraint, not because they particularly disliked killing Spaniards but because every soldier and sailor had his eye out for ransom money: the more prisoners they took alive, the greater their share. But there were many volunteer Dutchmen among the English soldiery, desperate men who had lost all. The people of the Netherlands had suffered dreadful atrocities at the hands of the Spaniards. The Dutchmen now paid it back with maniacal frenzy.

Raleigh had himself rowed ashore. His wound had now begun to hurt. In pain himself, he could sympathize with the pain of others. There was all too much to see. He wrote: "As the Spanish ships burned themselves the spectacle was very lamentable; many perished in the fires; many, half-burnt, their lower parts aflame, leapt into the water in hope that the water would put out the pain of their grievous wounds, but in the end they sank and drowned."

Raleigh was not the only one who viewed the destruction of Cadiz as appalling waste. A group of Spanish merchants, who traded throughout the Spanish Empire, whose merchandise lay in the warehouses which they now saw going up in flames, hastily sent a delegation to the English flagship and offered two million pounds if the English would stop the fight and withdraw from the city.

The English thought, "If they offer two million, the loot is surely worth four," and answered that they would assemble a committee at once and consider the matter and give the merchants their reply with all speed.

The merchants departed, disgruntled, with a fatalistic shrug. They knew the "speed" with which English committees conferred. They knew too that it is always useless to bargain with victors, who can always get all you offer and more just for the taking. Still, it had been worth a try: bankruptcy stared them in the face. Many a drowning man that day had grasped at straws.

The sack of the city continued all night, with all the horrors that occur when a mob of looters gets out of control, when darkness covers individual crimes.

Some semblance of order came with the dawn. Soldiers and seamen returned to the English ships; the captains regained control. That day the English Navy captured sixteen Spanish warships, still in good condition in the harbor, put English prize-crews aboard them and sailed them with their Spanish prisoners to England. Thirteen other Spanish warships had been destroyed the day before. In addition, the Royal Navy systematically looted, then burned, forty merchant vessels, confiscating their valuable cargoes. Such Spaniards as remained aboard were permitted to escape, since there was now no room in the English ships for prisoners and booty too; and even the Dutch were sick of the sight of blood.

The action at Cadiz was over; the English victory was complete, one more spectacular page in the brilliant annals of British naval history.

The English fleet sailed home in triumph. Behind them rose the smoke and the stench of the holocaust, befouling the Andalusian sky. Queen Elizabeth's royal standard fluttered from the mastheads of all her ships; captured

Spanish flags and Popish gonfalons, specially blessed and woven from the virgin wool of little lambs at Pascaltide, were used by the sailors at the latrines when they went to relieve themselves.

The financial loss to King Philip was virtually beyond estimate. His treasurer guessed it might come to forty millions of English pounds. The loss in warships was even worse: he would have to build many more ships before he could mount another invasion attempt.

In Madrid, pondering the news of the burning of Cadiz, he shook his weary head, muttered the last words from the Cross in the ancient tongue, "*Eli, Eli, lama sabachthani,*" and checked himself, "Nay, those were the words of the Son of God!" and struck his breast in a penitential gesture like that of the priest at the Mass when he says, "*Domine, non sum dignus.*" But his confessor promptly reassured him: when Jesus spoke those words from the Cross, He was merely quoting an ancient psalm, voicing the sadness He felt for ungodly men who forsake God and are themselves forsaken. "For it is clear, Your Imperial Majesty, that the Son of God, being one and the same with God Himself, cannot forsake God," and counselled the King to look rather to the Book of Job, who was chastened almost beyond endurance, but in the end God rehabilitated and rewarded him.

"Aye," said the King, "He chasteneth whom He loveth," and took heart.

With a stroke of his pen he repudiated all of Spain's debts. All 'round the world millions of his subjects went bankrupt. He resolved to build ships for another Armada. His faith never faltered nor failed.

Raleigh's wound healed slowly and painfully, despite all his medicines, but without infection. "Were more people to employ my special unguent," he congratulated himself, "and leave off the boiling oil and the red-hot cauteries of the surgeons, I trow there would be fewer putrid sores in this world." But it irked him that his leg was stiff. He limped for the rest of his life. He retired to Sherborne, where Lady Raleigh bore him another son.

In the Admiralty's public paper recounting the victory at Cadiz Raleigh was highly praised: "The chiefest for the sea service besides the Earl was Sir Walter Raleigh." And Raleigh himself in a separate letter for publication wrote: "The Earl behaved himself valiantly and advisedly in the highest degree, without vainglory or cruelty to the enemy, and hath gotten himself great honor and much love of all Englishmen thereby." But secretly he blamed Essex for Essex's inane unseamanlike commands, especially the endangering of the men in the boats; and he was jealous because Essex had got the lion's share of prize money, though this was in accordance with Admiralty usage: namely, that the Commander-in-Chief gets more than his subordinates. Raleigh's share was by no means inconsiderable; he simply thought he should have been the Commander-in-Chief.

In a testy letter to Robert Cecil he complained that many dishonest ship captains and commanders of the soldiers had stolen money and jewels and silver plate from the warehouses, "though they declare to be little what they have taken for themselves or naught."

Cecil thought this was very likely true; but a moment of great national victory is no moment to bring charges against the valiant men who have won that victory. Nothing was said of the matter. "For my part," Raleigh said, "I have gotten a lame leg and deformed." He conceded that everyone was kind to him, and declared with some irony, "There is no dearth of fair words and good usage. But I came out of this enterprise in possession of nothing but poverty and pain."

The diminutive Secretary of State, Elizabeth's "pygmy," rubbed his sparsely bearded chin. "Poverty?

Fiddlesticks!" Raleigh was one of the richest men in England. Secretly he had always envied Raleigh's commanding stature. Wouldn't it be nice if Raleigh were to lose that long and shapely leg! But Raleigh didn't, it only went gimpy; and Cecil wrote him a diplomatic letter congratulating him on his recovery. For Raleigh seemed to be rising once more in the Queen's capricious favor.

She had never actually stripped him of his title, Captain of the Guard. But ever since his marriage she had not allowed him to discharge the duties attached to that office. Now, after the victory at Cadiz, she reinstated him. Him, of all men, she could trust to protect her person, which was threatened.

Quite recently her Jewish physician had been falsely accused of plotting to poison her. Lord Essex, in a frenzy of loyalty, made it his personal business to prove that the physician was in the pay of the King of Spain; and indeed he unearthed some incriminating letters. King Philip, as always, had written to everyone close to Elizabeth, promising God's blessing and Spanish gold if only someone would murder her. Nothing was proved; Elizabeth refused to sign a death warrant. Without her consent, Essex had the Jew hanged. Elizabeth mourned, for she had liked the man, but once he was dead there was nothing she could do to bring him back to life, and Essex quite truthfully said that his death would prove a warning to others. Elizabeth thanked him for his loyalty. She still loved him, still wore the ring he had given her long ago.

Recuperating at Sherborne, Raleigh now received sad news. "Ah, would that that great Englishman had lived to hear of Cadiz!" Sir Francis Drake had died of a fever in the West Indies. Drake, like Raleigh, was a Westcountry man and distantly related. "He died in his ship," mused Raleigh, "and they buried him at sea. So it is with all of us; the sea claims us in the end; so will it be with me."

The death of Drake confirmed the Queen in her decision to rehabilitate Raleigh. Drake had known how to win sea battles, Raleigh also, especially at Cadiz. She must treasure, hoard up, favor such men, for word had come that the indefatigable Spider of Madrid was building another Armada. "How *can* he?" she wondered and answered herself, "With slave labor of course; alas, probably many of my own." For she knew that a quirk of Nature had brought a climatic disaster to Spain. There was no rain, the harvests withered and rotted, people went hungry.

But the same climatic phenomenon brought scanty harvests in England and Ireland also. "If, as I hear from my spies, King Philip constantly says 'He chasteneth whom He loveth,' it seems to me that the good Lord loveth us both and chasteneth us equally." She deputed Lord Burleigh to distribute such food as was available to the hungry, lest they revolt; and, confiscating all Raleigh's potatoes, had them transshipped to England, lest Raleigh, who disliked seeing children starve, give potatoes to starving Irish children.

Ancient Lord Burleigh looked very bad. All the time he was agreeing to carry out the Queen's commands he seemed only half aware of the world, reverting to calling Elizabeth, "my pretty little princess." Robert Cecil, his son, looked on, sadly shaking his head. "My father is failing," he said. "Little pygmy," said Elizabeth, not unkindly, "see to it you fail not your father, see to it my commands are carried out." Cecil said he would, and meant it.

Burleigh's last days were peaceful. "Thou'st done for me more than all others together," Elizabeth breathed in his ear, but he was deaf and could not hear her. "What did you say, my princess? Whatever you said, God bless you." "You too, my dear friend, as assuredly He will." "What did you say, pretty one?"

Peacefully he passed away, his pretty princess nursing

him to the end, spoon-feeding him like an infant, like the baby she never had had; how she'd have loved one! Just before he died he said, "What a beautiful girl thou art! How comes it to be that this beautiful girl hath in her nature that which shall make of our little island an Empire!" She closed his blind, dead eyes. "God knows, dear my Burleigh, but that I will do," and wept.

A contemporary wrote:

> His funeral was performed yesterday, with all the rites that belong to so great a personage. The number of mourners was above five hundred, with many officials wearing their golden chains of office. There were many noblemen and among the rest the Earl of Essex who, whether it were upon consideration of the present occasion or by reason of his own disfavor, methought carried the heaviest countenance of the company. As for the Earl, the Queen says he hath played upon her long enough, and that now she means to play upon him. But this is no doubt a mere pettifog wrought by her grief, for she loves him still.

The cause of Lord Essex's "disfavor" was an old one, one that never failed to exasperate Elizabeth. Another of her waiting-women, one of the most beautiful, not daring to marry, had fallen in love and become pregnant. Great physical beauty seems to have run in the Essex blood: the young and lovely girl was his cousin. The man she loved was noble, another Earl, the Earl of Southampton, and, by a quirk of chance, as handsome as she was beautiful. Both the Earl and the girl had hidden their love as long as possible, fearing the fury of the Queen.

Now the Earl of Essex came forward with one of the most heartwarming acts of all his romantic impulsive career. Risking everything, heedless of self, he bade the lovers have no fear. He arranged all the details for a marriage. Once they were married he took them to Essex

House, his own residence, where he sheltered and protected them, boldly avowing his part in the affair. All England applauded. More than ever Essex was their darling, their hero.

But he could not protect them long. In her loneliness, weeping, again betrayed, Queen Elizabeth clapped them both into prison, and Lord Essex again was forbidden the Court.

The next month Lady Elizabeth Vernon, now wife of the Earl of Southampton, gave birth, at full term, to a beautiful baby girl. Southampton held Essex in great affection for the rest of his life and was constantly in hot water as the result of his loyalty to his friend, as Essex went up and down in his rash and erratic career.

Sensing the temper of her people and needing brave men, Elizabeth shortly released them all, and Essex again took his place at Court. There was trouble again in Ireland.

It was a year of death among the great of her Age. Hard upon Burleigh's demise came news out of Spain that King Philip was in extremis. Philip had long foreseen the manner of his passing, meticulously arranged for everything in advance. He ordered brought to his bedside a shirt of lead in which his corpse was to be wrapped. He ordered artisans to construct a leaden coffin in which his corpse was to lie. Bravely he bore the pain that afflicted him in his last hours. His body had greatly decayed. All over it were suppurating sores. He stank. His son held his nose. In Sherborne Sir Walter wondered what the malady could be, guessed it must be the Great Pox contracted from Bloody Mary, his English Queen who, in turn, had got the infection from her father, King Henry VIII, who also stank before they buried him, stank from the billions of spirochetes that were in him, the Curse of the Tudors.

King Philip's fortitude passes belief: he never complained, never moaned as do ordinary men when racked with pain. He prayed to his Spanish God, sure that all was well—with Spain, with himself in the Afterworld, with that other Armada a-building and the utter downfall of that heretic bastard Queen Elizabeth. At one time in the course of his terminal illness his doctors pronounced him dead. Then at the touch of some relics he revived. He raised his hand to make the sign of the Cross, forgave his enemies, blessed his son, who fled, sick, from the death chamber; and then King Philip died. He was seventy-two years old. Never in seventy-two years had he made a mistake—this conviction comforted him. All 'round the world throughout the Holy Roman Empire on which the sun never set there were constant tolling of bells and Spanish prayers for the repose of his soul.

Philip's Imperial son, more than half demented, knelt in the cellars of the Escurial and prayed, "God in His Holy Trinity, bestow thy blessings upon my dear father," harkening enthralled to the solemn dirge of the subterranean organ, "and spare him the pains of Purgatory," and thought, "Now I am free."

Orchard men, who love fruit trees, have sometimes been witness to a curious natural phenomenon. Fruit trees bloom once a year, in the springtime, and display their blossoms, often most colorful, often sweet-smelling. Color and fragrance, full of the promise of nectar, attract bees, which fertilize the trees, having recently visited trees of the opposite sex and carried on their furry legs the golden fertilizing pollen. Then the blossoms fade, having fulfilled their purpose, and in their place appear the swelling baby fruit that will grow to maturity in the autumn. This is natural and healthy, and the cycle repeats itself year after year.

But sometimes a tree grows old and sick and blooms not once but twice, the second time just before winter sets in, a winter the tree will not survive. Some natural philosophers speculate that the tree possesses a dim consciousness, knows it is dying, senses, "You personally will not survive. Therefore blossom again, that your sons may live after you." Whatever the reason, moribund trees do occasionally blossom again just before they die.

In Ireland Edmund Spenser had married and his wife had borne him a son. She was the daughter of a penniless English soldier who had gone to Ireland to fight the Papists and seek his fortune. Through bravery, skill and furiously repressive measures he had found the fortune he sought, risen high in the English occupying army. More than a soldier, he was also a clever politician and wielded considerable influence when estates were taken from the Irish and bestowed upon deserving Englishmen. When he died his orphaned daughter inherited some of his traits, but a softer heart and more delicate tastes.

Her name was Elizabeth, like the names of so many girls in the age of the Great Queen. She was attracted to the pale and sickly Puritan poet. Through her influence he obtained his sinecure in the Chancery, his cottage at Cork, and after he married it was through her that he got Kilcolman Castle, through her he was able to stave off the creditors when he would not, or simply forgot to, pay the very nominal rent. He wooed her with love poems. When he married her he wrote the tender "Epithalamion" to celebrate their marriage, since then a treasured gem of Elizabethan poetry. Victorian ladies were cautioned not to read it; those who sneaked a look into it swooned and called for the smelling salts. "Epithalamion" is an explicit, detailed, erotic account of the ecstasy of married love, love never before experienced by Edmund Spenser, never so beautifully enshrined in verse by a great English poet.

The trouble erupting in Ireland was caused by the drought that had smitten the whole of western Europe,

Ireland, Scotland, England and Spain. Hungry inhabitants of those countries could not know that the blight was universal throughout all Europe, thought they were the only ones doomed to starve and reacted accordingly, blaming their natural enemies, as if those enemies had somehow cursed them with the drought. Tempers grew short and each man, bewildered, thought only of himself, of how he could survive, and of the children who looked to him for food, their bellies pitifully bloated. Desperate hungry men always take to thievery, murder, revolution. To make things worse, King Philip, just before he died, dispatched a contingent of Spanish assassins to Ireland, whose mission was to slaughter the English oppressors of his well-loved Irish Papists, snatching the food he was certain the English were hiding, denying the Irish.

Essex said to Elizabeth, "Ma'am, permit me to go over to Ireland and put things right, as I swear by the living God I will do."

Again she appointed him General in charge of more soldiers who, he assured her, would put things right in Ireland.

Canny Robert Cecil suggested, "Ma'am, hadn't Sir Walter better go too? Raleigh hath greater experience in Ireland," and forebore to mention that Raleigh had suffered fewer defeats and was far better balanced then Essex.

Queen Elizabeth promptly agreed.

Raleigh was commissioned forthwith to cross over to Ireland and help quash the revolt.

But when Raleigh found out that Lord Essex was again to be General and he was again to serve under him, he sulked and wanted no part of it, pleaded the sickness of his leg as an incapacity. Besides, Diana had taken all those potatoes.

To the Queen's great delight Essex's campaign against the Irish was a rousing success. He thoroughly vanquished the Irish, forever she hoped, and many Spaniards were killed.

In gratitude toward his faithful retainers Lord Essex began dubbing them knights right and left—any knight could make anybody else a knight. There needed to be no ritual, no kneeling, no ceremonial touching of shoulder with sword. The jollier sort, like Lord Essex, liked the ancient way: a good hard bash of the fist to the favored one's chest.

A contemporary wrote:

The Earl of Essex hath made many new knights, but I cannot yet come by the total; but marry! for a taste here be Sir Henry Lindley, Sir Harry Carry, two Lovelaces, Sir Ajax Harrington, Sir Jack Heydon, Sir Dick Morrison, all persons of no account, with many other English and even some Irish withal, which were a shame, to the number of fifty-nine in the whole. It is much marveled that this humor should so possess the Lord Essex; for, not content with his first dozens and scores, he huddles them up by half-hundreds; and it is noted that the Earl upon so little service, hath made in so short a time more knights than were all hitherto knighted in the realm; nor is it doubted that if he continue in this course he will shortly bring in tag and rag, cut and longtail, and so draw the Order of Knighthood into contempt of all men.

Queen Elizabeth sighed, as often she did in these troublesome days. But when, thought she, had her days not been troublesome? Lord Essex, her darling, the darling of England, was cheapening the honor of knighthood, revered since time out of mind, since that distant legendary age of King Arthur and his knights of the Round Table. She murmured, "Sir Walter called me 'England'; and now Lord Essex hath cheapened me." But Essex had won a notable victory. There would be no more trouble in Ireland. "*Video, taceo,*" she mused.

"Essex worsted the filthy vile whoreson Spaniards," and caressed the ring he had given her.

Essex returned to England to the universal applause of the people. Queen Elizabeth received him with favor, ordered fireworks set off in his honor over the Thames.

Proudly kneeling before her, tears in his large and limpid eyes, he said, "Madame, I did it for you."

She kissed him on the mouth, that common English salutation which so scandalized the Spaniards. "Thank you, my dear friend."

But the great victory of Essex in Ireland wasn't so great after all. The hungry kerns rose up in arms, they burned Kilcolman Castle. Spenser escaped by the skin of his teeth and his little son perished in the flames. "Goddamn them to deepest most fieryest Hell!" swore the gentle Puritan poet, then, "Oh my dear God, I beg of thee, please, please, if it please Thee, grant that my poor little boy didn't hurt too much in the fire."

This from the man who had conjured the Gods in most beautiful verse to grant him sons and sons of sons in his "Epithalamion." "*Pulvus*," mused Spenser in agony, remembering his Horace, ashes; "*et ombra*": naught but a shadow of loving remembrance.

Then he sat down, for words were his life, and penned against the Irish the most vicious political diatribe ever written against that hapless race by an Englishman. In essence he growled, "Destroy them!"

In England this was received with much nodding of heads and profound parliamentary agreement. His verses were famous. That the author of *The Fairy Queen* was in total accord with English parliamentarians was taken as assurance of English rectitude in foreign policy.

His castle in ruins, his son dead, Spenser went with his wife from Kilcolman to his little cottage in Cork, not caring whether he lived or died. The waning spark of life already was flickering out of his sickly body. He died.

They shipped his pallid and wasted corpse, so light that by now a child could have carried it, over to England and there he was buried in Westminster Abbey close to the grave of Chaucer.

Notables, noblemen, artists and poets went to his funeral. An extraordinary occurrence took place as his coffin was lowered into the earth. Many of the mourners had written him elegies. Mingling with the ceremonial dust cast upon the coffin little white sheets of paper on which the elegies were written fluttered down. Then the mourners threw into the grave the pens that had written them.

CHAPTER XX

AT SHERBORNE Sir Walter Raleigh lived in dignified retirement, possessed of all his titles and honors. But he wasn't wanted at Court. Elizabeth preferred her Essex, and, on the political level, was sensitive to the hatred her people felt toward Raleigh.

Raleigh had salvaged some potatoes, planted them, exulted when they flourished; and tobacco, to which he had now become addicted; and some sweet-savored spiny vegetables called pineapples, brought from Virginia, the only place in the world they were known, by one of his sea captains. The pineapples didn't do well.

Raleigh loved all growing things.

He set up a chemical laboratory and spent many hours each day concocting elaborate elixirs which he was certain would cure all human ills once he perfected them.

This was one of the happier periods of his life.

But his pen was busy too, as always. He wrote several letters to Robert Cecil, warning the Secretary of State that King Philip's naval ambitions had survived him, that another Armada was a-building and England had better beware.

Cecil, however, wanted peace with Spain, bent all his considerable talents toward that end and did not answer Raleigh's letters.

Then Robert Cecil's wife died, and his son, who was growing up and precociously literate, wandered around forlorn and unnoticed among Cecil's entourage of elderly statesmen, spies and parliamentarians and other high-placed officials who had no time for a lonesome little boy whom his father was too busy to notice.

At Sherborne Lady Raleigh heard of the child's predicament. "Water," she said, with her Westcountry accent, "that poor little thing!" The Raleighs had sons of their own, loved them dearly as they loved pets and gardens and all growing things, for they sensed that they held promise of life that endures when old lives pass away. "That poor little thing, walking about on those cold marble floors amongst men who say 'Yes, Master Cecil,' and 'No, Master Cecil,' and don't give a hoot if he eats right, or care if he gets a cough, and don't know when to put him to bed. It's a shame!"

Raleigh said, "Good Bess, I should have thought of that myself; it takes a woman to know these things; God bless you."

Shortly he offered the hospitality of Sherborne to Robert Cecil's son.

The ancient feudal custom of packing off noble sons to be brought up and taught good manners by other highly placed persons was not quite dead, was still remembered and thoroughly respectable. Cecil acceded with thanks and perhaps some relief—how *could* he care for his son? And hired governesses were undependable, felt no affection, sought only to please their masters.

So young master Cecil came to Sherborne, romped with the Raleigh sons, and Bess Raleigh grew to love him like one of her own. As for Sir Walter, he was delighted with the child, physicked the boy who had come to him pale, underweight and sickly.

Walter Raleigh's copious correspondence usually complained about something, asked for something, or, as in his letters to the Queen, struck a self-seeking note in high, flowery rhetoric. But his letter to the Secretary of State, one of his most endearing, came from the heart:

Little Will, he said, was thriving, putting on flesh, eating well and digesting his food and was happy; happy as he himself was to have him there, as was his good wife Bess. (It was noteworthy that in this letter he put on no airs and called her his "good wife," not "Lady Raleigh.")

The boy returned the motherly-fatherly love bestowed upon him. Once, when Raleigh was away trying to get his underpaid miners in the stanneries more pay, little Will Cecil wrote him a letter:

> Sir Walter: We all cry out and exclaim that you are absent, like soldiers who know not what to do when their Commander is not with them. Therefore I pray you, Sir Walter, leave off all idle matters and come home to us who love you.

This charming epistle was probably edited by Bess Raleigh but the boy, who had spunk, wouldn't have signed it if it had not expressed his own sentiments.

This period of his life, which Raleigh remembered as his happiest during all the long years that remained to him, was actually one of political rustication. He wanted instant war with Spain. The aging Queen and her Secretary of State were for compromise and accommodation. Lord Essex, reflecting the temper of his Queen, said, "To give that firebrand Raleigh his head were to embrue Your Majesty's kingdom red with blood and belike endanger Your Majesty's sacred person also." The Secretary of State thought the same. So did the Queen. Old Burleigh would have said, "Little princess, when women grow old they tremble at shadows." But Burleigh no longer was there to advise her.

At Court things went their merry English way, rapidly sliding downhill, amidst cheerful chatter and idle gossip—who was seducing whom and what shaggy Siberian bear would be bloodiest at the next bearbaiting in the bear garden, where the Queen had her canopied pavilion and clapped her pretty hands and urged the dogs on to their work, like all noble ladies at this popular sport.

Nor was there dearth of other amusement and gossip: the hanging of a Jesuit, the next poetic sermon preached by the popular Dean, John Donne, who saw visions in color and extolled the virtues of virginity, begat eight children and lost his mind; the appearance in the heavens of a blazing star that everyone knew caused the birth of a two-headed calf in Kent and foreshadowed the death of a Queen, or perhaps merely the plague; and an earl who lost his daughter's dowry on a wager whilst playing at tennis. Some of these things came true, just as when you say, "It is going to rain," and eventually it does, and you are accounted a prophet.

All this—the gossip, the cruel sports, the jolly amusements—coexisted cheek by jowl in the wide-open all-welcoming Elizabethan mind, which could entertain concepts that were mutually exclusive without questioning their contradictory nature. Elizabeth was the apotheosis of her age, an age that produced a host of genuises never before or since equaled in the English-speaking world.

Underneath all the trivia, failings and contradictions of her age there was, as there was in her, a solid foundation of sterling good sense.

At Elizabeth's Court, where Essex reigned supreme, fawned upon by all men because of her love for him, a deplorable event occurred.

Essex had access to her chambers night and day.

One day she rebuked him for some quite inconsequential misdemeanor. Brooding upon her rebuke that night he stormed into her chamber and shouted, "I didn't!"

She was in her shift, her shoulders naked.

Only Lord Burleigh had known, but one of her shoulders was slightly deformed, just a bit lower than the other.

The Earl of Essex looked, yelled, "Ha! Your body is as crooked as your mind!"

She stood up and walloped him a resounding slap, right on the cheek she so loved.

Essex, fuming, half drew his sword, thrust it back into its scabbard, knelt, wept, cried, "Oh my God, what have I done!"

Gently she raised him to his feet. Her face had gone white under her rouge. "You are beside yourself, my Lord Essex," she said. "Pray get you to bed and get some sleep, and try to behave yourself hereafter."

"Madame, dear Madame . . ."

"Get out!"

Raleigh always believed it was this bedroom incident that doomed Essex to death, not his subsequent rebellion, not his erratic behavior—he had always been erratic, she had always rather fancied it. No, not that. It was his discovery of a secret deformity. Physical vagaries ran in the family of Tudor: Bloody Mary's protruding forehead and squashed-looking nose; Bloody Mary's sterility; Elizabeth's mother's extra finger and Elizabeth's own awkward gait, caused by a twisted pelvis she cleverly hid and that nobody knew about, not even her Jewish physician whom Essex had hanged; worst of all, her own sterility, the sterility of one who loved children and could not bear them, loved beauty, fostered it in poetry, architecture, philosophy—but knew it did not exist in her own royal body, to all outward appearances so girlish, svelte, lithe and attractive no matter how old she became. Sometimes she mourned in secret, "Would God I were a mere peasant with a brood of brats about me to love!" But of course she wasn't, she was royalty, England, and, drawing herself up, remembering, she would say to herself, "*Video, taceo,* I cannot bear brats but burdens I can and I will, and belike my kingdom shall profit thereby; for all that I can, I shall do."

The Earl of Essex behaved himself thereafter, and all

went on as if nothing had happened—till something did, something big.

Despite his ineptitude as a soldier, his absurdity as a naval commander, his many defeats and repeated blunders, Lord Essex remained popular. Elizabeth retained him at Court and conferred honor after honor upon him. He lived far beyond his means. Elizabeth repeatedly paid his debts.

His estimate of his own importance, always great, now swelled to inordinate proportions. If Raleigh had a touch of paranoia, Lord Essex assuredly had more than a touch of megalomania.

He remembered that he was a true and direct descendant of the Plantagenet kings; why! his blood was more royal than Elizabeth's own. A mere Tudor slapping a Plantagenet! It was unthinkable; it should have been the other way 'round. And how it irked him that Sir Walter had disobeyed his commands at Cadiz and by so doing won part of the credit for that victory which should have been all his.

But now, out of Ireland, through Cecil's spies, ugly rumors began to filter back to Elizabeth. Essex really hadn't tried very hard. The rousing "victory" over the Irish had soon faded, and the rebellion which soon flared up again after his departure was actually caused by the Earl himself: he had secretly met with Tyrone, the rebel leader, a quick-witted able man who saw through the Earl at a glance, discovered his basic weakness, played upon it and thoroughly duped him. "If you were the King of England," said the Irish tempter, "would you make me Viceroy of Ireland?"

Essex was startled. Visions of the grandeur of sovereignty dazzled him. Elizabeth's death was surely not far away. There were many other claimants besides the feeble Scottish King? Why not himself? Was he not a Plantagenet?

"I would," he answered the Irishman.

Robert Devereux, Earl of Essex, scion of the royal Plantagenets, King of England! The name rang in his ears like a joyful carillon of bells at his coronation. King Robert, restoring the ancient Plantagenet dynasty. "They were really much like me," he thought, "me, who have their blood . . . ," The chivalrous knights, the victorious warriors, the romantic poets—they lived long, long ago, but not too long ago to revive them for the glory of England and the good of his people, *his* people—"Yes, much like me." And what would this paltry Westcountry upstart be then, he thought. But no, he wouldn't punish Raleigh too severely; after all, he *had* done some minor service; just put him back in his place where he belonged.

For a while, when these rumors were at their height, Queen Elizabeth held him in house arrest. It was hard to prove the meeting with Tyrone. Nor, in her heart, did she really want to believe it. Impossible that Essex would stoop to conspire with an Irishman! Besides, the people were murmuring against Raleigh. Essex had cleverly had it bruited about that Raleigh had started the traitorous gossip. Cecil shook his head, knew that Raleigh was not at fault; but suspected that if Raleigh had not actually started the rumors it was quite possible that he had done nothing to stop them.

So Cecil held his peace; had the truth come out it would have destroyed the Earl. Elizabeth deemed it impolitic to destroy the best loved man in England; the worst hated got the blame.

Shortly the Earl was back at Court. Raleigh remained at Sherborne, conscious of his unpopularity but pleased and surprised that the powerful Secretary of State still seemed to trust him, for Cecil left little Will in Sir Walter's and Bess Raleigh's loving care.

Only the great heads of state in Europe and the more powerful English nobility knew the truth, and each only a part of the truth, each being encouraged to believe that his own private ambitions were to be rewarded when God, in His wisdom, should take to His own the magnificent Queen who had reigned over England for forty-four years. The astute little hunchback was secretly playing all sides against all others, a valuable skill in a diplomat, requiring an especially high order of tact. Elizabeth had not named her successor; he must keep on good terms with everybody and wait upon events, for Cecil, the peaceful, feared civil or foreign war. Be it said to his credit that in this he had the good of England at heart.

Now the time of year arrived fot the Queen to make public her Honors list: the elevation of new lords, issuance of new patents of nobility, bestowal of coronets, the coveted right to add another stripe of ermine to a ceremonial cloak, the granting of pensions, the creation of admirals, generals, masters of artillery, and a host of useless old feudal honors that gave their recipients no duties but gave them great credit with tailors and tradesmen. Raleigh got nothing; Essex, much, but he thought he deserved more. This was the spark that nearly ignited the flames of a civil war, and brought on the Essex Rebellion that broke Queen Elizabeth's heart.

The angry Earl wrote to King James of Scotland, asked him to raise an army, invade England and take over the realm. The Queen had not nominated a successor, he said to King James. King James would never be King of England except by invasion to assert his rights, there being so many other claimants. Sir Christopher Blount, a respectable man, Essex's father-in-law, seconded the invitation.

In every country in the world it was high treason to invite a foreign army to invade a nation; it was then, still is.

The Secretary of State intercepted the letter, read it, sent it on to the King with a letter of his own: the Queen of England, he told King James, contrary to the Earl's assertion, had indeed nominated a successor, King James himself; her Privy Council had been told and applauded; she had simply not made the fact public, being in excellent health and not wishing to cause unrest. There were evil men among other aspirants who would stick at nothing, warned Cecil, not even the murder of James himself, to eliminate Her Majesty's nominee, the best qualified successor to the throne.

As a result, King James did not even answer Essex's letter—but it had charmed him. "No wonder the people love the dear lad," he thought; "he's so very understanding. And I hear he does not befoul his bonny mouth by taking tobacco."

King James had his spies at Elizabeth's Court too. They gave him an altogether different version of Elizabeth's health. He had only to wait, probably not very long. Then he would honor Lord Essex as the handsome young fellow deserved.

Receiving no answer from Scotland, Lord Essex took matters into his own hands. He gathered together all his new knights and a few armed followers and marched on Queen Elizabeth's palace, planning to take her hostage and await the revolution. Blount accompanied him, to give the rebellious force an appearance of legality. So did Derrick, the public hangman, as a personal bodyguard, for Essex kept shouting, "Traitors are plotting to murder me, a plot is laid against my life!" Derrick was to deal with them.

Essex was sure that the populace would rise and join him, that his little force would become an army.

But as he passed through the streets, not a man stirred from his place; they looked on in silence, many in tears. Clearly their darling was out of his wits, his eyes were wild, his yelling frenzied and incoherent. Most of his followers deserted him, fearing hanged necks and sundered quarters. The hangman slunk back to his favorite alehouse, not wishing to be seen with an unsuccessful traitor, ready to assume whatever new duties his office might require of him.

What had threatened to become a revolution had dwindled to the size of a street riot.

Essex suddenly underwent a¹ curious alteration of mind. The Queen was in danger! He must save her!

"To the Queen! To the Queen!" he shouted. "Walter Raleigh hath plotted to murder her! To the Queen!"

But Elizabeth was in no danger. The Secretary of State had seen to it her palace was guarded securely by soldiers.

"Shoot! Shoot!" cried the Earl. "Save the Queen!"

Faced by the stern-faced militia all but a handful of Essex's followers melted away without firing.

Now all the strength that excitement had generated in his body throughout the day drained out of him. His body ached, he wanted to go home. When he came to his home, Essex House, he found the gates shut and guarded by soldiers in the livery of the Queen's Guard. He whimpered, "Raleigh hath plotted my death to my very doorstep."

He drew his sword and would have fought his way in and very likely died on the spot; but a courier rode up on a foaming horse with an order from the Secretary of State: no harm was to come to the Earl.

Elizabeth had said, "I will not have him slain·in the gutter like a vulgar man of no consequence," adding, "Tomorrow he shall be arraigned with decorum and decency, like the great English peer that he is."

That night a herald in a crimson tabard rode through the streets of London shouting that Robert Devereux, Earl of Essex, was a traitor, accused of high treason, having risen in rebellion, with others, against the Queen's Majesty.

Essex did not hear the dire proclamation. He was peacefully asleep in his own bed at home in Essex House, where the servants tiptoed about and spoke only in whispers, and his father-in-law slept not at all that night, longing to live, knowing he would not.

A contemporary wrote: "The general opinion is there will be no great number of executions, for the Queen is very gracious and much inclines to mercy."

But of course there would have to be some. The city was still edgy, bewildered, the Queen thoroughly frightened. The contemporary continued: "There are captains with trained bands to the number of two thousand or more men from the neighbor shires hereabout, and they keep continual watch and ward day and night throughout the city."

The Queen now called Raleigh up to London, and for a while he stood outside her door, her Captain of her Guard in full discharge of his duties, not for her amusement, not to weigh tobacco smoke, not to write her love poems—she was terrified of assassination. In the chaotic state of London, with "trained bands keeping watch and ward night and day," she never could know who among her most trusted courtiers might not be a secret assassin, bent on her murder, since a man can smile and smile and be a villain.

With all Raleigh's petulance he had proved his devotion to her time after time. He was the one true friend she could rely on to thrust his own breast between her and a sudden unsuspected dagger.

Raleigh appeared as a witness at the arraignment of Lord Essex. He gave his testimony in dignified factual words, not at all prolix as was his wont. He was promptly acquitted of "complotting" to murder the Queen, Lord Essex or anyone else, and Elizabeth returned him to his duties, though not for long.

When Lord Essex awoke from his sleep he felt refreshed and strong again. At his arraignment his behavior was carefree and confident. A contemporary describes it:

The Earl of Essex and Sir Christopher Blount, the Earl's father-in-law, were arraigned this day at Westminster before 25 of their peers, whereof were 9 earls and 16 barons. The only matters objected were his coming in arms into London to raise rebellion and his brabble at his house against the Queen's Guard.

He answered he was driven for safety of his life, and wished only to prostrate himself at Her Majesty's feet and there divulge such matters against his enemies as would make them odious and remove them from her person and recall him to his former favor.

This was the sum of the matter, but the worst of it all was his many and loud protestations of his faith and loyalty to the Queen and State, which no doubt convinced and carried away the great part of his hearers, but I cannot so easily be led to believe protestations against manifest proof.

I must needs say that one thing sticks much in many men's minds: that whereas on Sunday divers preachers were commanded to tell the people that, among his other treasons, he hath complotted with Tyrone and turned Papist, to the end that he become King of England; yet there was no such matter mentioned at the arraignment though there was time enough for it, from nine in the morning till almost seven at night.

Thus Elizabeth tried to save him to the end, suppressing evidence she could not believe and did not wish to. Perhaps in time he would recover his wits.

At his arraignment Lord Essex tried to be flippant, made jokes and cast up his eyes in amazement when Raleigh was sworn. "That paltry fox!"

The contemporary wrote:

At his coming to the bar his countenance was somewhat unsettled; but later he showed much boldness and resolution and contempt of death. But whether this courage were borrowed or feigned, it were hard to judge. I hear he begins to relent of his impudence, nay, hath confessed the whole plot and accused divers persons not even suspected including his own sister. It is doubted she knew of the matter.

As for his father-in-law:

He spoke very well, as a man that would live, pleaded hard to acquit himself, but all in vain, for it cannot be; whereupon he descended to entreaty and moved great commiseration, being generally liked; but methought somewhat too low and submiss, and seemed too loath to die.

Both Essex and Sir Christopher were tried by their peers before the House of Lords.

English lords did not take an oath, did not place their hands on the Bible and swear to tell the truth as was customary in lower courts. Ancient tradition took the truth of an English peer for granted.

The House of Lords condemned them both guilty of treason. Each lord merely rose, doomed them, saying, "Guilty, upon mine honor."

Now there was nothing left but to wait for their execution.

The dire death warrant to execute them was duly engrossed, presented to Elizabeth for signature. She refused to sign it, till something that Raleigh had repeatedly warned her would occur, occurred.

A second fleet of Spanish warships set sail against England. Papists were landed in Ireland and cordially received by Tyrone.

But Cecil had heeded Sir Walter's warning, dispatched a strong force of English soldiers to Ireland. When the Spanish Papists came ashore the English slaughtered them all, as was customary. This was not yet known in England.

The contemporary wrote:

There be yet no news out of Ireland, for the wind sits in our teeth and no vessel hath yet crossed over.

And he added some medical bulletins:

Here be an outbreak of the Small Pox, though some call it the Great, and many run off to their country estates.

When news finally came it was good. The contemporary wrote:

The Armada of the King of Spain hath utterly wrecked and foundered by the storms I spoke of in my last; and those of the Spaniards that survived have returned to Spain much discomfited. Tyrone runs up and down distressed, and offers to surrender upon any conditions that spare him his life.

Once more the troublesome Irish were subdued; once more a Protestant wind had saved England from invasion

Before the news came, however, while the invasion issue still was in doubt, Queen Elizabeth reluctantly signed the death warrants of Lord Essex and his father-in-law, Sir Christopher Blount.

Blount was the first to go.

Derrick, the hangman, liked very high gallows. "The people can see better and enjoy the spectacle more." And the more they saw and enjoyed, the greater the gratuities he received.

Derrick's name is long forgotten as a hangman; but after four centuries his name still survives in those very high "derricks" that are useful in constructing our skyscrapers.

Blount died like a true Elizabethan.

The Captain of the Guard was required by law to witness all executions of traitors.

"Sir Walter," said Blount, "I thank God you are

present, for I had an infinite desire to speak with you. For the wrongs I have done you, for my ill intents toward you, all past and most sorely regretted by me, I beg your forgiveness before I die."

Raleigh was shaken, pulled out and lighted his pipe to steady his nerves as he stood beside the man whose head was about to be severed from his body.

"Good Sir Christopher, thou'rt no traitor; and were it to lie with me, thou'dst be set free forthwith, but I can do nothing."

Every man at his execution was allowed a death speech. Usually they composed them in advance and committed them to memory.

When Sir Christopher began his there were impatient murmurings among the crowd. This was not what they wanted to hear.

Raleigh imperiously silenced them; Sir Christopher had his say. Many spectators yawned.

The hideous death for high treason, the half-hanging, the cutting down while still alive, the disemboweling, the slicing off of the genital organs, their burning in a fire prepared for the purpose, their being flung into the traitor's face, the sawing up of his body into four quarters immediately thereafter—this punishment was quashed in this instance by the Queen, though announced as reserved for some others involved in the same conspiracy, more as a warning than as what she actually intended to do, for later she pardoned them all.

Sir Christopher was merely to be beheaded.

Cecil sent a message to Derrick. "Are you drunk?" for he usually was.

"I am not, not today, not as yet."

"Do not get drunk, for I have orders to hang you higher than Haman if you do."

"Sir, I'll chop clean, and get drunk afterwards."

"You filthy whoreson rogue."

While Sir Christopher Blount declaimed his long-

winded death speech, forgiving his enemies, acknowledging his sins, blessing the Queen, asking prayers for his
soul that so soon would depart, granting a sum of
money to the ringers of the passing bell, another gratuity
to the hangman, double if he did his duty at one stroke,
praising the Captain of the Guard (on which there were
hisses), blessing his son-in-law (on which there were
cheers and sobs)—while this was going on, concessionaires passed among the crowd selling roast chestnuts
and sugarplums.

Blount was little known, they little cared to hear him.
They were waiting for the next.

Then Derrick raised up his axe, brought it sharply down
and chopped off Blount's head in one stroke, just as
he'd promised.

Essex was next. This is what they wanted to see,
mourning, weeping. He mounted the platform.

His mind had undergone another strange alteration.

All that was good in his generous nature came out in
his final moments.

"Where is Sir Walter?" he asked. Hisses. He held up
his hand; the crowd instantly fell silent, bewitched by his
noble appearance, awed by the black mourning garb he
had donned to memorialize his passing.

Walter Raleigh came up and stood beside him. He was
shaking. His lighted tobacco pipe was still in his hand.
He sought to hide it in his pocket. "No," said the Earl,
"It pleases me. Take your tobacco, Sir Walter, for it
shows me you sorrow at my death."

Then came his death speech, not very coherent but
gentle and mild. He forgave all his enemies. He blessed
the Queen. He denied (convincingly to the audience) all
intrigue with the enemies of England, especially the
Irish. In a welter of self-accusation, which his hearers
did not believe, wept to hear, he declared himself to
be the "most vilest and loathsomest traitor that ever was
born in this England." He placed his hand on Raleigh's

shoulder. "I was ever thy friend." There were screams of fury.

Then he declared to the Anglican Archbishop who was with him, "I thank God, Your Grace, that my sinful days are now at an end. Do thou, good my Lord Archbishop, pray for my soul." The Archbishop nodded, unable to speak, choked with grief. Then Essex raised his head and cried in a loud clear voice, "God bless Queen Elizabeth! God bless England!"

Then he lowered his head to the block and the hangman chopped it off.

In her palace Queen Elizabeth wept, and kissed and kissed his ring. "Would God I could have spared him!" Distress at his loss caused her fear of assassination to somewhat diminish. "Essex is dead; I too must die; what matters it how!" She had heard the hisses. She ordered Sir Walter back to Sherborne. He still might be useful sometime, she thought, when she was herself again. Meanwhile she gloomed and sorrowed and twisted and twisted and twisted Lord Essex's ring with pale and shaking fingers, somewhat gouty and painful by now. In her dreams he still lived. When morning came he was dead. Often she imagined she had not slept at all.

Cecil now called back his son, turned him over to the care of hired governesses. It would never do at this critical moment to seem to favor the worst hated man in England.

He waited to see whether the Queen would live or die, elaborating a policy to take care of either event.

The Queen did not die. Cecil now put in a good word for Raleigh. He counselled the Queen, "Keep him away during this period, but keep him available for service. He will never desert you." She agreed. Raleigh was the last of the old coterie of her courtly lovers, of so long, so very long ago, those happy days.

In Sherborne Sir Walter loaded some muskets and stationed some of his trusty ruffians night and day around the house with orders to shoot if enemies came to kill him; and planted some ingenious land mines that would explode when stepped upon in case enemies came by the back way through the gardens.

There he dwelt, secure with his Bess and his sons, whom his men kept clear of the mines, explaining their purpose. How wise was their father, how he must love them, to keep them thus safe from his enemies, God rot 'em!

Captain Keymis was with him now, promoted to major-domo in charge of these operations. Sherborne looked like a flowery English country estate. In actual fact it was a booby-trapped fortress. Walter Raleigh had no desire to die.

In Scotland King James mourned the death of Lord Essex. "How I'd have favored the laddie!"

But Elizabeth had formally designated him her successor, there were more bonnie laddies, he never said a word.

He knew from his spies that Queen Elizabeth had developed strange timorous symptoms. Every night she slept with a rusty old sword poked under her bed. Who might not be lurking there! "Silly old maid," chuckled his Scottish Majesty. "Maybe she hopes it's a boy and wants to ferret him out, then scream she's raped." King James liked both men and women; but if *he* had been poking under a bed he'd have preferred to flush out a boy, no danger of royal bastards resulting, always embarrassing to kings; and boys are such very pleasant company.

To James's disgust Queen Elizabeth recovered her health. It was time for her to address her parliament, her House of Lords, the Commons, her people. Being somewhat short of breath she asked them to hear her out of doors. There it was easier for her to breathe, and she wouldn't demean herself by sniffling or coughing into her handkerchief. It was November, the erratic English weather was muggy outside.

"This were a speech should be written in gold, for our sons and posterity," said a member of her Commons after she made it. No one knew it was to be her last.

In a beautiful gown, head erect, majestic, she greeted them. She said:

We perceive your coming is to present thanks to us. Know that I accept them with joy and more esteem than any treasure or riches, for these we know how to value at their worth. [She shook her head, paused.] But loyalty, love and thanks, I account them invaluable. And though God hath raised me high, yet I account this the glory of my Crown: that I have reigned with your loves. That God hath made me Queen I do not so much rejoice as to be Queen over so thankful a people, to conserve you in safety and preserve you from danger.

That Queen Elizabeth assuredly had done.

I was never greedy, a scraping grasper, nor a strict fast-holding prince, nor yet a miser. My heart was never set on worldly goods, but on my subjects' good. What you bestow on myself I will not hoard up, but bestow it on you again, yea, mine own properties I account yours, and your eyes shall see it spent for your welfare.

They all stood up and doffed their hats, even those who were privileged to wear them in a sovereign's presence.

It is not my desire to live or reign longer than my life and reign shall be for your good. And though you have had, and may have, many and wiser princes, yet you have never had nor ever shall have any that will love you better.

Smiling, she held out her hand. Awed, they pressed forward to kiss it. Kneeling, they muttered their thanks.

[267]

Speechless with foreboding, they departed to their homes.

Then she returned to her palace, greatly fatigued and, in a melancholy mood which persisted for weeks, she took to her bed. In Scotland King James said, "Ah, soon."

Then summer came. She was better again. She went hunting, galloped sidesaddle ten miles on a spirited horse in a single day with a bow in her hand, and brought down a quail. A foreign visitor wrote home, "Tonight I saw Her Majesty walking sprightly about in her garden like an eighteen-year-old and late into the night she frolicked and danced with a handsome young page, who sweated like a dog out of fear of her; but she mopped his brow with her handkerchief and gave it to him for a token and said, 'You pretty boy'; on which he fled from her presence."

In Scotland King James heard of the incident, grumbled, "Will the bald old biddy never die?" She was seventy years old.

Her good health didn't last. Neither had Spenser's, that strange late blooming. Winter came on and the Queen became melancholy. She grasped a friend's hand. "I am not well," she said.

Again she took to her bed, but often arose. She was convinced that if she remained in bed she would never leave it.

Her physicians offered her medicines, sharpened lancets to bleed her, brought leeches in jars as a substitute when she stoutly refused to be bled. They prepared an elaborate unguent concocted of arsenic, water pepper, kill-ridge and whites of fertilized eggs to paste on her scalp, guaranteed to balance the humors and restore her to instant health. But her scalp was bald and she refused to expose it. "Pay the good doctors," she said to her purser, "and send them away, for they mean well." They departed richer for their efforts, sorrowing because the Queen had rejected their help, which they honestly believed would have saved her.

[268]

Walter Raleigh had a nostrum too. That too she refused.

Then, worn out, she turned her face to the wall and peacefully died between the hours of two and three in the morning, her mind at ease and her thoughts set on the life to come. An Archbishop was with her; gently he closed her eyes and prayed, "Ascend into Heaven, thou greatest of England's Queens."

In Scotland King James said, "At last!" But he too had shed tears at the news of her death. "She was a miracle."

In England at that time the death of a sovereign was subject to ancient protocol. Much of it was pure ceremonial, without much heart. But when Elizabeth died all England sorrowed. Few could remember when she had not been Queen, so long had she lived and reigned. There was a nervousness, a tremor amongst her people at her passing. What would come next? Would it be good or bad? But the sorrow in the hearts of her subjects was real, whatever might come.

Her funeral procession slowly wended its way toward Westminster Abbey. Her coffin was mounted on a cart drawn by horses caparisoned in black velvet, specially chosen big black gelded beasts that were trained to walk slowly with heads erect.

Noblemen, privileged to honor her, held aloft on high poles starch-stiffened banners on which were painted the coats-of-arms of her royal ancestors.

Upside down, there followed on poles the Spanish flags her armies and navy had captured in so many victories. Young people wondered, "So many! We never knew! What glory!" Nor did they know that Queen Elizabeth had made England great, the England they lived in and whose greatness they took for granted; but they were sobered and sensed all that she had done for them, long before they were born.

There followed her women-in-waiting, in mourning caps and cloaks, all noble, many pretty and young with questing eyes, preserving a proper decorum whatever might pass through their heads.

Then followed her heralds, pursuivants, lord mayors and other feudal officials who traditionally accompanied a dead sovereign to his grave, many dressed in regalia that hadn't been brought out of cedar closets since fathers and grandfathers had packed them away four generations ago.

Then followed Her Majesty's Guard; Sir Walter Raleigh, their Captain, his tall stature towering above the others, valiantly trying not to limp, led them to her grave, where Elizabeth found peace at last.

King James the First succeeded peacefully, not a voice being raised in murmur against him, to the throne of England, the throne of his dreams. The age of Queen Elizabeth had ended; another age began.

Walter Raleigh lived far into it.

CHAPTER XXI

A CHANGE in the leadership of a nation is always welcome, especially when there has been one leader for a very long time, as was the case with Queen Elizabeth. People welcome such a change simply because it *is* a change, and think that things will be better.

No one could deny the late Queen her greatness; but after all, she was a woman, the weaker sex as all men knew. In France and in most other states of Europe women were held unfit to be sovereigns by reason of their constitutional frailty.

With the accession of James to the throne of England, England now had a King. Everywhere he was received by cheering crowds. In every town through which he passed in his royal progress toward London he was met by some dignitary with a longwinded but sincere speech of welcome. Church bells pealed carillons of joy, preachers preached sermons of loyalty, there were displays of fireworks and in the streets the common people toasted his health in bumpers of beer thoughtfully supplied by the local authorities who wanted a brave display—for the new King had power to bestow many favors, power to take away old ones.

With him in his coach rode his Queen, just barely entering upon her thirties, sister of the King of Denmark. Her blond Scandinavian beauty captivated the English. Nor was the King himself at all bad looking. His face was sensitive, graciously smiling at the fervor of his welcome; he waved a limp-wristed languid hand to his people, acknowledging their cheers. "Naturally the King is fatigued after his long journey from Scotland," they said. They welcomed him the more because he was known to be a man of peace. The Spanish wars had cost them dear.

King James had a genuine affection for his children. Once or twice he held up his infant son. "Shall I let them see our baby Charles?" he said to the Queen, whom he always consulted in matters of importance. "Yes, do," she agreed. Even little Charles's big bosomy Danish wet nurse raised no objection. The weather was warm.

Here, thought the people, was a truly handsome and normal Royal Family, no wigs, no crooked shoulders, no hunchbacks; but instead young, with all their teeth, no wrinkled and sallow complexions; and all could see that the roses in the cheeks of pretty Queen Anne never came out of a rouge pot.

Outside the coach, in English dress, on a white palfrey, rode Prince Henry, the King's nine-year-old son, heir-apparent to the throne. The spirited lad was tall for his age, broad in the shoulder and lanky of limb; he had chafed a bit at being told to ride a horse he deemed more suitable for ladies, but his mother had said, "This is your father's day, Henry; when you are Prince of Wales you may ride anything you like."

Prince Henry was already possessed of the great dignity and manly beauty that Queen Anne bequeathed to her sons.

Behind the coach rode a contingent of Scottish Guardsmen in tartan cloaks, curious bonnets and kilts, with claymores hung from their belts where Englishmen wore smaller swords, tassels on Argyle stockings that left bare a considerable gap of hairy leg and knobby knee before reaching the kilt—a colorful exotic display for the uninstructed English. But the Scotsmen seemed a friendly lot, laughing and joking amongst themselves in a language totally incomprehensible to the English. When bands of English musicians greeted them with stately Elizabethan music, answering bands of Scottish musicians replied with a skirl of bagpipes that sounded for all the world like the screamings of angry birds of prey. It was noted that the Scotsmen handled their big horses with extreme dexterity. Many were glad that they came as friends.

There was also a mounted English contingent of Guardsmen, signifying by their presence the union of the English and Scottish Crowns.

There followed some pack wagons that contained King James's favorite possessions, his Scotch whisky, bound volumes of his essays, his poems, his translations of Latin and French dramas, all in Scottish dialect, his acronyms and his much-prized *Daemonologie*, a treatise denouncing witches and advocating the strongest measures to suppress them. He himself had studied how to recognize them, instructed others how to go on witch hunts, had flushed out several covens of the creatures in Scotland where, after a fair trial, he reverently burnt them all.

The King looked out on the English countryside, the velvety close-cropped greenswards, the carefully tended hedges, the flowering gardens—how different from wild and craggy Scotland with its stingy rocky soil! How much more to the taste of an artist and scholar. "And"—a typically Scottish observation—"how vurra vurra rich!" And how safe he felt in the hands of these well-behaved English people, now *his* people, he had almost forgotten. In his weak well-meaning heart he determined to rule them wisely and well.

At the death of an English sovereign many changes took place. Parliament was prorogued, sent home, waited to be called again when the new sovereign should choose to assemble them again under new writs stamped with the new sovereign's new seal, the old one being voided and broken up.

Persons holding high office during the pleasure of the late sovereign, like Walter Raleigh, habitually stayed away from the new sovereign until he should renew or take away their honors, posts and positions. Above all it was counted bad manners for them to appear in person before the new sovereign for any reason.

It was not in the nature of Walter Raleigh to submit to this time-honored and very sensible protocol, which he deemed humiliating.

He therefore took horse, garbed in the livery of Queen Elizabeth's Captain of the Guard and, just outside London, rode up and stopped the whole procession.

Presenting himself at a window of the royal coach, he delivered to King James a beautifully engrossed parchment, welcoming His Majesty to England. He, and many others had signed this welcome, he said. He said, "Overcome with the emotions that every good Englishman cannot but feel, that Your Majesty hath graciously deigned to come and reign over us, I took it upon myself as Your Majesty's Captain of the Guard, to arrogate to myself the honor of being first to greet Your Majesty and present this pledge of our loyalty."

James frowned. Raleigh wasn't his Captain of the Guard. In fact he had other plans for that post. But he looked for guidance to the Queen. "He means well," she said. "Hear him out."

James took the parchment, smiled, answered, "Thank you, Sir Walter."

Raleigh had another request. He asked that His Majesty would see fit, quite soon, he hoped, to continue him in all his offices—his wardship of the stanneries, his title of Admiral, his many estates, his monopolies.

King James said, "Of course, Sir Walter. I propose to deprive none of my loyal subjects of his justly won honors."

Then Raleigh presented the King with a long composition of his own, in the manner of a state paper, as if he were still advising Queen Elizabeth. He entitled it *A Discourse Touching at War with Spain*, advocating immediate war. James glanced at the title. It was the last thing he wanted. He said, still smiling, "I canna digest so much at a sitting, but rest you assured, it shall be read."

Raleigh wheeled about, doffed his hat with a flourish and congratulated himself that he had done a good day's work.

King James looked at his Queen. "I dinna like the mon."

"I do," said Queen Anne.

"You do?"

"I do."

"Oh well then, well, well, oh well—we shall see," and he took a nip of whisky from a silver flask artfully concealed in a small compartment prepared for the purpose in the coach wall.

Raleigh had one more scheme up his sleeve to consolidate the gains he was sure he had made that day. He rode up to Prince Henry, expecting a weakling.

They looked at each other, smiled, instantly liked and admired each other. The heir-apparent was still too young to understand the sexual ambivalence that bedeviled his father; but Prince Henry was a man, Raleigh was a man, and there, at that first meeting began the close comradeship that lasted as long as Prince Henry lived.

Raleigh had memorized a speech that he hoped would advance him in the Crown Prince's eyes, but found himself speechless. He grasped and kissed Prince Henry's hand, and all he could mutter was, "God bless you."

Henry said, not in Scotch but in excellent English, "You too, Sir Walter." Both meant it.

When young Henry reported this seven-word dialogue to his father, who could never avoid a pedantic pun, King James said, "M'lad, I've heard *rawly* of that mon." The prince and his father both laughed; it was one of the King's wittier quips; everyone knew that many raw things were said about Raleigh.

Mingling in and out amongst King James's carefree suite on the road toward London and the throne of England were two young men whose future seemed brilliant. They are worth naming in view of what Fate held in store for them.

One was an Englishman, Thomas Overbury, returning from a holiday in Scotland. He was twenty-two years old, clever, inordinately ambitious, a worldly-wise bachelor with a string of conquests under his belt and much knowledge of the vagaries of the love lives of men and women. He himself preferred women but he was tolerant of those who deviated from the norm, convinced that they couldn't help it.

In Scotland on his holiday he had happened upon the other, a Scot named Robert Carr. Carr was extremely handsome, dimpled of cheek and thirteen years old, just the age that James loved most in boys: their pubescent bodies charmed him. Everyone whispered that Carr was the King's current catamite; they were often together. To Carr it was enormously flattering, this fondling of a King, but it was also somewhat confusing.

Thus it was that Robert Carr turned to his older — older! twenty-two! — friend for counsel.

Overbury said, "He's clean, no pox, he won't harm you; humor his fancy and you will rise far, likely an earl, and" — he mimicked the Scotch dialect — "verra verra rich siller."

"Aye," said the youngster, chuckling a bit, "I have never been rich and no Scot would let pass a chance for siller. Will he hurt me?"

"Has he so far?"

"No, he is very gentle. But his Queen — doesn't she mind?"

"Laddie, the Scandinavians understand these things

far better than we do; that's why they're so broad-minded."

"I do so like her."

"She likes you too."

"Approves of me, and—everything?"

"Thoroughly. Queen Anne understands her King."

Be it said for King James that he always consulted his Queen before he chose a new boyfriend. If she said No, the boy had no chance. She genuinely liked Robert Carr.

Her relationship with her husband was a strange one. James was always good to her. Together they had borne children; both loved them, both doted upon babies; together they planned goodly futures for them, as all happily married couples do.

King James had access to his Queen, body and bed, at any time and was always welcomed with affection. Sometimes at night he would start up in bed and whisper, "Someone is at the casement! Someone is coming to murder me!" She would comfort him, soothe him, call for a light and say gently, "See, Jamie boy? There is nobody there." "But I swear I heard something!" "Only the wind, dear, only the wind."

He would drop off to sleep again, his head on her breast like a frightened child, and have bad dreams about witches and warlocks.

But largely she lived apart from him in her own lavishly furnished apartments, not out of fear or revulsion, but simply because their interests and tastes were so different. The King was busy all day long with affairs of state, meeting with his Privy Council, granting audiences to foreign ambassadors, laying down a foreign policy from which he never deviated: peace for England. Always, outside his door, often beside his chair at these audiences, stood his Captain of the Guard, a giant of a man, a Scotsman in Scottish dress, with a face grim as a hangman and a glare that scared the daylights out of the ambassadors. Raleigh had been dismissed from his captaincy the moment King James assumed the Crown.

The Queen approved of James's peaceful policy, tactfully encouraged him in it. Wars cost a great deal of money. She loved dancing, jewels, frilly dresses, plays and light music, and squandered great sums on them. A war would force her to economize, curtail her amusements, which charmed the whole Court: they were so endearingly feminine. Scottish King James, quite un-Scottishly, never once begrudged her a penny.

To the English, at least in the beginning, the Royal Family presented a most attractive picture: a devoted mother, a loving father who worked very hard at his job, and extremely handsome children.

True, His Majesty *did* have some quirky personal habits, but much was forgiven the private life of a King, and he hanged almost nobody. He issued a blanket order to all his justices to grant instant royal pardon to children who, hungry, stole food: the statutory penalty for doing so had always been death, and had always been carried out. Even panders and bawds and cutpurses and highwaymen were given light sentences.

But a contemporary wrote, tongue in cheek: "Today His Majesty rode out a-hunting and brought down a lark right skilfully, on which he repeatedly clapped his hands for joy." He did not dare add—King James's spies were everywhere—that the Tudors had brought down huge stags and wild boars, lustily whooping and shouting at the kill, and even Queen Elizabeth had loved fox hunting. The new Stuart Dynasty was decidedly daintier.

King James's foreign policy was successful. Many years would pass, long after Walter Raleigh was headless in his grave, before England had another war.

King James had a horror of bloodshed. As a little boy in Scotland he had seen, heard, big hairy foul-mouthed desperadoes burst into his mother's bedroom and slaughter an innocent man.

[278]

As a scholar and student of history he had studied the ancient wars of the Greeks and Romans: nothing good ever came out of those wars and the nations declined thereafter. Peace, any peace, was better than war.

Did not the Bible adjure you to beat your swords into ploughshares? Did not Christ Himself preach peace? Did there not lie in the beautiful Hebrew word for peace, *shalom*, the salvation of mankind? Currently he was deputing an assembly of scholars to translate the Vulgate into English, which has ever since been known as the King James Bible.

There were his better impulses.

His worse were astute: he saw how he might benefit from the religious chaos rampant in Europe.

He wrote to the Pope of Rome, in flawless classical Latin, that he, King James, Head of the Church of England, had been born and baptized a Roman Catholic and was much drawn to the Old Religion, could easily be persuaded to return to the fold, bringing England with him. Nay, he proposed to arrange a Catholic marriage for one of his daughters when a suitable Catholic prince should present himself and the children grew just a bit older. Meanwhile, would His Holiness, gloriously reigning, inform the King of Spain? He had need of funds for a splendid tomb he was building for his martyred mother, Mary, Queen of Scots.

Spain instantly responded with a large grant of money, and the costly tomb was constructed, King James pocketing most of the funds and instructing Robert Cecil, his Secretary of State, to tell the artisans to whistle the wind for the rest, which would come in time.

James's Queen was Lutheran. He wrote to her brother, the King of Denmark, that he was at heart a devout follower of Martin Luther, had constructed a private chapel where the Queen might pray her Lutheran prayers. It had been costly. Would His Danish Majesty kindly advance him the funds to pay for it? He himself could not, being Head of the Church of England; there had been some murmurings when Queen Anne refused to take the sacraments after the Anglican Rite, but he, King James, would defend to the death the right of his Queen to practice her own religion. The King of Denmark paid.

As for the Kirk of Scotland, King James informed them, in code through his emissaries, that never for one moment had he deviated one jot or tittle from the true, austere, predestinarian faith of the land of his birth. One had only to wait a little while and everybody would be Presbyterian. The Kirk of Scotland responded, in code, with secret thanks and a grant of money to further the Cause, which was obviously predestined.

Through Spain and the Pope, news of the King's imminent return to Catholicism seeped into Ireland. The miserable kerns had nothing to offer, but they quieted down, ceased to pillage and burn, and prayed for King James, who reminded the Anglican bishops in Ireland that some ancient feudal payments were now due him if they wished to remain in their sees. They paid.

Peace, peace everywhere.

Robert Cecil said to him, "Well doth Your Majesty designate Your Majesty's rule, so recently entered upon and so splendidly successful, by the cognomen 'king-craft.'"

King James patted his shoulder. How he relished the term "cognomen." People must really appreciate him. His Secretary of State must have looked it up in a dictionary to please him. And, as if accidentally, he let his hand wander from the shoulder-patting to stroke the hump on Cecil's back, which, to those instructed in the occult arts, always brings good luck and wards off witches.

No one since Lazarus had recently been raised from the dead, and King James didn't quite dare attempt the feat though he had books that told him how. He greatly mourned Lord Essex, the bonnie lad he had never had a chance to favor. So he did the next best thing.

By virtue of his sovereign power he reversed the attainder of Lord Essex, purged the "corruption of blood" that attainder entailed, restored him posthumously to all his titles, honors and estates and vested them in Lord Essex's son, who was much like his father, just as good-looking, just as impetuous and of course much younger. "No wonder the old Queen loved him," James thought to himself as he buckled on the new Earl's belt of office, graciously smiling, thrilled at the touch of the young man who, kneeling before him, placed his hands between his and swore fealty in accordance with the ancient feudal ceremony.

Somewhat sententiously King James said that night to his Secretary of State, "Today I have righted a great wrong. Queen Elizabeth thought she had an Earl of Essex in the palm of her hand, but never actually did; but I have, as today you have witnessed."

Cecil said, "Of a truth, Your Majesty most certainly has."

Cecil thought, "Of a truth, it's the other way 'round."

Even with peace in both his kingdoms, even with foreign money pouring into his coffers, King James still needed more to support the Queen's amusements and his own.

At a stroke of his pen he created eight hundred and fifty new knights, graciously reminding them that some ancient feudal "aids, reliefs, wardships and scutages," terms long forgotten, customs long disused, were now due and payable to him personally, their sovereign lord, by reason of his knighting them.

They paid, some to impoverishment. It was a great honor to be called "Sir," even if you were a country bumpkin, and to have your lady called "Lady Bumpkin," and to watch the local farmers doff their sweaty caps and the local farmers' wives curtsey as you and your lady walked grandly past. Thus, by his kingcraft, King James created a large and loyal following in addition to garnering huge sums that were his alone to expend.

Monopolies were another prerogative of the sovereign. He reviewed them all. Some he abolished, those that bore most heavily on the people and caused grumbling. Most, so old that the people were used to them, which constituted a hidden tax and did not raise prices, he kept for himself. Some that Elizabeth had granted to her favourites he took away and gave to his own favourites. Raleigh lost all his monopolies. But he was by no means poor. He still had his Admiralty pay and perquisites, his revenues from the stanneries, all his titles (except his Captaincy of the Guard) and much hidden income from the privateering activities of a small fleet of ships that he owned, chartered or bought shares in. And of course, his many estates.

Now, suddenly, King James informed him that he was to lose his prestigious London residence, Durham House, and gave him a week to move out. Raleigh was reminded that the place was Church property; that Queen Elizabeth had taken it away from a bishop; that he, King James, as Head of the Church of England, had decided to give it back to a bishop. He gave it not to the old one, who had died, but to a new one whose support he might need. This move on the King's part was far-seeing and wise; it would quash any rumors that might leak out that he was a Papist, a Lutheran or a Presbyterian. It would prove beyond cavil that he was a true Anglican. Kingcraft. King James's art of pleasing everyone.

Raleigh was dismayed.

"We are bankrupt!" he said to his Bess. "We will starve in the streets!"

Lady Raleigh smiled at his characteristic hyperbole. "You are still Governor of the Isle of Jersey," she said.

"Aye, that I am," he said with a twinkle in his eye.

The Governorship of the Isle of Jersey was one of the minor favors Queen Elizabeth had given him, charging him only three hundred pounds for the post. In return he was entitled to levy, collect and keep the taxes.

The island lay in the English Channel just south of his native Westcountry, a few hours' sail away. The Queen had chosen him for his fluency in French, though the patois of the natives proved hard for him to understand at first. There he lived for a space during the latter part of her reign, detesting the isolation, the primitive backward natives. Till he surveyed the coast with his sailorwise eye and schemed up a scheme that added materially to his wealth. Here was the very place for his privateer ships to put in if chased by a Spaniard! The waters were treacherous, full of twisting currents that only an Englishman could cope with, and best of all, far too shallow for Spanish ships, which quickly turned tail and gave up the chase and sailed away to deeper-draught waters.

After that he felt kinder toward Jersey, even toward the natives. He imported and planted potatoes and beheld with delight and astonishment that they grew bigger, matured earlier and tasted better than Irish potatoes. He levied few taxes, because the natives were too poor, and was content to take taxes in kind; he was particularly fond of the Jersey venison. And he let them have all the potatoes they wanted in return for their labor in tending the plants. They didn't want many. Their culture was French and the French did not take to the bland starchy tubers. So Raleigh shipped them to England, where they were eaten by the poorer sort with large families, which everyone knew became larger the more potatoes the fathers ate.

No one but the Secretary of State knew that Raleigh was using the island of Jersey as a base for his privateering against the Spaniards, and the Secretary of State said not a word—he had invested in the enterprise himself, charging Raleigh only the most reasonable of bribes. When the Spanish ambassador protested that strange ships without flags were using the Isle of Jersey to prey upon Spanish shipping, Cecil said blandly, "It must be those Huguenot French pirates. Only they know those treacherous waters."

"Heretics!" hissed the ambassador. "They are always troubling us."

"Our English Governor of Jersey," Cecil said, "is in semi-retirement, raising potatoes and sending them over to us." Knowing that harvests were poor in Spain, he suggested, "In the friendly atmosphere now happily existing between our two countries, I am sure that His Majesty could arrange a trade agreement to ship you large quantities of this nutritious new food at a very low cost. The Irish practically live on it—it is a thoroughly Christian food."

But the Spaniards didn't like potatoes either and nothing came of the matter, though King James was thanked for his generous gesture.

Raleigh protested vehemently at his eviction from Durham House. The simple logistics of moving his horses, men, servants, furniture out of the house in a single week were insuperable. In the end he was given three weeks. Much of the old bishop's plate and most of his excellent wine cellar Raleigh casually appropriated, knowing it would never be missed, and disposed of it to Isaac Ehud at one hundred percent profit, since it had cost him nothing. Isaac was very old now, but his son carried on the business. "I am very glad to see you alive, Sir Walter," he said. "I once feared . . ."

"You will never see *this* head stuck up on a pike on your bridge!" Raleigh said.

He never did. No one ever did.

Raleigh still had Sherborne, his ships and his other estates and titles except his Captaincy of the Guard, which he didn't much miss. "To protect that half-man half-woman? Not me! His Queen, his son, his babies, oh aye, with my life! But him? Never!"

In Sherborne, awaiting King James's next move, Walter Raleigh sat himself down with his busy pen to write *The History of the World.*

Like Machiavelli before him, whose *Prince* he had read, Raleigh's *History* was cleverly designed to influence and instruct an heir to a throne.

"When it's done," thought Sir Walter, "I shall dedicate it to Prince Henry; nay, I shall sign my own name to it."

Further admiration could not go.

King James, coveting auctorial renown, had written many anonymous treatises, later modestly letting it leak out that he was the author. Raleigh was contemptuous of James, but James's son, Prince Henry, he loved.

Drawing upon his immense erudition, carefully selecting those incidents in the lives of the ancients most likely to appeal to a manly young prince when he should come to rule over England in his father's stead, Raleigh scribbled and scribbled with his pen, putting it all down on paper, his handscript so hurried as to be virtually illegible.

Occasionally Prince Henry would come to visit him at Sherborne. Occasionally Sir Walter would read him a chapter heading. "That is very good, Sir Walter! I shall weigh its import. Where did you learn so much?"

"By living, Your Highness."

The young prince would have liked to call him "Walter," and had once tried. Raleigh had stiffened. Raleigh would have liked to call him "Hal," harkening back to the days of Queen Elizabeth's father, but of course he was far too old-fashioned, far better disciplined. Prince Henry was always "Your Highness" as long as he lived.

King James did not fancy these visits to Raleigh. He would ask, "Where is our boy again this nicht?"

His Queen would answer, "Down at Sherborne, I expect, listening to Sir Walter's *History*."

[285]

"Is he safe, our prince? 'Tis a dark long muddy way down to Devon, and highwaymen aboot, belike."

"He is safe, dear, don't be afraid. Master Secretary has him followed everywhere with armed men to protect him. Didn't you know?"

"Aye, I knew. He's a clever little humptyback, is my Secretary. But I'm never quite sure till you tell me."

"Quite safe, dear."

"Oh well then, oh very well. But I dinna like that rawley rogue."

She laughed, mimicked his Scottish accent. "Dinna be too sure o' yoursel', King James. Sir Walter's no rogue."

"Madame," said the King, "I can speak excellent English when I try. I am studying their language from one of my English dictionaries."

"Your English subjects will like you better when it comes naturally." They both laughed good-naturedly. King James's English subjects liked him very well, so far.

Then, just at that time when Raleigh felt most safe, most secure; just at that time when his future looked brightest, when the reigning King had frowned but a little upon him and the King-to-be loved him like a father —just at that time disaster struck. Fortune spun her fickle wheel.

Sir Walter Raleigh was accused of high treason and clapped into the Tower.

CHAPTER XXII

KING JAMES's flirtation with so many religions brought dire consequences to a great many persons, and to Raleigh in particular.

Two Catholic priests had seen the King, been received with favor. Yes, declared James, he greatly favored the Old Religion, the religion of his martyred mother; one had only to look at the splendid tomb he had built to perpetuate her memory. The priests were naturally delighted. If they waited a while, they sincerely believed, England would be Catholic again.

But once King James felt secure on the English throne he no longer needed the Catholics. It came to the ears of the priests that he had laughed and said, "Na, na, I dinna require the help o' the Papists noo."

Distraught and deceived the two priests conspired to kill him and raise to the throne of England a Catholic Queen. The new Queen was to be Arabella Stuart. Her Stuart blood was as royal as King James's own. Her pedigree was impeccable. She was Catholic to the bone. She was next in direct line of succession to England's throne.

The plot spread. There were many crypto-Catholics in England. Spanish gold was creeping into their purses; Spanish promises of high positions encouraged them. Robert Cecil himself was on this secret payroll.

King James got wind of the plot through his spies, but

he never suspected Cecil, who had taken a leaf from the late Queen's book: *video, taceo:* knowledge was power. To keep silent would enable him to ally himself with the winning side if everything turned upside down, as usually happened when dynasties changed.

Cecil had a brother-in-law, Lord Cobham, as foolish and weak as Cecil was clever and cautious.

When Cecil began to draw away from Raleigh, sensing the King's dislike of him, Raleigh set out to cultivate the friendship of Lord Cobham. Raleigh had always been close to the Court; to lose contact with the powerful Secretary of State terrified him; what better continuing contact could there be than the Secretary of State's own brother-in-law? He used all his great power of persuasion, turned on all his charm, and Lord Cobham was easily charmed. Soon they were boon companions.

Lord Cobham was deep in the priestly plot, heavily subsidized by Spanish bribes. Sometimes he hinted that Raleigh might benefit also from certain secrets he knew; but Raleigh would treat it as a joke, laugh and say, "I've been offered fortunes more than once to throw in my lot with Popery; but I have spent my life fighting it —in Ireland, France, Holland, the New World, and I'm far too old to change now"; and would speak of other things, discouraging such dangerous confidences. Still, he heard a little, more than he wanted to, and was afraid that Cobham would soon get himself into trouble.

Soon Cobham did, and with him Walter Raleigh.

The priests hired two down-at-the-heels assassins, filled their purses with Spanish gold, promised much more once they should murder the King. King James's spies ambushed them, killed them, stole their purses, threw their bodies into a swamp and rode back to report to His Majesty that His Majesty's sacred person was now safe; and were suitably rewarded by the Secretary of State for their loyalty.

Then the priests were taken into custody, promised

their lives if they would divulge who was implicated with them in their treason. Fearful of their necks and disemboweling, they confessed everything, hoping to save their lives. They were asked, "And the Lady Arabella?" No threat or torture could make them implicate her; she knew nothing, they said, which was true. King James was satisfied: Lady Arabella was important to his kingcraft; she could not marry without his permission and he planned to marry her to a suitable foreign prince to bolster his shaky position in Europe.

Thus it was that Lord Cobham and Sir Walter Raleigh were shut up in the Tower of London to await trial, accused of high treason, the most heinous of English crimes. Far into the twentieth century it was still possible, though in fact never done, for an Englishman convicted of high treason to be publicly beheaded; and there is nothing in the unwritten British Constitution, so much more flexible than ours, to prevent the old treason law from being speedily revived if Parliament should decide it expedient to do so.

It was summertime, and very hot. The moat around the Tower of London was scummy-green. The river Thames, where the city garbage wagons dumped their loads, stank; and the tides washed the garbage back and forth, never entirely out to sea since the busy wagons always dumped more. Rats from the ships in the harbor greedily ran down the mooring lines, dived into the water and fed on the garbage, so much more to their taste than the slim pickings left by the sailors. Some of these rats came from Spanish ships, a trickle of trade being now a reality between England and Spain as relations between the two countries continued to improve. Some of the Spanish ships had touched at ports in Spain's Far Eastern possessions. Some of the rats were infected. Having gorged themselves on garbage they swam ashore to die.

Plague broke out in London. The weekly count of

dead rose to a staggering two thousand. Everyone rich enough fled from the city till the plague should die out as it had always done in the past. Only the very poor and some militiamen on triple pay remained, while criminals looted the shops unchallenged and often fell dead in their tracks, the loot still clutched in their hands.

The jury charged with the arraignment of Raleigh, Cobham and others involved in the treason plot and the judges who would try them fled to the palace of the Bishops of Winchester, a delightful spot in Surrey, fifty miles west of London, seven hundred feet above sea level, where the air was crisp and clear and the prevailing westerly winds were counted upon to blow the infection that hung over London out to the sea in the other direction toward France and the Netherlands. This intelligent empirical precaution had always worked in the past. Rats do not swim across the North Sea.

Raleigh and Cobham were locked in a coach surrounded by guards whose duty was to prevent their escape, but turned out to be to protect them from the fury of the populace, who threw stones and screamed curses at the man they blamed for the execution of their idol, Lord Essex. Locked in the coach, they arrived safely in Surrey where they were promptly arraigned before the grand jury. Robert Cecil was one of the jurors.

The priests' depositions were read. Lord Cobham, the evidence stated, had been heard to utter foul and treasonable threats: "The King must be killed, and all his brats!" The priests' evidence further stated that Walter Raleigh had favored the cause and planned to seize the Royal Navy.

Here Cecil became seriously alarmed. The priests' evidence against Raleigh was pure hearsay; but Cecil knew how popular Raleigh was with sailors. The arraignment was held in public, the whole Royal Navy was hearing about it. It would be a disaster if they mutinied. Even before the trial, he stripped Sir Walter of his Governorship of the Isle of Jersey, privately telling the Spanish ambassador that he had quashed the piratical activities of the French Huguenots who had been using that isle for their headquarters and, sadly shaking his head like a man who had just heard distressing news, avowed that some English sea captains might also have been suborned. The Spanish ambassador was delighted and rewarded him with an increase in his Spanish pension.

Cecil by now was certain that Raleigh would be condemned. But he still professed friendship, struck a cunning pose as an impartial unbiased juror. Contemptuous as he was of his brother-in-law, he did not want to see him die. And if he were to save Cobham he must, of necessity, save Raleigh, against whom the evidence was flimsy and hearsay.

Raleigh was interrogated before the jury. In a dignified manner he admitted that he had indeed heard from Cobham some hints of a plot of some sort, but he had believed Cobham was joking, and in any case, had taken no part in whatever was brewing.

Then Cobham burst out, "Oh, you traitor! You wretch! It is you who have led me into this villainy!" and delivered himself of a wild incoherent confession in which Raleigh was the instigator and he but a guileless innocent, hypnotized by the vilest most ambitious man in England, and the worst hated as everyone knew. There were solemn nods of understanding among the jury; everyone knew *that*.

Cobham confessed that he was to receive six hundred thousand pounds from the King of Spain. With this vast sum he was to go to the Isle of Jersey, where Raleigh, having taken over the entire English Navy single-handed, was to inform him how the money might best be spent to murder the King and his brats, set Arabella Stuart on the throne and further advance the cause of Spain.

In a curtained alcove, hidden from the jury, sat King James, listening. Now he had heard all he could stand.

Frightened half out of his wits he fled from his hiding place and went weeping and trembling to his Queen. "It is murder they plot!" he blubbered. "Me, you, all our children! And back of it all is that demon Raleigh!"

She tried to soothe him, but she too was frightened. There was evidence aplenty that conspirators were plotting to murder the Royal Family, and that they had been discovered, and Raleigh seemed one of them.

The jury indicted them all.

Now there was nothing to do but to try them.

The two priests were not tried. They were immediately hanged, drawn and quartered and their tonsured heads were stuck up on pikes on London Bridge till the ravens picked them white, down to the skull. They went bravely to their hideous deaths, praying their Spanish prayers. Cecil, who understood Spanish, as well he might, heard one of the priests quote an old Spanish proverb: "In a hundred years you will all be bald," and heard him remark, "We shall not have to wait so long."

All the rats that were destined to die, now died. The bubonic plague kills quickly. The westerly winds continued to blow their pure and cleansing breath over England, purging the realm of infection. The garbage wagons continued to dump their loads into the Thames as usual, but the count of plague-deaths dropped to zero and did not rise. It was now safe to return to London. There Raleigh's treason trial took place.

It is one of the most redeeming features of King James's baffling character that he was genuinely interested in justice, he who had been brought up in Scotland where torture, the iron maiden, the boot, were common. Ofttimes he was heard to mutter, "Na, na, use only the more tender tortures," when criminals were interrogated.

Not only did he conceive of himself as a scholar, poet, historian, cryptographer, enemy of witches, tobacco and all other nastiness, but he also took pedantic delight in the quibbles and quiddities of his lawyers. It is owing to James's interest in the letter of the law that Raleigh's trial is so thoroughly documented. "How do you construe the French words in the Treason Act, '*ou par aillours*'? Do they mean 'in some other place,' or 'in some other manner'? It might make a difference," he asked his Attorney General.

The Treason Act was written in 1351, centuries before, when Anglo-Norman was the language of the law.

The Attorney General, Sir Edward Cope, answered, "Sire, it matters not a whit where treason is committed or in what manner. All, all of these traitors are guilty."

"I think so too," said the King, glad that his attorney, who would prosecute Raleigh and the others, saw no loophole in the law that might save them.

From the Tower Raleigh sent Lawrence Keymis with a letter to Cobham. Keymis was permitted to attend him because, reasoned Cecil, if anybody knew Raleigh's secrets it was sure to be this dog-devoted sea captain of his. But Keymis did not ride out of the Tower unchallenged. Guards instantly surrounded him and took him to a dungeon, where a rack stood ready awaiting an occupant; and beside the rack stood Derrick, the public hangman.

Derrick had not improved his public image since he chopped off the head of Lord Essex, the public idol. He was hated. Once, moved by pity, Derrick had used a cold iron instead of the red-hot one, to brand on the breast of a nine-year-old girl the "T," for thief, when the hungry child was caught stealing a loaf of bread, a hanging offense; and Derrick was soundly whipped for his lapse. Now he was harder, followed his orders to the letter.

"You have a letter," said Derrick to Keymis.

"That I have," answered Keymis. " 'Tis addressed to Lord Cobham from my master, Sir Water Raleigh."

"Read it to me."

Keymis handed it to him. "Read it for yourself."

Derrick could read, a little, but he could not make out Raleigh's scrawl. A clerk read it, made a copy of it and handed it back to Keymis. "Send it on," said the clerk, and Keymis rode out of the Tower.

Shortly thereafter Keymis was prey to a phenomenon common amongst soldiers but new to himself. They go into battle, as Keymis so often had done. They experience no fear. Then, when the danger is over and they are safely back behind their own lines, they get the shakes: they tremble, calling to mind the bullets that missed them. And so it was with Keymis. The remembrance of the rack, clear as day in his midnight horror, set him into a sweat. He had nightmares that night. When he awoke in the morning he thought, "The damned thing wasn't even used, maybe wasn't even meant to be!" and he was ashamed of a weakness he construed as cowardice. "I could have withstood it for my master!" and he gave vent to a spate of good round Elizabethan curses: "That he-she, whoreson, shit-abed foreigner of a Scot, that calls himself a King!"

Here the reader must pause and acquaint himself with some long-disused Elizabethan words. The word "whoreson" connoted no particular derogation, did not mean literally "son-of-a-whore": and was employed as a generic term of abuse, often with levity. It simply meant "an extremely unpleasant person." "Shit-abed" was somewhat more opprobrious. It meant exactly what it means today, though the word "shit" was not accounted vulgar as it is now, when it is seldom used in polite conversation. In our own time President De Gaulle has resurrected the term in its original sixteenth-century sense, "shit-en-lit," meaning a scaredy-cat weakling who befouls his own bed. De Gaulle's use of the old term caused consternation among radio and TV commentators, who did not possess the French President's scholarly background. King James, when he was scared, was known to shit in his bed, to the great annoyance of his fastidious Queen, who would have someone clean him up before she kissed him again. "He-she," of course, is self-explanatory. "Son-of-a-bitch," so popular today, had not as yet become part of the English language. Shakespeare, who was growing in popularity as a playwright, invented it in one of his theatrical productions.

With the reader's pardon for this digression, we now return to our narrative.

Raleigh's letter to Cobham declared: "My good lord and my singular good friend: I protest by the living God that I never accused you of anything, far less of treason against the King, less even than that (though that were enough) of murderous designs against His Majesty's children, one of whom, Prince Henry, by the purest chance, I spoke to on His Majesty's progress to London, *preux chevalier* like another Bayard, tall in the saddle, instinct with the majesty of England! God grant him long life to further our glory!"

(Raleigh knew that his letter would be intercepted, read. He knew the King's love for his son.)

And further to Cobham: "As for the allegation that I accuse you of plotting with Spain to 'murder the King and his brats,' believe me, my friend, 'tis a Spanish plot in no wise contrived against you but against me, for as the Bible hath it: They seek my life, to take it away."

Then Raleigh grew too clever, stating: "If aught in our jocular converse hath come to the ear of His Majesty seeming to point to treason, know that you and I, in our talks in these parlous times, never were heard by two witnesses; and two are required by the common law of the realm to convict."

(Here Raleigh's legal lore was old-fashioned and wrong, as was shortly brought out in their treason trial.)

He subscribed himself, with many a flourish of pen, "Your devoted servant and friend, Walter Raleigh."

Cobham wrote back: "My dear friend: I

never thought for a moment you accused me of treason. 'Tis slanderous tongues, as you so aptly put it, that malign us. God save the King!" It was signed 'Cobham.'

At the very same time he was writing this letter to Raleigh, Lord Cobham wrote another to King James, repudiating the letter to Raleigh. Raleigh, said Cobham to James, was exactly as treasonable as he, Cobham, had accused him of being in the first place, plotting a war with Spain.

Then Cobham had copies of all the contradictory letters delivered to Robert Cecil, the Secretary of State. Cecil clapped them up in his secret casket, musing, "Treason assuredly is afoot, somewhere, by someone."

As for King James, frightened half out of his wits, he said, "Traitors complot to imagine and compass the death of my family, and me! But truth will out. I will instantly bring them to justice!" and his Queen had to have him cleaned up again, so frightened and trembly was he.

Sure of his innocence, feeling doubly secure with Cobham's letter in his pocket, Raleigh jauntily awaited his trial and acquittal. He was jolly in the Tower and joked and smoked with the Warden, who visited him daily and supplied him with all the necessities of life and many of the luxuries, which Raleigh cheerfully paid for in gold on the spot. "My purse is in that coffer yonder," Raleigh said. "Look in, heft it if you like—it is heavy—so as to assure yourself that I shall pay my way." It was half a question; Wardens of the Tower had been known to steal from rich prisoners; Raleigh wanted to be sure he wouldn't be robbed.

"Sir Walter, I don't dare; it could mean my head; I am under strict orders not to touch your possessions." Then the Warden would scuttle back to his own apartments, open the windows, take a bath and chew cloves, lest the odor of tobacco cling to his garments and breath. He never knew when one of King James's spies just might pop in to inquire how Sir Walter fared and whether he had divulged anything that might strengthen the flimsy evidence against him.

Raleigh wondered why no one came to visit him in the Tower. He still had friends, or so he thought. Not among the common people; he had heard their hisses, heard the thumping of their hurled stones against the barred coach. Not among the courtiers, who were jealous of him. He thought of writing to Cecil, but was too wise to do so because Cecil was to be one of his judges. Delicacy forbade him writing the Queen or Prince Henry, whom he knew to be friendly. No one came to visit him but Bess, and she knew nothing. "I was asked to go to Sherborne," she said, "till this nonsense is over."

"Who asked you to go?"

"The Queen; no doubt she meant to spare my feelings. She spoke most kindly of you."

"Did she intimate what the verdict will be?"

"Her Majesty seemed completely in the dark."

"Naturally she couldn't tell you even if she knows. You look fit, my dear Bess."

She smiled. "I am untroubled of heart, my dear, for the outcome is certain."

Raleigh nodded, but he was troubled. Surely one of his ship captains should have come to pay his respects by now.

So he sent Lawrence Keymis to sniff the judicial wind, to report back with any intelligence he might be able to gather. Keymis came back with a gloomy face.

"Well, man?" said Raleigh offering him a pipe, which Keymis eagerly accepted.

"Thank you for that," he said gratefully. "I have had to avoid taking tobacco for days."

"So? Then you've been at the Court! Good, good. Tell me all."

"Could I have a bit of a drink first?"

"Of course, of course. I forget my manners; I beg

your pardon. Truth to tell, I was worried at first. No one came to visit me. What shall it be, my dear Lawrence, Spanish sherry, good Huguenot Burgundy, some Papist whisky from Ireland, the only good thing the scurvy kerns ever produced, good English beer—no, you can get that anywhere—"

"Have you some brandy, Sir Walter?"

Raleigh's happy face grew taut. "Aye, Lawrence," for he knew now that the news was bad. "Say on, my friend, whatever it is."

"I went to the Court indeed, Sir Walter. The Secretary of State received me."

"Was Cecil cordial?"

"He smiled like a Cheshire cat, tried to draw me out."

"What did you say?"

"That I knew of no plotting by anyone against the King's Majesty, far less any plotting by you."

"What did he say?"

"The whoreson cripple said—"

"Hush, Lawrence, sh-h-h!"

"—that he had ever held you in esteem and doubted not that justice would be done in your trial."

"In other words, he said nothing."

"Nothing to snare him, nothing at all."

"How looked he, the Secretary of State?"

"Dwindled, peaked, pale about the gills, or so it seemed to me. Then I made cautious inquiries among your friends at Court."

"Have I any?"

"Aye, but they pull in their horns and speak only in generalities."

Raleigh shook his head. The judicial wind smelled bad.

"I did hear that it's whispered the King has forbidden the Royal Family to see you or communicate with you in any way."

Raleigh mused, "Then they must have wished to, or it would not have been necessary to forbid them"; then, "Say on, Master Keymis."

[298]

"Then I walked through the streets, to listen to the common people, whether news of the trial was big news or little. It is big news. It's on every scurvy gossipy tongue amongst the people."

"Who hiss at my name, no doubt." It was scarcely a question. Keymis bowed his head, muttered, "Aye," and continued, "Then I went to the taverns that line the dockside to hear what sailors had to say."

Raleigh brightened. "Surely they—"

"They weren't there," Keymis said.

Then the weather was foul indeed, Raleigh knew. "Poor souls, they dare not show their faces. They are afraid. Who wouldn't be!" for it was clear to him now that the verdict would be guilty, and anyone who cleaved to him would be suspect of treason no less than he. Misprison of treason—knowing about it and not divulging it—was a hanging offense, or worse.

His face was so woeful that Keymis sought for something, anything in the gossip he had picked up to cheer him. "The King is frightened himself!" he said, and added, "He stuffs his britches with cotton so full that his backside looks like a fat whore's, so as to be deeper than a dagger thrust; and under his doublet he wears a coat of mail. He stinks like a bilge, and the Queen cannot coax him to remove all this protection even to bathe."

Raleigh smiled tightly. "Not much like his mother, is he!"

Everyone at the Scottish Court knew that King James's beautiful mother, Mary, Queen of Scots, was accustomed to bathe daily in her favorite imported French wine, a habit she had picked up from the ladies of the French court when she was Queen of France before her husband, the King of France, died and she reluctantly returned to the land of her birth to be Queen of Scotland, where she demanded, and, incredibly, got, from the thrifty Scotch Treasury, a special allowance to pay for her wine baths. Queen Mary often regretted that her Scottish Treasury refused to pay for milk baths for her ladies-in-waiting, another French custom. The Scots deemed it spendthrift and unnecessary. Queen Elizabeth, of course, during the years that she held her prisoner, would have none of such nonsense, deeming it decadent: all right for French women, if that was how they wanted to behave, but intolerable in manlier Tudor England. She was also jealous of the Scottish Queen's alluring femininity, and above all her ability to bear children. No one knew, no doctor could guess, why it was that the Stuart blood was clean and the Stuart Queens prolific; while the manlier Tudors were cursed in their blood and the Tudor Queens were barren.

"Not a bit like her mother," said Raleigh. "Take your rest, Master Keymis. You have done well and told me all I wished to know." For a moment he let his hand rest affectionately on Keymis's shoulder. "Good night, dear friend."

Keymis did not like the look on his face. "I am not at all fatigued. Shall I not stay with you for another pipe or another drink."

"Good night, Lawrence."

Keymis accepted his dismissal with misgiving.

Raleigh now knew what, in love and honor, he must do.

Unquestionably the verdict would go against him. All his estates, all his ships, all his titles, all his financial interests in all his profitable ventures, everything, money, jewels, everything down to the shirt on his back and the clothes of his wife and his sons—everything would revert to the Crown. King James would have it all, and his family would be destitute.

But if he should die *before* the court adjudged him guilty, none of this would happen. Everything he possessed would go to Bess and his sons.

"The matter is really quite simple," he said aloud to the empty apartment, and laid hold on his dagger and, baring his breast, thrust it into his body.

But Raleigh did not kill himself. At the touch of the dagger his courage failed him.

Keymis was roused from his fitful and troubled sleep by a guard, and rushed into Raleigh's cell, where he found him weeping, not out of pain but shame. "I couldn't do it," Raleigh moaned. "I couldn't, I don't know why, I meant to but I couldn't," he said, and reproached himself for a coward.

"That you are not, Sir Walter," said Keymis, who examined the wound and found it superficial. "I will cauterize it at once. It will quickly heal."

"No thank you," said Raleigh, who now wanted to live, whatever befell. "None of your sailor-man's hot irons." His voice was stronger, more hopeful, his tears had stopped. (In sea fights there were always plenty of hot irons handy, superficial wounds were seared shut with red-hot cauteries.)

He instructed him. "Beat up some eggs like an omelette and pour into the omelette some poppy juice, and make a gruel of it and apply it to my wound."

Keymis scurried off to the Warden with his master's unusual request for eggs in the middle of the night; the Warden took him to the larder and, wondering what strange hunger had overtaken his precious and profitable prisoner, followed Keymis and the eggs back to Raleigh's cell, where he found Raleigh bleeding from the self-inflicted wound. "Good God!" he cried, for he would be blamed for Raleigh's death if Raleigh died.

Keymis beat up the eggs into a yellow froth and poured into the mixture a measured amount of the pain-killing poppy juice from Raleigh's well-stocked medicine chest of drugs, smeared it on his chest and applied a plaster.

The Warden reported to Robert Cecil, "Through no fault of my own, my lord Cecil, Sir Walter Raleigh attempted this night to take his own life; but owing to my vigilance the same was prevented."

Cecil sighed. "It had been better for him and his family if he had succeeded," and told King James of the incident. James muttered, "The rogue seeks to rob me!" and gave instructions for stricter guards to be set over Raleigh, and had his own surgeons examine the wound every day lest it prove mortal. It did not. It healed quickly.

Then the traitors were tried.

Cobham, being a nobleman, was tried for his treason by a court of his peers. Each peer adjudged him: "Guilty, upon mine honor," and the horrible sentence of death with all its ancient obscenities was pronounced against him.

Raleigh was tried by a civil court with Sir Edward Coke as the Prosecuting Attorney for the Crown, Robert Cecil being one of the jurors.

Coke, the Prosecuting Attorney for King James, asked Raleigh, "How do you plead?" and Raleigh replied, "Not guilty."

From the first he was vilified by the Prosecuting Attorney. "Ha! say you, 'Not guilty'? I will prove thee the most notorious traitor that ever came to the bar, for I 'thou' thee, thou villain."

Then there was read the opening speech for the prosecution: that Raleigh had plotted a bloody attempt to kill the King and his royal progeny; that he had suborned Lord Cobham in his murderous schemes; that never in England had there been a like treason; that Raleigh had plotted to put Arabella Stuart on the throne after King James's death and so change the religion of England into Popery.

Coke: And so I charge you: that with your other treasons you would alter religion.

Raleigh: My innocence is my defense. Prove one of these lies and I will confess the whole indictment, confess that I am the horriblest traitor that ever lived, worthy to be crucified with a thousand thousand torments. Prove one!

Coke: One? I will prove all. Thou hast an English face but a Spanish heart.

Raleigh: Your words do not prove it.

Coke: You are the absolutest traitor that ever came out of the bottomless pit of the lowest hell.

Then came Cobham's letter to Cecil, in which he confessed his own treason and blamed Raleigh. Cecil said blandly, "I know of no such letter."

Coke: It is known to us, and it proves the treason of this viper.

Raleigh: If Cobham be a traitor, what is that to me, a faithful vassal of the King?

Raleigh still felt reasonably secure: he had Cobham's letter in his pocket. He demanded that Cobham be brought into the court to confront him.

Coke: No, he hath already confessed his treason. What boots it for one lying traitor to face another? No.

Raleigh: My lord Cobham is your only witness against me. Two are required to convict.

Coke: That law has been repealed.

And indeed it had, and Raleigh's legal lore was long out of date. If, said Coke, one man should sneak into the King's bedroom and murder him, that man would still be a murderer even though there had been no witnesses. Raleigh sighed; nothing could be truer; how long it was since he had studied law! But Raleigh still had Cobham's letter.

Coke: Thou'rt the most execrable traitor that ever lived.

Raleigh: You speak indiscreetly, barbarously and uncivilly.

Coke: I lack words to express thy viperous treasons.

Raleigh: I think you lack words indeed; for you have spoken but one thing half a dozen times.

There were murmurs of approval and stifled laughter at this.

Coke: Ha! We have to do with a man of wit. But I will now make it plain that there never lived a viler viper upon the face of the earth, as all the world shall see.

Here Coke produced a letter from Lord Cobham. In it Lord Cobham retracted all his retractions and leveled all his original accusations against Raleigh.

Among the spectators, at first so hostile, a subtle change had begun to take place. Sir Walter, though his legal knowledge was defective, had conducted himself with dignity and intelligence. The Prosecuting Attorney had sunk to the lowest depths of invective. The English sense of fair play was outraged.

Raleigh now drew from his doublet his own letter from Cobham, Cobham's unqualified assertion of his innocence. He passed it up to Cecil and asked if Cecil would identify the writing of his brother-in-law, Lord Cobham.

Coke instantly objected: My lord Cecil, my lord Cecil! Mar not a good case!

Cecil reduced him to silence with a sharp rebuke. "Do not presume to come here to tell me what to do. You are more preemptory than fair-minded, Master Attorney," and forthwith the powerful Secretary of State read Lord Cobham's letter aloud. "The script is the script of my Lord Cobham," said Cecil after reading the letter.

There were murmurs of applause among the spectators.

One of the spectators, a Scotsman sent by the King to observe the proceedings, hurried off to inform him of all the conflicting evidence, also the reaction in favor of Raleigh. King James was in a quandary. Scholarly, pedantic, he saw all the flaws in the case against Raleigh.

"We mun wait for the verdict," he said, half fearing that Raleigh would escape.

In the court Coke found his voice again, and in a long vague rambling speech charged that Cobham's letter to Raleigh must be a forgery and repeated all the accusations he had made against Raleigh during the trial.

The jury retired to consider their verdict.

In fifteen minutes they filed back into the court.

The verdict was "Guilty"; and again the horrible words of the death that a traitor must suffer were heard in the silent courtroom.

A contemporary wrote:

Never before was a man so hated and then so popular in so short a time. The Scotsman that first brought the news to His Majesty declared, but not to His Majesty, "Before the trial I would have ridden a hundred miles to see him hanged, but after hearing him speak I would ride a thousand to save him." It is buzzed about that Master Secretary of State was observed to dab at his eyes when the verdict was pronounced; but whether he wept out of sorrow, as some say, or whether the effluvia sprang from the weakness of eyes it were hard to say, as for some time his health is much decayed.

Raleigh and Cobham were immediately remanded to the Tower to await execution, which was expected to be swift.

CHAPTER XXIII

THE VERDICT delighted King James. But he was bewildered and angered by the sudden turnabout that occurred among the spectators at the trial. "From the worst hated man in England to the best admired, full in the face of the evidence, all in the space of one day! Mon, mon, I dinna faddom the mind of my English subjects. It could never have happened in Scotland."

Cecil advised him, "It is the English sense of fair play, Your Majesty. We quickly turn about to favor the underdog."

"But the verdict was 'Guilty.' "

"True, Your Majesty."

"And the sentence shall be executed."

"If Your Majesty so decides."

The King mused, "Truth to tell, the rogue defended himself with dignity and wit, though inept in the law," and added, "I mun sleep on it, Master Secretary. I am no bloodthirsty mon. But the verdict was 'Guilty.' "

"Aye, 'Guilty' it was, Your Majesty."

"And the jury took only a quarter of an hour to reach it."

"I know."

Cecil's face was sad. If Raleigh were hanged, drawn and quartered so would be his brother-in-law, Lord Cobham.

The King said with a snicker, as if he relished the

thought, "The privy parts are cut off, you know, and burnt; and you will be there to witness."

"Majesty, spare me, I beg of you."

The King, who trusted him, said, "Oh well, very well; I mun try to think o' somewhat to spare you, Master Secretary; but pardon a traitor I never will. Never."

From the Tower on the eve of his death Raleigh wrote a cringing letter to Cecil:

To speak of former times were needless, for Your Lordship knows how long I have loved you and have been favored by you, but change of times have worn out those remembrances and, I fear, in the state wherein I stand, you bear me no favor. Compassion there can be, for it is never separate from honor and virtue. Sir, what malice may do against me I know not. My cause hath been handled by strong enemies. If, in the power of the law, all that is suspected of me be laid to my charge, leave me to Death.

Your Lordship is now a counsellor to a merciful and just King, and the King hath given you to defend his subjects from undeserved cruelty. *Potentia non est nisi ad bonum:* the Law ought not to overrule piety, but piety the Law.

How therefore I shall be judged I know not. I desire nothing but to be judged by mine own merit.

If I should say to the King that my love so long borne him might hope for some grace, it were taken for presumption, because he is a King and my sovereign. Yet you, my Lord, can plead for me to the King. For the King is a true gentleman and a just man and as such he oweth unto me merciful respect, for he knows I would hazard my life for him against all men.

For yourself, my Lord Cecil, for me sometime a friend that is now a miserable forsaken man, if aught remain in your heart of good, of love or compassion, Your Lordship will show it now, when I am not worthy to deserve it to plead my cause. Know that I will follow you without mark or cover to the end.

(signed)
W. RALEIGH

Cecil was deeply moved, for in his heart he respected Raleigh. In his craintive devious heart he was still the little son of old Lord Burleigh, Queen Elizabeth's beloved counsellor, and the magic of the great Queen was strong in him, as it had been in his father: he'd truly have hated to see Raleigh die.

This time he did not clap up a letter in his secret coffer. He showed it to King James. It had the effect that Raleigh hoped for. It saved his life.

But King James did not go back on his word; he did not pardon. He "digested" the dilemma and compromised with his conscience. He elaborated a stratagem that pleased everybody—Cecil, Cobham, himself, his Queen, the Spanish ambassador—and which, to his credit, proved his genuine horror of bloodshed.

For the moment, however, all went forward as the verdict of guilty and the law required, and the execution of the traitors was set for the morrow.

In the Tower, awaiting his death, Raleigh scribbled a beautiful poem. He conceived himself a pilgrim, wending his weary way through this transitory life toward Heaven.

Pilgrims walked on foot to Jerusalem. Traditionally they carried with them only four objects: a begging bowl in the shape of a scallop-shell—they were forbidden to carry money—a staff to lean upon—there were weary miles ahead and feet might falter—a "scrip," or knapsack—and a bottle of water—there were terrible deserts to cross.

Raleigh wrote:

[308]

> *Give me my scallop-shell of quiet,*
> *My staff of faith to walk upon,*
> *My scrip of joy, immortal diet,*
> *My bottle of salvation,*
> *My gown of glory, hope's true gage:*
> *And thus I'll take my pilgrimage.*

He envisioned his gory death. No one was permitted to enbalm a traitor. His body would be quartered, sawed asunder, like that of a well-butchered pig, mutilated and left to rot wherever King James might deem it most edifying to exhibit his two legs and two arms, together with whatever remnants of his body might adhere thereto. There would of course be no head.

His poem continues:

> *Blood must be my body's balmer;*
> *No other balm will there be given,*
> *Whilst my soul, like quiet palmer,*
> *Travelleth towards the land of Heaven,*
> > *Over the silver mountains,*
> > *Where spring the nectar fountains,*
> *There will I kiss the bowl of bliss*
> *And drink mine everlasting fill*
> *Upon every milken hill.*
> *My soul will be a-dry before,*
> *But, after, it will thirst no more.*

When King James, who wrote competent poetry himself, saw this poem, as shortly he did, he said to Cecil, "Master Secretary, men say he's an atheist, but atheists don't write like that." "He's no atheist," Cecil replied, "just quirky and crank."

From the Tower on the eve of his death, Sir Walter wrote to Lady Raleigh:

You shall receive, dear wife, my last words in these, my last lines. My love I send you, that you may keep it when I am dead; and my counsel, that you may remember it when I am no more.

The letter was prolix, precise, logistic like the letters he wrote about provisioning his army in Ireland.

I would not present you with sorrow, dear Bess; let sorrow go to the grave with me and be buried in the dust. And, seeing that it is not the will of God that ever I shall see you in this life, bear my destruction gently.

He lists his several counsels:

First, I send you all the thanks my heart can conceive or my pen express for your many troubles and cares taken for me, which—though they have not taken effect as you wished—yet is my debt to you none the less. But repay it I never shall be able to in this world.

There is in his next adjuration the Raleigh concern about money, transfigured, now that he was about to die, from greed to a dead man's provision for his family:

Secondly, I beseech you for the love you bore me living, that you do not hide yourself many days, but rather by your diligence seek to better your miserable fortunes and secure the rights of our poor children. Your mourning cannot avail me, that am but dust.

Then he bequeaths to her all his landed estates, monopolies, jewels, "ventures in shipping," furniture and other valuables, wishing they were more. He carefully lists the amounts owed him, telling her how and from whom to collect them, and asks her to pay some debts he may owe, "which I may have forgot; howsoever, for my soul's health, I beseech you to pay all these poor men."

Then follows a counsel that any woman but a Throgmorton might have resented:

When I am gone, you shall be sought unto by many, for the world thinks that I am very rich; but take heed of the wiles of men, for they seek after rich widows, as the Bible hath it, Like a lion greedy of prey; though I do not dissuade you from marriage if the man be honest. As for me, I am no more yours, nor you mine. Death hath cut us asunder; God hath divided me from the world and you from me.

Then the tenderest note of all:

For their father's sake, remember to our poor children, who comforted you and me in our happiest hours, dear wife, that they be children of a true man who despiseth Death in all his ugly misshapen forms.

God knows how hardly I stole this time, when all the world sleeps and the dawn creeps in through the bars of my cell and soon, very soon, soldiers will come to separate me from the living. I can write no more. Time and Death call me away.

And Raleigh's benediction:

The everlasting, infinite, inscrutable almighty God, that is mercy and goodness itself, true light and true life, keep you and yours and have mercy on me, and teach me to forgive my false accusers and persecutors, and send us to meet in His glorious Kingdom. My true wife, farewell. May God hold you in His arms.

King James now set in motion the cunning stratagem he had elaborated. It had all the drama of a Shakespearian play. It was acted out with success and, for a time, the world accounted him a wise and merciful Prince, whose dearest desire was peace abroad and tranquillity at home.

Lord Cobham was solemnly marched to the scaffold to the doleful beat of a dead march on muffled drums. There stood a priest in the black vestments worn at a Mass for the dead, to shrive him at his passing, pray for his soul so soon to depart, exhort him to confess his treasons and acknowledge the justice of the King.

There stood Derrick the hangman, black-hooded, one hand holding a razor-sharp knife, the other the axe.

There, in a brazier, smoked the red-hot bed of coals. All eyes were fixed upon it. Its purpose was to burn the privy parts that the sharp knife would slice off the traitor's body when, cut down alive from half-hanging, still conscious, he must witness his ultimate degradation. This was the most dramatic moment in the execution, men waited breathlessly for it; it held a peculiar fascination for them and ofttimes they went home sexually stimulated to demonstrate their own virility. Compared with this moment the sawing asunder of the traitor, now mercifully dead, was as nothing.

Cobham strode to the edge of the platform to deliver his death speech. His manner was debonair. "How brave he is," they thought. He spoke at length in a loud clear voice. "Will he never finish?" they murmured.

Not only did he confess his treasons. Again and again he lauded the King for his strict administration of the law of the land. Ruled by such a King, he said, every man would receive justice. He asked the crowd to obey, respect, thank God for such a Prince, for such rectitude.

Not once did he ask for pardon for himself. The crowd sensed something suspicious in his unconcern.

Then he spoke of Raleigh. For the first time his cultured voice began to growl. Everything he had said of Raleigh was true, he said. *He* was the traitor, Raleigh; and he reiterated all his accusations, expecting hisses and hoots; but there was a stillness from the crowd.

Then he said, "Derrick, do your duty," and stood up straight, the very image of a lord whose noble ancestors dated back to Magna Carta.

Derrick prepared to discharge his office.

Then suddenly a courier rode up with an order from King James. The execution was to be postponed pending further investigation. Cobham, whom Cecil had quietly tipped off in advance, shouted, "God bless King James!" and was remanded to the Tower.

Having postponed the execution of Cobham, the King could not but postpone the execution of Raleigh. Thus Cobham and Raleigh were both clapped up in the Tower.

For the two traitors shut up in the Tower, reprieved but not pardoned, subject at any moment to the execution of their death sentences, there now began a long period of imprisonment.

We, in our twentieth century, have seen condemned criminals in prison spend fourteen years on Death Row. The outside world quickly forgets them. There are new crimes daily to beguile us with more up-to-date horrors. Raleigh might have put it, *"Plus ça change, plus c'est la même chose."* Or, since he was writing his *History*, quoting everything from Herodotus to Ecclesiastes: there is no new thing under the sun.

Lord Cobham lost everything, languished in prison till he died, forgotten.

With Raleigh it was quite otherwise.

London now lionized the old Elizabethan. King James greatly disliked Raleigh's popularity, but snickered, "At any time I can instruct my judges to execute the verdict of 'Guilty,'" and felt himself secure in his kingcraft. But not quite as secure as he had felt when he first assumed the throne. There was scandal a-brewing, scandal in which he himself was involved, scandal he was trying to cover up because it might backfire to his detriment. He sighed, "Oh wirra, wirra, how does the blatherskite do it! The carriages that parade every day to wait for the rawly rogue's salutation from his prison walls!"

And in this his peculiar warm all-welcoming heart was also involved.

His strong-minded Queen had her carriage driven

daily under the walls of the Tower, where she would wave to the traitor, wait for his doffing of his jewel-studded hat, his stately old-fashioned bow; and pause and send an equerry to inquire how he fared, how was his *History* progressing, how were his chemical experiments progressing, did he need anything? And King James, who loved his pretty Queen, could not find it in his heart to forbid her to drive her carriage anywhere she pleased.

Nor could he forbid Prince Henry, whom he also loved, from riding into the Tower to listen, rapt, to Raleigh's *History* and Raleigh's tales of wars long past and dangers run.

Nor could he prevent that remarkably seductive young man, George Villiers, whom his Queen preferred to Robert Carr—"You must be tired of Carr by now, aren't you, Jamie boy?" "Aye, I suppose I am if you say so; yes, really I am"—he could not prevent George Villiers, who could smell cream and land on his feet like a cat, from riding past the Tower walls, manly-beautiful like an Apollo, from waving a cheery greeting to Raleigh.

With all this going in Raleigh's favor, King James relaxed the stern restrictions he had placed on Raleigh when he first confined him to the Tower. He gave him a chemical laboratory in which to pursue the perfection of his elixirs. He permitted Lady Raleigh to visit him any time she wished, also Raleigh's sons, servants, retainers, Lawrence Keymis, anyone he asked for, and to stay as long as they liked. And Raleigh, despite his self-pitying bewailment of "poverty," was still immensely wealthy; he paid for it all, while complaining to Bess, "I am being bled white."

"You are still alive, my dear."

"For the moment, dear Bess."

CHAPTER XXIV

THERE WERE certain advantages in being a prisoner in
the Tower. Raleigh could not, for example, be accused
of complicity in the murder plot that took place outside the walls of his prison.

King James was indeed growing tired of Robert
Carr, since his Queen told him he ought to be. But
King James could not forget the happy nights when he
walked hand-in-hand with him while the distant moon
half withdrew above the clouds as if to give them
privacy, shedding a mystic beauty on the mists that lay
over the moors; when he would kiss him occasionally
as they philosophized in soft low lover-like tones on the
excellence of Attic friendship and when, as such friends
do, gently, endearingly they fondled each other's genitals,
the very embodiment of close and enduring friendship.
No, he could not forget. And now that his friend was
in trouble he stuck by him and protected him.

Unlike Queen Elizabeth, King James never got jealous when his lovers got married.

In the exercise of his kingcraft he had arranged a
marriage for young Lord Essex, son of the bonnie lad
who had not lived to receive his favor. It was politically
advantageous, designed to unite the religious factions of
his court. And it pleased the King that young Lord
Essex now had a most beautiful bride, for he loved the
contemplation of her beauty just as he loved to con-
template the beauty of his Queen.

Lady Essex was born a Howard, sprig of a noble genealogical tree that produced some of England's best and most famous men as well as some of England's worst and most depraved. Far back (some said more recently), she was blood kin to the man she married. By common assent Lady Essex was the most desirable woman in England. To add to her perfection of face and body she was possessed of a sexuality that glowed from within, magnified, transfigured her beauty.

If King James had been born a private person history would have preserved no account of his existence—another weak well-meaning man who wished to offend no one, hurt no one, above all shed no blood; a learned man who read his Bible assiduously and sincerely believed himself to be like one of the multitude that Jesus addressed in the Beatitudes: Blessed are the merciful, Blessed are the peacemakers. And no man ever so took to heart the oft-repeated adjuration, Love one another. Though of course King James felt free to interpret that adjuration in his own very liberal fashion. Now he was caught up in the quandary of his loves, surrounded by persons stronger than himself, turbulent spirits in a turbulent age.

For he was not born a private person, he was born a King. Hence sprang the necessity for his lies, his waverings, his advances and retreats, his turnabouts, and above all his skilful foreign policy that promised everything to everybody and for a very long time was successful. Here indeed King James was a peacemaker.

The trouble that Robert Carr was in was this: King James received through his spies secret intelligence that Carr and Lady Essex had been observed to kiss and embrace each other at frequent assignations, had been heard to whisper words of love.

Thought King James, with an inward chuckle, "Who wouldn't love Bobby Carr?" and shrugged the matter off for the moment, till the spies reported something worse: Lady Essex was talking about a divorce.

"Canna the woman haud her clack!" growled the King to himself—he thought and prayed in Scotch, though more and more he spoke in public in English, as his Queen had advised him to.

A divorce would upset his policy of unifying the contentious religious factions of his Court. Lord Essex was a Protestant, Lady Essex was a Catholic. "Oh wirra, wirra, my troubles! And the scandal!"

But he rose above his troubles and elaborated a stratagem to end, or at least cover up, the threat of scandal. He sent for Thomas Overbury.

The King had continued to favor Carr, and Carr had risen in honors, as had Overbury, who had found Carr in Scotland and ridden with him in the suite of the King on his progress to London to assume the crown. It seemed a very long time ago.

"Sir Thomas," said the King when Overbury was presented to him, "there is trouble a-brewing for your good friend and mine, Robert Carr. Do you know aught of it?"

"Nothing, Your Majesty."

"You know Lord Essex, of course."

"Of course."

"And his lady, you know her? A most beautiful woman."

Overbury frowned. "Your Majesty, all the world knows Lady Essex, in the common as well as the Biblical sense of the term."

(And Adam knew Eve, his wife, and she conceived. . . .)

Scholarly King James relished the play upon words, but shook his head. " 'Tis no time for a paronomasia. 'Tis a very serious matter. Lady Essex has fallen in love with Robert Carr. But that," said the King, brushing it aside as if it were nothing, remembering that his mother also had had lovers, "that poses no danger of scandal if a woman is discreet; half my Court is in bed with the other half, contracting the pox I dare say. No, Sir Thomas, the danger of scandal lies in the fact that Lady Essex is talking about a divorce from Lord Essex. It would be a catastrophe."

"On what grounds, Your Majesty?"

"Impotence," said the King, with pity in his face.

"I can hardly believe it."

"I must find out. It must be a fearsome thing to be impotent, not to be able to love. Go to him, Sir Thomas. Ask him to his face. The poor man must be suffering the tortures of the damned if it's true. Tell him you come from me. Tell him anything you please about Lady Essex, which he probably knows anyway. Tell him whatever he says will be kept in my heart, my lips will be sealed on my honor as his King, who reversed his father's attainder and restored him to honor. Tell him I love him like a son, like his martyred father, maybe more. He will answer you truthfully."

Overbury did as the King bade him, talked to Essex, and Essex, grateful to his King, answered him truthfully as the King had predicted. Yes, he was impotent with Lady Essex, always had been, he didn't know why, he wasn't with other women. Yes, he knew, to his shame, about Robert Carr and Lady Essex; but in honor he had not said a word, had not denounced them. He too feared scandal, feared to besmirch his good name so lately restored.

Overbury burst into a fury, called the wife of the pitiful young man a whore to his face.

"Sir Thomas, you forget yourself," Essex said with great dignity.

Sorry that he had hurt the young cuckold, Overbury rode back to report to the King.

"You should not have added to his pain," said the King, mildly reproving him. "But there will be no divorce, that I vow."

There never was.

After Overbury had left, Lord Essex got to brooding. He blurted out to his wife everything Overbury had said about her.

She answered, "There will be no scandal, no divorce, my Lord Essex," in a formal voice that sent an icy chill down his spine. "I will be more circumspect in the future."

She was, and the matter seemed to blow over.

But Overbury also got to brooding, and foolishly circulated among his friends, in manuscript, some verses entitled "The Wife," a thinly disguised narrative that, to an instructed eye like King James's, told a sordid story of impotence and adultery, the story of Lord and Lady Essex.

King James was furious: Overbury went to the Tower.

Overbury was little known and soon forgotten. Only the principals knew who the characters in "The Wife" really were.

But Lady Essex did not forget. She said to her lover, Robert Carr, "Sir Thomas will not remain long in the Tower, nor in this life," and told him how she proposed to murder him.

Carr, infatuated, agreed to do what he could to help. "He is, after all," said Carr, "a wicked man, who said there was nothing wrong if I did certain things with the King when he first took a fancy to me, things I knew were wrong. He said I would rise far if I did them."

"And so you have, sweetheart," she said, loving him with a love that had been hideously transmogrified into lust, "and higher still you shall rise, for the King still fancies you."

"But I'm damned if ever again I'll . . ."

"You certainly won't, not with me handy to drain you so limp that that droopy-cod Lord Essex were a Priapus beside you!"

Lady Essex knew from experience that knowledge of

a rival often restores vigor to even the most torpid of husbands, and Lord Essex knew that he had a rival. It behoved a prudent adulteress to keep an impotent husband impotent, lest he do something foolish, like falling in love with his wife and murdering her lover.

So she consulted a prosperous witch, who lived on London Bridge in deceptively humble surroundings, in a tumble-down shack in the poorest part of the Bridge community. Lady Essex, heavily veiled to preserve her anonymity, explained her problem. The witch-woman nodded sagely. She had, she said, the very thing; and produced a little wax figure of a man-doll, "and the man will lose all feeling down there, numb as a corpse, with insertion of the pins," she said, but she cautioned, "No pins in the heart, ducks, not in the heart, or the man will die. Or would you want . . . ?

"No, not him," said Lady Essex. "It would cause comment."

All practitioners of black magic sold such images, and the belief that you could kill a person by sticking pins into a wax doll was widespread. King James himself, in his *Daemonologie*, had spoken of the practice with respect.

The witch-woman weighed Lady Essex's words, "No, not him," and cannily guessed that her customer would not be averse to murdering someone else; but she did not bring up the point immediately.

Knowing that ladies who came to purchase something to make a husband impotent often simultaneously purchased something to make a lover capable of loving all night long, the witch-woman suggested a love potion, guaranteed to be made of the purest potato juice with a tincture of cantharides: "You know, ducks, those little green flies from Spain, very rare, absolutely dependable. Why, I've had men of eighty—No? He isn't eighty? Sixty? No? Well then, all the more potent in a lusty young man!"

"The young man I know doesn't need it," said Lady Essex, her voice husky, looking forward to her next meeting with Carr.

"Aye, that I can hear in your voice, even through a veil, and a lucky man he is. I see you have no further need of my art. Now my prices are nominal, but of course . . ."

"I do need something further from you," Lady Essex said.

She had an enemy, she said, who was trying to kill her. He was now confined to the Tower, a known criminal; but he had powerful friends on the outside. She lived in constant fear of her life, she said. Her enemy might make use of his outside friends to poison her, make it look like a natural death; did any such poisons exist? She made her voice sound little and help-less.

The witch nodded her head to encourage her. "Oh, the rogue, the vile rogue, and you so young! Aye, my dainty ducks, such poisons do exist; and your enemy ought to be given a taste of some, for as I see it, it's his life or yours."

"I'm afraid it is," sighed Lady Essex.

"I can supply the poison," said the witch, and indeed she had everything from arsenic to wolfsbane, but these were so commonly employed in murders that doctors readily recognized them in corpses and traced them to their source; and whoever had sold them was promptly burned at the stake. "It must be something subtle, some-thing to cause death from natural causes." She seemed to be casting about in her mind, but actually she knew exactly what to sell to this cool self-possessed young lady.

"What does your enemy drink?" she asked.

Lady Essex replied, "Wine, I suppose."

"Good," said the witch. "Put what I shall give you in his wine, and your enemy will die a natural death."

"How soon?"

"Soon or late, depending on how much you put in his wine, how often he eats, the strength of his constitution—there are many variables. You must watch how he responds, decide for yourself how soon you wish God to take him unto His own." She paused. "If your enemy is in the Tower I know not how to get the poison into his wine."

"I do," said Lady Essex.

She departed, lighter in the purse by several hundred pounds, heavier by a small wax doll and a bottle of blue vitriol.

Behind her the witch spat into the Thames and shivered with fright. "I never served a customer who terrified me before." She was glad that the cool cruel veiled woman was out of her shop.

Now it was time for Robert Carr to play his part in the murder of his friend by poison. Highly placed as he was it was easy.

First he bribed the Warden of the Tower. For a heavy fee the Warden agreed that Sir Thomas Overbury was to be permitted certain attentions. "He is my close friend," said Carr, but he isn't very well. I want every care to be taken to preserve his health." Very commendable, thought the Warden, who lost money when rich prisoners died, and nodded his head in agreement.

Overbury would require his own suite of servants, Carr said: a special cook to cook his meals, since Overbury had a delicate stomach. And an apothecary, in case Overbury required medicine at any time. He himself, Robert Carr, would send over some cases of light wine for his friend. Could this be arranged?

Nothing could be simpler, said the Warden. "Sir Walter Raleigh also has his own servants in attendance upon him. It is quite usual among my more prominent residents." With every mark of sincerity he praised Robert

Carr's solicitude for his friend. He was thoroughly duped. He had no notion that he was sealing the doom of Sir Thomas Overbury, not then, not for a very long time. And even if he had had, he'd have been helpless to prevent what was about to occur, because Robert Carr was so close to the King. All he could have done would have been to disclaim any knowledge of the matter.

Carr then found a competent apothecary named Franklin, and hired him away from his shop at so princely a fee that Franklin rented his disreputable shop to an equally disreputable character, and took up residence in Overbury's apartment in the Tower, to watch over him and minister to him. "It's probably not for long," said Carr. "My lord," said Franklin, "for as long as your lordship requires. 'Tis an honor to serve you."

Carr then found a vile creature named Mrs. Turner. She was the widow of a physician, whose practice had been devious and unprincipled: those of his patients who died he sold to the "resurrection men," graverobbers, who sold them in turn to legitimate medical societies to be anatomized—the medical societies were always short of prime cadavers and had to turn to such ghouls for material to carry on their research, which was scientific and fruitful. By "anatomizing" a cadaver they could spot evidence of poisons in the organs they examined, tested chemically, scrutinized under their primitive microscopes, thus laying the basis for all modern postmortems. Naturally they were much feared by criminals, and respected by everyone else.

Carr hired Mrs. Turner to prepare Overbury's meals.

Very shortly Overbury became ill.

Blue vitriol is copper sulphate. All metallic poisons are irritant poisons. They attack the mucous membranes of the body—the nose, throat, intestines—causing great pain and thirst.

Overbury grew pale. He experienced tingling sensations in his limbs; then they would become numb. He had bad dreams and muttered in his sleep like a man in a delirium. His appetite failed owing to the pain in his stomach. "You really must eat something," said his cook. "See what I've prepared for you, Sir Thomas, so very good; it will restore your strength." Looking at her as she bent over his bed, Overbury thought her the kindest person in the world.

"I am very thirsty," he said. "Do give me a glass of the excellent wine that Robert sent me." It always eased his stomach pains.

It always contained the blue vitriol that was killing him. Blue vitriol has a sour taste, but the wine was flavored with honey to mask it.

"Thank you," Overbury would say, grateful to be out of pain.

Overbury had a strong constitution. He lingered weeks beyond Lady Essex's expectations, till she grew impatient and said to her lover, "We must double the dose. This very night. See to it!"

Franklin, the apothecary, was sleeping off a boozy imbibition of beer. So Mrs. Turner sent the apothecary's apprentice, a youngster so obscure that nobody ever noticed his presence, to prepare Overbury's fatal cup. The lad seems to have been possessed of some native intelligence. He tasted the stuff Mrs. Turner told him to put into Overbury's wine, screwed up his face into a wry grimace, got scared and said nothing to anyone.

That night Overbury died in great pain.

With unseemly speed Robert Carr had his corpse carted out of the Tower before sun-up and buried in a secret place.

Only now did the Warden of the Tower suspect something amiss. Not only had he lost a most profitable prisoner, but he shrewdly guessed that the unholy coterie that ministered to Overbury in his cell, even Robert Carr, the King's favourite, might have had something to do with his death and his precipitate burial.

The Warden therefore sought out some means of divesting himself of his wardenship, which he rightly deemed to have become a hazard. He offered the wardenship for sale, and quickly found a buyer named Helwys, who was delighted to get so coveted a position and a little bit suspicious because he had got it so cheaply. Cautiously he questioned Mrs. Turner and the apothecary, but of course learned nothing from that precious pair. Only the frightened apothecary's apprentice seemed to be hiding a secret, and he would say only, "I wouldn't drink any of Mrs. Turner's wine if I were you, Master Helwys," and then the lad disappeared into foreign parts unknown with a large sum of money obtained no one knew how. The new Warden thought, "I wonder he was allowed to live."

He was allowed to live because Robert Carr was not at heart a killer, any more than King James.

Helwys felt somewhat safer in his new job as one by one the persons in the poison circle began to leave the Tower, Franklin the apothecary back to his shop, with Mrs. Turner to perform small jobs of deviltry for him. They dwelt in obscurity, well supplied with money, knowing that their lives hung by a thread if they were caught doing anything as spectacular as the thing they had just done, knowing they would instantly be dispatched.

When Robert Carr reported the unfortunate death of Overbury to King James, the King said, "Too bad, too bad; Sir Thomas introduced you to me. I always liked him for that." He was much more interested in Carr's insistence that he be allowed to marry Lady Essex, and sighed, "You're too good for that lady, lad," but Carr was obdurate.

There was now only the thorny religious question of the divorce to be faced. The King had vowed that there would be no divorce, nor was there. But an annulment was another matter entirely: every Christian

Church, from the Presbyterian Kirk of Scotland to the College of Cardinals in Rome, recognized impotence in a husband as valid grounds for declaring a marriage null and void *ab initio*, from the very beginning, as if the marriage had never occurred: it simply had never existed.

Nothing was now required but to prove that the union had never been consummated, that the wife was still a virgin.

Forthwith King James, albeit reluctantly, deputed a panel of experts to examine into the virginity or non-virginity of Lady Essex. The panel was comprised of midwives of unblemished reputation plus a covey of physicians and, as a contemporary wrote, tongue-in-cheek, "seven bawdy bishops."

A heavily veiled woman alleged to be Lady Essex appeared before the panel. No one saw her face. Owing to her high rank, the panel were told, as well as to her maidenly modesty and the delicacy she felt at being forced to submit to such an examination, Lady Essex was permitted to conceal her features. Historians are almost unanimous in believing that the veiled woman was actually Lady Essex, despite the obvious opportunity for substituting a real virgin: King James had personally appointed the panel and King James was a stickler for legal details.

But of course there was nothing to prevent King James from dropping a hint that he hoped the panel would find Lady Essex a virgin, which is precisely what they did.

The midwives peeked under her farthingale, while the bishops looked away in well-simulated embarrassment, and in less than a minute the midwives solemnly declared that Lady Essex was a virgin. Since her reputation was well known, one of the bishops was later heard to remark, with a wondering shake of his head and a show of faith well befitting his high office, "Today I have witnessed a miracle the like of which hath not been seen in this world since the star shone over the stable in Bethlehem sixteen hundred years ago."

The marriage was dissolved, null and void *ab initio*. Lord Essex held his peace, in dignity and shame, glad to be quit of the adulteress. Robert Carr then married her, spent his nights and days in an ecstasy of pleasure that drove him to the verge of madness over the possession of the most beautiful body in England.

King James then decided to give Robert Carr and his virgin bride a sumptuous estate in which to spend their honeymoon. Carr suggested Sherborne. James instantly agreed.

Since Raleigh had failed to commit suicide Sherborne had now become Crown property. If Raleigh had killed himself, Sherborne would have gone to his son, as was his intention and the motive for his suicide attempt: Sherborne would have been beyond the reach of King James. But Raleigh had failed and now lay condemned to a traitor's death, reprieved but not pardoned, legally dead. Traitors' estates reverted to the King.

The prospect of imminent loss of his favorite home struck Raleigh like a thunderbolt, gave him nightmares; but a legally dead man was helpless.

Bess Raleigh was equally appalled. In a pitiable state of depression she wrote to King James:

> I beseech Your Majesty, in the mercies of Jesus Christ, to signify your gracious pleasure concerning myself and my poor children. Your Majesty hath disposed of all my husband's estates, save one small farm which Your Majesty bestowed upon my husband in Dorsetshire for his lifetime.

But she knew that a man who is legally dead possesses no lifetime. The King could take this small farm from the traitor at any moment. She continued:

[327]

I beg that it will please Your Majesty, out of your abundant goodness, to relinquish Your Majesty's right in the reversion of that small farm, and suffer my poor harmless children to enjoy the same, in imitation of the most just and merciful God, who, though He punished the fathers, yet gave the land to the guileless and innocent children

("I dinna faddom the lady's reference," mused James to himself, wrinkling his scholarly brow. Didna the Bible punish the bairns unto the third and fourth generation?) But the King, who loved children, was touched by her appeal. Didna Jesus say: Suffer little children to come unto me, for of such is the Kingdom of Heaven. "Aye that He did, and Lady Raleigh shall have her little farm. But *I* will have Sherborne for Robert Carr!" Bess Raleigh concluded:

We shall ever pray to God for the continuance and increase of Your Majesty's dearest comforts.

CHAPTER XXV

PERHAPS he had high blood pressure. Only a twentieth-century sphygmomanometer could have diagnosed his condition, and in Raleigh's time there was of course no such instrument in existence. But certain it was that the imminent loss of Sherborne caused him great mental anguish; and certain it is to this day that inordinate worry sends your blood pressure soaring and exacerbates your condition; and no modern doctor is ever surprised if suddenly something pops in your skull when, close to his patient and knowing your background, he sees you suffer a cerebral hemorrhage.

One morning Sir Walter Raleigh awoke to find that he could not move his left arm or left leg. In a fuzzy befuddled state of mind he thought, "How queer. That's my good leg," but he was much too sick to think further than that, nor did he very much care. Nor did he know that the left side of his face was also paralyzed, or that his left eye was open and staring. "Half my master," thought his servant, seeing the staring eye, "is ready to put the dead penny on!" and gently closed it lest it dry out and go blind, and fled to the Warden to report Sir Walter's sudden decline.

Before the servant closed the left eye Sir Walter saw double. "Only one servant usually attends me at breakfast," he thought. "Now two? Good! Who deserves it more than I!" and forthwith lapsed into a dreamless

coma, in which he lay for three days and three nights.
Consciousness dimly returned.

Now we know, as no one knew then, that Nature was healing him: the blood that had burst into his brain was being absorbed, the lesions turning into scar tissue: Raleigh's apoplexy was not to be fatal. It was merely Nature's warning of things to come.

He was aware, as consciousness returned, that there were people in his room, concern on their faces, asking him questions: his servant, the Warden, King James's physician, Prince Henry. He heard, understood the questions, tried to answer. But he could only mumble, with half his mouth, the other half drooling. Tenderly Prince Henry wiped it with a handkerchief, nigh upon weeping. On which Sir Walter lapsed again into a dreamless sleep, but this time more healthy as Nature healed him.

Nobody knew he was healing. Prince Henry said to his mother, "Visit this good man before he dies," for death seemed just around the corner. "I have always admired him greatly," said the Queen; and forthwith her carriage entered the Tower and she sat for hours by Raleigh's bedside, comforting him by her presence, patting his ring-bejeweled hand which, as he healed, now no longer was paralyzed and tenderly grasped hers in thanks.

"It was," said the King's physician, who was also the King's spy, "like a miracle, as if Her Majesty possessed by her touch, like Your Majesty, a divine healing power."

"Vurra like," said the King; for he often touched for the King's evil and conceived that his Royal touch cured other evils also, including apoplexy.

But he wasn't too pleased when, a few weeks later, Sir Walter Raleigh completely recovered. Nor was he pleased that large crowds gathered below the walls of the Tower to cheer the return to health of the old Elizabethan.

King James's popularity was waning. The cost of his pleasures and the Queen's rose every day. Parliament, which held the purse strings, stubbornly refused to vote funds to pay for the Royal Family's extravagances. Thereupon the King dismissed his Parliament, determined to rule without it. He had a perfect right to send Members of Parliament back to their homes, and he promptly took advantage of that right. He was honestly convinced that he ruled by Divine Right of Kings, was responsible to God alone. Hence, a Parliament had no say in fiscal matters, only he, King James. If Parliament refused to vote him funds he would obtain funds by other means.

He asked Robert Cecil how this could be done.

Cecil had a ready answer: "Your Majesty hath by ancient right the power to create English nobility," he said. "Such right hath never been questioned since time out of mind."

"So I have," said the King, harkening back to King William the Norman.

"I suggest to Your Majesty," said Cecil, "that a new order of nobility should be created." There was, Cecil said, a place in the ladder-scale of honors, ranking just above a knight (which Raleigh was) and just below a baron, that might be called a "baronet."

"Your Majesty could sell the baronetcy," Cecil said; and suggested a going price of one thousand pounds.

This King James did; and suddenly there arose to power some thousands of new nobles, anybody who happened to have a thousand pounds to buy the title "Bart." From this cynical sale dates the title England has to this day. Many baronets have proven excellent men, though those who first bought the title were anything but.

But the ancient nobility of England detested Cecil for this sale, and Cecil became the most hated man in England.

Still it wasn't enough, and King James's money problems continued, for he simply could not curtail his expenses.

As King James's popularity declined, as Robert Cecil came to be hated, laughed at, scorned for his diminutive stature and the hump on his back, a nostalgic generation was growing up. The days of the late great Queen seemed golden days. Little children, who could not possibly remember Elizabeth, would gather under the walls of the Tower to catch a glimpse of Walter Raleigh, who seemed to epitomize an age that had passed but must have been good.

Bejeweled and tall, erect, with gray in his beard, he, who had always loved children, would doff his hat, wave to them and give them a stately old-fashioned bow that made them feel proud and sent them home to their mothers with oddly mature words of praise in their childish mouths that greatly puzzled their parents. Yes, thought the children, those must have been golden days.

All this Sir Walter took only as his due.

With time on his hands Sir Walter's busy pen was busier than ever, not only with his *History* but with his perennial preoccupation, ships. Just as his *History* was written to instruct Prince Henry, so was his monograph on the architecture of ships written to instruct the heir to the throne, to instruct him that ships of the Royal Navy would always protect England against enemies, and that his was the way to build them.

Thus he specified from the Tower:

MOST EXCELLENT PRINCE:

1/ A warship should be strong built;
2/ Swift in sail;
3/ Stout-sided;

4/ Her ports so laid that her great guns be serviceable above water in all weather;

5/ That she hull and trim well, whether upon or before the wind;

6/ A ship of six hundred tuns will carry as good ordinance as a ship of twelve hundred tuns, if she turn about fast and thus double her broadside;

7/ To make her strong, watch over the workmen, that they exercise their skill and shirk not;

8/ To make her swift, lay out her bows before and her quarters behind, that she forge ahead with speed and likewise, when required, backwards; and make sure that she neither hang in the water nor take green seas, but lie clear above it;

9/ Stout of side by providing a long deck, shaving off from above water to the nether edge of the ports; which done she will carry her ordinance ready to shoot in all weather.

There were further technical specifications, then:

Above all things, have care that the great guns be four foot clear above the water, for if the ports lie lower it is dangerous, the great guns wetting and idle; and by that default was a goodly ship and many gallant gentlemen lost in the days of Henry the Eighth before the Isle of Wight in a ship called by the name of *Mary Rose*.

In a ship called the *Mary Rose** the father of Raleigh's cherished cousin and trusted sea captain, Sir Richard Grenville, had drowned. Raleigh never forgot, and fully expected to share the same fate: the watery death of so many Westcountry mariners. "There are much worse deaths," he mused. "Perishing in your ship is much better than dying of apoplexy; yes, there are much worse deaths." There certainly were. Raleigh's own.

---

* Footnote: Far into our own century there have been ships in the British Royal Navy named after Raleigh's *Ark Royal* and Grenville's *Mary Rose*.

Just as he had harkened, rapt, to Raleigh's *History*, so also Prince Henry harkened to Raleigh's long-proven expertise in the building of ships. Ships not only protected the sceptered isle of England, as Shakespeare phrased it, ships sailed all 'round the world; and in his manly expanding mind Prince Henry sometimes imagined himself striding the quarterdeck, a sailor, an explorer, a mariner like Raleigh. Sir Walter mused, "Here, when I am gone, is a King that will build a navy as I would have built it myself, forever protecting us!"

Dearly he loved him, as you love a child in whom you see yourself mirrored, and the love was mutual. Once Prince Henry said to Raleigh, "Sir Walter, you have taught me much." Raleigh replied, drawing himself up, "Such is my intention," and the young prince wasn't offended despite Raleigh's incredible self-assurance.

Prince Henry was useful to Raleigh in minor ways. Once Raleigh said, "Your Highness, kindly procure me a two-fathom length of copper tubing. I should like it tomorrow."

"What in the world—copper tubing, Sir Walter?"

"I am perfecting my Golden Elixir," said Raleigh, and stared down the incredulous Prince.

"Oh very well," said Henry. "I suppose it can be arranged."

Raleigh needed the copper tubing to distill a medicine that he firmly believed would cure all human ills.

Next day Raleigh got his copper tubing, "perfected" his elixir and, having made careful note of all the weird things that went into it, bottled up some demijohns of it, thanking Prince Henry, who said, laughing, "Don't ever use that stuff on me!"

Raleigh said, "Highness, I shall never have to." But he did, when the time came to do so.

Most of the Golden Elixir was pure brandy. Some was sassafras and potato juice. Some was a decoction of meadow saffron. But in Raleigh's notes there is a curious mention of "that other, only a smidgin."

What "that other" was is not known to this day.

But the British Royal Navy swore by it, took it when sick and seems to have benefited from it for a very long time: two centuries after Raleigh and Prince Henry were dust in their graves the navy hoped for health from Walter Raleigh's Golden Elixir.

None of this pleased King James. Even so small an amount as a fathom or two of copper tubing irked him. His Admiralty had signified to His Majesty that ships of the Royal Navy should be copper-bottomed, and here was a waste, albeit small; but no Scot can abide a waste and the King blamed Raleigh. He said to his son, "Ye love the rawly rogue, d'ye not, my bairn?"

"Aye, but not half so much as you, Father."

"Wirra, wirra, wirra," moaned the King. "I fret me sair," and inquired, "What says your mother?"

"She loves him too, but not half so much as you."

The King muttered, "Absalom, Absalom, my son, my son."

"What?" said Prince Henry.

"Naught," said the King.

"Father?"

"Aye, fruit of my loins?"

"Oh, for goodness' sake, stop it."

"I shall. I will. What is it, Henry?"

"Set him free, this Raleigh. I ken his quirks, but much, much he hath to advance Your Majesty."

"Son, son," with tears in his eyes, "call not your father 'Majesty.'"

"Majestic I deem you. I beg you, set him free."

"Is that what you want?"

"Please, if it please you, Sire."

The King said, "Sire is a good word, a classic word, do you know what it means, the word 'sire,' my Henry? Sire means 'father,' and that assuredly I am of you, my son. And mark you"—King James was off again on his acronyms and philogistics—"'Son' has another interesting designation, signifying male offspring, which you most certainly are, male, oh so male; but did you not know—of course you did not—that the very same term signifies 'Son of God'? Hm, hm, hm. One day I shall compose a monograph on this interesting subject, Son of God. For there's no question that I rule, like God's Son, by divine Right of Kings. Yes, I shall compose that monograph."

"Father?"

"Yes, son?"

"You'll set him free?"

"Aye, I will set him free—or at least let him out of the Tower, which he seems to have transformed into a court of his own, what with you and your mother paying him daily visits, to say nothing of the rabble who gather in crowds to catch a glimpse of him and cheer him."

King James could not stand up to his manly son, or his spendthrift Queen, or indeed almost anyone else with a will stronger than his; and as usual promised everything to anybody, serene in the conviction that he was answerable to God alone. But there was a stubborn streak in him.

Prince Henry said, "Sire, when you set him free, will you not also grant him full pardon for the conviction of treason found against him by the Court?"

The King said, "Henry, when you are King, you will discover that a King does not pardon convicted traitors. No. You can ease their confinement, postpone and forget their execution, but never pardon. To do so breeds dissension, begets a bevy of other ambitious plotters and traitors, undermines the foundation of the King's authority and poses a threat even to the life of the King, as history is witness since Caesar's time—I could not abide the assassination of a King Henry, son and heir of King James. Do not ask me again to pardon the traitor, my son. 'Tis your own good, your own life I protect."

Prince Henry nodded, forced to agree. His father

[336]

was exercising true kingcraft. For Raleigh himself had read to him from his *History* countless instances of good kings who were killed by traitors, and worse kings mounted the throne only to be killed by other traitors, and after them worse and worse kings, only to suffer the same fate, till the title King became a laughingstock and once, in ancient Rome, was actually auctioned off to the highest bidder.

"I will not ask it again," he said, "for I acknowledge your wisdom in this matter."

King James was immensely gratified. Prince Henry suggested that Christmas would be an appropriate occasion for the King to let Raleigh out of the Tower. The King readily agreed. That was the time of year when everyone gave gifts, made good cheer, was happy; and a generous regal gesture would be greeted by the people with general applause. It might even restore some of his waning popularity.

Henry brought the good news to Raleigh in the Tower. "When I am King," he said, "Sherborne shall be yours again, never doubt it, Sir Walter."

Raleigh too was immensely gratified. But Prince Henry was still young and King James was in excellent health, like all the Stuarts, and would likely live many years; and Raleigh felt put upon at the prospect of waiting so long for the return of his favorite estate.

Cleverly mixing praise of the Prince with his congenital proclivity to self-pity, convinced that he was being wronged, he made a little speech: where, he asked Prince Henry, would he and Lady Raleigh live during all those years? He had no home, save that one small farm in the Westcountry. Then, reverting to Sherborne, "I understand it is to go to Robert Carr, your royal father's handsome—I had almost said beautiful—favourite and his very good friend. Sherborne has always been lived in by men. And now, belike, it will be lived in by faggots."

Prince Henry blushed red as a beet. "Faggot" was a

term of reproach applied to loose and compliant women. Henry fancied Robert Carr no more than did Sir Walter Raleigh, for he now knew more about the sexual ambivalence that sometimes afflicts even a King.

"I will see to it that doesn't happen," he said. "My father is pressed for money. I will ask him to rent Sherborne, for Carr would get it free; and you shall have most of the rent."

He asked his father. His father consulted Cecil. Cecil saw a chance to get a good round sum of ready cash to pour into the rapidly dwindling royal coffers; and advised the King to do as his son suggested, which James promptly did.

Then the King had a message for Carr, presented regretfully but with finality: he, the King, found it necessary to rent Sherborne, and he, Robert Carr, must live elsewhere till other arrangements could be made. To sweeten the bitter pill, the King presented Carr with a grant of money plus considerably more out of his privy purse, in short, bought him off. Robert Carr was delighted; he was still in his master's favor; his clothes were never so resplendent, his tailors never so well paid.

The King also promised Walter Raleigh, at Henry's insistence, a goodly portion of the Sherborne rent.

Thus everyone was pleased: Carr was appeased, and the populace was delighted: their old Elizabethan was to be released, they all assumed pardoned; Robert Carr, whom everyone disliked because of his influence over the King, seemed to be losing favor and was not to have Raleigh's Sherborne. For a while King James was popular again, smiled graciously from the windows of his coach when his people cheered him. This had not happened for a very long time.

But Christmas had not yet arrived, the weather was still summer-hot and humid, and Raleigh grew lonesome in the Tower. Sensing the wind had veered in his favor, he besought the King to permit Lady Raleigh and his family to share his confinement. This request King James graciously granted, carefully letting it be known that Lady Raleigh was not a prisoner, could come and go as she pleased.

Richly dressed, she arrived in a handsome coach, followed by a suite of servants, her tall sons on horseback flanking the coach. It was clear to the people that generous King James had not beggared his prisoner of the Tower.

Thus it was that King James's kingcraft had accomplished much. At home and abroad he had brought about peace. No Spanish invasion threatened. Ireland was quiescent. Where lately his people had hungered, Nature suddenly turned about and bestowed upon western Europe a succession of bountiful harvests, and his well-fed subjects were in no mood to murmur. Patently he and God had accomplished that which Bess Raleigh had termed his "dearest comforts." His mind was at peace, and some ugly skeletons that stank in the closets bade fair to stay there, forgotten.

Then it was that the apothecary's apprentice who had tasted Overbury's fatal cup, the youngster whom James could not bring himself to kill but let live, foolishly talked. In a Brussels tavern, to make himself look big, having drunk too much wine, he declared that he knew a secret, that nobody else knew, that would cause their hair to stand on end. Sir Thomas Overbury, he said, had been poisoned in his food by Robert Carr and his beautiful wife. This was duly reported to King James through his spies. "Wirra, wirra, wirra," sighed the King. "Now is a scandal; and now my poor Carr will suffer, and I canna protect him."

King James was far too intelligent to delude himself that his were the only spies who had heard the foolish babbling of the apothecary's apprentice in the Brussels tavern. England had always had enemies jealous of her growing power, always been spied upon. Certain it was that they would have heard with glee of the youngster's indiscretion. To add to England's enemies he knew that he himself had made many more. "Wirra, wirra."

He consulted Robert Cecil, whom he still trusted though he knew that Cecil had replaced Raleigh as the worst hated man in England. Cecil already knew through the Spaniards who paid him his pension that the apothecary's apprentice had opened a Pandora's box of furies that threatened his pension, and secretly blamed the King's soft heart for letting the youngster live.

"I see naught," he blandly advised the King, "but to institute a thorough inquiry into the matter, and if there be guilt, let the guilty be punished."

"That I will," said the King.

Then there was held the most gruesome trial ever held in the reign of King James.

CHAPTER XXVI

THE POPULARITY that King James had achieved by his generous treatment of Sir Walter and Bess Raleigh was short-lived. He bitterly regretted taking the advice of his still-trusted Secretary of State "that the matter be thoroughly inquired into, and if there be guilt, let the guilty be punished." Perhaps, mused the King, with the exercise of kingcraft, I could have hushed up the scandal a while longer.

"But the puir mon is sick," he remembered. Perhaps Cecil was not in full command of his faculties.

Sick he assuredly was. A contemporary wrote:

> He hath a swelling in his thigh which, increasing daily, was at first thought good; molifying medicines were applied, and the surgeon cut it, but then it grew angry and gangrened, and the matter running out of it was very venomous and so poisoned the surgeon who lanced it that he hath ever since lain at death's door.

Cecil was too sick to attend the inquiry, which was thorough. All who heard the evidence were sickened by the details and furious at the highly placed persons involved: patently there was corruption in King James's Court. A forlorn unimportant forgotten prisoner in the Tower had been cruelly poisoned, and King James had hushed up the scandal to shield his weak and worthless minions, especially his favourite Robert Carr and his beautiful bride.

The contemporary wrote of the poisoned man:

> There was nobody with him when he died, but the foulness of his corpse left aspersion that he had died of something worse than the pox. He was a very unfortunate man, for almost nobody remembered or pitied his plight, and his very friends speak but indifferently of him.

Once again the peculiar English sense of fair play, inborn and working contrariwise, was outraged. The London populace, long inured to the spectacle of public executions, who never turned a hair at the savage torments they saw inflicted, turned out in throngs to witness and cheer the inquiry and the executions that followed, hissed and sneered as one by one the principals denounced each other:

Sir Thomas Overbury's jailor swore he knew nothing of the poisoning, wasn't believed, blamed the apothecary.

Franklin, the apothecary, flushed out of his shop and haled into court, swore equal innocence, was equally disbelieved, blamed Mrs. Turner.

Who was equally disbelieved. She claimed that Helwys, the Warden of the Tower, bore the ultimate responsibility.

The Warden of the Tower conceded that he had indeed been aware of certain special attentions accorded Sir Thomas before his unfortunate death, but maintained that he had acted upon direct orders from Robert Carr and his Lady, who seemed to have taken Sir Thomas under their special attention. Indeed, said the Warden, Robert Carr had told him exactly that, "special attention," in so many words. "Naturally I did not interfere in the affairs of so eminent a personage."

Robert Carr, still handsome and beautifully dressed,

cast his eyes about the court for some sign of the King; surely the King would remember, forgive. But King James had fled weeping to his Queen, who tenderly dried his eyes and counseled him, "There, there, Jamie boy, don't cry, don't cry. Robert Carr is a rogue, and growing old. George Villiers would serve you better, and not marry a whore," and King James was appeased.

Before the whole court Robert Carr stoutly maintained his innocence, swore he knew nothing of the crime; and such was his eloquence that many believed him.

But then his Lady took the stand. To the disgust and astonishment of everyone present she pleaded guilty. Yes, she said calmly, she had brought about the poisoning of Sir Thomas Overbury because he had called her a whore; and hatred blazed from the snake-hypnotic eyes of the most beautiful woman in England. As for her husband, she said, turning upon him with scorn, he had arranged all the details. She had had only to ask him and he, Robert Carr, had suborned all the other accomplices.

Then glancing gravely down, she crossed herself like one who has just confessed to a priest, and said in a sweet low voice, "I am sorry for my sin, and I cast myself on the mercy of God and the King's Gracious Majesty."

Derrick was busy that day. He hanged Mrs. Turner, Franklin the apothecary, Sir Thomas's jailor and Helwys, the Warden of the Tower.

Robert Carr and his Lady, King James imprisoned in the Tower—perhaps after all he remembered the tender intimacies, the long sweet walks hand-in-hand under the misty mystical Scottish moon. He must have, for he could not bring himself to hang his erstwhile lover, and since not him, neither his Lady. But their careers and influence were at an end; and when, later, he pardoned them, nobody cared, and when, later still, they died, nobody even took notice, since people have short memories: Time and Death never pause.

The most welcome death was that of Robert Cecil, the Secretary of State, who quietly passed away, his frail body worn out and eaten up with disease. To the King's dismay there was found among his secret papers irrefutable evidence that he had been in the pay of Spain. "I could never have believed it," sighed the King. "Another scandal, for this too will come out," as indeed it did, adding to the odium that the worst hated man in England carried with him to his grave. The Queen suggested, "George Villiers has a good eye for figures, better than Cecil's."

In the Tower Sir Walter Raleigh received concise details of all this from a source far better informed than any spy, Prince Henry, who visited him daily. Raleigh shook his head sadly at the news of Cecil's death. "The late great Queen used to call him 'little man,' and little he turned out to be"; then in anger, "And they accused *me* of taking bribes from Spain!" Henry laughed good-naturedly. "No, not you, not from Spain anyhow." Raleigh looked at him sharply; the Prince was wise beyond his years. But Henry continued, with some distaste, "The Queen, my mother, has found a replacement for Robert Carr. I hope he'll prove better."

"He could hardly prove worse, whoever he is," said Raleigh, who disliked talking to Henry about his royal father's weakness.

Henry went on, "He's a true Englishman, Sir Walter, cultured, good-looking of course, inordinately vain but immune to flattery, which he detects at the first word; he is brave even to rashness and greedy for wealth— which a good Scot like my father will understand. I think my mother has made a good choice. When I am King I may need such a man as George Villiers."

Raleigh nodded in half approval. Since there was

sure to be a male favourite as long as King James was King James, perhaps a man like George Villiers would do the least harm. He seemed to have many of the qualities of Raleigh's own Westcountry mariners.

"He likes ships, as I do," said the Prince, "and no doubt the King will take renewed interest in the Royal Navy." He seemed almost to be pleading a cause, almost to be asking Raleigh to overlook James's notorious character flaw.

Raleigh said gallantly, "Your Highness's royal mother is a wise woman, and England can thank God that His Majesty harkens to so good a counsellor."

Hidden in the womb of History, long after both Henry and Raleigh were dead, lay the terrible fate of George Villiers who, when he died the second richest nobleman in England, died of an assassin's dagger thrust through his heart.

"When I am King . . ." Prince Henry had said. But he never was.

Christmas was only two months away. With Christmas would come Raleigh's release from the Tower. King James had promised, and now that the Overbury scandal had reduced him to ridicule and contempt, he meant to keep his promise. Releasing the old Elizabethan would please the people and restore much of his former popularity. Why, he might even be cheered again!

Though late in the year the weather turned unseasonably warm. Bess Raleigh and her sons spent much of their time in a London town house that Sir Walter had bought her. She could not abide the stench of the moat that lay at the foot of the Tower, nor the miasma that rose from the Thames that daily washed its sewage and garbage back and forth with the tides on the other side. Sir Walter was used to it after his long confinement, but he said to his wife, "Dear Bess, 'twere better you take the boys down to our little farm, where the Westcountry air is clean," but she preferred to stay in London to be close to him, saying, "It's not so bad in the house away from the river, and there's not so long to go now, only till Christmas." He kissed her, jubilant at his imminent release. Only two months! A free man again.

Then came another death, a death that changed the history of England. If Prince Henry had lived, the deplorable story of the Stuart Dynasty would have been different, and probably baby Charles would not have had his head chopped off, nor would a dictator have arisen in place of a King—but the historian can only record, not speculate on what might have been.

Sweating in Raleigh's study, Prince Henry suddenly took it into his head to go for a swim. He dove into the Thames, stayed only a few minutes, came out cool and refreshed.

"Bathe yourself thoroughly when you go home," Raleigh admonished him sternly. "Your Royal Highness stinks like bilge water."

Prince Henry laughed. "The King has a tub full of sweet pure water, drawn from a palace well. It is full of perfume. Robert Carr used to use it all the time. Tomorrow when I visit you I shall be fragrant as a flower. Au revoir, till tomorrow, Sir Walter."

"Au revoir, till tomorrow, Your Highness," said Raleigh laughing heartily at the notion of a perfumed Prince. Henry usually smelled like saddle leather and the horses he rode fast and hard, good manly smells, soldierly smells, lacking only the smell of gunpowder, "and I trow that will come in time," Raleigh mused, utterly delighted with his royal protégé and friend, his King-to-be.

But Prince Henry did not return the next day, nor the next nor the next. Not really alarmed, but missing his company, Raleigh sent Lawrence Keymis to the palace to inquire how he fared. Keymis was received with politeness by an equerry, but informed that His

Royal Highness was indisposed, running a fever, and that No, he could not see him. The physicians were bleeding him. Keymis came back with the same report every day for a week.

"You did not see the Prince?"

"No, Sir Walter."

Raleigh cursed the King's order that kept him shut up in the Tower. He remembered the Prince's swim in the Thames. "He smelt like bilge water." He remembered how ships' bilges served as sumps into which all the ships' latrines vented, and how sewage was daily dumped into the Thames. He was thoroughly alarmed. The Prince might have swallowed some infected Thames water.

At length he sent for his wife. "Good Bess, beg an audience of the Queen. Entreat her to let me come to see Prince Henry, though I go shackled in chains on a hurdle! Notify to Her Majesty that I have a medicine that will cure Prince Henry's illness. Will you do so, my dear?"

"I will try," she said, "though I doubt if I'll be received. The King's physicians forbid all visits, they're so busy bleeding him and now, the word goes, they're blistering his scalp to drive out the fever. But I'll try."

Lady Raleigh was instantly received by the Queen, whose face was ashy pale. King James stood beside her, tears running down his cheeks into his sparse auburn beard. Lady Raleigh delivered her message. "Sir Walter hath perfected a Golden Elixir, that he firmly believes will cure the illness of His Royal Highness," and declared that Sir Walter desired to administer it, "though he knows he is a prisoner, though you let him out of the Tower if only for an hour, though you bring him here under heavy guard and in chains, for he loves Prince Henry like one of our own sons." Lady Raleigh spoke with some bitterness, but it was lost on the distraught royal parents.

The Queen said, "Sir Walter shall be brought hither with all speed; his only guard shall be our royal Guard of Honor."

The King sobbed, "My son lies speechless, motionless in a coma. My physicians give me no hope. Oh Henry, my son, my son!"

Raleigh was instantly sent for. It was a long time since he had ridden a horse. It took all his will power not to look awkward as he mounted, throwing his stiff right leg over the saddle and easing his foot down into the stirrup. "I'll be goddamned if I look like a cripple in front of Her Majesty's Captain of the Guard!" He swore so loudly that the burly Scotch Captain, who did not know that the prisoner had once held the same title, turned his head and looked at him curiously.

Then they rode like the wind.

The palace gates flew open.

Raleigh approached the bed of Prince Henry. The room was full of the fetid smell of the Prince's bloody stool. There on his cheeks were the telltale splotches, there was the labored breathing, the brow on fire with fever. It was the bilge-water fever that Raleigh had seen many sailors die of. He hoped he wasn't too late.

Gently he raised Prince Henry's hot dry head, tenderly he spooned some of his Golden Elixir into his mouth, repeating the dosage again and again till the Prince had swallowed perhaps half a cupful. For a long time nothing happened. Then suddenly there was a twitching in his cheeks, he opened his eyes, recognized Raleigh. Seemingly without effort he raised himself almost to a sitting position, grasped Raleigh's hand and said distinctly, "Sir Walter! It was good of you to come to see me. I have been ill."

Then he sighed, lay back on his pillow and dozed off to sleep with a smile on his lips.

The King and Queen, who witnessed this demonstration of Raleigh's Golden Elixir, deemed it a miracle. It was the first time Prince Henry had moved in days. Raleigh rode back to the Tower jubilant. It is no small thing to save the life of one's future King.

Next day Prince Henry died.

Christmas came. Christmas passed. The Tower moat froze over and little children with Holland skates skated upon it, ofttimes falling flat on the seat of their pants, laughing and standing erect again, the picture of health.

So also the Thames was healthy, with chunks of ice in it. Foul it continued to be, but it no longer stank of bilge water. And nobody went swimming in it, not in that frigid weather; and so nobody got typhoid fever, which is what modern medicos think Henry died of. But Walter Raleigh, still wealthy, still respected, indeed held a little in awe by the Royal Family by reason of his Golden Elixir—Walter Raleigh remained shut up in the Tower.

"I am forgotten," he fumed with a sailorman's curse, "forgotten like Overbury, and here I shall eat out my guts till I die, die, die!"

When Prince Henry died Raleigh no longer had any motive to continue his *History*, for now there was no King-to-be to instruct. He wrote of it: "Whereas this book, by the title it hath, calls itself *The First Part of the General History of the World*, implying a second and third volume, which I also had included and hewn out, now it hath pleased God to take that Glorious Prince out of this world. His unspeakable and never-to-be-enough-lamented loss hath taught me to say with Job: 'My harp is turned to mourning, and my organ into the voice of them that weep.' "

So ended, in dolor, Raleigh's *History of the World*.

He sent the manuscript to King James, who riffled through it. James's scholarly mind was delighted with its erudition, its long and accurate quotations from many of the ancient Romans that he himself admired; he was astonished to discover that Raleigh was at heart a true Christian, though somewhat irreverent, who constantly extolled the superiority of Christianity over even the wisest and best of the ancient pagan philosophers. Most of all the King was touched by the last sad words in which Raleigh mourned, as did the King, the death of Prince Henry.

King James had it published. But he had it published anonymously, without Raleigh's name. It was instantly popular and ran through many editions. But the secret leaked out that the work was the work of Sir Walter. The King grumbled, "He is popular enough, and I saw no reason to make him more popular still."

Then, on closer inspection, the King found some comments that implied that kings were no better than anyone else, on which he withdrew the book muttering that it was "too saucy in censuring princes." But the precious *History* remains to this day as a window into a vastly complex and many-compartmented mind, grown mellow through years of misfortune and frustration. This is not, of course, to say that Raleigh's mind had lost its cunning.

One morning he woke up in a cold sweat. He had dreamed a terrifying dream. He was in the *Ark Royal*, fighting a sea battle against a Spanish galleon. A Spanish cannonball shot off his right arm. Then another shot off his right leg. And when he woke he could not move them. "Here I shall die of apoplexy," he muttered. "Would God that the dream were true and I had died at sea!" It was the death he had always envisioned for himself as most desirable.

One of his servants brought him his breakfast. Raleigh told him curtly to leave it by the bedside. The servant was surprised by the brusqueness of his manner and asked Lawrence Keymis to look in on him. "Sir Walter seems not to be himself this morning."

Keymis came, looked down at his master, grew greatly alarmed. There was a weird wild look in Raleigh's eyes that Keymis had never seen before and, well as he knew him, could not comprehend. "I must fetch your Lady at once," he said.

"God rot ye, Keymis, that you shall not, not till I'm better!" and softer, "It's not like it was before Lawrence, not half so bad. Then I couldn't move or speak. Now look."

With an effort he propped himself up on his pillows using his left arm, then lay back smiling. "Bess would only tell the Queen and the Queen would pity me and tell the King and the King would send his doctors to bleed me white and belike poison me in my food like Overbury, nothing would please him more. No, no thank you; there's much to do, much I have in mind, so many, many important things."

Keymis did as Raleigh bade him, shielded him from prying eyes, and when next Bess Raleigh visited him he seemed quite himself again, walking about his cell unaided, full of business, talking more rapidly than was his wont, skipping from one subject to another.

"Are you feeling well, my dear?"

"Pish, pish," he said, laughing. "It is nothing." He had had, he admitted, a touch of jail-fever, but he had physicked himself with his Golden Elixir, which instantly cured it, as it would cure any other disease if taken in time. "If His Majesty's judges were to come to me to be physicked they would not so often die of the jail-fever they contract from the miserable wretches they constantly send to the gallows. But do you know, Bess, if they were to come, not a drop would I give them, not a drop!"

He asked after his sons.

"Little Carew will grow up to be a big tall man," she said, "and Wat [Walter Raleigh junior] already is. I'm afraid he got into a tavern brawl again, broke a lot of bottles over the heads of some waterfront ruffians and had to run for it." She smiled.

Raleigh shook his head. "Young Wat needs discipline, discipline, needs to tether that temper of his, rash, so foolish rash."

Lady Raleigh said, still smiling, "He is much like you when you were young, my dear. It's in the blood, instinctive with him. He's safe at home now, with nothing worse than a pounding headache."

(It is fashionable in our own time among a certain group of socio-ethnico-bio-psychiatrists, to assert that no such things as instincts or hereditary traits exist; that everything is environment; but most of us cannot afford to be psychoanalyzed, nor can we spare the time; and so we are unable to benefit from their therapy; and so most of us stubbornly cling to the outmoded notion that instincts do exist and heredity is very important. Of course, in Raleigh's time there were no socio-ethnico-bio-psychiatrists, so the Raleigh family could not benefit from their wisdom either.)

On Raleigh's desk was a sheaf of disorderly papers. He scrawled another note. "That reminds me of something," he said. "I must have money, lots of money. I have a project in mind, Bess, a project that will free me forever and make us richer than Villiers."

"Haven't we enough, Walter?" She was a bit alarmed by his febrile activity.

"Not nearly enough for my project, not nearly."

She prepared to go. "Dear Water," she said, lapsing into their Westcountry dialect, "it frets me mich to see you gadding so frantic about. Get Keymis to give you a sleepy draught, sleep sound, and—forgive me, dear—remember your age and be calm lest you suffer worse than a touch of jail-fever." He glanced at her sharply, but she had not guessed.

He kissed her good-bye and said in a calm controlled voice, "It is just that my project exhilarates me."

[352]

Then he returned to his desk and dipped his every-busy pen in ink.

He addressed his first letter to a Huguenot sea captain in France. For some years Raleigh had secretly lent the captain a vessel for the purpose of preying upon Spanish shipping. For political reasons the French government blinked at such acts of piracy; for reasons of personal greed the Huguenot sea captain was delighted to make use of Raleigh's ship and always expressed his gratitude by smuggling back to Raleigh a goodly amount of the gold, silver and jewels he had stolen from Spain. Lady Raleigh hid the treasure chests in the wine cellar of her little Westcountry farm.

About a year before, young Walter had seriously wounded a man in a duel. Raleigh bribed the captain of a merchant vessel, plying legitimate trade with France, to smuggle the obstreperous young man over the Channel to his Huguenot friend, who was charmed by the young man's high spirits. When the trouble blew over and the wounded man – a person of no account – recovered, when young Walter was no longer looked for, young Walter returned to England. Now Raleigh was writing his Huguenot captain asking for a large sum of additional money, promising to repay it a hundredfold when a project he had in mind was certain to be successful. He described that project, but not in detail. "There lies at a certain spot that I know well on the shore of the Orinoco river in Guiana, which by rights I still own – the late Queen having given me the whole of the American continent – a mine of gold that I propose to put to good purpose."

He had planned his project, Raleigh said, to take place at about the time when the Spanish treasure fleet yearly sailed for Spain, but assured his Huguenot friend that there was nothing to fear, "for if I should be intercepted by the fleet I shall know how to deal with it, as I did at Cadiz, in the days of Elizabeth."

Raleigh was reliving those great old days, but they were long since past. Not a Tudor now but a Stuart sat on the throne of England. Peace with Spain was the English policy now. Not a thrifty Elizabeth but a spend-thrift James, who weakly wasted his money with oddly un-Scottish abandon, controlled the destinies of England.

It was no secret that he and his Queen squandered fortunes on her pleasures and his favourites.

To one of his favourites, the current one, George Villiers, Raleigh sent another letter, enclosing a gift of money and a ring worth nearly a thousand pounds. Villiers was already a nobleman, had just been raised to the coveted and lucrative post of Gentleman of the Bedchamber, "which I deem a most appropriate title," mused Raleigh with a chuckle. But such a man had the King's ear and could further Raleigh's Guiana project. Villiers replied with a gracious letter, assuring Sir Walter that he held him in high esteem. Since Villiers accepted presents from everyone else who sought through him to gain the King's favor, there was nothing unusual or uncharacteristic in his accepting Raleigh's. He often squeezed "loans" out of rich courtiers, promising to re-pay, without the slightest thought of doing so.

Villiers had a personal reason to be gracious toward Raleigh. Villiers was afraid that King James, the source of all his growing riches, would soon be forced to cut off the stream of gold that flowed into his pockets.

In Parliament the Puritan faction was growing stronger every year. Frugal, strict in their private morals, they detested the waste and immorality of King James's court. They were among the most avid readers of Raleigh's *History*, especially the portions that were "saucy in censure of princes," for they believed, like Raleigh, that kings were no better than other men.

Though growing in numbers, the Puritan members of Parliament were not yet strong enough to topple the throne or chop off the head of Baby Charles—that lay in the future, when Baby Charles grew up and became King Charles the First—but already the Puritans were strong enough, by ancient right, to niggle, carp, delay, frustrate the granting of funds to the Crown. This they were constantly doing when King James constantly demanded money. And just as constantly he would prorogue Parliament, send them packing, determined to rule without them, scheme to get money elsewhere.

Thus it was that Villiers looked with a favorable eye on Raleigh's project to sail to America and bring home to England the fabulous riches that Raleigh assured him lay there for the taking on the banks of the river Orinoco in Guiana. King James was also intrigued. But above all, he warned Raleigh, there must be no conflict with Spain, or he'd have no part in the enterprise.

Raleigh assured him that Guiana was an independent kingdom, ruled by an Indian Emperor, and that Spain recognized his sovereignty. In this there was a grain of truth. The Orinoco was so remote and the Indian chief who ruled Guiana was so unfriendly that the Spaniards had long neglected the place, never having found any gold there themselves.

James asked George Villiers to inquire of the Spanish Ambassador if this were so, "but cautiously, cautiously, George. You know why."

The reason why was this: King James had long tried to arrange a marriage between Baby Charles and the little Infanta of Spain, scheming as always to get money, demanding a million pounds "to further the Old Religion, in which I myself was baptized," but the King of Spain said No. For he sensed the rising Puritan power in England. The last thing he wanted was an English civil war, in which he would lose a million pounds.

"I will inquire cautiously," said George Villiers, and inquired not a word of the Spanish Ambassador. Then, later, with a perfectly straight face, he said to King James, "I have cautiously inquired, Your Majesty, and

[355]

Sir Walter's assertion that Guiana is a sovereign state appears to be true."

Raleigh's demands were exorbitant. He wanted no fewer than fifty fighting ships for the expedition. England had always been strong on the sea, strong she must continue to be. There was danger, he said, from pirates attacking the fleet that would bring the treasure home.

King James said, "I can lend you a few, I don't know how many. I leave all such matters to my Admiralty advisers."

"So they be manned by brave seamen, fewer will suffice," Raleigh replied. "Sailors know me, Your Majesty; they have fought under Admiral Raleigh before." King James nodded thoughtfully. But he did not reply, so greedy was he for the gold of Guiana, his last hope to rule without a Parliament. He knew that sailors had long since forgotten their aging Admiral, his prisoner of the Tower.

He gave him few indeed: four leaky ships manned by discontented riff-raff from waterfront stews, whose principal complaint, once they sobered up and went aboard, was that there were maggots in the biscuit, and the "salt pork," their favorite meal, tasted queer. Well it might. Villiers had exacted forced "loans" from the ships' victuallers, and they in turn had been compelled to substitute horse meat for salt pork. The horse meat came from spavined beasts so weak and old they scarcely had the strength to haul a drayload of beer barrels. Villiers assured King James that the ships were the best to be had.

Raleigh was not to be fobbed off with so small a fleet. He fired off a spate of letters to rich London traders, promising in the King's name, which the King did not deny, fantastic profits for the loan of their ships in a venture that the King himself approved; and James sent Villiers to assure them that this in fact was the case, but cautioned them not to noise it abroad. "It is a private undertaking, George. Any incautious gossip will cause

[356]

other traders, not in on the secret, to demand to join. Sir Walter seems to have chosen only the best and most reliable firms. I don't know how he knew."

The memory of tradespeople is long; longer and even more detailed is the memory of their ledgers. Many of the traders whom Raleigh had written were as old as he, remembered the free-booting days of Queen Elizabeth, when piracy and patriotism were virtually synonymous, and Westcountry sea-captains sailed out of Plymouth, returning with the spoils of captured Spanish ships and highly ransomable Spanish prisoners; remembered when Raleigh was really an Admiral. And in their secret account books were carefully set down the enormous profits they had made. With Raleigh in charge of another expedition—who knew?—the good old days might come back again. Their ships were far better than the King's, their crews better, if only by a little: competent seamen but inordinately greedy and undisciplined. Corruption and cynicism had infected the merchant marine as well as the Royal Navy.

"He knew," Villiers replied to the King, "because he remembered the traders that made fortunes preying upon Spanish shipping in the Old Queen's piratical days, Your Majesty. Of course, they're much more respectable now that Your Majesty is at peace with Spain."

"Elizabeth was a pirate at heart," growled the King. "It must never happen again."

With the ships of the traders and the King's disreputable hulks, Walter Raleigh assembled a fleet of thirteen of the best merchant vessels that England had to offer during the reign of King James. Of them all one was superbly good, the *Destiny*. Raleigh had had her built to his own specifications, paid for her out of his own pocket, would still have owned her if a man legally dead for fifteen years could have owned anything. Now she belonged to King James, whose Admiralty told him that *Destiny* was every whit as valuable as the *Ark Royal* and others of the Royal Navy that Raleigh had built.

On a hot summer day in June of the year 1617, *Destiny* leading them, Sir Walter Raleigh set sail with his fleet on a fair following wind toward the river Orinoco that lay with its fabulous riches in the Indian Empire of Guiana, far to the west beyond the sun. "I can see it now!" Sir Walter said.

"Father, in this dim light?" The tall young man beside him smiled.

The sun was setting.

Sir Walter had taken young Walter with him, out of a father's love and out of a lively concern that brash young Wat would get into trouble again. There would be long days and long nights during the voyage for a father to teach a son the lore of the seaman's craft, the necessity for discipline, caution, foresight aboard a ship. For in a ship, as in life, he said, one must often deal with liars, rogues and scoundrels, tall-talkers, opportunists, devious men who will do you in if you're not on your guard. And in the men he thus described Walter Raleigh genuinely saw not a jot of resemblance to himself.

CHAPTER XXVII

ALMOST AT ONCE Raleigh's fleet began to dwindle away. A moderate storm arose, and King James's four rotting ships were forced to put about and return to England. Ocean water poured into their bilges through weak worm-eaten sides. The bilge pumps wouldn't suck, the leather hoses being full of holes or missing altogether, having been stolen. No one blamed the crews, who were glad to escape with their lives. One look at the sorry spectacle of the ships, so low in the water that their ports were submerged, caused seamen who saw them to ex- claim, "It's a miracle they didn't go down to the bottom!" On the advice of his Admiralty King James let it be known that his ships were sturdy and strong; the storm was represented as having been a most violent tempest, a veritable hurricane.

This advice was sound and statesmanlike: no nation happily at peace with the whole world, seeking trade, must ever admit even in isolated cases (as those four old hulks must surely have been) that there existed any flaw in ships, seamen, cannon or morale, all the essential elements that constituted a peaceful nation's strength and good will, lest enemies rise up, sniff out a weakness and take advantage of it. "Aye," mused the scholarly ever-fearful King, remembering a verse in the Reve- lation of Saint John the Divine, which he construed as revealed particularly to himself: "Without are dogs and sorcerers, murderers . . ."

Worse now occurred.

The five staunch ships that the traders had provided defected. Their greedy undisciplined crews turned pirate. Sighting some inoffensive French vessels, merchant ships, they promptly attacked, overwhelmed and looted them. Then they too returned to England, laden with the French spoil, which was considerable. "We acted," they blandly averred, "on direct orders from Sir Walter."

"Now the rawly rogue is turned pirate," sighed King James. "It was only to be expected." But he eagerly grabbed the French loot, being pressed for money, save only that portion which the delighted traders stole from him and secreted in their own private coffers. To the furious French he sent a cunning note of apology, promising them greatly expanded trade, vast profits, on a most-favored-nation basis; peace, trade, money. King James was achieving his ends, but, a contemporary wrote:

> Here be some ship captains, stolen away from Sir
> Walter Raleigh, who give out that he is turned pirate;
> but the world hopes that they speak out of malice, and
> there is no such matter.

King James reflected, "At least he did not turn pirate against Spain. If he does I will have his head."

On the quarterdeck of the *Destiny* Sir Walter scanned the horizon in vain. Nowhere were there to be seen the sails of the King's or the traders' ships. "No doubt I outran them in that little blow," he said with a chuckle. "No doubt I'll see them lumbering after me soon, trying to catch up with me." Affectionately he patted the sturdy oak rail of his speedy ship. "My *Destiny* carries us fast, eh Wat?"

"Fast, Father, fast," young Walter said. Neither of course knew whither the nine other ships had disappeared, what they had done or that they would never see them again.

Raleigh glanced aft. "Look how my stout-hearted

Keymis brings up my rear. Set him for a model, lad, copy his ways. Never was a skilfuller seaman! Heroic!"

But young Walter said, "Keymis is a subordinate, a follower, else why is he bringing up the rear instead of leading, like you?" and his eyes, looking up at his father, told him, unspoken, " 'Tis you are heroic."

With this filial tribute his father quite characteristically agreed, but he could not read his son's heart as he could read his eyes. Young Wat in his brash young heart was just a bit jealous of his father, who of course seemed incredibly ancient to him. "He is grown old, over-cautious, my father; but I am young, and I will out-Raleigh Sir Walter!" Nor did Raleigh remember that Bess had said, "He is just like you when you were young."

"Patience, patience, lad," Raleigh said. "You will lead in time, no doubt of it, but first you must learn to follow, if only to observe the mistakes that leaders make, profit by your observation and not repeat their mistakes."

Wat Raleigh pondered. He thought his father the wisest man in the world.

"I shall certainly try," he said.

Raleigh made a perfect landfall. *Destiny* leading, he entered the muddy mouth of the Orinoco with his fleet, now reduced from thirteen to four ships. All around lay steaming jungle. Up from the river at night rose the noisome stench of rotting vegetation. Myriads of mosquitoes swarmed and hummed in the air. Crocodiles swam in the sluggish stream and sometimes ate monkeys that failed to detect their ancient enemies, being intent on the business of spanking their babies, as is the habit of mother monkeys. Overhead screamed unknown birds of gorgeous plumage and buzzards with razor-sharp hooked bills that fed on the offal so copiously supplied by the river, vomiting it up when they over-gorged themselves, fouling the decks of the ships.

"An unsavory place," Raleigh said, "but the headwater

of the river in the Indian Empire of Guiana runs sweet and clear, as is attested in the writings of many explorers since the time of Columbus."

The Orinoco has many tributary affluents: some are dead ends, some turn back upon themselves, mere circles around low-lying islands of vegetation all composed of putrefaction. Some of these islands actually float, break loose and further confuse the mariner. The stench was dreadful.

Often he had to anchor and wait for Indians to peer out of the swamps. He would heave them gifts of mirrors, little tinkling bells, hatchets and copper bangles, all safely lashed to floating hogsheads. Then they would paddle out in canoes to pick up the gifts.

"Guiana, Guiana?" he would ask.

The Indians had taken them for Spaniards, who made slaves of them and whom they hated. But no Spaniard had ever given them gifts, so these white men must not be Spaniards. They knew that Spaniards had many enemies, white-man enemies, who had fought many wars with Spain. Hoping that these were such, the Indians pointed out the true channel upriver; and paddled away with their gifts.

As the little fleet pressed westward toward the upper reaches of the Orinoco, the river began to clear, the current to run less sluggishly; and the air began to smell cleaner, healthier. "Just as I predicted," Raleigh said through chattering teeth.

He had taken a chill, felt cold despite the sun that shone warm on the spotless decks, now cleansed of the bird droppings by sailors with holystones, mops and clear river water, singing at their work.

Then Raleigh fell gravely ill. Every day he shook with a chill. Wat Raleigh covered his father with blankets. Then the chill would pass, he would sweat till the blankets were wet, throw them off and beg to be fanned. His belly was bloated and tender.

[362]

He dosed himself daily with his Golden Elixir. The brandy in it would put him to sleep, give him a good night's rest; but next morning the alternating fever and chill would return. At length he became so weak that he had to be carried about in a chair. His mind would wander, he would give conflicting orders, forgetting what orders he had given an hour before.

At this point Keymis took over command, and ordered the fleet to anchor, fearing that his master would die. For if Raleigh died the expedition was at an end. Raleigh, not Keymis, held the King's commission to bring back the gold of Guiana.

Then, as can happen in the still-mysterious disease of malaria, a sudden remission occurred. Such remissions often occur for very long periods; and then, just as suddenly, years after the sufferer has left the area where he contracted the disease, the disease strikes again, no one knows why. Raleigh did not live to experience this puzzling medical phenomenon.

Raleigh's symptoms entirely disappeared. The chills and fever left him. He completely recovered his wits. Though still weak he ordered Keymis, "Take the fleet upriver and find the mine. Guiana is only a day or two sail away. Take young Wat with you. As yet he knows only sea-sailing. He must learn to navigate rivers too, like me, at Cadiz, on the Blackwater, many rivers. I will tarry here in *Destiny* till I grow just a bit stronger."

Keymis cried, "I cannot leave you here alone with one ship, Sir Walter."

Raleigh laughed, "*Destiny* sails fast, my good Lawrence. I can overhaul you in a day. I shall be with you, with my son, when the Emperor receives us."

Keymis did as his master commanded, he always did. Raleigh bade his son a fond au revoir, with much sound advice on the manner of dealing with princes when, in a day or two, the Indian Emperor would receive them all in his golden palace.

Raleigh expected to regain his strength much sooner than he actually did. Each night he would sink exhausted on his bed. Each morning he would arise, less fatigued but still reluctant to meet the Indian Emperor till he could make a better impression: "Just a day more. England must not hobble up to his golden throne, stiff of leg and pale as a sheet."

Keymis, expecting the *Destiny* to appear at any moment, sailed bravely upriver till he came to the spot where the mine was supposed to be, near the miserable Indian village of San Thomé. There he disembarked his troops and began to search for the mine.

All was a myth.

There was no mine.

There was no sovereign state of the Indian Empire of Guiana.

There was no Indian Emperor, no golden palace.

This was Spanish territory, always had been, and the Indians who inhabited the place were Spanish slaves, who hated their Spanish masters and were in turn hated and feared by the Spanish. The principal occupation of the Indians was raising tobacco. They were perpetually in a mood to revolt, but the whips of the Spanish overseers kept them down. Some fast Spanish ships were ready and manned to carry the Governor and his garrison to safety if the Indians did actually revolt. All this gradually unfolded to Keymis and his men in disaster and death.

When the Spanish garrison saw strangers in broad daylight rummaging up and down the riverbank they hailed them, demanded to know who they were, why they were armed and whence they came. The challenge was not unfriendly; they hoped they were Spaniards, come to reinforce the garrison, though they didn't look Spanish and neither did their ships.

Keymis answered them in English.

"English!" screamed the garrison. "English pirates!" and instantly fired upon them and raced off to inform the

Governor. Keymis fired back and took cover among the bushes by the riverbank till nightfall.

As night came on he and his men advanced upon the town. There was a further exchange of gunfire, with casualties on both sides. But the English far outnumbered the Spanish, who fled to the ships already prepared for the purpose.

Seeing the Spaniards scrambling into the escape vessels the Indians rose in revolt with whoops and shouts and slew many, including the Governor; but the rest of the Spaniards got away and set sail toward England and Spain to protest the breach of the peace.

Then, in the dark, the Indians attacked the English, for, as one young Indian, who had sailed in an English ship said apologetically, "All white men look alike to us"; then the English killed him.

And then the English stormed the town. Keymis tried in vain to keep young Walter safe in the rear. But the Raleigh blood was up, the Raleigh compulsion to excel and, for young Wat, the joyous longed-for chance to out-Raleigh Sir Walter. He drew his sword, tossed his jeweled cap in the air, shouted, "Follow me, men!" and led the charge. And was immediately cut down and hacked to pieces.

Then the English burnt San Thomé to the ground. Such Indians as they were unable to massacre melted into the forests.

Keymis loaded his ships with the spoils of San Thomé. The treasure of Guiana amounted to a few hundredweight of tobacco. With a heavy heart he sailed downriver to report to his master.

In the great cabin of the *Destiny* Walter Raleigh received Keymis's report first with disbelief, then with mounting anger. He reproached him for seeking the mine in the wrong place, berated him as an unskilful navigator, heaped scorn on his head for mistaking an

Indian village for the golden palace of the Indian Emperor.

And when at last Lawrence Keymis, trembling, head bowed and tears streaming down his cheeks, told him of the death of his son, Walter Raleigh flew into a rage.

"Ignorant rogue! Self-saving man! How comes it to be that my son is dead and you are alive? Out of my sight, you whoreson coward! Out! Out!"

Keymis tried to explain, but Raleigh screamed, "Out! Out! Out!"

Keymis retired to his cabin, heavy with grief and a deep sense of personal guilt. He had failed his master. Dogs have been known to die of starvation on their masters' graves.

Seated in his chair, with a mumbled prayer, he drew out his pistol and blew out his brains.

The latter days of Sir Walter Raleigh present unmistakable evidence that he was never the same after Lawrence Keymis's suicide.

In London the Spanish ambassador demanded immediate audience with King James in the dead of night while James was reading some of his poems to George Villiers, who professed to admire them. Occasionally the King would pat his hand. "I've done vurra guid wi' me poems, dinna ye think, George?" Villiers thought the King had done very "good" with everything, especially himself. He had just made him an earl.

The Spanish ambassador was admitted, glowering. Villiers and James assumed a less intimate posture.

With the slightest of bows the Spanish ambassador informed the King that Sir Walter Raleigh had broken the peace, had turned pirate and burned down a Spanish town in the New World, massacring many Spanish citizens. Sir Walter had already landed at Plymouth in the Westcountry. He demanded that Sir Walter be turned over to the Spanish authorities for transportation to

Spain, where the Inquisition would fairly inquire into his behavior and, after finding him guilty, release him to the secular arm for the just punishment of his misdeeds. Then, shouting "Pirate!" in James's face, he turned his back on the King of England, stalked out of the chamber and slammed the door after him. Even the servants winced.

King James went pale and trembly, turned paler still when Villiers remarked, "You know what the Inquisition will do. They'll take weeks to kill him."

"He is already under sentence of death," James said.

Then the King's genuine horror of bloodshed, and his kingcraft, saved Walter Raleigh from a death far more hideous than that he was shortly to die.

It mattered not a whit to King James that Raleigh must die. What mattered to him was that Raleigh posed a distinct embarrassment to his kingcraft: there was that saucy *History* of his, so avidly read by the Puritan Members of Parliament, more numerous every year, ever ready to deny him funds that the Crown so desperately needed. How he wished the confounded old Elizabethan would disappear, vanish on a broomstick; or that he would actually turn pirate and sail away in his *Destiny* — anything to rid him of his presence. But here was Sir Walter Raleigh landed in Plymouth, in England; and the King's spies reported that lank-haired Puritans greeted him with nasal hymns as he rode up toward London, ghost-pale on a horse caparisoned in harness bedecked with jewels.

The King asked his newest earl, "Why, why, my dear George, *why* does he return?"

Villiers replied, "He is back in the days of Elizabeth. Her minions were a queer breed. They died with her name on their lips, lauding the majesty of England's sovereign, even when they died at her command. Aye, very queer."

"He must die, of course."

"Calling down blessings on Your Majesty, I doubt not,

[367]

even as he dies. It is said that he said of Elizabeth, 'Thou art England!' In his old-fashioned mind it may be that he thinks of you as the same."

"I canna faddom him."

George Villiers gently mimicked the King's Scottish accent. "And ye canna dispose of him wi'out due process of law."

"Of course not. I am noted for my devotion to due process of law."

"Nor kill him secretly on his ride up to London."

"I had thought of it."

"The Puritans would count him a martyr."

"God damn the Puritans."

"It were better, belike, to give him a guard of honor, led by some person that's faithful to Your Majesty, preferably a Westcountry kinsman—he has shoals of them—and let him ride bravely for all to see, here into London; and here confront Your Majesty and answer for his crimes."

"Dear George, thou'rt a canny counsellor! Well you deserve the ermine on your cape."

"But do not turn him over to the Spaniards, lest you make small the image of England, which is grown big in the eyes of the world since the days of the Spanish Armada."

"I couldn't anyhow, George," said the King. "He shall die, but not at Spanish hands; and as painlessly as I can contrive."

"It is said he is daft, since the death of his son."

"Traitors are often daft. 'Tis no matter. They must die."

"And a witch."

"Witch or no, if daft he be I will not burn him, though I burn witches that be not daft. Wurra, wurra, sweet my George! Would that the rawly rogue had the wit to absent himself out of my kingdom."

"It is not in his nature, Your Majesty."

[368]

Forthwith King James deputed Sir Lewis Stuckley, a distant Westcountry cousin of Raleigh, to join him as he rode northward toward London, ostensibly to act as an honor guard but with private instructions to cozen him into absconding, anywhere, out of the realm of England, out of King James's dilemma; to turn pirate if so he pleased, or flee to his Huguenot friends in France, or join the Barbary Corsairs, anything, anywhere that would alienate his Puritan followers and rid the realm of a troublemaker. Thus King James, his kingcraft.

Raleigh greeted his kinsman with joy, an embrace, but was horrified at Stuckley's insinuations.

Stuckley said, "Sir Walter, it is likely you'll be called upon to answer for the burning of Spanish San Thomé; and I fear me the answer will be death. I beg you, flee from the wrath of Spain, as you value your life!"

Sir Walter said, "Cousin, I value not my life, since it does not exist. For fifteen years I have had no life, being legally dead during all that time."

"Then why repair to London?"

"To kiss my Bess and assure my one remaining son, Carew, that he suffer not the fate of his father; and further assure that what little remains of my wealth revert to him, not to that he-she coward of a Scot that sits on Elizabeth's throne—my dear, dear Diana, lost, lost, lost forever to me! That is why, Sir Lewis, that is why," and Stuckley could not shake him.

As they rode past Sherborne Raleigh remarked, "But once all this was mine."

In London Sir Walter was immediately clapped into the Tower. He left it only once before he died. Below the Tower walls Puritans chanted dismal hymns to honor him. King James said to Stuckley, "Manage a means to let him escape."

Stuckley said to King James, "He seems to want to die."

Villiers said, "He tried that once, tried to commit suicide like Keymis, could not bring himself to do it. He does not want to die. He wants to live."

Said the King, "I dinna faddom Sir Walter Raleigh," and knew not what to believe.

Confronted by a problem beyond his capacity to resolve, King James went to his Queen for comfort and advice.

"The Spanish ambassador all but spat in my face! Turned his back on me, on *me!* Then he stalked out of my private chamber, slammed the door after him! Oh Anne, dearest Anne, wise Anne, he was threatening war, war with Spain. What shall I do? For all I desire in this world is peace."

Queen Anne, who loved her husband, patted his soft white hand, soothed him. "Aye, Jamie boy, England needs peace and you will contrive it, I know you will. Fret not yourself."

"Raleigh has broken the peace with Spain. Spain knows it. I know it. Everyone knows it. Unless I execute him there will be war."

"Do not kill that foolish good man."

"I do not want to, truly I don't, any man. But he stings like a gadfly, comes home when he could have escaped. If only he'd take his own life. Stuckley says he wants to. Villiers says he doesn't."

"Villiers is usually right."

"Then kill him I must."

The Queen said, "If you kill him the Puritans in Parliament will hold back the funds that we sorely need." She was thoughtful and just a bit frightened. "So sorely need, James."

"I know."

"If Sir Walter were mad . . . ?"

"Oh, he must be. I have always thought him mad."

"But if the world is convinced he is mad?"

The King slowly nodded. "Perhaps. Perhaps. Perhaps even the Spanish ambassador would be appeased if it

[370]

were proved that Sir Walter is mad," and, his kingcraft enlightening him, he said smiling, "It should be easy to prove. He wants to live."

Forthwith King James sent a messenger to Raleigh in the Tower. The substance of his message was this: "It is bruited about that your brains are decayed, that shortly you will escape and that no man will blame a madman for aught that he does or attempts." And the King added some canny encouragement: Sir Lewis Stuckley himself would make the escape easy.

Now Raleigh, who truly wanted to live, knew what to do.

Hitherto his movements had been sternly restricted. Now the restrictions were suddenly relaxed. He was permitted access to his medicine chests that before were denied him.

He smeared his face with an ointment that caused it to break out in dripping pustules and sores. He crawled on all fours in the confines of his cell, barking like a dog. He knew exactly what he was doing. The ointment was harmless. But it looked dreadful.

Now the King sent his personal physician, ostensibly to physick him, actually to let it be known to the world that Sir Walter was daft.

But Raleigh's cantankerous nature led him into a foolishness. To the King's physician he bragged that he was only feigning madness, like King David when once, in particularly dire circumstances, he "changed his behavior and scrabbled on the doors of the gate, and let his spittle fall down upon his beard." Cried Raleigh, "Now I can escape with impunity. I have the King's word," and he laughed like a maniac.

King James said to Stuckley, "Let him escape. Prepare a boat to get him out of my realm."

Stuckley did. One dark night the Tower guards were withdrawn to enjoy a feast which the King said they deserved. Stuckley and Walter Raleigh walked away un-challenged through Traitors' Gate and embarked in the boat prepared for the purpose.

"It is witchery, Your Majesty."

"No, Excellency, it is madness."

Said the Spanish ambassador, who wanted no war with England, appeased, "If it's madness my King will leave him to his own sorry end, which is certain to overtake him," and King James and the Spanish ambassador toasted each other in a cup of most excellent sherry, for each knew that the King of Spain was also mad. King-craft. Peace. Trade. And a good round pension from England for the Spanish ambassador.

Then occurred one of those unlooked-for accidents that perpetually frustrate the best laid schemes of the rulers of nations.

In the early morning light Stuckley descried the sails of a Spanish fleet making toward England. It was noth-ing but an assembly of merchant vessels, laden with Spanish products, destined to turn about and go back to Spain with holds full of English products.

Such was the peaceful and profitable trade now exist-ing between the two nations.

But Stuckley panicked, imagined that Spain had sent an armada for the sole purpose of capturing Sir Walter Raleigh.

He immediately ordered the boat to turn back. He returned to England. He returned Walter Raleigh to the Tower. He returned to King James to report. The King sighed, "Stuckley, you acted the fool."

"Majesty, I acted as best I knew how, in Your Maj-esty's interest. Belike I acted wrong. But I was afraid."

King James could understand that.

"I will not punish you, Stuckley, fool and coward though you be. But your name will stink Judas-like in the nose of all England. Betake yourself to some hidden place, some out-of-the-way estate of yours, lest you suffer the Judas fate, lest Sir Walter's friends rip out your guts. The rogue hath many. And now I must kill him."

Sir Walter never again left the Tower but to die. On two counts he was condemned: the old count of treason, a new count of breach of the peace with Spain. His execution was scheduled to take place with unconscionable speed, within twenty-four hours.

During his last night of life, from his cell in the Tower, he penned to his Bess and the world he was shortly to leave, a most beautiful poem:

> *Even such is Time which takes in trust*
> *Our youth, our joys and all we have,*
> *And pays us but with age and dust;*
> *Who, in the dark and silent grave*
> *When we have wandered all our ways,*
> *Shuts up the story of our days.*
> *And from which earth and grave and dust*
> *The Lord shall raise me up I trust.*

He wrote these words on the flyleaf of his Bible. It was found in his cell after he was beheaded.

CHAPTER XXVIII

WHEN A MAN is about to die of a terminal disease, such as cancer, twentieth-century doctors, who assess these things, have often observed that the patient loses all fear of death. Hitherto he might have struggled, screamed, yelled at those about him, his doctors, his nurses, relatives, cursing them in a paranoid fury because he conceived them against him. Then a curious change can occur. Soft as a feather descending from the dread death-angel's wing there comes upon the dying man a profound acceptance of what is about to occur and a peace in the soul that passes the understanding of the doctors. Though they do not understand it, the doctors are glad when it happens, for it is far better to witness the death of a man with all his wits about him than the raving death of a maniac.

No man had more wanted to live than Sir Walter Raleigh.

But the logical mind that had designed the British Royal Navy, the logistical mind that had explained to the Admiralty in countless explicit papers exactly how much of what was required to sustain seamen in whatever enterprise was required of them—that mind informed Walter Raleigh that further life on this earth was not to be, and with knowledge of certain death, all that was great and good in him came to the fore and upheld him to the end: his wit, his gaiety, his poetic, punster-prone love of words, tobacco, wine and an abiding devotion to his Bess, the Throgmorton girl whom he had seduced under the very nose of furious Diana, the Bess he had so loved but so often been absent from, to whom he had written his exquisite death-poem, who now came to visit him in Bloody Tower on his last night of life.

"My dear, my Bess!"

For a moment she clung to him, stifling her tears.

" 'Tis the end, you know."

She said, "I know."

She kissed him, weak and trembling.

He said, "Wife, thou'rt my sweetest friend in this sorry world. Come now, come now, sweet Bess. Fret not."

She tried to be gay. "Your gray beard tickles my cheek."

They had grown old, his beard was gray, as was her hair.

He quipped,

> *"I've not the knack*
> *And not the time*
> *To dye it black,*
> *So die it rime."* *

She answered, hugging him, "I will not fret, dear heart," and, smiling, "You've changed not a whit, my husband; and this—" she tweaked his tickling beard, "—I will treasure it always." And then, still smiling, her weakness left her. Standing erect, Throgmorton-proud, she said, "Good-bye, sweet heart. You will always be with me."

He said, "Good-bye, dear wife," and they parted; but this was not the last she saw of him.

Powerful forces were brought to bear to save Raleigh's life even at the last minute. Queen Anne wrote to

---

* Footnote: In modern English this line would read: Therefore let it die the color of rime, that is, hoarfrost-gray.

George Villiers, hoping that the favourite she had raised to power would intercede with King James:

My dear Friend:
If I have any power or credit with you I pray you to let me have a trial of it at this time, that you deal sincerely and earnestly with the King that Sir Walter's life may not be called in question.
If you do, and success answer my expectations, assure yourself that I will take it extraordinarily kindly at your hands; and so shall remain as one that wishes you well —

The Queen added a broad hint that she would use her influence with the King to continue Villiers in favor:

— and one that desires that you always remain, as always you have been, a true servant to your Master.
(signed) ANNA R.

Villiers' sharp eye caught the hint, but he could do nothing except greatly ameliorate the usual procedure in a traitor's death: Lady Raleigh might be present at the execution if she wished; the body would not be sawn asunder; the head would not be impaled on a pike on London Bridge. King James remarked, "All shall be as you ask, George." Villiers said, "It will also quieten the Puritans," and kingcraft answered, "Aye."

Raleigh's son, Carew, also wrote a letter to the King, couched in the stately style of the Book of Common Prayer—he had inherited much of his father's skill with the pen—petitioning humbly for his father's life almost as if he were praying to God. Carew begged that:

It may please Your Majesty mercifully to look down upon the distressed estate of my poor father, sometime honored with many great places of command by the most worthy Queen Elizabeth, whereof she left him possessed at her death as a token of her good will to his loyalty.

Great Lord, whose princely goodness once saved him from destruction, conceit not too grievously the error of a dispirited mind, torn with every misfortune.

And, Great Lord, though merit and reason cannot require, yet let the privilege of old age and the innocency of a fatherless child beg mercy of Your Majesty, from the image of God, Who pardons the greatest offenses to the meanest suitor.

Carew Raleigh had no political following, and his letter moved King James not a whit. But the King was pleased to be addressed as the Image of God, pleased that the son of the most popular traitor in England seemed to confirm the Divine Right of Kings; and tossed the letter to George Villiers. "Save that," he said, for he knew he could put it to political use. Villiers saved it, and thus it has come down to us over the centuries.

The King was a stickler for the letter of the law, especially when it redounded to his credit. He resolved that the people must know that nothing was stolen from Walter Raleigh, that nothing crept into the pockets of corrupt and greedy jailors as was customary.

He sent a treasury official to the Tower to take from Raleigh everything of value and published the list, letting it be known that Lady Raleigh might have it, even though he, the King, was legally entitled to all that a traitor possessed. This was sure and canny kingcraft. He knew it would please the people. Here is the list:

IMPRIMIS, In gold about fifty pounds in his purse and own custody.

Item: a Guiana idol of gold and copper.

Item: a jacinth seal, set in gold, with a figure of Neptune cut in it.

Item: an emerald set in gold.

Item: a loadstone in a leathern purse.

Item: an ancient seal of his own arms, in silver.

Item: one ounce of ambergris, not taken from him but left him for his own use.

Item: one green spleen-stone, out of Guiana, where the natives cure disorders of the spleen withal.

Item: one wedge of fine gold, at 22 carats.

Item: one other wedge of coarser gold.

Item: 63 gold buttons with sparks of diamonds.

Item: a chain of gold, with sparks of diamonds.

Item: one diamond ring of nine sparks.

Item: one sea-captain's whistle, gold, set out with small diamonds.

Item: one ring with a diamond which he weareth on his finger, given him by the late Queen.

Item: a sprig jewel in the shape of a flower, set with soft stones and a ruby in the midst.

Then, as was customary, King James sent a clergyman to the prisoner's cell to comfort, counsel and console the man about to be put to death. To Raleigh he sent a high-ranking Anglican priest, Robert Tounson, Dean of Westminster.

I was commanded [says the Dean of Westminster], to be with him both in prison and at his death, and this, the manner of it, is true.

Raleigh seems not to have behaved quite as the Dean counseled him.

He never made mention of his former treason, but only desired to clear himself of new imputations, namely the charge that he had broken the peace with Spain. He had heard that the King was displeased at it, but how, he demanded, could he have broken the peace with Spain and Spaniards who, within these four years, made war, not peace, on his Englishmen, bound them back to back and drowned them?

[378]

The sticky business of the burning of San Thomé
came up. Raleigh, who had not personally witnessed the
incident, avowed what he believed to be true:

> As for the burning of the town, he said it stood on the
> King's own ground, and therefore he did no harm to
> Spain in that.

The Dean described Sir Walter's mood on the eve of
his death:

> He was the most fearless of death that ever was known,
> and the most resolute and confident, yet with reverence
> and conscience. When I began to counsel him not to
> fear death, he seemed to make so light of it that I won-
> dered at him.
>   I told him that others, in better causes than his, had
> shrunken back and trembled a little; and this he denied
> not, but gave thanks to God he had never feared death:
> and if fear of death in those others seemed grievous to
> them, it was but their own opinion and imagination;
> but as for him, he had rather die, as soon he would,
> deeming it better so than to die of a burning fever.

The October wind blew cold and whistled about the
Tower. Sir Walter began to fear that he would shiver
when they killed him and count it a weakness.

The October wind blew up from the common cells
below and the oubliettes lower still, fraught with the
noisome smells of hopeless fearful men and the stench of
putrid death, decay of corpses. "Phaugh!" said Sir Walter, and mulled with a red hot poker a flagon of
brandy, and dropped a morsel of ambergris into it, which
instantly dissolved, and tossed the brandy into the fire.
There was a quick blue flash of flame, white smoke,
and suddenly the air of his cell was suffused with a warm
sweet lingering fragrance. "That is better," he said.

> I was feign [said the Dean] to divert my speech another
> way, and wished him not to flatter himself, for I told

him this extraordinary boldness came from false ground. Heathen men, I told him, had set as little by their lives as he did and died as bravely. He answered that no man, except that he loved God and feared Him, could die but with cheerfulness. Other men might make show outwardly but felt no joy within. He satisfied me very Christianly, as I think he did all his spectators at his death.

After he had received communion in the morning he was very cheerful, and hoped to persuade the world that he died an innocent man.

This startled and frightened the Dean.

Thereat I told him that he would do well to advise what he said: pleading his innocency was an oblique taxing of the justice of the King. I put him in mind of what he had done formerly, and though belike thereof he was clear, yet for some other matter he now was guilty, and now the hand of God had found him out. And I put him in mind of the death of Lord Essex, how it was generally reported that he was the great instrument of his death. To which he made answer that nothing of the sort was true, but that my Lord of Essex was fetched off by a traitorous conspiracy against the late Queen.

He was very cheerful the morning he died, ate his breakfast heartily and took tobacco and made no more of his death than if he had been to take a journey, inasmuch as Sir Lewis Stuckley is grown very odious.

Bereft of all but his cloak, kindly left him to shield him against the wind, and his hat, Walter Raleigh marched to his death, trying in vain not to limp.

He strode to the edge of the platform, elevated so all could see. He delivered his death speech. Few heard him. His voice was squeaky and old, virtually inaudible. In substance he exculpated himself from all the crimes charged against him. Mostly he lauded the late Queen. He thought he was heard, but he wasn't. He thought he was heard when he saw people weep. He had spent much time composing his death speech, was glad when he thought they heard him, which they didn't.

He saw his Bess in a coach draped in black, rejoiced she was here at his death.

He took off his hat, tossed it to a friend. "Friend, thou'lt make better use of this than I, for I come to the parting," smiled and inquired, "Do you know of a plaister to glue back a head once it's off?"

Then he went up to the hangman, who was to decapitate him. "Let me feel the axe."

"It is not permitted, Sir Walter."

"Fellow! Let me feel it!"

Awed, the hangman did.

" 'Tis sharp medicine, but 'twill cure all my troubles, sharp, very sharp, Master Hangman. How art thou called, Master Hangman?"

"Derrick, Sir Walter. I am called Derrick."

Raleigh mused, "I knew another Derrick, long long ago. He was a charming lad."

"I know not, Sir Walter. I doubt if he's kin of mine."

"So do I," said Sir Walter, "much, very much do I doubt it," and he looked at the block.

"Master Hangman, when I stretch forth my arms, strike! And strike clean, d'ye hear? One blow." And Raleigh bent his head to the block.

"I hear, Sir Walter." But the tone of command in the last Elizabethan unnerved the hangman, he trembled, struck not once but twice, and Raleigh's head dropped into the basket prepared for the purpose. "Dear Jesus, he's smiling!" cried Derrick, and got very drunk that night.

From her black-draped coach Bess Raleigh saw her husband's head drop into the basket.

"Now," she said quietly to an equerry.

Derrick still stood on the platform. Bess Raleigh's

equerry pushed him aside. "His head, if you please."

The equerry had in his hand a scarlet bag.

Derrick said, "No, I must hold it up by the hair and shout 'So die all traitors to the King's Majesty.' "

The equerry said, "His head, if you please. Here. In this bag, or yours will follow, as certain it will, now or later," and history tells us that Derrick was later beheaded for some later crime.

He dropped Raleigh's head into the equerry's scarlet bag. Bess Raleigh drove off with it in her black-draped coach.

King James could have stopped, but did not, these bizarre proceedings. He was glad to be quit of Walter Raleigh. "What she does with his head I dinna give a hoot," he said to George Villiers, who said, "You are shut of him now, and a head can do you no harm," and they patted each other's hands and smiled.

Raleigh had written in one of his poems, "Blood must be my body's balmer, no other balm will there be given, whilst my soul, like a white palmer, travels to the land of heaven, over the silver mountains."

But this was not to be. There were expert embalmers in England, men who preserved against rotting the bodies of traitors who had been sawn into four quarters; and some of the best Bess Raleigh had hired to preserve her husband's head.

Their recipe for preserving such parts of a dead body as the sovereign wished to have exposed as a warning to others was well known and, there being so many traitors, widely practiced. It was as follows:

First, you immerse the parts in a boiling bath of sea-salt and cumin seed for about twenty-four hours. Then you carefully remove the parts from the boiling bath, taking care not to let it dehydrate: you anoint it with oil, any oil will do but goose grease is the best, second only to chicken fat beaten with egg white, the yolks of the eggs having been separated lest they impart a yellow cast to the flesh. Then the parts, in this case Raleigh's head, would look quite natural for a very long time, except for some slight shrinkage as the years passed, scarcely noticeable.

All this Bess Raleigh did, and paid the embalmers well. With her own hands she closed her husband's eyes, which had melted. "Now," she said, "he's himself again." Gently she combed his hair. "Once it was black, my sweet, when we were young, and so was mine."

She placed Raleigh's head on a sort of shrine, a little box, where she could always see it. Frequently she invited friends to see it also. Frequently she kissed his dead lips. "See, he smiles, he always smiles when I kiss him." "Indeed, he is smiling," they would say, pitying her. By now they all knew that Lady Raleigh was not quite in command of her senses.

Bess Raleigh lived on to the astonishing age of eighty-four years. She outlived the death of King James. She outlived the death of Queen Anne. Living but one short year more, she would have lived to witness the death of Baby Charles, who became King Charles the First, whose head was chopped off, just like Sir Walter's.

Carew Raleigh took care of his mother in her old age. "Keep your dear father's head by you always," she would say. He would say, "Yes mother, I will"; and when she came to die Carew kept his promise. For many years he kept it by him in his home, though of course in a manner more sane. Then he too came to die, and with him in his coffin was buried the head of his father. He did not bequeath it to his sons.

In England the Raleigh descendants live on to this day, epigoni of their multi-talented progenitor, the Last Elizabethan.

Theirs is a glorious heritage.

[383]